The Pleasures of Autumn

'Evie Hunter' is actually two authors who met at a creative writing workshop in 2010 and discovered a shared love of erotica. Since then, while they have both written fiction in other genres, they have also written a number of BDSM-themed novellas together. *The Pleasures of Autumn* is their third collaboration on a novel, following the publication of *The Pleasures of Winter* (2012) and *The Pleasures of Summer* (2013).

Praise for previous *Pleasures* books

'Ah, Oh, Ah, OMG! Damn You Evie Hunter! Are you trying to kill me? What a freaking read! I love love love love every single second of this steamy, exciting and thrilling read! You all know how much I loved the first book, *The Pleasures of Winter*, and I didn't think I would enjoy this as much just because *Winter* was just perfect but . . . The amazing Irish writing duo have did it again! I was hooked from page one and left breathless by the end . . . *The Pleasures of Summer* is a book that will capture your very being. You will fall in love with the characters and get so caught up in the story that you will forget everything around you. I highly recommend the "Pleasures" series to anyone who loves a good erotica read that has depth.' 5/5 *Totally Bookalicious*
(full review at: http://totally-bookalicious.blogspot.ie/2013/06/ double-review-pleasures-of-summer-touch.html?zx=92a1b025942114ac)

'I loved *The Pleasures of Winter*, so I hopped on the opportunity to read this book [*The Pleasures of Summer*] . . . I wasn't disappointed. These

characters were created with precision. They have depth and scope of where they are going. They clash and create chemistry like any great romance. The heroine doesn't roll over and play dead, she gives it as good as she got it. Watch out people, I'm telling you this writing duo is one to watch. They've knocked it out of the park with two in a row . . . If you want a well-written book to read after *Fifty* or even better than Gideon Cross, look no further. Not only do you get all the tension with a hell of a pay-off, you get a believable HEA at the end. Masterfully written, artfully told, and yummy to read.' 5/5 *My Book Boyfriend* (full review at: http://mybookboyfriend.blogspot.ie/2013/06/ the-pleasures-of-summer-pleasures-2-by.html?zx=7e2a07f2382adc48)

'Blushworthy scenes, graphic. *50 Shades*-ish but with a feisty, strong female character and intelligent writing. Epic romance, hotter than the hottest of summers!' *Between the Lines* Twitteresque Book Reviews on *The Pleasures of Summer* (full review at: http://betweenthelinesisanendlessstory.blogspot. ie/2013/07/twitteresque-book-reviews-friday-night.html)

'Evie Hunter does it again! Honestly, this book was just as good as the first one [*The Pleasures of Winter*] . . . This novel had me and wouldn't let me go. I never had a reason to stop reading this book, and I'm so glad that I did get the chance to read it. As erotic literature goes, I'd say this novel would be in the top ten of amazing books to read in the genre.' 5/5 *Manhattan Reader* (full review at: http://headstrong-tomgirl.blogspot.ie/2013/06/ the-pleasures-of-summer-by-evie-hunter.html)

'*The Pleasures of Summer* by Evie Hunter is NOT just an erotic romp through the world of the Dom/sub relationship, there is a plot – honest – and it's a good one, filled with tension, danger and a kidnapping or two! Summer and Flynn are both well-developed (very – had to say that), dimensional (very – had to say that, again) and their bickering and bantering back and forth is actually chuckle-worthy at times.' 5/5 *Tome Tender* (full review at: http://tometender.blogspot.ie/2013/06/the-pleas-ures-of-summer-by-evie-hunter.html?zx=c6d5aac4bee7872f)

'I loved *The Pleasures of Winter* so much that when I received this second instalment, I dove right into it! There is still plenty of S-E-X, but the storyline is different from the first with different characters . . . The makeup sex was HOT!!! It made me wish there was more book when I was finished reading (I am soooo looking forward to *The Pleasures of Autumn*).' *Nightly Reading*
(full review at: http://nightlyreading.wordpress.com/2013/06/10/the-pleasures-of-summer-by-evie-hunter-review-guest-post-in-my-mailbox-video/)

'These authors certainly know how to write good erotic fiction because once again the sexual parts were sizzling hot but I didn't feel like they overwhelmed the actual storyline . . . I was utterly gripped by the action-packed events leading up to the end, it was so exciting and really got my heart pounding. This will be added to my one-day read list because I just couldn't put it down and I can easily say that Evie Hunter's books are so much better than the *Fifty Shades* series thanks to the fantastic storylines and wonderful characters.'
Me, My Books and I
(full review at: http://memybooksandi.wordpress.com/2013/06/24/the-pleasures-of-summer-evie-hunter/)

Quotes from *Goodreads.com* user reviews:

'These hot D/s books are entertaining and well rounded. Meaning there is so much more going on emotionally than the hot one-on-one time. The struggle with your own self-doubt, and being comfortable with who you really are and not what you think people want you to be, all come to play here as well.' 5/5

'Evie Hunter knows her way around describing headboard rocking, and she will leave you panting.' 4/5

'Firstly, I have to say that *The Pleasures of Winter* was one of my favourite books of 2012. I loved Jack and Abbie and was looking forward to another taste of Jack. So when I read the blurb for *The*

Pleasures of Summer and realized that it had a different hero, I wasn't expecting to like it as much. I was totally wrong. Ms Hunter has done it again. Talk about a page-turner. . . . This is more than just a love story. The sexy scenes are HOT.' 5/5

'Flynn is another swoonworthy lead male and I would give my left leg to be stranded in that Scottish cottage with him (*fans self*). He's too yummy for words! I love the writing team that makes up Evie Hunter, they truly are talented. I am seriously excited to read *The Pleasures of Autumn*.' 4/5

'*The Pleasures of Summer* is a must read for those who like to take a walk on the wild side. This is a sexy, no-holds-barred read all wrapped up in a thrilling adventure.' 5/5

The Pleasures of Autumn

EVIE HUNTER

PENGUIN
IRELAND

PENGUIN IRELAND

Published by the Penguin Group
Penguin Ireland, 25 St Stephen's Green, Dublin 2, Ireland
(a division of Penguin Books Ltd)
Penguin Books Ltd, 80 Strand, London WC2R ORL, England
Penguin Group (USA) Inc., 375 Hudson Street, New York, New York 10014, USA
Penguin Group (Australia), 707 Collins Street, Melbourne, Victoria 3008, Australia
(a division of Pearson Australia Group Pty Ltd)
Penguin Group (Canada), 90 Eglinton Avenue East, Suite 700, Toronto, Ontario, Canada M4P 2Y3
(a division of Pearson Penguin Canada Inc.)
Penguin Books India Pvt Ltd, 11 Community Centre,
Panchsheel Park, New Delhi – 110 017, India
Penguin Group (NZ), 67 Apollo Drive, Rosedale, Auckland 0632, New Zealand
(a division of Pearson New Zealand Ltd)
Penguin Books (South Africa) (Pty) Ltd, Block D, Rosebank Office Park,
181 Jan Smuts Avenue, Parktown North, Gauteng 2193, South Africa

Penguin Books Ltd, Registered Offices: 80 Strand, London WC2R ORL, England

www.penguin.com

First published 2013
001

Typeset in 12.5/14.75pt Garamond MT Std by Palimpsest Book Production Ltd, Falkirk, Stirlingshire
Printed in Great Britain by Clays Ltd, St Ives plc

A CIP catalogue record for this book is available from the British Library

ISBN: 978-0-241-96666-2

www.greenpenguin.co.uk

Penguin Books is committed to a sustainable
future for our business, our readers and our planet.
This book is made from Forest Stewardship
Council™ certified paper.

To the men in our lives who inspire
the heroes in our books

Prologue

Standing in the wings, she drew in a deep breath, savouring the moment. It was always like this – the final nervous minutes before the spotlight came on, when she left the real world behind and became a fantasy.

Adjusting her corset, she checked that her pasties were in place over her nipples and plumped her pale breasts a little higher. Her trademark red sequined costume was a perfect foil for her pale skin and glossy raven wig. Her dresser had laced her tightly tonight, emphasizing her tiny waist and long dancer's legs.

'Your whip, *chérie.*' A bare-chested dancer handed it to her.

'Thanks, Gabriel.' She flashed him a smile before clapping her hands. 'Places, everyone. We're on in three.'

Six glorious specimens of oiled male perfection moved quickly to do her bidding, taking their places beside the gilded chaise longue on which they would carry her onto the stage. Male dancers only, her contract stipulated. Years of back-stage bitchiness had taught her a valuable lesson. She never shared a stage with another woman if she could help it, but it didn't stop the gossip. One rumour hinted that she had been offered a million dollars by an Omani prince in exchange for a single night in her bed.

She had laughed out loud when she heard that one.

'One minute,' the stage manager barked.

She took her place on the chaise, lounging with contrived indolence. Like a woman waking up after an afternoon of passion with a lover, or perhaps two lovers.

'Ladies and Gentlemen, on the final evening of her farewell UK tour, for one night only . . .'

His voice faded as she blanked it out. She closed her eyes. The heady sense of anticipation made her tingle as it always did – music, the swish of curtains, followed by the hot brightness of a single spotlight.

The scent of the predominantly male audience wafted to her nostrils; expensive cologne, mingled with an undercurrent of lust. Her nipples peaked behind the confines of her corset. A woman's high-pitched laugh was silenced by the spectacle of her entrance onto the stage.

Sinead O'Sullivan opened her eyes and became Lottie LeBlanc.

Like a jaded cat, she yawned and stretched and came to a sitting position in a single fluid movement. Her impossibly high heels dangled over the side of the raised chaise and she stared pointedly at her lead dancer. Following a single crack of her whip, he knelt, pressing a tender kiss against her ankle before bending his head to form a human footstool.

A bald man in the front row shuddered as she walked the length of her dancer's naked back before stepping onto the stage.

Behind her elaborate red mask, her eyes swept the thronged venue. It was standing room only – except for the owner's box, which was empty – a fitting tribute to one of the top burlesque performers in the business.

According to gossip, she was a woman with a string of lovers, a fortune in diamonds and a reputation for unsurpassed notoriety.

If only they knew the truth.

She loved the sense of power that performing gave her. As she slowly removed one diaphanous layer after another, she played with the audience, making each man believe that she would be his. A quick change of costume transformed her from twenties vamp to Chinese courtesan. The silk-draped bed was a perfect foil for a lustful concubine, awaiting her master's pleasure.

Every glance, every step of her routine was choreographed and rehearsed to sensual perfection. When she tossed a sheer black stocking into the crowd, the audience went into a frenzy of delight. As she unlaced her shimmering corset, the bald man wiped his forehead with a linen handkerchief. She cast the sequined bundle to the side of the stage, standing before her admirers, wearing nothing but a tiny jewelled thong, embroidered with a dragon.

A flash of movement caught her eye as a man entered the empty box. Her carmine-tinted smile froze on her face. She knew him – Niall Moore. CEO of Moore Enterprises, a company specializing in black ops and rescuing damsels in distress.

Well, she wasn't a damsel and she certainly wasn't in distress.

With his long fair hair tied back from his face, he looked like a Viking. The stark symmetry of his knife-edge cheekbones and strong jaw line would have captured her attention anywhere. There was something about the big man that had set her heart racing from the moment she had seen him. Strange he should turn up so soon after their first meeting. Not that he would remember her anyway. A week earlier, he had looked straight through her. As if her serious bespectacled everyday self didn't merit his attention.

But not tonight. Tonight his rapt gaze was as eager as the rest of them. His steel-grey eyes glittered and there was a hint of sensuous promise in his smile. She was willing to bet that his mouth could reduce a girl to a quivering jelly.

If it wasn't so dangerous, she might have been tempted. But despite the rumours to the contrary, Lottie always went home alone.

Distracted by his chiselled beauty, she almost forgot her next move, but recovered quickly. Throughout the routine, her attention was constantly drawn to the box above the stage. An uncharacteristic whim made her toss him a souvenir stocking, and left her pleased when he pressed it to his mouth in a silent kiss.

She turned her back on him. She couldn't afford to lose her concentration and flirting with someone who could connect her with her other life was too dangerous.

A giant champagne glass rose from beneath the stage accompanied by roars of approval from her audience. It was bath time. Stepping lightly up the ladder, she removed her thong and rewarded her fans with a flash of naked derrière before sliding into the warm water.

She stroked her breasts, knowing that every man in the auditorium was imagining what her skin felt like. Rolling over, she splashed playfully, sending droplets of water to cool her overheated admirers. She washed her long legs with a slow sensuous movement, taking satisfaction when she noticed Niall's fists clenched on the gilded edge of the box.

Toes gripping the edge of the glass bath, she raised herself on her arms in a wet and wanton offering that gave him a perfect view of her naked body. Grey eyes narrowed in a heated stare that sent a thrill straight to her core.

Naughty Lottie. You really shouldn't tease.

The music rose to a crescendo and the curtain fell for the final time, shielding her from thunderous applause. She hurried from the stage – Lottie never did an encore – and into the tiny dressing room that was already filling with flowers.

Sinead removed her dark wig and contact lenses, wiped off her make-up and took a quick shower, rinsing Lottie away for the last time. Her faded jeans and T-shirt hung on the costume rail. She dressed swiftly and pulled a woollen beanie over her long, damp hair. Without the elaborate stage make-up, the mirror revealed a slender woman with a pale, nondescript face. She might have been a waitress or a student.

A tap on the dressing-room door announced the arrival of more flowers, this time a lush display of orange tiger lilies.

'For you, *chérie*.' Gabriel had already changed into a pair of dark jeans and a T-shirt. A subtle waft of aftershave announced that he had a date.

She took the bouquet from him. 'For me? Oh, you shouldn't have.'

'I didn't.' He grinned. 'You have enough admirers already.'

The crisp white envelope that accompanied the flowers contained a card with a London telephone number. She inhaled the fresh scent from the bouquet and tore up the card.

'Are you sure you want to give all this up?'

Gabriel knew her well. Lottie had put her through college and given her the confidence to pursue her dream career. But now that it was within her grasp, she was having second thoughts. 'I'm sure. I have a whole other life planned.'

'*Oui*, but there is still time to change your mind . . .'

'I won't.'

As he was closing the door, he inclined his head. '*Au 'voir*, until Paris.'

With a final glance at the mirror to be certain that Lottie was gone, Sinead slipped from the dressing room and went to the stage door at the back of the theatre. At the top of the narrow street, several limousines were waiting. It was the same every night she performed – rich men, all hoping for an encounter with the glamorous dancer. But no one noticed the girl with the backpack, walking along the rainy streets to the bus stop.

In a late night grocery shop she picked up a half bottle of wine and a tin of tuna for the cat next door. She would miss his furry company when she moved to Geneva. Climbing the stairs, she let herself into her apartment and shrugged off her jacket. Most of the crates were packed and ready, waiting for the removal men.

There was just one more box to be done. Armed with

a glass of wine, she set to work on the last of the boxes from beneath her bed. The glossy photographs of Lottie, she placed in a folder and put into the top of one crate. They could go to Paris with the rest of her costumes and stage props.

In her folder were photographs spanning seven years of Lottie, from nervous backing dancer to headline act. She flicked through them, pausing when one caught her eye. Ian. Her first boyfriend when she came to London. He had arrived at the theatre one night with a group of drunken friends, never expecting to see her on stage. Sinead cringed when she remembered the aftermath. It had been one of the worst nights of her life.

Ian was furious and ashamed when he discovered that she took her clothes off for money. He had called her a whore. She hadn't dated much after that and had always worn a wig or a mask on stage. How could she expect anyone to understand about Lottie? No man could. Sinead tore the photograph in half and bundled the rest into an envelope. They could go to Paris as well, until she decided what to do with them. She'd already had offers for her entire collection of costumes and memorabilia, but she wasn't ready to let them go just yet.

A meow on the balcony caught her attention and she let Mr Fish inside. 'You're just in time for the party.'

While he ate, Sinead leafed through her mail. Among the final utility statements and auction catalogues was an envelope with an Irish stamp and her grandmother's spidery handwriting. Granny O'Sullivan was a witch. Sinead poured a second glass of wine before opening the envelope.

Along with the note saying that she was praying for her

and wishing her well in her new job, was a religious medal tied onto a piece of blue ribbon. She sighed. Granny O'Sullivan had finally gotten over her fear of flying and acquired a passport. Her uncle Tim had probably given his mother an entire plane to herself. God help Lourdes.

She had cleared her student loans and now it was time for Lottie to disappear. Her increasing fame brought with it the danger of discovery and there was no way that any respectable museum would employ an exotic dancer as a curator. She had one more show to perform in Paris and after that it was adieu, Ms LeBlanc.

Sinead undressed and before she climbed into bed, she checked the contents of her briefcase one final time; airline ticket, passport and a letter of appointment to her new job at the Rheinbach museum in Geneva, the most prestigious private museum in Europe.

The start of her new life.

I

Geneva – three months later

'We know who the thief is,' the director of the Rheinbach museum told him. 'Your job is to get the ruby back.'

Niall Moore sat up a bit straighter. This seemed too easy. 'If you know who has it, surely it should be simple to recover it?'

Günter Rheinbach shook his head. 'It is never simple. The thief was caught but unfortunately was granted bail and had an opportunity to hide it. The police have already searched and found nothing. The Fire of Autumn is officially missing.'

Niall looked around at the museum director's office. Although it held the clutter he suspected was endemic to anyone involved in the museum world – books, computer print-outs, a box of amber fossils, a broken diamond necklace, old mahogany and leather furniture – it also contained the control panels for a state-of-the-art security system and doors with metal frames and triple deadlocks.

As a security expert, Niall knew this set-up had cost a small fortune and should have kept out thieves. There were only a handful of hackers in the world who could have broken into the Rheinbach and gotten out undetected. There was almost nothing he would have added to the system to reinforce it. Whoever pulled this off was good.

'How did you catch him, sir?' he asked Rheinbach.

'Her,' the museum director corrected him. 'It was one of the curators. I still find it difficult to believe she did it, considering the chance we gave her. She was the youngest curator we have ever hired. At the time, we thought it was a coup. We were stealing an expert from under the noses of the other museums and art collections.' He sighed. 'They're going to laugh when they hear about this.'

Rheinbach picked up his pipe, peered at the empty bowl, shrugged and put it between his lips. He looked at home sucking the curved stem. He was grizzled and turning grey, with a face weather-beaten from mountain expeditions in the Alps, which were visible through the window. He looked even more out of place in his formal business suit than Niall himself did.

'Filthy habit, I know,' Rheinbach said. 'But this pipe is over two hundred years old and I cannot bring myself to throw it away.'

Niall nodded. He had his own addictions. Who was he to judge anyone else? Some day, he would stop hoping to meet that elusive woman who could match him as an equal. He would stop wasting his time chasing her through the clubs and battlefields of the world, and concentrate on being a doting uncle. In the meantime, he had a job to do.

'Can you tell me what happened?'

Rheinbach put the pipe down again. 'She walked in here late one night. Said hello to the night watchman as she passed him, went to the jewel room, somehow she opened the case where the Fire of Autumn is kept, took it and left. She was quite blatant, didn't attempt to hide from the CCTV cameras. The police are authenticating the tapes now. The mystery is how she opened the case. I'm the only person with access to the pass-code.'

'And what she did with the jewel,' Niall reminded him.

He scowled. 'Yes, that too. We knew she had a passion for stones, especially this one, but we never guessed that she would do anything like this.' Rheinbach switched his scowl to Niall. 'The ruby is on loan to the museum. I want you to find the Fire of Autumn, before word of this gets back to its owner. Can you do it?'

Niall nodded. 'If the price is right.'

He kept his expression neutral, but inside he was cheering. This couldn't have come at a better time. His security company, small, select and highly specialized, was in trouble. He had lost one of his most skilled operators just after he expanded into Europe and now two more were injured. The move had been costly. This job could be the one that saved his company.

He withstood Rheinbach's probing examination stoically. He knew that in spite of his formal suit, he didn't look like a businessman. He was too big, too muscular, and his hair, though neatly tied back, was too long. But his background in the Irish Rangers and running his own security company made him the best in the business.

Money was something Rheinbach understood. After some intense haggling, they agreed a price for the job. Niall was to find the ruby and return it to the museum before the stone went back to King Abdullah. Piece of cake.

'And no publicity, of course,' Rheinbach warned, before handing Niall his copy of the file containing the thief's details.

He glanced at the photograph on the file first. A mousy-looking woman, with large glasses and hair pulled back into one of those complicated and unflattering plaits women were so fond of. Her mouth was set in a tight line, as if someone had cracked a dirty joke and she disapproved.

She looked like someone who would fine you for returning a library book late rather than an audacious jewel thief. And she looked familiar.

He turned his attention to the personal details, and his jaw dropped.

Sinead O'Sullivan.

It couldn't be. Sinead O'Sullivan was the niece of one of his biggest clients, the billionaire aviation magnate, Tim O'Sullivan. Their paths had crossed briefly a few months before when O'Sullivan's daughter Summer was kidnapped. He didn't recall ever talking to Sinead. She was just there – mousy and a bit old-fashioned. He examined the photo again. He could well believe that this woman was sought-after as a curator, but not that she was a jewel thief.

'Are you sure she's the thief? She doesn't seem the type.'

'There's no doubt that it was her, her fingerprints are all over the place, she was seen by a witness. There is also CCTV footage of the theft,' Rheinbach said grimly.

'In that case, consider the jewel as good as back in your collection.'

Niall left the museum, glancing back at the building, which looked like something out of a Disney fantasy, all turrets and towers and pointed windows overlooking the lake. But looks were deceiving; this building was as secure as Fort Knox. It was almost as deceptive as Sinead O'Sullivan's appearance.

He considered the best way to investigate her.

Niall turned up the collar of his long woollen trench coat. Geneva was picturesque. The fountain splashed in the sunlight, but a cold wind blew down from the Alps. He took his phone off silent and it rang seconds later.

'Damn it, Moore, do you never answer your fecking phone? I've been ringing you for the last hour.' Tim O'Sullivan's voice boomed out, startling the couple standing at a tram stop.

'I've answered it now,' Niall said. He knew that it was never a good idea to make excuses to O'Sullivan. He took it as a sign of weakness.

'I've a job for you.'

'I'm already on a job.'

'Drop it. You're on a retainer to me. If you don't do the work when necessary, you're in breach of your contract.'

Fuck. O'Sullivan paid well but he was demanding, and if Niall didn't produce the goods, the Corkman would have no hesitation in blackening his name and his company throughout Europe. And he had an idea what O'Sullivan was ringing about.

A second later, Tim confirmed it. 'Did you hear that those gobshites in Switzerland have arrested my niece? They're accusing Sinead of stealing.'

'Yes sir, I heard about that.'

'As if my Sinead would steal their poxy jewel.'

Despite himself, Niall smiled. 'The Fire of Autumn is hardly poxy. It's the largest ruby in the world and worth over $50 million.'

13

'Fecking nonsense, the whole thing.' O'Sullivan made a disgusted noise. 'Anyway, I've put up a million Swiss francs in bail. I want to make sure it stays safe. You're to get to Geneva, make sure she obeys the conditions of her bail and turns up for court.'

'That's all?'

'What else is there?' O'Sullivan snarled. 'Make sure my money doesn't go walkabout.'

Niall's thoughts whirled. There was no conflict of interest here, he could keep an eye on Sinead and find the ruby at the same time. Two satisfied customers. Win-win.

'As long as you tell Sinead about it.'

He considered his next move, but it was obvious really. Sinead O'Sullivan was alone in a strange city, accused of a serious crime, under stringent bail conditions. She needed a friend. He wracked his brains, trying to remember anything he could about Sinead. He wondered if she had a boyfriend. There was something about her being a straight-A student who never got into trouble. Considering that picture, he wasn't surprised there was nothing about boyfriends.

Moore Enterprises had one operator who specialized in seduction, but Andy was busy right now. Besides, sending in Tall Dark and Handsome was probably overkill. There was no point in overwhelming the poor girl.

Looks like he would have to do it himself.

Twenty minutes later, he had found his way to the address listed on the file. After holding the main door open for an elderly lady with two poodles, he climbed the stairs to the fourth floor apartment and knocked on her door.

When it opened, he smiled. 'Hello, Sinead. I'm Niall Moore, your uncle sent me.'

No. No. This was not happening. Sinead closed her eyes and opened them again but he was still there. Niall Moore was standing on her doorstep, grinning down at her. She hadn't seen him since her last night in London, when he had stared at her with such heat in his eyes that she thought she might spontaneously combust.

Unfortunately, that scorching look had been directed at her glamorous alter ego, Lottie LeBlanc, not at plain Jane museum curator Sinead O'Sullivan.

His eyes flicked dismissively over the damp towel wrapped around her head and her sensible blue woollen dressing gown before returning to her face.

'You might want to . . .' Niall brushed a finger along the edge of her chin and scooped up a creamy drop of moisturizer before offering it to her. Trying not to cringe, she scraped the gloopy substance from his index finger and rubbed it into her hands. Oh, great. She thought her day couldn't get any more bizarre but this took the biscuit.

She had been arrested before breakfast. Had spent hours being questioned by a plodding Inspector Clouseau look-alike at the police station before her uncle Tim had arranged her release. She had come home to find that her apartment had been ransacked. A polite note from the police announced that they had taken certain items away for further examination.

With typical Swiss efficiency, an itemized list accompanied the note. Sinead shuddered when she thought of what their forensics department might do with her scarlet rhinestone-studded corset. At least the rest of her costumes were in storage. She would have to sort them out at some stage but . . .

'Sinead?' Niall prompted, and she stepped back to allow him to enter.

He glanced around, taking in the scattered paperwork, the empty shelves where her collection of books had stood. Even the tiny excuse for a kitchen hadn't escaped their attention. The contents of her fridge had been thoroughly searched, the bags of frozen vegetables opened, even the tray of ice cubes had been defrosted.

Niall whistled. 'Good party, was it?'

Sinead shot him a look that would melt steel. 'Would you like to tell me what you're doing here?'

He ignored her glare. 'You could say that I was in the neighbourhood. Tim said you were in some kind of trouble.'

The unwelcome sympathy in his eyes made her turn away. She didn't want his pity. Oh god, Tim. Her determination not to cry almost broke. The awful phone call when she had to explain that she had been arrested for stealing; her uncle's stunned silence on the other end of the line – a miracle in itself, given his encyclopaedic knowledge of swearwords – and then the torrent of expletives that had followed.

Niall dropped his holdall on the floor, shrugged out of his coat and hung it on a hook beside the door. 'Let's get this place cleaned up before we talk.'

She watched as Niall crossed the room and began to re-shelve her scattered books. Her inner control freak itched to remind him to file them according to subject, but it didn't matter now. Nothing mattered. She had been suspended from her job. The police had branded her a thief. None of her colleagues at the museum would tell her what was going on. Every one of them had politely referred her to Günter, but the director had refused to take her calls. It was her worst nightmare come true.

Well, almost her worst nightmare.

How could anyone believe that she would steal from her own collection? And to imagine that she would be stupid enough to take something like the Fire of Autumn?

The Fire was unsaleable. It would be easier to flog the Mona Lisa at Sotheby's. A stone like that couldn't disappear. It was ridiculous. None of the wealthy private collectors would touch it.

Throughout the long hours in the cell, she had mentally gone through her list of contacts in the stolen art world. One of them must know something. She would start contacting them tomorrow, put out a few feelers and see if anyone had heard a whisper.

'Sinead?'

She blinked. She had zoned out again, clutching a leather-bound volume about medieval silversmiths. She couldn't concentrate on anything. Niall was talking to her and she had missed what he was saying. He took the book from her hand and she didn't protest when he filed it next to one about Victorian mourning jewellery. She would fix it later when she could think clearly.

Niall was holding her hand, stroking her wrist gently. His touch was warm; his familiar Irish accent was soothing. 'You can tell me. It's okay if you did it. We can sort

17

this out quietly. Maybe you made a mistake, you were tired . . .'

Somewhere in her foggy brain an alarm bell went off. Sinead pulled her hand away. Was she the only sane person left on the planet?

'Do I look like a kleptomaniac housewife who drops a lipstick into her handbag when she's doing the grocery shopping? I am not a thief and I did not steal the jewel.'

Niall stood up. 'Great. I'm sure the judge will be delighted to hear it. Now, how about you get dressed while I unpack?'

'Unpack?' He was staying? He couldn't be serious. The tiny spare room had a single bed that would barely hold a three year old and there was only one bathroom. 'You can't possibly stay here.'

'Your uncle paid a million francs to get you out of jail. Until the trial is over, he's instructed me not to let you out of my sight.'

Sinead folded her arms across her chest. He meant it. Niall Moore was going to hang around here, like a bad smell, until the trial was over? That could be months away. She stared into his flinty gaze, trying not to flinch. She could see how it would intimidate someone who was working for him. Even more eerie was the way he could flip from tender to tough in a heartbeat.

How was she going to find the real thief if he was following her around, watching her every move?

Her cousin, Summer, said that Niall didn't do serious relationships and Sinead wondered idly if he had ever lived with a woman. She was sure that they must have female security operatives, but probably not too many.

Anyway, it was none of her business. She would have to find a way of getting rid of him. But nicely. She didn't want Tim revoking her bail because she wouldn't co-operate.

Sinead smiled sweetly at him. 'Fine, if you're sure you want to. Let me show you the spare room.'

She tried to keep her face straight as she led him to the guest bedroom. Sinead pushed open the door and turned on the light. A bare light bulb illuminated the room.

A brightly coloured duvet cover announced that she was Little Miss Fussy. The girls at the museum in London had bought it for her as a joke. They knew Little Miss Fussy slept alone.

She had been called worse things than that. It wasn't her fault that she liked to be organized. She stifled a grin as she watched Niall survey his new home. He'd be lucky to last the night. By morning he would be gone to some plush hotel.

2

Niall dropped his bag on the bed, and took off his coat. He couldn't take his eyes off her face. At close quarters, her eyes were mesmerizing. In the photo, her spectacles had obscured her best feature. Now they were on full view and he couldn't stop staring. Niall wondered absently how she managed to wear glasses. Surely those ridiculously long lashes must catch against the lenses?

The expression in her narrowed eyes jerked him out of his reverie. 'Take a picture, it will last longer,' Sinead snapped.

Her lips were pressed together in a stern line. He wondered if it was her default expression, or was it just him that pissed her off. He had to admit that he hadn't exactly made a great first impression.

It was a pity really. Looking at her objectively, he realized that she wasn't bad looking. With a bit of effort, she'd be quite passable.

He examined the ugly dressing gown she wore and wondered what was underneath it. Not that he fancied her, but he was a man after all, with all the functioning body parts and an adequate supply of testosterone. A woman's dressing gown begged to be opened.

He leaned in a little closer so he could peer down the front of it. While her face was still greasy with whatever gloop she had slathered on it, the skin at her neck was white with faint veins under it, and for a fascinated moment, he allowed himself to watch the pulse of an artery. It sped up under his gaze.

The appeal of vampire novels made more sense now. He had a sudden urge to bite that delicate skin and mark it. He didn't understand the surge of possessiveness that swamped him.

His gaze dipped to where the edges of the dressing gown met. From his superior height, he could look down and see a hint of cleavage. It was a very nice cleavage and surprisingly bountiful for such a skinny woman.

He was losing it. Since when did he get turned on by old-maid librarian types? Young old maid, he amended. According to her file, she was twenty-seven, despite the fact that she could easily pass for a woman in her late thirties.

Sinead finally realized where his eyes were straying, and yanked the edges of her dressing gown closer together. 'God, you're disgusting.'

'Have you ever seen *The Secretary*?' he asked. Maybe she was secretly kinky and he was picking up the vibes.

She glared at him. 'No, and don't change the subject. If you have to stay here, you can keep your eyes and your hands to yourself. I'm not going to be harassed in my own apartment.' She took a breath, and her eyes clouded. 'For as long as I still have it.'

Oh yeah. She was now out of work, and Geneva wasn't exactly a cheap city to live in. He wondered what would happen to her when he found the ruby. Even if she managed to escape a jail sentence, she'd never work as a curator again.

What had possessed her? he wondered angrily. It wasn't as if she was short of money. She might not have a share of the O'Sullivan fortune, but she was never going to starve. And someone with her education and CV could always have found a good job. Now that was gone.

And jail was still on the cards. The Swiss were not fond of thieves. They could well make an example of the Irish-woman who had dared to steal a historic jewel from under their noses. Even her blue eyes and white skin wouldn't save her.

'What colour is your hair?' he asked. It was still wrapped in a white towel.

She stared at him for a long moment until he wondered what he had said wrong. It had been a reasonable question.

'I can see I made a big impression on you.'

Now it was his turn to stare. 'What do you mean?'

'We met less than four months ago in London. And you clearly have no memory of it.' Her voice was even, but he could hear a trace of hurt.

Oh fuck.

'I'm sorry. But I was working on your cousin's kidnapping, I didn't have time to check out the talent.'

'I'm glad that my red hair qualifies me as "talent". I'm going to dry it off and get dressed. You can unpack and settle in. I have to go to the police station to hand in my passport,' she said bitterly. She closed the door of the bedroom firmly behind her.

When the noise of the hairdryer assured him that she was fully occupied, Niall left his room and carried out a rapid search of the small apartment. The kitchen yielded nothing except a suspicion that she was on a permanent diet or didn't shop enough. There were a few bags of frozen vegetables, half a dozen eggs, a tiny carton of skimmed milk and a box of cereal that looked like something scraped off the bottom of a hamster cage. There was an open bottle of Swiss white wine with one glass gone from it. She clearly didn't entertain.

In the open-plan living room, he found a large collection of old books, many of them antiques and valuable in their own right. He wondered cynically if any of them had come from museums whose staff didn't know they were missing. Most of them related to fine arts and jewels. One was a history of the Fire of Autumn. He flicked the pages, eyebrows rising as he noticed the list of former owners of the ruby. It seemed to have gone from India, through the dowry of Margaret Theresa of Spain, to Napoleon Bonaparte, to Archduke Ferdinand, to the Nazis before King Abdullah purchased it from Harry Winston.

With that history, it made a sort of twisted sense that someone like Sinead could give in to the craving to own it. It wasn't just a jewel – it was a piece of history.

Tucked into the back of the book was a newspaper cutting with a photograph of Sinead holding a large ruby. Below a headline crowed about the Rheinbach scoring a coup by being able to put the fabled ruby on display for the first time in almost one hundred years.

The rest of the apartment was surprisingly bare. She had a long couch that might be more comfortable than the child-sized bed in the spare room, several floor-to-ceiling mirrors, a framed photograph of herself and her cousin Summer; arm in arm at their graduation from Trinity College Dublin and a beaming Tim O'Sullivan in the background.

He wondered why Sinead's parents were not in the picture. Surely they would have been at her graduation? He sent a quick email to Andy to check them out.

The hairdryer switched off, so he sped up his search. Nothing much out of the ordinary, unless he counted the drawer in the tiny hallway, which yielded a pair of Gore-Tex ski gloves, perfect for a Swiss winter – and six pairs of opera gloves.

The door of the bedroom opened and she came out, dressed in jeans and a bulky jumper. It was a kaleidoscope of colours, unlike anything he had ever seen before, and it swallowed her slender body.

'Where did you get that?' he asked. He couldn't decide if he loved it or hated it.

She shrugged. 'Granny O'Sullivan knitted it for me, with all the odds and ends of leftover wool from things she had knitted for other people.'

He couldn't suppress a pang. His own mother was a knitter, and he'd had to suffer horrors from her needles. Did she really think that an undercover operator would wear a bright red sweater patterned with dog heads? But at least she had knitted it with new wool.

'Come on,' he said, his voice a little rougher than he was expecting. 'You can hand in your passport at the station and then I'll buy you dinner.'

His rented car, or rather his Jeep, was just like him. It was large and imposing, from the don't-mess-with-me chrome grill to the dashboard that lit up like a cockpit when he turned on the ignition. What was it with men and cars? Her cousin Summer used to joke that the bigger the car the smaller the . . .

'Is something amusing you?'

'No.' She flushed under his intent gaze. It probably wouldn't apply to Niall anyway. He was probably big all over. She was almost 5' 7" and taller when she wore heels, but he made her feel tiny and feminine. Sinead plucked a bobble of wool on her sweater. She had meant to go shopping for clothes, but never seemed to find the time.

Why on earth had she worn this? Her outfit would look more at home on the ski slopes than in a restaurant. She wished that she'd brought some of her Lottie clothes when she moved from London. Her first dinner date in months and she was dressed like a frump.

She couldn't believe that Niall Moore was actually here. He had been centre stage in her fantasies for weeks after the night in the theatre, but he didn't even remember what colour her hair was. She felt like a pathetic loser. Sinead cast a sideways glance at him from beneath her lashes. Everything about him was calm and controlled. He projected an air of quiet confidence that almost made her relax. He touched the indicator and turned onto Rue de Berne before parking the car near the police station.

She gripped the door handle. 'I'll be back in a few –'

'I'm coming with you,' he said in a tone that brooked no argument.

Sinead didn't protest. She would be glad of his company on the walk of shame. Just then his phone rang. From the expression on his face, it was a private call and she heard the tinny echo of a woman's voice. He put his hand over the mouthpiece and shrugged apologetically. Of course someone like him would have a girlfriend; he probably had a string of them.

Sinead slid from the car and made her way to the station. She would have to do this alone.

A wraith-thin man with spiked blond hair and a leather jacket did a double take as they passed each other at the entrance. 'You too?' he laughed.

Sinead glared at him. Idiot. He must be drunk. 'Do I know you?'

'I'd never forget a performance like that. You were sooo hot.' He leered at her.

Sinead froze. A performance? It wasn't possible that this man could have recognized her as Lottie. 'You're mistaken,' she said with as much confidence as she could muster.

'Baby, how could I forget? The way you worked that –'

'You heard the lady. She doesn't know you. Take a hike.'

She hadn't heard Niall approach. How could someone so big move so silently? The menace in his tone was unmistakeable and the man slipped away, disappearing into the crowd on Rue de Berne. Relieved, she smiled up at him.

'That was one of my female operatives on the phone,' he explained. 'She's having a little trouble with a client. She's on a 24/7.'

Sinead turned away. A 24/7? He meant a job. She had probably misinterpreted those looks he had given her earlier at the apartment. She was obviously suffering from sexual deprivation.

She had thought that giving up Lottie would mean the start of a new life. No more working late nights and weekends. No more being afraid to date a guy in case he found out about her other life. But the months without Lottie had been, well, dull. She had lost something. A bright spark of energy had disappeared from her life and she couldn't remember the last time she had –

'Good evening, Mademoiselle O'Sullivan.'

Sinead recognized the middle-aged man as one of the detectives who had questioned her earlier. He flicked an interested glance at Niall before returning his attention to her. 'I have something to return to you. One of my men may have been a little over-zealous during the search of your apartment.'

Her heart dropped. They had taken some of her books, bank statements, papers relating to the museum and the rhinestone-covered corset she had worn on her first show and had never been able to part with. She doubted he was returning a book. She breathed a sigh of relief when he handed over the corset wrapped up in an opaque evidence bag.

Sinead signed the paperwork for the bag, handed over her passport and took the card which showed her next court date, before she hurried from the station. She had spent too much time here today.

She checked the remand date when she was in the Jeep. Tuesday week. They were obviously keeping close tabs on her. Well, she supposed a million francs bail made her a sort of criminal celebrity.

Niall eyed the bag. 'Something important?'

'Just some clothing.' She smiled. 'Now, feed me. I'm starving.'

In a small corner booth of an Italian restaurant, Niall ordered salmon, while she ordered a chicken breast and salad without dressing. A glass of white wine took the edge off her nerves and the grim reality of the day finally hit her. She was on bail for a crime she hadn't committed. Uncle Tim's money was the only thing between her and a prison cell. She had lost her job and her reputation as a curator was almost destroyed.

As if he could read her thoughts, Niall covered her hand with his. 'Everything will be okay when the stone turns up, I promise.'

She managed a half smile and wished she was as certain. 'I hope so.'

Niall leaned back in his seat, dwarfing the small booth. 'So tell me how you ended up in Geneva.'

'I got a job offer at the Rheinbach. They needed someone to take care of their jewel collection.'

'Sounds like you took care of it a bit too well.'

She narrowed her eyes at him. What was wrong with him? He was supposed to be here to help her. 'Look, I've worked with precious stones and priceless works of art for seven years. I'm a professional curator, not a thief.'

The waiter arrived with a basket of grissini and a bowl of olives drenched in olive oil. She shuddered at the thought of the calories in those, but took a breadstick and crumbled the end of it.

'So why do you think they've arrested you?' Niall asked.

'They said they found my fingerprints in the jewel room.' She snorted. 'Of course they did. I work there.'

'There has to be more evidence than that.'

'Do we have to have the interrogation with dinner? I'd rather eat on my own.' Sinead put her glass down and slid from the booth.

'Oh, come back. You have to eat. I promise not to ask you any more questions.'

Sinead settled back into her seat. 'Sorry, it's been a horrible day and I'm stressed.'

Niall changed the subject. 'You're not much like Summer.'

Funny how much it still hurt to be constantly compared to her famous cousin. 'We can't all be socialites,' she snapped.

'I just meant that you're quieter than she is.'

Despite herself, Sinead smiled. 'Did no one ever tell you that it's the quiet ones that you have to watch out for?' Quiet wasn't a word she would use to describe her cousin. 'Summer was a handful. Uncle Tim relied on me to get her through school without being expelled.'

'Was that a tough job?'

Sinead took another sip of wine. 'You have no idea. She was a magnet for trouble.'

'You were probably as bad.' He popped an olive into his mouth.

She laughed at the idea of that. She had always been the good girl, the one who didn't break the rules. 'Yeah, right.'

'That hair doesn't lie.'

Offended, she straightened her spine. 'What's wrong with my hair?'

He grinned, pleased with her reaction. 'Nothing. I love it, but it's not the hair of a demure girl who never gets into trouble.' He munched another olive. 'There's something about redheads that does it for me, all that fiery passion waiting to be unleashed.'

'My passions are not for unleashing, thank you,' she said primly. 'They're fine just where they are.'

Now he looked interested and leaned forwards. 'Come

on, tell me, what does it take for you to let go? What arouses you?' He had stopped eating while he waited for her answer.

She was flabbergasted. 'What? Do you always talk to complete strangers like this?'

'We're not strangers.'

'Yes, we are.'

The waiter arrived with their food before he could reply. She was grateful for the chance to change the direction of the conversation. Niall Moore was an investigator, but she didn't want him digging too deeply into her life.

Her chicken was as she had specified, grilled and skinless, with no sauce. Her salad was fresh and crisp. The waiter set bottles of olive oil, vinegar and lemon juice on the table, so that she could mix her own dressing.

Niall sliced into his fish. 'So, what did you study at college?'

'History of art and after college I went straight into Sotheby's.'

He leaned forwards. 'Really? That seems like a fast move.'

'I have a talent for spotting fakes, Mr Moore.'

Niall laughed. He had a nice smile and she began to feel more cheerful; at least he had stopped asking questions about the theft. 'Is that a jibe? I'm solid all the way through.'

'Merely an observation. Just what did my uncle tell you?'

'Not a lot. Only that you were on bail and that he wanted someone to take care of you.'

She let that one pass. She doubted if Niall was lying, but he wasn't being entirely truthful either. 'I see. Well, I'm used to taking care of myself.'

Niall frowned. 'You didn't do such a good job this time. You're under arrest and charged with a serious crime.'

'And do you usually move in with your clients?'

'No, only the pretty ones.'

She rolled her eyes. 'Save it for someone who believes you.'

Niall laughed. 'Worth a try. Besides, you really are pretty, in a buttoned-down sort of way.'

She did feel that she had lost something of herself since she moved to Geneva. She had lost the Lottie sparkle.

'Really? It's amazing how many times a day I hear that.'

Niall ignored her sarky tone. 'But you don't make the most of yourself. That sweater swamps you.'

She knew that she shouldn't have worn it but she wasn't prepared to listen to him telling her that. 'You wouldn't say that to me if I was a man. I may have to put up with you staying at my place, but don't push it.'

He raised his glass to her. 'Prickly, aren't you? You're probably hungry. Here, have some fries.'

'Fries? No thanks.' She pushed the basket of fries away, and watched him dig in. She shuddered when he dipped them in mayonnaise. How could he do that?

They ate in silence for a few minutes, until Sinead had eaten as much as she would allow herself. She put down her knife and fork and waited for Niall to finish.

She saw him glance at the food remaining on her plate. He stretched his arm across the table and put his hand over hers. 'Stop worrying. Talk to me. Tell me what's going on. I can help.'

Sinead stared down at their hands. His was warm and

broad; hers was pale and small in comparison. 'I swear to you that I didn't steal the jewel. I love my job, I would never do anything to jeopardize it.'

'Then who did?'

She only wished she knew. 'I have no idea.'

Niall paid the bill and they strolled to the car park. There was a chill in the air that even a Granny O'Sullivan sweater couldn't keep out. She shivered and Niall was immediately all concern. He shrugged out of his coat and wrapped it around her. The woollen coat almost reached her ankles and she caught the faint scent of his aftershave as he pulled the collar up around her, a heady blend of citrus, leather and sandalwood – sexy and intensely masculine. She resisted the urge to bury her face in the collar and sniff.

Something flickered behind his brooding gaze. The events of the day had definitely addled her brain. She was tempted to stand on tiptoe and kiss him. As if he had plucked the thought from her head, Niall brushed his lips against hers in a barely-there kiss.

Her pulse hammered at the touch of his lips and she pulled away. Had he just done that? Kissed her? She had been right about that mouth and the encounter left her wanting more.

'Sinead, I can help, but only if you trust me.'

She hesitated. It would be nice to trust someone, to be able to lean on him and share everything. She could never seem to break through the barriers she had built around herself. Something always held her back.

All of her friends were still in London. Her cousin Summer was in South America. She barely knew a soul here in Geneva and it was months since she had really talked to anyone. What would happen if the police started snooping around and found her connection with Lottie? She dreaded to think what the museum would do if they found out that their curator was a former burlesque dancer. They would believe that she was lying about stealing the Fire of Autumn. She needed to talk to someone.

'Niall, I –'

The sound of a car alarm shattered the moment and they broke apart.

On the drive back to her apartment, Sinead watched the city shut down for the night. It was barely 10 p.m. She had never known a city that went to bed so early. She tapped her fingers against her thigh. There was no way that she could sleep yet.

Up ahead she spotted an off-licence. The lights were still on. There was a nice bottle of Bushmills whiskey back at the apartment. 'Pull over here. I need to get some ice.'

Niall watched her as she hefted a bag of ice into the back of the Jeep.

'What's that for?' he asked. 'Because if you are thinking of getting kinky, I should warn you I don't put out on the first date.'

She glared at him, her eyes dark under the streetlights. 'Idiot. I don't do kinky. I don't do anything.' She sounded almost triumphant.

Niall's finely honed instincts, which had saved his life on too many occasions to count, went on the alert. There was something off about Sinead O'Sullivan. He had the feeling that she was hiding something. There was definitely something going on beneath her placid surface.

Had she stolen the Fire of Autumn? She was lying about something.

What had she said? 'I don't do kinky, I don't do anything.' Somewhere in that statement was a lie, and a lie she was proud of. So Ms O'Sullivan had hidden depths? This assignment was starting to look a whole lot more interesting.

'So what's with the ice?' he asked, forcing his attention back to the road.

She shrugged, the movement almost lost in her big sweater. 'I fancy a nightcap, that's all.'

He drove on, the ice rattling every time they passed over a speed bump.

Her apartment was warm and quiet, and very small. It was going to be interesting spending so much time at close quarters with her. As she fiddled with the door key, he caught her distinctive scent. The smell of the shampoo had faded, leaving pure woman. He filled his lungs with it. He had no idea why women insisted on paying a fortune for all sorts of fake perfumes, when they already possessed the most enticing smell in the world.

He grinned. Well, second most enticing smell.

She turned and caught his expression. 'What are you laughing at?'

'Just thinking about smells I love.'

He held the door open for her. She headed straight for the kitchen and rooted in one of the cupboards. With a shrug, she took out two water tumblers and the bottle of

Bushmills. 'Hmmm, I love the smell of the sea. And cut grass.'

'Everyone loves those. What about ones that are personal to you?' He sprawled out on the sofa and watched her splash whiskey over ice-cubes before she handed him a glass.

Sinead took a sip of her drink and considered. 'The smell of boxty cooking. Granny O'Sullivan used to make it.'

'What about bread baking? Did your mother bake?'

Her expression clouded and she shook her head. 'I don't remember.'

Interesting. Reference to her mother closed her down. 'Let's see. I love steak of course. And the smell of onions frying. And bacon!' He smacked his lips.

'Saturated fat!' But she was interested again. 'Have you any idea of the dangers of processed meat?'

Niall patted his stomach, still flat, thanks to a punishing workout routine. One thing about the Rangers, they didn't take on weaklings or let them get lazy. He had been at 5 per cent body fat when he left the wing. Even now, he was around 7 per cent and planning to stay there. 'I think I can handle the odd slice. So what smells do you love?'

'Eyelash glue.'

Niall sat up straight. She couldn't possibly need eyelash glue with those lashes. They were already longer than most fakes. But she went on before he could demand details.

'Saddle soap. And newborn babies.'

He wasn't going to touch that one. He had a fleeting vision of Sinead holding a red-haired baby and found himself becoming strangely intrigued. Not somewhere he wanted to go. She'd probably put the baby on a timetable. 'You have a thing for horses?' he asked instead.

'There was a really cute stable boy who used to clean the tack for the O'Sullivans,' she said with a sly, unexpected grin. Then she sobered. 'Not that he had eyes for anyone except Summer.' She was matter-of-fact about it, as if being ignored in favour of her cousin was something that happened a lot.

She topped up their drinks. Funny, he had no memory of emptying his glass. 'So what is your favourite smell?'

He leaned back on the sofa, stretching out so that his foot touched hers. 'Fresh pussy juice, of course.'

She choked on the sip of Bush and coughed so hard Niall got up to thump her on the back. Eventually she caught her breath and pulled away, glaring at him.

'And this is why I'm still single,' she told him.

She clambered to her feet, slightly unsteady after the whiskey and headed for the bathroom. 'I'm going to bed. You can stay up if you like but this apartment building has a late noise rule, so don't put on loud music or make a racket. In fact, it would be better if you didn't shower until morning.'

She closed the door in his face, and, a few minutes later, he heard her brushing her teeth.

With a sigh, he went into the tiny spare room. The bed was going to be grossly uncomfortable for a man of his height.

He'd had a couple of hours' sleep when he was woken by noises from Sinead's room. Not bothering to put anything on over his boxer shorts, he hurried into her room, but came to an abrupt halt when he saw that she was still asleep.

She twisted in the bed, her limbs caught up in rumpled bedclothes. She slept in panties and a short camisole that looked damp. 'No,' she murmured. 'Please, don't go.' Her eyes remained closed.

Niall put his hand on her shoulder to wake her. 'Sinead, it's okay.'

She flinched. 'No, no, no, no. I won't.' Her voice had gone up an octave, more like a child than the assured woman she seemed to be.

He shook her again and she batted his hand away. She was deep in the grip of whatever nightmare she was enduring. 'RoRo!' Tears leaked from under the closed eye-lids.

Ah, damn it. Niall could never bear to see a woman crying. Not like this. He climbed into her bed and pulled her firmly against him. 'Shush, shush, it's all right now,' he said, much the way he had to his sister Alison when she was a kid.

Sinead struggled feebly against him for a few minutes, then settled with a sigh, and relaxed into deep sleep.

He would stay here for a few minutes, Niall assured himself. He wasn't enjoying holding her like this. He didn't miss a woman in his bed. This wasn't even his bed. But it was more comfortable than the lumpy child-sized mattress in the spare room. He stretched out his long legs. A few more minutes of comfort, to make sure she was sleeping soundly, and then he'd return to his own room.

Just a few more minutes . . .

3

Her head was pounding and her mouth tasted like something had died in there. Sinead tried to groan, but her throat was parched and it came out as a cough. She pressed a hand against her thumping forehead. How much whiskey had she had to drink last night? A heavy arm snaked across her waist and she was dragged against a large warm body. Niall palmed her breast with a possessive grip. He snuffled against the back of her neck before his steady breathing told her that he was still sleeping.

Oh god, I didn't. Please don't let me have fallen into bed with him.

Sinead risked a peek beneath the duvet. In the early morning light, she could see she was still wearing her panties, so they hadn't had sex, but the strap of her camisole had fallen from her shoulder and Niall was taking full advantage of her exposed flesh. The desire to wriggle free wrestled with the unfamiliar pleasure of sharing her bed with a man. Hedonism won. Niall was still asleep and it wouldn't do any harm to enjoy this for a few minutes more. She closed her eyes, savouring the pleasure.

The chest that pressed against her back was almost completely smooth. The muscular thighs that spooned hers were strong. On the small table beside the bed was a clasp for his hair. The sight of it made her want to turn in his arms. Before Niall, she had dismissed long hair on men as an aberration, something for rebellious teenagers or ageing rock stars. He had definitely changed her mind.

Niall reminded her of a pirate from an erotic romance novel. She would love to see him standing on the deck of a frigate, wearing a pair of indecently tight pants, a white linen shirt and his hair loose about his shoulders. He could carry her off to his cabin, tie her to his bed and . . .

Something hard stirring against her thighs startled her. The hand on her breast was no longer still. Niall rolled her nipple between his thumb and forefinger as he slowly plumped her breast. God, that felt good. Sinead wriggled her hips experimentally against him and was rewarded with a lazy thrust.

Her aching nipple protested when it was abandoned and Niall's fingers trailed slowly down her abdomen, learning each curve of her ribs and the soft rounding of her belly until he reached the lacy edge of her panties. She held her breath as he paused there as if waiting for permission to continue. A small whimper of excitement escaped her throat and her hips moved in invitation.

His hand slid beneath the scrap of silk and he hissed when he realized that she was completely smooth. In Lottie's line of work she couldn't be bothered with the endless maintenance. She was as bare as an egg, thanks to a series of laser treatments. His searching fingers slid between her folds and brushed her clit.

'Oh god,' Sinead moaned.

He nuzzled the tender part of her neck where it met her shoulder and bit down gently. 'Say my name.'

The rough command in his voice sent an unfamiliar

tingle through her. She didn't want him to stop. 'Niall.' His name came out in a breathless plea.

His fingers pumped her aching wetness slowly, drawing moisture from her before he brushed her clit again, sending a pulse of pleasure zinging through her. 'Oh yes. Like that.'

She clenched her inner muscles, trying to draw him inside her again. He stilled and she huffed an impatient breath. 'Please. Please, Niall.'

He traced over her tender nub, building sensation with every touch. She was so close and it had been far too long. His other hand caressed her breasts, pinching the sensitive peaks between his fingers until she was breathless and achy.

Her pulse raced, every nerve ending tingled. Tiny fireworks exploded behind her eyes. She was there. Her words an incoherent jumble interspersed with his name, always his name.

He bit down lightly on her shoulder again and it was enough to send her over the edge. She was a floating, boneless, trembling creature on a stormy sea of pleasure and he was her anchor; holding her close as the waves of ecstasy crashed over her and ebbed away.

Finally she was able to open her eyes again. The bedside clock still ticked out its steady rhythm, but her world had shifted on its axis. She wanted to say something, to thank him, but her voice didn't seem to work.

Niall dropped a kiss on her shoulder. 'You go shower while I make us some breakfast.'

He climbed out of bed and paused beside the door. 'Sinead, can I ask you something?'

She rolled over and caught her breath. Holy hell. Had she just spent the night with him? Niall in a pair of boxer shorts was too much man for someone who hadn't had a lover for a while. For anyone female. She realized that she was staring and he was still waiting. 'Yes,' she said, hoping it was the right answer.

'You were having a pretty bad dream last night. Want to talk about it?'

She forced herself to smile. 'Thanks, but I'm fine. It's just an old nightmare.'

He nodded and shut the door behind him.

Sinead ran her hand along the warm part of the bed where he had lain. Her first sexual encounter in more than a year but he hadn't kissed her or permitted her to touch him in return. Everything had been about her. Niall had been in total control and while she wasn't sure if she liked that, her languid body certainly had.

How long had that taken? Minutes? Sinead cringed as she realized how wanton and needy she must have seemed. She flushed, wishing she had behaved with more dignity.

She must have had the nightmare again. Usually she woke in a sweat, battling with the sheets, trying to remember what had left her throat raw and her face wet with tears. This time, instead of spending the rest of the night staring at the ceiling, she had spent it in his arms. She inhaled his scent from the pillow and smiled.

Only then did she catch a glimpse of the bedside clock. 7.30. She had a moment of panic that she was late, before she remembered. Instead of being due at her desk that Monday morning, to work on plans for the exhibition, she was on bail. She was jobless and the highlight for the next week would be meeting her lawyer and wondering how quickly the Swiss authorities would try her for stealing the Fire of Autumn.

They were convinced they had arrested the right person. She knew they were wrong and she had an incentive to find who really did it. She couldn't lie in bed all day. She had a thief to catch, but at least she was no longer alone.

After a quick shower she went to the kitchen to find that he was using every saucepan she had. 'What are you doing?'

'Eggs,' he announced. 'Boiled, scrambled or fried. Take your pick. You don't have any other real food here.'

'I don't eat in the mornings.' It was true. Most days she ate a piece of fruit on the way to work and was on her second cup of herbal tea by eleven.

He raised one blond eyebrow in disapproval.

'Except at weekends,' she said, trying to placate him. She did need his help if she wanted to get out of this mess.

'Pretend it's the weekend,' Niall said as he dished up four eggs onto his plate and poured himself a mug of coffee.

Sinead opened the container of organic muesli and poured fat free yoghurt over it before sprinkling some myrtle berries on top. She hunted for the grater and finely shredded half an apple on top, squeezed lemon on the other half and put it into the fridge for later. Finally she sliced a finger of fresh ginger into a glass and poured on boiling water before topping it up with cold.

Niall watched in fascination. 'Are you for real?'

'What?' she snapped.

'You're not actually going to eat that ... that stuff? I wouldn't give it to a hamster.'

Sinead dug a spoon into her bowl and raised it to her mouth. The yoghurt had softened the grain mixture. It might not look like the most appetizing thing in the world but it was full of nutrients. She took a mouthful and chewed.

And chewed. The oats weren't quite softened yet. Maybe she should leave it for a while longer.

'I dare you to swallow it.' His grin was openly challenging.

With a last vigorous chew, Sinead swallowed and smiled at him. 'Says the man who has just eaten three eggs for breakfast. Maybe you should add some roughage to your diet.'

'Four eggs, and my diet is fine, thank you. What's up with you that you don't have any real food in the house?'

'I have real food.' Well, she had until yesterday. The police had taken away the oddest things for examination and the rest she had dumped because she didn't know how long it had been out of the fridge.

'You need a bit of meat on you. You're too thin.'

She snorted. She had gained ten pounds in the last few months. Since she had given up being Lottie, her weight had crept up. She had been a plump teenager and dancing kept her weight under control.

She had always loved dancing. The ballet classes she had been dragged to with her cousin had started a life-long addiction, but it was the dance classes taken during college that had transformed her. Latin, Tango and Zumba kept her fit, but her first burlesque class was a revelation. She discovered that putting on a mask or a costume enabled her to leave shy Sinead behind and become someone who was flirtatious, sexy and confident.

Her early dance training had given her the poise and flexibility to become a professional and when she had arrived in London, she had braved her first audition. The hours were better than waitressing, but harder on her feet. Even though she performed only part time, to fit in with her MA studies at Sotheby's, Lottie quickly became a star on the burlesque circuit.

Moving to Geneva and working extra hours to master her new role at the museum had taken its toll in a way she hadn't expected. While trying to impress her employer with her serious, studious side, she had lost something.

She hated to admit it, but she missed being Lottie. Her alter ego wouldn't have allowed Niall to bully her in her own home and Lottie wouldn't have permitted him to leave her bed this morning without a rematch.

'You didn't seem to mind earlier.'

And that was obviously the wrong thing to say. He put down his knife and fork, reached across the breakfast bar and touched her cheek.

Sinead stared at the button of his shirt, unwilling to raise her eyes to meet his face.

'Look at me.'

She kept her eyes fixed on his shirt button, hoping that he would stop. Instead his hand cupped her face and he raised her chin until she was forced to look into his eyes.

'That was concern. Not criticism. And as for earlier, I liked you just fine.'

The smouldering heat in his eyes told her that he meant

it. He released her chin and leaned back but not before she realized that she was shaking.

This thing that had flared between them – whatever it was – was dangerous. And Sinead O'Sullivan didn't do dangerous and certainly not with someone like him. This wasn't a nice safe fantasy. It was happening too fast, and she didn't like the feeling of being out of control.

'Finish your breakfast and put on some more coffee. I'm going to take a shower and when I come back, we're going to talk about the ruby.'

Sinead sat at the breakfast bar again and took another spoonful from her cereal. Niall was right. This wasn't food. She looked longingly at the bits of scrambled egg on his plate. It did look good, but she didn't have time to make herself an egg white omelette.

After scraping out her bowl, she went to the bookshelf. The cover of the notebook stated that women who read were dangerous. Inside the back cover was a scribbled list of names. She had hauled the battered notebook through school, college and her years in London. Among the names of school friends and work friends were a few special contacts. People she had done some private consulting for when they wanted to expose a fake, or find out if something was worth buying if the provenance couldn't be completely authenticated.

When she got some privacy, she would make a few calls.

Niall shuddered as he touched himself in the shower. God, what had got into him? He never shared a bed with a woman. Oh sure, he loved women, loved their shape and smell and the feel of their soft flesh under his hands, but he never stayed the night. They played, and then she left or he did.

What had happened last night that he had ended up sleeping in Sinead's bed, and not just sleeping, but holding her in his arms? God, he was getting soft.

All but one part of him. He looked down ruefully at his engorged penis. It had been in a state of semi-arousal since he woke up. Cooking, and looking at her repulsive breakfast, had calmed him enough that he could conduct a rational conversation. She had looked up at him with those damnable eyes and reminded him of how he had woken up. His cock sprang to instant life and he'd had to take refuge in the shower.

He remembered the way her bottom, surprisingly full for such a slender woman, had nestled into his groin. It had been perfect, round with soft flesh covering firm muscle. He wondered idly if she lifted weights.

Her breasts had been a revelation. Somehow she had concealed them under the ugly clothes she wore and he had convinced himself she was flat chested. Niall swallowed. She was so far from flat chested; her breasts were beautiful, high and succulent and topped with prominent nipples that firmed up as soon as he touched them.

His fingers flexed as if he were still feeling them and his hips bucked.

There was no way that his erection was going anywhere.

He rooted around in Sinead's collection of beauty products, wondering what women did with all of them. They must have a purpose, or they wouldn't buy them, but he doubted it. There, that one looked as if it would do. He opened the bottle of Nuxe oil and poured a stream of it into his palm. The smell wafted to his nose, hinting at Sinead.

His erection swelled more urgently.

Niall turned his back so that the shower beat down on his shoulders, and slathered the scented oil down his chest and to his cock. He smoothed it on, poured another dollop of oil and rubbed that around his balls as well as his cock.

He closed his eyes and imagined that the hands caressing his chest belonged to Sinead. He kept his touch light, as if she was exploring for the first time. She'd be tentative at first, he decided, and then she would gain courage. Her fingers would dig into his ribs, run through the meagre strip of hair on his chest. As a teenager, he had hated not having as much body hair as the other kids at Mount Temple. Now he was glad of it. Otherwise Sinead would never explore his chest with her lips like this . . .

The heat of the water on his back was nothing compared to the heat of her mouth as she licked and kissed her way from one nipple to the other. Ah, now she was nipping at one and sucking it into her mouth. The edges of her teeth were sharp and arousing.

Through his eyelashes he glimpsed the water beading on her skin, made it glow in the dim light of the shower stall. Her wet hair, plastered against her head, made her appear younger. She bit one nipple, making him shudder. As his hands moved down his body, so did her mouth.

Sinead was kneeling in front of him, her eyes large and beseeching. Drops of water caught in her outrageous eyelashes. His hands slicked down his cock, pointing it at her open mouth. His fist tightened as her mouth closed over the tip. He groaned and braced himself against the wall.

His bath-time fantasies had always featured Lottie LeBlanc and her amazing champagne glass routine. In his dreams, she had emerged from her on-stage bath, stalked naked over to him and taken his cock in her mouth with all the skill of a courtesan. Now she had been replaced with Sinead O'Sullivan's more hesitant but equally enthusiastic effort.

Sinead licked and sucked, running her tongue over the head of his cock, drinking down the drop of pre-cum, murmuring her approval of his length. Her hands ran up and down his thighs, before cupping his balls with gentle fingers.

As his excitement mounted, her grip became less gentle. Her teeth rasped along the stem of his penis and her fingers pinched his sac while the other hand pressed on the sensitive spot behind it.

It was too much. His back tightened and his hips flexed, thrusting his cock more deeply into her mouth. She hummed in approval, tightening her lips and sucking harder while she held onto his balls.

As his orgasm gathered, he opened his mouth and gasped. His legs shook. The pressure and pleasure as he exploded, jet after jet, was almost too much to bear. He opened his eyes and, for a fleeting second, saw an image of Lottie kneeling at his feet.

4

How long could one man spend in the shower? Sinead glanced at her watch. Almost twenty-five minutes now. It must be the long hair. As if he had heard her thoughts, the bathroom door opened. Amidst a cloud of steam, Niall emerged, a towel slung low on his hips.

Sinead averted her eyes and pretended she was reading. Eye candy didn't begin to describe it. She knew he was big, but Niall was seriously built. He looked like a cover model for a *Men's Health* magazine bodybuilding special. He whistled as he crossed the hall and disappeared into the guest bedroom. Her libido perked up. She couldn't believe that she had actually shared a bed with him. Had spent the night lying in his arms and then this morning he had . . .

Stop that. This thing – whatever it was – was only happening because they had been thrown together by the theft. It wasn't real. When this horrible mess was over, he would return to his own world and she would still be here.

She tossed the magazine aside – it was upside down anyway – and she hoped he hadn't noticed. Sinead stretched. Despite the earth-shattering orgasm earlier, she was stiff from the hours she had spent sitting in the police station the previous day. She wondered if Niall would be amenable to some exercise. She needed some time away from him. And with a body like that, he must do some serious workouts.

Maybe she could suggest a trip to her dance studio and leave him to work out in the gym while she got some exercise? She didn't care what class she took. An hour of Zumba would take the edge off.

When she danced, her mind was free to wander. She could put any problem at the back of her brain and a solution would usually pop up by the time she was ready to shower.

Sinead hurried to her bedroom and tossed some exercise clothing into a bag. This mess about the Fire would be sorted out soon. She hadn't stolen it and there couldn't be any real evidence against her. Of course her fingerprints were all over the jewel room – she worked there – duh! But when the police interviewed the security guards and watched the CCTV footage, they would realize they had made a mistake. All she had to do until then was keep calm and try to find the real thief.

'Going somewhere?' Niall's voice startled her. The man was half cat. She wished that he wouldn't sneak up on her like that.

'Dance class,' she said. 'If I sit around here all day I'll go crazy.'

He shook his head and she sighed, determined not to fight with him. She tried to sound reasonable, 'Look, I need to exercise and they have a great gym there.'

That sealed the deal.

At the studio, Sinead stared at the display board in the lobby. It was all classes aimed at housewives or mothers with young children. No Zumba until this evening, but there was pole-dancing starting in five minutes.

'Do you know that your mouth twitches when you're trying not to smile? As if the smile is trying to escape.'

She glared at Niall. 'I do smile.'

'Not enough.' He tapped the end of her nose. 'I'll see you in 90 minutes.'

'Arrogant ass,' she muttered, to his departing back. By the time she changed and found the right studio, class had already started. Sinead took a place at the back and warmed up before approaching her pole.

The other students appeared to be beginners. She should have checked that. It didn't matter. At least she was dancing, and she could do her own thing. Sinead warmed up, then moved into a body wave, lifting off the floor, undulating her hips in a slow provocative wave. Sinead smiled at the simple pleasure the physical exercise gave her. It had been a while, but she hadn't forgotten everything. Next, she grasped the pole and spun, going from a simple front hook to a back hook to a fireman spin to get back into the swing of it.

She jumped and swung high, arching her back as she spiralled around the pole, her hair flying out behind her. Next, she tried a flagpole move and her lats screamed in protest. Ouch. That hurt. How had she lost her dance fitness so quickly?

If Lottie was here she would have laughed her head off. She swung up on the pole again, determined to get it right.

When the music changed she realized that she had an audience. 'Sorry,' she said sheepishly. It wasn't fair to show off in a beginner's class.

The teacher clapped her hands. 'Take five, everyone.'

The other students dispersed, giggling, and the teacher approached Sinead.

'Sorry, I didn't mean to . . .'

'Don't apologize.' The blonde smiled. 'I haven't seen you perform since the club in London. I thought you had a gig with Cirque in Paris?'

Sinead froze. This was the second stranger in two days to recognize her. 'Um, no. I don't,' she mumbled, playing along. What the hell was Cirque?

'Well, you should. You're wasted here. Geneva's so dull.' The blonde didn't wait for her response. She scribbled on the back of a card and handed it to her.

Sinead glanced down at the card. Tasha. She definitely didn't know her. It must be a case of mistaken identity.

'Tell them I sent you. They'll have no problem finding you work.'

'Thanks.' Sinead smiled politely. 'I'll do that.'

The studio door opened and the students filed back into the room.

Niall racked the 265 kg squat bar and stepped back, panting. Amazing how a couple of days away from the gym could hurt him. He'd made up for it now, and had the proof in his shaking muscles. But the heavy lifting routine had helped him clear his head. Now that he had a break from Sinead's heady scent and mesmerizing eyes – where had that thought come from? There was nothing special about her eyes – he could think clearly.

He had to remember that he had two jobs here, and neither of them involved playing knight-errant. Recover the Fire of Autumn for the museum, and make sure Sinead turned up for her court dates and obeyed her bail conditions. She was the one who had got herself into this and he was not here to rescue her.

He was still at a loss to know why someone with so much going for her had stolen the ruby. It didn't make sense, and anything that didn't make sense bothered him.

He dashed through his shower, refusing to think about his shower earlier this morning.

Sinead was waiting for him outside, foot tapping while she checked her watch. The librarian was back. She was still dressed casually, in jeans and a baggy T-shirt, but her face was closed off, hair scraped back into a tidy but unattractive bun. She had gone back into her shell again. 'You took your time,' she snapped.

'A guy's got to moisturize, you know,' he said.

Her mouth tightened. 'Not funny.'

'Look, how about we go for a walk and discuss the situation?' He wanted to change the subject but he did need to talk to her.

She nodded grudgingly. 'We're not far from the lake. We can do the Lake Shore Walk.'

The thirty-one-mile walk that circled the lake was one of the biggest tourist attractions of Geneva but the locals all loved it too, and at this time of year, when summer was over and the city wasn't yet inundated by skiers, it was relatively peaceful.

Sinead walked along briskly, not looking to see if he was following. Amused, he strolled along, his long legs allowing him to keep up with her. Did she ever slow down, he wondered?

'So tell me about the night of the theft,' he said.

She turned her head to look at him, but didn't slow her pace. 'There's nothing to tell. I was at home, having a quiet night in. When I got up the next day the police were camping on my doorstep and I was arrested.' Her face was calm but there was a slight, betraying wobble in her voice.

'Do you have an alibi for that night?'

'Only my paint brush. I was painting over those yucky beige walls in the bathroom.'

Niall had no trouble recalling the pale green walls with a few small shells stencilled on them. At one point this morning, he had focused on one of those shells while the pressure mounted in his balls. He forced his mind back to the business at hand.

'Did anyone see you?'

She shook her head. 'I was alone all night. I even drank my coffee black because I was too busy painting to go out for milk.'

'What was on the radio?'

'I have no idea. I was listening to music on my iPhone.'

How could someone as intelligent as Sinead have left herself without an alibi? As it stood, there was nothing, absolutely nothing, to back up her claim to have spent the evening at home. She wasn't stupid. In fact, she was so intelligent he bet that she scared most men away. Why hadn't she set up an alibi? Why leave herself vulnerable like this?

'You're very calm,' he observed. 'In your place, I'm sure I'd be sweating bullets.'

She stopped and swung around to face him. The lake behind her wasn't as blue or as bright as her eyes. 'Look, I know I didn't do it. Yes, it would be nice if I'd been in the gym or out with friends who could vouch for me. But I didn't do it. They have excellent security at the museum. When they examine the evidence properly, they'll find out it was someone else.'

'Rheinbach said your fingerprints were found at the scene.'

She made a rude noise. 'I'm the curator. My fingerprints are all over the museum. There isn't an exhibit there that I haven't touched at least once. Your fingerprints are all over my apartment now. It doesn't mean you burgled me.'

'And he said that people saw you.'

She shook her head. 'That's not true. I wasn't there. Maybe the thief wore my lab coat or something. If they question the witnesses properly, or look at the CCTV footage, they'll see it wasn't me. It couldn't be me, because I wasn't there.'

The obvious answer was usually the right one, and all the evidence pointed to Sinead as the thief. But her certainty was convincing. Was it possible that she had been framed? If so, he realized, his job of tracking down the missing ruby would be a lot harder. And instead of being free to go chasing it, he was stuck here looking after Sinead O'Sullivan.

She took a breath. 'Until the police do their job, I'm trying to look at this as an unexpected holiday, a chance to get my apartment fixed up the way I want it. I'm just scared that when it's all over, my reputation will still be tarnished. "There's no smoke without fire" is what people will say. I don't want to spend the rest of my life proving I'm not a thief, not to you or anyone else.'

She didn't wait for his reply, but turned and marched on.

Bloody ass. Sinead tramped along the path, trying to put distance between them. Did he think she had stolen the Fire? It was too stupid to contemplate.

Her phone vibrated in her pocket and she fumbled as she pulled it out. She didn't recognize the number. 'Hello?'

'Miss O'Sullivan, this is Gerhardt Arnheim of Arnheim Associates.'

It was the lawyer she had contacted the previous day. Her Uncle Tim had recommended him. Mr Arnheim had sounded none too pleased at being called on a Sunday morning, but as soon as she mentioned Tim's name he had changed his tune. Now he was all urbane politeness.

'Is this a good moment to talk?'

'Of course.'

'I'm afraid that matters have dis-improved, as you say.'

That didn't sound good. 'In what way?'

'The police have completed their preliminary enquiries and are happy that they have sufficient evidence against you to proceed with a prosecution.'

A fist squeezed her heart. Her shock must have shown, because suddenly Niall was beside her. He touched her arm and mouthed a question to her. She opened her mouth to respond but the words wouldn't come out.

'Miss O'Sullivan?' the voice on the phone continued.

'Yes,' she croaked, in a voice that didn't sound like hers.

'I've requested copies of their files and any other evidence that they may have. In the meantime, I suggest that we meet as soon as possible, so that we can discuss your defence or your guilty plea.'

'I didn't do it. I didn't . . .' The phone slipped and tumbled from her hand and was caught by Niall.

He spoke into it. 'This is Niall Moore. I'm looking after Sinead. Can you give me your address? Yes. I know the place. Yes. Okay. We'll see you there this afternoon.'

He disconnected the call. 'I'm sorry.'

Niall's expression said it all. They were going to prosecute. She was going to have to stand up in a courtroom full of people and be accused of stealing. Even when she was declared not guilty, when they discovered that it was all a horrible mistake, her reputation would be tainted forever.

And they would find out about Lottie. She could just imagine her grandmother's face when that came out. Her knees trembled. The muesli she had eaten for breakfast threatened to make a reappearance.

'Breathe, Sinead. Just breathe.' Niall helped her along the path to a wooden bench and they sat and stared at the lake. He held her hand, rubbing his thumb along her knuckles. His face was unreadable.

Niall wound an arm around her shoulders and pulled her against his chest. The slow thump-thump of his heart steadied her nerves and her racing pulse returned to normal. She felt safe in his arms, protected.

'Sinead, I have to ask you some questions and I want you to answer me. No matter how hard it is, you must tell me the truth. You know me. You know that you can trust me.'

'I know.' He was probably the only person in Geneva that she could trust.

'Tell me what happened on the day of the theft, every-thing that you remember. Every detail, no matter how small or insignificant. Even the smallest thing could be important.'

Sinead snuggled closer. 'It was a normal day. I did lots of admin work, insurance for the show, a meeting with the Finance Unit about next year's budget, that sort of thing. In the afternoon, Günter and I looked at the final proofs for the show catalogue and approved some of the souvenirs for the gift shop.' She laughed. 'Günter hates anything tacky.'

'Go on,' Niall prompted her.

'Afterwards, I went home and painted the bathroom.'

'That was it. No visitors? No phone calls or emails once you got home?'

She shook her head. 'I didn't bother turning on the lap-top.'

'What about cameras in the lobby?'

'I don't think they work properly. We had a burglary a couple of weeks ago and the security system was damaged. The building manager is still waiting for the insurance company to settle the claim.'

He sighed deeply. 'So no one else saw you? There was no one in the lift? Or in the hallway?'

Her stomach gave another little flip. This was serious. She had no alibi for the evening of the theft. 'No one.'

He moved back so he could see her face.

'Did you steal the jewel?'

The question blindsided her and she jerked away from him. 'How can you ask me that?'

'I am asking you that, and I won't be the last. Answer

the bloody question.' There was an edge to his voice that made her shiver and she wasn't sure if it was fear, or a warped sense of excitement at his command.

'I swear on my life that I didn't take the stone.'

'And is there anything else that you need to tell me before we meet your lawyer?'

Sinead hesitated. Should she tell him about Lottie? If the case went to trial her past might be exposed. *Don't be silly. That won't happen. This is all just a horrible mistake.* Besides, what would Niall think of her if she told him the truth? Oh, he might enjoy watching Lottie dance on stage, but in real life no respectable businessman would want to be associated with an exotic dancer. And he would probably have to tell Uncle Tim. No. She couldn't risk that. Her uncle would be furious if he discovered that she had put herself through college that way, rather than asking him for money. She couldn't tell Niall about her past. Lottie would have to remain a secret.

'Sinead,' he prompted her for a response. 'Is there anything else?'

She forced a smile onto her face. 'No. Nothing.'

Satisfied, he pulled her back into his arms again. Despite the chill breeze from the lake she felt warm. She relaxed and burrowed deeper into his coat.

'Comfortable?' Niall's voice rumbled against her ear.

Mmm, I could get used to this. She almost said the words out loud and stopped. What am I doing? Niall wasn't her boyfriend. He was an investigator her uncle had sent to keep his one million franc investment safe. Niall was only doing his job. Nothing more. She was crazy to think that it was anything else.

A light bulb went on inside her head. *Idiot.* Why hadn't she thought of it sooner? He was the perfect solution to her problem. Niall was an investigator. He had contacts and he was used to dealing with all sorts of crimes and underworld characters. She couldn't rely on the police to protect her and she didn't know anyone else she could trust. She had some money, thanks to Lottie. It wouldn't have to be a charity case. She could pay him.

She reached for her bag. She didn't have much cash on her, but she supposed she should give him something to retain his services. Sinead emptied the contents of her purse into her hand. One hundred and twelve francs and fifty-eight centimes.

'There.' She pressed the money into his hand. 'It's a retainer. I know that you cost lots more than that but I have money and I can pay you the rest when I get to a bank.'

'Pay me for what?'

'I want you to investigate my case.'

5

She was so intense, clutching a handful of Swiss francs and looking at him so hopefully. Something inside Niall melted. It was totally irrational, but he couldn't bring himself to believe that she was the thief. He had no idea how it would affect the two other cases he was dealing with, but he knew he had to help her prove her innocence.

Behind her glasses, her eyes were big and round. They looked at him with a combination of trust and pleading. She really did believe that he would find the ruby for her, and clear her name.

She wasn't the thief. Relief filled him.

'I'll do it.' He bent his head to brush her lips with his, intending it as comfort and confirmation of the deal.

Sinead's lips were soft and sweet, with a hint of peach-flavoured lip balm. It was a contrast to how sharply she could speak and he allowed himself to enjoy the taste of her. The iron lady had a soft centre. For a moment, he thought she was going to pull back, maybe even slap him. Instead she leaned into his kiss and tentatively returned it.

She parted her lips under his, allowing him a tantalizing taste of her mouth.

Without warning, hunger roared through him. This wasn't enough, would never be enough. Niall pulled Sinead into his arms, enjoying the feel of her body against his much bigger one. She might be small, but she wasn't delicate. Through her bulky clothes, he could feel her vitality and resilience.

He slid his hand into her hair, holding her head still so that he could deepen the kiss. He tightened his grip and tilted her head back, changing the angle. She gasped, but didn't resist. Niall slanted his mouth across hers, eager to taste it. She moaned slightly, the tiny sound egging him on. He plunged his tongue into her mouth, invading it.

Her mouth rose hesitantly to touch his, giving him silent permission to carry on. God, she was so sweet. How had he missed it? He swept his tongue across hers while tightening his arms around her.

His cock rose, hard and demanding, but he ignored it. Kissing Sinead required all his attention. He pulled back slightly, so that he could see her face, flushed and tempting.

Her eyes opened. 'What?' she said, dazed.

But he kissed her again before she could go on. This time, he sucked her lower lip into his mouth and nipped it. She jerked but didn't recoil. He soothed it, a tiny kiss asking forgiveness before plunging back into her mouth. She kissed him back.

He could do this for hours. Days. Months. How had someone as sharp and controlled as Sinead O'Sullivan concealed this much sweetness and passion?

She moved so that her breasts were pressed against him. They were round and lush. He had felt them while he was in her bed that morning and was impatient to see them in daylight. With her colouring, they'd be pale and delicate, and would mark when he sucked on them.

He couldn't wait. He slid a hand beneath her sweater, eager to examine them more carefully. The bra she wore underneath was some sort of lace, and he could feel her nipple rising, hard and proud, into his hand. His mouth watered for the taste of her.

A disapproving cough sounded, alerting him to the presence of a couple of elderly walkers and reminding him where he was. Out in the open, on a seat on a walking trail that saw thousands of people pass every day. From the expression on the faces of the Swiss couple, he had already gone too far.

With an effort, he set her away from him, but held her upright until her breathing steadied and she had command of herself again.

God help him, he loved seeing her like this, all dazed and uncertain, with her lips slightly bruised and her hair mussed. He wondered what it would look like spread over his pillow. He was determined to find out, and soon.

Unlike most redheads, her eyelashes and eyebrows were dark, giving her face definition and making those startling eyes even more dramatic. Perhaps that was why she wore such unflattering glasses. Eyes like that could get a girl into trouble.

'You're staring,' she said.

'Eyes like yours should be illegal,' he said.

For once, he silenced her. She opened her mouth but no words came out. He liked this feeling.

'I have no idea what you are talking about.' But her prim tone didn't deceive him; the half smile pulling at her lips told another story.

'I'm on to you.'

Her expression changed for a moment.

'You know that if you went to work with eyes like that,

and your hair loose, no one would believe you had a brain in your head,' he continued. 'You deliberately dress down so that you can be taken seriously.'

'I dress appropriately for my job,' she protested, but he could see she was pleased.

'And the glasses? Your eyes aren't that bad. You could probably manage without them.'

She shrugged. 'I'm safe to cross the road without them, if that's what you mean, but I can't read road signs at a distance. And I don't find contacts comfortable to wear for long periods. Glasses are not a big deal.'

'They hide your eyes, and that's a crime.'

He took her arm and they walked together back along the path. Now, in spite of the sexual tension simmering between them, they were more relaxed. They stopped at a lakeside restaurant for an early lunch.

Sinead busied herself mixing vinegar and lemon juice and a sinful drop of oil on her salad, before she looked over at Niall's plate. After the workout at the gym, the steak looked large and appetizing.

'That's a big steak.'

Niall cut into it. 'Hey, I'm a big man!'

Oh, he was. He made her feel small and delicate.

'There's a lot of me to keep up.'

That phrase called to mind an image from her bedroom earlier that day that heated her cheeks. Not one she wanted to think about when he was sitting across the table from her. 'Haven't you heard that too much protein is bad for you?' she asked instead.

He put down his knife and fork. 'You don't buy all that crap, do you? It's cheap processed low-fat food that will kill you.' He looked at her plate in disgust. 'How small a portion of chicken can you eat? It's not big enough for a cat.'

It did look small beside his lavish meal, but she wouldn't admit it. 'There's nothing wrong with my chicken. At least it's healthy.'

'It wouldn't keep an ant alive. You need feeding up.'

To her mortification, he looked her up and down, bending over and pushing the tablecloth aside so he could examine her jean-clad thighs.

'You have great legs.'

She jerked the tablecloth down. 'Keep your hands above the table where I can see them.'

'Spoilsport.' But he didn't look upset.

'It's the red meat talking. You have testosterone overload.'

'Come on, you'd be upset if I didn't have enough testosterone to appreciate a woman with sexy thighs. Have you ever considered wearing stockings and a suspender belt?'

She froze. That was a staple part of Lottie's costume. 'Is that all you think about? Sex?' she demanded. She took a gulp of wine, and Niall re-filled her glass.

'No, I also think about guns and blowing stuff up. Particularly those hideous clothes you wear.'

'What's wrong with my clothes?' she asked, offended. Her clothes might not be fashionable, but they were good quality and comfortable.

He pointed at her with his fork. 'That baggy thing

drowns you. You might have no breasts at all. And the stuff you wear to work makes you look fifty. You're allowed to wear sexy stuff when you're off-duty.'

'I have to dress seriously, if I want to be taken seriously.' He had no idea what it was like being a woman in a male-dominated world.

'You take it too far.' Maybe he realized he was pissing her off. He cut a piece of his steak. 'Here, try a bite.'

'Are you kidding? There's blood on it.' She hated blood. The sight of it made her feel queasy.

'It's rare, the way it should be.'

'What did you tell the waiter – shave its ass and take its horns off?' She looked into her glass in surprise. How much had she drunk? Maybe she should have eaten more breakfast. 'Sorry, this has gone straight to my head. I haven't eaten much all day . . .'

'So you're a cheap date? I must remember that.' He looked way too happy about it.

She couldn't resist payback. 'I bet all your dates are cheap, especially if they wear skimpy clothes.'

He winced. 'Some of those are damned expensive.'

Sinead speared a leaf of lamb's lettuce and then wondered what to do with it. 'You pay too? My. My. You get more appealing by the minute.'

The waiter cleared away their plates and brought them coffee she had no memory of ordering.

Niall peered at her over the edge of his cup. 'So how long is it since you got lucky?'

She spluttered a mouthful of coffee over the table. 'Lucky? Some of us have more to think about than sex.'

He would probably laugh at her if she said it was more

than a year. Or that the encounter had left her edgy and unsatisfied and she had spent hours staring at the ceiling hoping he would wake up and go home.

'That long, huh?'

'What do you mean that long? I'll have you know that I . . . I . . . I don't want to talk about this.' She wanted to smack him.

'Oh yeah, it's been a loooong time, hasn't it?'

She looked around her at the other tables. They were definitely attracting attention. 'Stop that, people are staring.'

'Sure they are, at your sexy thighs.'

'Oh. You are infuriating.'

'One of my best qualities,' he agreed.

Sinead huffed a breath and turned her attention to her coffee, pretending to ignore him, but each time she risked a glance at him across the table, he was smiling.

At the car park, they parted company. She would go back to her apartment and tidy it up, while he would return to the museum to start his investigation.

On his second visit to Rheinbach, Niall was again struck by the contrast between the building's fairy tale exterior and old-fashioned reception area – the main hallway's marble floor, its panelled walls, the classical statues on either side of the cash desk – and its state-of-the-art security system. Once inside, the display rooms were modern, with hidden lighting and security cameras monitoring the glass cases where the more valuable items were housed.

Niall examined an exhibit of rubies of different sizes

and clarity and wondered what their combined value might be.

Günter Rheinbach was eager to show him the case where the Fire of Autumn had been displayed. It had a special security system, more complex than the rest, with an access code that only Günter was supposed to know.

Back in the lobby, one other old-fashioned feature was a flesh and blood security guard who checked everyone who entered or left the building. Jean-Baptiste Moutier was nervous about speaking to Niall, but certain about what had happened the night the ruby disappeared. 'Mlle O'Sullivan came in, signed the book and went to her office.' He held out the book for Niall to see.

Niall flipped through it. Sinead had a pattern of working at night, often calling in and doing a couple of hours when the museum was closed. He examined the signature and frowned. It looked the same, but there was something a little off. He'd have an expert examine it, he decided.

'Are you sure it was her?' he asked Moutier. 'It was a cold night, everyone was wearing bulky clothes. Could you be mistaken?'

'Oh no. I see her often. I could not mistake her. Nice lady, always asks about my daughter's dance classes.' He frowned. 'She wished me "Good night" that night, but I don't remember her asking about Michelle.'

'She was thinking about the theft, had no time for pleasantries,' Günter pointed out.

Niall asked a few more questions, but didn't manage to get any more information. Günter tapped him on the shoulder. 'If you've finished here, come to my office. I have a copy of the CCTV footage. You can see for your-self what happened that night,' he told Niall.

The image was low resolution, but the quality was good enough for Niall to see clearly. First, there was a quick image of a woman wearing a long coat and fur hat coming into the museum. The time stamp on the image showed 2345. Light glinted on her spectacles. She took them off before signing the book the security guard held out to her.

Niall was shaken. That bulky coat made it hard to be sure, but the woman on the tape looked a lot like Sinead.

The tape flickered forwards, showing the woman going to Sinead's office. When she emerged, she was wearing a lab coat with something in the pocket and her head was down as she fiddled with it. Ice coated Niall's spine. She was very familiar.

The woman walked to the Fire of Autumn display case. She had her back to the camera. Niall could see her remove something from her pocket, but not what she did with it. For long moments, all he could see was her slender neck bent with a tendril of titian hair loose over the collar.

The door of the case opened. She reached in and lifted out the ruby, then turned so that the camera had a full view of her face.

Niall stopped breathing. It was Sinead. There was no doubt about it. He had examined those spectacular eyes barely half an hour ago. Now, they were facing the camera, looking at it as if she knew it was there and was challenging it. Even those extravagant lashes were the same. She took her glasses out of her pocket, put them on and turned back to her office.

Two minutes later, she emerged, wearing the heavy coat, with her hair tucked into her furry hat.

'Have you seen enough?' Günter asked.

'More than enough.'

Somehow, Niall managed to behave normally while he took notes, arranged for extra information to be sent to his computer, and took his leave of them.

All the while, a voice in his head was repeating over and over, taunting him. *You have been had. Sinead O'Sullivan has played you.*

6

'What?' Sinead took a step back as Niall advanced towards her. His grey eyes were as cold as the Atlantic Ocean in winter. He couldn't be saying these things to her, not after what happened between them this morning. Not after that kiss in the park.

'You heard me,' Niall spat. 'You're a lying, deceiving bitch and to think that I fell for it. Where is the stone?' He opened and closed his fists as if he could barely control his rage.

Fear crawled up her back like an icy finger. She had a sudden flashback to the makeshift commune in Mayo – the man's voice raised in anger and the sound of her mother sobbing, while Sinead clutched a small hand beneath the threadbare sheets of the single bed in the next room.

She took a deep steadying breath. *Calm down, you've been through worse. You can handle this.*

'I don't know what you mean.' She was proud that her voice sounded steadier than she felt.

'You're lying!' There was no doubt in his voice. 'That's just to start with. What about cheating and stealing, huh? Don't bother keeping up the act. I saw the CCTV footage from the museum.'

What had happened since he left? 'Niall, I don't understand. Calm down and explain to me what you saw.'

He paced the floor. 'Jesus, you're good. Not so much as

a flicker of guilt. I've dealt with some psychos in my time but you . . .' He spun around to face her. 'I saw the fucking footage with my own eyes, Sinead. I saw you take the stone.'

She swallowed hard. This was a nightmare. She believed that it was a simple case of mistaken identity but Niall had seen the tapes and he had no doubt that she was the thief. Could it be her sister?

'And to think that I trusted you, that I . . .' His short laugh was full of bitterness. 'God, you were good. Shy, sweet little Sinead O'Sullivan.'

Like a predator stalking his prey, he advanced on her. Her heart thumped but she held her ground. She wouldn't give him the satisfaction of showing that she was afraid.

Niall stroked her cheek with his index finger before capturing her chin and raising her face to meet his scornful gaze. 'Are there any depths you wouldn't sink to? Would you have fucked me to make sure that I was on your side?'

His hand left her face and traced a path between the hollow of her breasts. 'Or would you have done it because you like it, hmm?'

Despite herself, she arched towards him.

He lowered his head until his breath fanned her cheek. 'Oh, I think that you would like it. Wouldn't you? All that pent up frustration. Was that why you went off like a rocket when I touched you? How long has it been since someone took you to bed and gave you what you needed?'

She swallowed hard. How could she have trusted him? Sinead pushed against his chest and Niall moved back a half step.

'Say the words, baby, and I'm all yours.' He dropped his voice. 'Three little words. Fire of Autumn. Where is it, Sinead? Where have you hidden it? Are you working alone or do you have an accomplice?'

She put her hands over her ears, not wanting to hear any more. She needed to think. Niall knew her. He knew what she looked like. Whoever had stolen the jewel had looked exactly like her and there was only one person that could be.

Roisin – her sister. Her heart pounded so hard, she thought it was trying to burst from her chest. 'I want to see it,' she said. 'I have to see that tape, now.'

'Be my guest.' His mouth twisted in a sneer. 'I believe the police have forwarded a copy to your lawyer.'

Sinead glanced at her watch. 'Fine. Give me a few minutes to get changed and we'll go there.'

On shaking legs she walked to bedroom, but paused at the door. No one believed that she had a sister. Her Uncle Tim had tried to comfort her, telling her that sometimes when little girls were lonely, they needed an imaginary friend. He thought Roro was someone she had dreamed up to help her get through her childhood traumas. Without knowing her father's full name, she had never been able to find him or her sister. But if what Niall said was true, this theft was the proof she needed.

Two strangers thought they had recognized her. What had the woman at the dance studio said? 'I thought you had a gig at Cirque in Paris.' It wasn't a whole lot to go on, but it was a start.

Sinead hurried inside and closed the door before he could see her tears. *Think. Think.* If she could find her

73

sister and the stone, she could get her life back. But she would have to do this alone.

She couldn't depend on Niall to help her. She couldn't depend on anyone. *Oh, toughen up. What did you expect? That Niall was some kind of knight in shining armour?*

If she packed a bag he would know immediately that she planned to run. Riffling through her lingerie drawer, she grabbed a couple of pieces and shoved them into her handbag along with a scarf and a pair of sunglasses. She couldn't risk using her credit cards. The police would trace her immediately. Reluctantly she put them back into the drawer.

She picked up her ATM cards for her Irish and English bank accounts and a small pile of bank notes. By the time the police got around to freezing the accounts, hopefully she would have cleared them out.

Her eyes were puffy and her nose was red, but when she repaired her make-up, she almost looked human, and not as if her life was falling apart. With a final glance around her bedroom, she walked to the door. The apartment was the first home of her own, and now she had to leave it.

Niall stood up immediately when she entered the living room. She didn't look at his face, afraid of what she might see there. 'I'm ready.'

They drove to the lawyer's office without saying a word. Niall announced his arrival at the receptionist's desk in the lobby, and they were directed to the elevator. On the fifth floor, another secretary showed them into Gerhardt Arnheim's office. The mahogany desk was an original, probably two hundred years old. At a polished meeting table near the window were three chairs and a laptop, already switched on.

The doors opened behind them and the lawyer swept into the room. 'Miss O'Sullivan.' He offered his hand, all formality.

He was younger than she expected. His old-fashioned manners gave him an air of gravitas beyond his years. She wondered idly how many generations of Arnheims had sat in the chair behind the antique desk.

They followed Gerhardt to the conference table. Sinead found herself caught in his steady blue-eyed stare. Tim O'Sullivan had chosen well; she felt as if the lawyer could see right through her. She wondered if he was comparing her to the woman on the CCTV tape.

'I must apologize, Miss O'Sullivan. I'm afraid there is no good news. The police are eager to put the case before the –'

'May I see the tape please?'

Gerhardt masked his puzzlement with politeness. 'Of course.'

Sinead sat impassively as the footage displayed on the screen. Images of the various exhibition rooms in the museum passed in quick succession before he paused and pressed play. She took a deep breath. The jewel room of the Rheinbach museum – her favourite place in the world, or at least it had been.

A woman entered. Sinead caught a flash of red hair, the same colour as her own. Sinead recognized the lab coat as hers immediately. It had an ink stain on the pocket where a cheap pen had leaked into the fabric. The woman approached the display case at the centre of the room, and Sinead's breath caught in her throat.

The face on camera was a mirror image of hers. The mouth, nose and eyes were almost identical to the ones that stared back at her from her bathroom mirror every morning. Anyone looking at the tape would immediately believe that it was her.

She steeled herself, resisting the temptation to reach out to touch the flickering screen. Tears welled up and she swallowed hard. She couldn't cry now. Roisin. It had been so long. More than twenty-three years since she had last seen her, but the ache in her heart told her that it was real. Roisin. Her sister. Her twin. Sinead almost said her name aloud. *Where did you go? What happened to you?*

Conscious of both men watching her reaction, Sinead tried to keep her face impassive. There was no point in hiding this any longer. She cleared her throat. 'There's something you should know. I should have told you before this. I have an identical twin.'

Niall closed his eyes and then shook his head slowly. 'Is that the best you could come up with? You actually expect me to believe something like that? For fuck's sake, Sinead, do I look like an idiot?' He took a deep breath. 'I've seen your file. The Rheinbach ran a detailed security check before they offered you the job.'

He had seen her file? Niall was working for the Rheinbach?

His words hit her like a punch.

Niall had been investigating her all along – the kisses, the touches, the tender looks – none of it was real. If

Niall and Gerhardt believed that she had stolen the jewel, she didn't have a prayer. She would be locked up in prison before the month was out.

After a moment of silence, Gerhardt pressed the control and Roisin's image disappeared from the screen. 'I'm sorry, Miss O'Sullivan, but I'm sure that you realize now that there is little we can do by way of a defence in this case. We can –'

Sinead's stomach heaved. 'Of course. I understand completely.' She stood up on shaky legs. 'If you gentlemen would excuse me, I need to use the bathroom.'

Gerhardt was immediately all concern. He directed her to a room at the end of the hall. Inside, she splashed her face with cold water. This was the end of everything. Her sister was alive, but the life she had worked so hard for had been destroyed in a single night.

Sinead examined her ashen face in the mirror, comparing it with the face on the tape. Identical twins were not really identical unless they worked at it, but the clothes, the hair. It couldn't be a coincidence. Roisin must have studied her to see how she dressed and wore her make-up. Her sister had pretended to be her to steal the Fire of Autumn. She had set Sinead up to take the fall for the theft.

I have to get out of here or I'll end up in prison.

Sinead opened the bathroom door a crack. She waited until Gerhardt's secretary was called away and then she hurried down the emergency stairs to the next floor where she summoned the lift.

In the marbled lobby the young receptionist seemed surprised to see her return alone.

'Please don't tell my husband that you've seen me,'

Sinead said. 'But I really need a cigarette and he hates to see me smoking.'

'Of course.' The girl smiled.

Sinead hurried outside. She raised her hand to hail a taxi before she remembered she couldn't use her credit cards. She had barely enough cash to pay for the journey. Instead she dug a ticket out of her wallet and hopped on a tram to the main train station. She glanced at her watch. Twenty minutes had passed. She wondered how long it would be before Niall came searching for her. With any luck, he would check the apartment first before calling the police. She had no doubt now that he would turn her in.

A sharp stab of pain hit her in the chest. She was stupid to feel like this. It wasn't as if they were lovers. It had been a ploy all along. She barely knew him.

Cornavin railway station loomed up ahead. Before she entered, Sinead pulled on the headscarf and sunglasses. She walked through the station as quickly as she could, staying close to crowds, trying not to draw any attention. She checked the display. There was a train to Paris leaving in less than ten minutes. She would be there in three hours. Sinead purchased a ticket at the machine and hurried to the platform.

Afterwards she wasn't sure how she had held her nerve. What if they stopped her when she tried to board the train? But her ID card received no more than a cursory glance and she found a seat. Only when the train pulled away from the station did she relax. A steward pushing a trolley through the carriage offered coffee and snacks. She had enough coins left for a bottle of water, so she purchased one and took a deep gulp. She had done it. She was leaving Geneva behind her.

And Niall, a small voice inside her head reminded her. She would never see Niall Moore again.

She closed her eyes and let the recent events wash over her. His kiss, the way that he held her, the way that he had set her body on fire when he touched her.

Then she thought about Roisin. The strange man at the police station who was convinced that he knew her, and later the woman at the dance studio. They didn't know her, but they obviously knew her sister. She had spent years hoping to meet someone who had met her sister. Hell, who believed that she existed. And now she met two in forty eight hours? What were the odds of that?

Sinead stood up, and pulled down her handbag from the luggage rack. The dance instructor had given her contact details for a club, Cirque. She still had the card somewhere. There it was, with a Paris number scribbled on the back and the name Clothilde. It was a start. She could use it to find Roisin.

Find her sister and get her life back.

Niall listened with half an ear as Gerhardt Arnheim droned on about the technicalities of the Swiss judicial system and how Sinead would plead and what defence he could muster. Most of his attention was on the memory of Sinead's face as she had watched that tape. He'd had to battle his own rage at being played for a fool, but he was used to keeping his attention on the important things. He had already seen the tape, so he watched Sinead watching it.

For most of the tape, she had been shocked, but there at the end, her face had changed. There had been something – recognition? And then a smile, instantly suppressed, before her eyes filled with tears. He was going to find out what that was about.

'If she pleads guilty and returns the ruby, I'm sure we can get her a reduced sentence, no more than seven years,' Gerhardt said.

'Seven years?' Shocked, Niall was recalled to his surroundings.

'Oh, I'm sure she'll go to a minimum security prison. She will be thirty-four when she gets out, still quite a young woman.'

The thought of Sinead locked up for seven years twisted his guts. Sure, she was a lying little bitch, but she was too alive, too sexy, too passionate to rot in a cell for seven years.

'Obviously, her sentence will be substantially longer if she doesn't return the ruby. She would be looking at twenty years.'

'I'll talk to her,' Niall said grimly.

Gerhardt looked at his watch. 'If you want to include me in the discussion, I suggest you do it soon. I have another appointment in ten minutes.'

She'd had enough time to herself, Niall decided and strode out of the office, intent on dragging Sinead back in to face facts. It was time she stopped playing games and told the truth.

'Where's the bathroom?' he demanded of the receptionist. She pointed to the end of the hall.

He paused outside the door marked 'Dames'. Even a

former Ranger hesitated at some things. He listened, and above the sound of running water, he heard a female voice speaking French. Could that be Sinead?

Geneva was a multi-lingual city where English was widely spoken. Gerhardt and Rheinbach had both spoken English to him. But the night watchman, Moutier, only spoke French and said that Sinead chatted to him regularly. He waited, and eventually a teenager came out, lips dramatically outlined and a phone clutched in her hand.

Damn it, he would have to go in.

Niall pushed open the door, saying firmly, 'Sinead, you have to come out and face the music.' He swept the small facility with a glance. Two open cubicles and only one person still here.

The grey-haired woman engaged in painting her eyebrows flinched at his violent entrance. Her hand slipped and one perfectly drawn black eyebrow now dipped into her left eye. '*Monsieur*,' she said with awful dignity. '*Qu'est-ce que vous faites ici?*'

Muttering an apology, Niall backed out, then realized that Sinead had given him the slip. Without a word to the lawyer standing gaping at him, he raced out of the building and into his Jeep. He feared he would break the suspension the way he sped over the speed bumps on the way to her apartment.

Her arrival in Gare de Lyon was uneventful. There were no armed police waiting to arrest her. At an ATM machine, she took out the maximum she could from Lottie's account. She wasn't going to risk using a Sinead O'Sullivan card.

Staying at a hotel was out of the question because they would insist on taking a copy of her passport. Sinead switched on her phone and checked her contacts in Paris. She couldn't make a call in case Niall used it to trace her; even switching the phone on would reveal her location. But there was someone here who could help her, so she risked it.

By now, Niall would know that she had left. He was probably searching Geneva for her. If she failed to turn up for her remand date in court, her uncle's bail money would be forfeit. She couldn't let that happen.

She had to find her sister by then or some evidence to convince the authorities that she hadn't stolen the jewel, but to do that she needed to find out about Cirque.

The internet café near the station revealed a little about the club. Like Crazy Horse and Bobino, Cirque had become a Paris institution since it was taken over two years before by Clothilde de Marseilles. Cirque promised an edgier experience than the other Parisian tourist traps and was now the premier BDSM club in Paris.

Clothilde had also gained a reputation for hosting exclusive private BDSM parties. Her girls were reputed to be very beautiful and very talented. Sinead winced. Talented at what?

She had performed some BDSM-inspired routines on stage and she could wield a whip with a certain amount of skill but it looked like her sister was doing it for real. Sinead reached for her water bottle and gulped greedily.

Being an exotic dancer was bad enough, but Granny

O'Sullivan would have a fit if she knew about this. Sinead had heard about twins having the same illnesses at the same time, or even knowing when the other one was in trouble. But this? Was the desire to perform some kind of a twin thing? The O'Sullivans were the type of family who sang at parties, but she had never heard of any of them being on stage. She wished she knew more about her father.

She logged off the computer and paid the attendant. It was time to get out of here.

On a narrow street in Montparnasse, she pushed an elaborate iron gate open. Sinead stepped into a lush courtyard garden, a quiet oasis amidst the bustling neighbourhood shops and restaurants. She closed the gate behind her, shutting out the evening traffic. The smell of garlic, onions and spices wafted on the air, reminding her that she hadn't eaten since lunch. Her stomach rumbled. He was home. She only hoped that he didn't have company.

Sinead pressed the bell and waited.

Without much hope, Niall pressed the buzzer. Nothing. He didn't have a key, but that wouldn't stop him. Carefully keeping his back to the security camera at the end of the hall so that his body obscured his hands, he picked the lock on the front door. Pathetic security.

If he had the right to interfere in her life, he would make Sinead move to somewhere with a better system. Her apartment door was no barrier either. It took him a mere fifty seconds to unlock that.

The apartment was neat and orderly, the way they had

left it this morning. There was no sign of hasty packing or a sudden departure. He did a quick search, looking for clues. Her well-worn wheelie bag, the one designed to fit as carry-on luggage on all O'Sullivan Airline flights, was still there. So were all of her clothes. She wasn't running.

He searched the apartment quickly. At least he didn't have to worry about disturbing things. If Sinead didn't want him riffling through her things, she should be here to stop him.

His eyebrows rose at the contents of her underwear drawer. For someone who managed to look so buttoned-down and conservative, Sinead had a remarkable love of fine lingerie. Despite himself, his fingers lingered on the silk of a pair of black panties hand-painted with roses.

With a jolt, he remembered the morning he had woken in her bed. She wasn't just well-trimmed, she had been bare. What sort of woman took the trouble of getting all of her body hair removed, and possessed dozens of pairs of expensive panties? Well, one sort sprang to mind.

Niall felt sick.

He finished searching the lingerie drawer, but found only one small vibrator and some spare batteries. So organized, Ms O'Sullivan. Taking no chance that weak batteries would get in the way of her orgasm.

Ten minutes later, he admitted defeat. There was no sign of a hurried departure.

He pulled out his work phone. 'Andy, do a check, see if you can find out where Sinead O'Sullivan is.'

His best operative's voice was full of glee. 'Don't tell me she's done a runner on you? Dude, you scare off the ladies.'

'Shut up, McTavish.' Niall didn't have time for a slagging match now. 'Run a search on all the airlines out of Geneva, car hire, credit cards, anything that might tell us where she's gone.'

'She stood you up?' Andy was still trying to piss him off, but Niall could hear the computer keys clicking as he searched.

'Consider this a million franc date. If she doesn't show by tomorrow week, Tim O'Sullivan will lose a million francs in bail money. Think he's going to be pleased about that?'

There was silence while Andy worked. A few minutes later he said, 'Sorry, man, no sign of her on any passenger list out of Geneva. She hasn't hired a car and she hasn't used her credit card, either.'

'Try her phone.'

Click, click, click went the computer keys. 'Dead. Not registering anywhere. She must have switched it off.'

Damn it.

'But it was last active at Gare de Lyon. Is that any use to you?'

'She's in Paris? Great work, Andy.'

'Is this a good time to ask for a raise?'

Niall laughed. 'Get your ass to Paris and we'll discuss it.'

7

Gabriel was barefoot. An open shirt revealed a tanned six-pack that would make most men envious. His hair was damp as if he had recently gotten out of the shower. Chocolate-coloured eyes widened in surprise before crinkling in genuine pleasure. '*Chérie . . .*'

Only then did she realize how glad she was to see him and that she had nowhere else to go. She threw herself into his arms. 'Oh, Gabriel.'

He held her tightly, stroking her hair and murmuring soft nonsense until, with a muttered '*merde!*' he released her and raced to the kitchen. Sinead smiled at his retreating back. Gabriel had been the unofficial cook for her troupe of dancers when they were performing in London. There had been many laughter-filled evenings around the table of his rented apartment, drinking wine and listening to Cesária Évora singing 'Sodade'.

In the large kitchen, Gabriel poured her a glass of wine from an open bottle, but he wouldn't allow her to talk until after she had eaten, making sure that she cleaned every scrap from her plate. Gabriel went to the cave in the basement and returned with a bottle of wine. 'Bring the glasses, *s'il te plaît.*'

She followed him to the sitting room, kicked off her shoes and sank into the deep linen cushions of the mocha coloured couch. He switched on a lamp and lit a candle on the mantelpiece before pouring wine for both of them and settling down beside her. He studied her face, noting the dark circles and puffy eyes. 'You look like shit.'

She made a face at him. 'That's the kind of compliment a girl loves to hear.'

He gave a Gallic shrug that conveyed more than a lengthy conversation. 'I take it that your visit means that you're in trouble. Or perhaps you've fallen madly in love with me?'

'Idiot. You know I'll always love you.' She squeezed his hand. He was one of her closest friends, but they hadn't spoken in a couple of months. Gabriel was right to be mad at her for not keeping in touch. 'I'm in so much trouble.'

Out it tumbled in fits and starts in between sips of wine; the theft of the stone, being arrested and her uncle bailing her out of jail.

He whistled. 'A million francs? *Chérie*, you have gone up in the world.'

'Oh, shut up.' She glared at him. 'You haven't heard the worst bit yet.'

'There is worse? I think I need another drink.' He topped up their glasses and sat down, stretching his arm along the back of the couch behind her.

Apart from Niall, she had never mentioned Roisin to anyone. The rag-tag camp she had lived in until she was four years old had good reason to avoid anyone official. Drug dealing and petty theft were rife and families appeared and disappeared, sometimes overnight.

Sinead took a deep breath. 'I saw the CCTV footage of the theft at the museum. It was my twin sister.'

'You have a sister?' Gabriel looked dumbfound. '*Chérie*, why did you never mention her?'

'Because sometimes I almost believed that I had imagined her.'

She took a deep breath and carried on. 'My mother was a bit wild. She ran away with a man when she was seventeen. Anyway, they ended up living in a commune in the back end of Mayo. That was where Roro and I were born. We slept in the same bed, wore each other's clothes and were never apart until my dad left and took her with him. But just after they left my mother died. I was brought up by my grandmother. I found out later that my mother died because she'd had an ectopic pregnancy.'

Sinead picked up her glass but her hand shook and a drop of wine sloshed onto her hand. It wasn't just talking about her past. It was everything about the last few days. Meeting Niall, losing her job, finding out that her sister was alive.

Gabriel sat up quickly and took the glass from her, setting it down on the table beside his own. He licked the spilt wine from her hand before pulling her into his arms. '*Mon Dieu*,' he murmured against her hair. 'Why didn't you tell me any of this before?'

'I couldn't. I couldn't tell anyone. It was years before I went to therapy. Granny and Uncle Tim were great, but who would believe a child? There was no proof that Roro ever existed. The other people from the commune scattered. No one remembered her. How could a child just vanish like that, and no one noticed or cared?'

'Did you try to find her?' His voice was gentle, but Sinead couldn't look at him.

'I couldn't. I didn't know my dad's full name. Only that he was Peter. Not a lot to go on.' She shrugged. 'Father unknown.'

She gave up the battle against tears and sobbed into Gabriel's shirt. After a few minutes he pulled out another tissue and used it to wipe her face. '*Petit chou*, what am I going to do with you?' He tossed the tissue when it was wet.

Sinead sniffed and searched her bag for yet another tissue and found the printed pages from the internet café. 'She has some connection with this club. Can you help me?'

Gabriel took the pages from her and shook his head. A slow smile spread over his face. 'I know it well, *chérie*.'

'Then let's go.'

He looked at her doubtfully. 'It's going to be quiet on a Monday night. And you won't get in dressed like that.'

He fingered her shapeless, long-sleeved T-shirt with distaste.

'I can't wait. I'm on bail and the clock is ticking. The longer I wait, the harder it will be to find my sister. You still have my Lottie clothes, don't you? Surely there's something there that's suitable.'

It felt like the longest day of her life, but she couldn't stop now.

Gabriel led her into the night air and to an old building on the other side of the courtyard. They walked up two flights of narrow stone steps on the outside of the building, then he unlocked a green door leading into a tiny studio apartment.

It had become a store room for her stage costumes. Sinead remembered the images from the Cirque Noir website. The costumes were a bit more hardcore than what she usually wore on stage. Did her sister wear clothes like this too? She had devoured books and articles about twins and knew that they often had similar interests, but this was unnerving.

The studio was crammed with boxes containing shoes, headdresses, masks – all the trappings of seven years of performances. She really should sell them, but that would be like saying goodbye to Lottie and she wasn't ready to do that yet.

'Hey, do you remember these?' Gabriel produced a tissue-wrapped bundle from one of the boxes.

When she opened it she found a pair of purple sequined nipple covers. Sinead smiled. 'That audition was the first time we met. Remember?'

'How could I forget?'

In the communal dressing room, another contestant had swopped Sinead's pastie glue for eyelash glue. The pasties had stayed in place until mid-way through her routine, when one had flown off and struck the stage director in the eye. Mortified, she had left the stage, vowing never to audition again.

Gabriel was the one who had returned the errant pastie to her outside the theatre. They had gone for coffee and had been friends ever since.

The studio was so full, Sinead would have had no idea where to start looking, but after a few minutes Gabriel gave a triumphant cry. He found the right box and carried it back to the apartment. Sinead knelt on the floor and delved into it. The black catsuit had been made to measure. 'I hope it still fits me,' she said ruefully.

'Mmm.' Gabriel sounded uncertain. 'Now that you mention it, your derrière does look a little more luscious than before.'

'Bastard.' She threw a studded glove at him. He laughed as he caught it.

'Don't worry. The leather will stretch and soften with the heat of your body. You can use the shower in my room while I make you up a bed.'

The warm water of the shower played against her skin. Sinead welcomed the needle-like sensation of the jets. Despite the age of the building, Gabriel never skimped on plumbing. It was a while since she had stayed here, and longer still since they had been lovers. Now, they had settled into an affectionate, intimate friendship.

Trust Gabriel to sense that she had moved on. Damned Frenchman, she could hide nothing from him.

When she emerged from the bathroom, Gabriel was dressing. His chest was bare and there was a faint sheen of oil on his skin. His dark latex pants left nothing to the imagination, but she had often seen him wear less on stage.

She wiggled her way into her costume. 'Zip me up, will you?' she asked, as she turned her back for his attention and breathed in.

'Relax, *chérie*, I was teasing you earlier. You're still hot, but performing a routine on stage is no preparation for the real thing. We need to have a little talk about the club tonight.'

'Why?'

'Have you ever been spanked?'

She glared at him, affronted.

Now, if Niall Moore had suggested it, she might have considered it. He was big enough and strong enough to put her over his knee if he wanted to. The man who had brought her to an earth-shattering orgasm had been controlled and experienced. She wondered what it would take to break that control and make him . . .

Sinead realized that Gabriel was waiting, an expectant look on his face. 'In your dreams.'

Gabriel laughed. 'You're not a natural submissive then. Okay, we can work with that.'

'What do you mean, work with that? Do you think I'm going to let some guy boss me around?'

'Why don't you tell me?'

'Bloody men,' she muttered. 'Now, where are my shoes?'

'Temper, temper,' he said. 'This is not a performance on a stage where you can switch off your smile when the lights go down. You can't walk into a club like Cirque and start asking questions. You'll be out on the street on your pretty ass before you know it.'

He was right. 'What do you suggest?'

'It looks like your sister was able to pass for you in your world. There is no reason why you can't do the same in hers.'

He opened the closet and reached for a black leather holdall. 'You remember the routine we did in Barcelona with the whip and flail?'

Sinead nodded.

'Perhaps we can replicate that, but first we need to find out whether your sister is a Domme or a sub.'

Wincing, Sinead eyed the collection of whips and flails in the bag. She didn't know what half of the other stuff was for, but she could guess. 'What if she's a sub?'

Gabriel gave her a grin that was wickedness incarnate. 'Then I get to spank you.'

Niall scowled at the computer screen in the small Paris office of Moore Enterprises. Where the hell had Sinead O'Sullivan gone? It was as if she had dropped off the face of the earth. How had she managed to give him the slip so neatly?

There were seasoned operators in the SEALs and SAS who couldn't do what she had done. All of his suspicions about her flared up again. No matter how beautiful her eyes were, or how innocent she seemed, Sinead was clearly an experienced strategist who knew how to circumvent the law.

He had tracked her as far as Gare de Lyon, but only because she had switched on her phone for a couple of minutes while she was there. She hadn't made any calls – that would have been too easy. He'd have been able to track down the other number in minutes. But at least he knew her location four hours ago. Since then, nothing.

At this moment she was in Paris and could take a train to anywhere in Europe. He was watching for her credit card to pop up as soon as she used it, but there was no sign. She probably had a spare one. Or cash stashed some-where. Or hell, maybe she was desperate enough to hitch-hike.

He flicked back through her credit card records. Never

in his life had he seen anyone so respectable. College, work, travel for work, virtually nothing else. Everyone had secrets. Hell, he had some humdingers himself. But Sinead's life appeared to be pristine. If Mother Teresa was a museum curator, she would have a record like this.

The only odd thing was regular payments for more dance classes than he would expect from someone so buttoned down, but he supposed it was her alternative to sweating it out in a gym.

While he continued to search, an alert came in from one of his team of geeks that someone else was searching for Sinead. He checked it out.

Fuck. The information request had come from Blackstone's head of European ops. Why was that bastard looking for Sinead?

Ever since he'd found Darren Hall on top of an unwilling woman in Iraq, he'd hated the bastard. Not that he'd had much time for him before that. He seemed to think that being a former US SEAL made him a minor deity, and his opinion of women had turned the stomach of every SEAL who had ever served under him. And they were a tough bunch of men.

Hall had barely escaped a dishonourable discharge from the SEALs. Now, he was working for Blackstone, a shadowy security company that was prepared to break the law if that's what it took.

If Hall was searching for Sinead, something was going badly wrong. In fact, something already was. Sinead had a $50 million ruby stashed away somewhere. The museum director wasn't the only person who would want to get his hands on it. The chances were that every bad guy in

Europe was after it. And Hall was one of the nastiest scumbags around. He didn't play nice when it came to getting what he wanted.

Niall needed to find her before Hall did.

As the taxi picked its way through the rain-soaked Paris streets, Sinead couldn't get Gabriel's words out of her head. Spank her? He wouldn't dare.

'Nervous, *chérie?*'

The amusement in his voice made her yearn to slap him. Maybe she had sadistic tendencies after all. She hoped that Roisin was the same. 'I'm fine. So what's the plan when we get there?'

'We will make a little tour, let people know that you have arrived and then we will go to the bar and wait.'

'Wait for what?'

'For one of your sister's playmates to come to us.'

The taxi pulled up outside the neon-lit theatre. Gabriel paid him and they stepped out of the car. A burly security guard nodded to him and they passed the queue of customers and were ushered into the lobby.

Sinead had been expecting something seedy – she had performed in her own share of dumps when she was starting out as a dancer, but this place was more like a five-star hotel. A matching pair of cantilevered staircases led to a bar on the upper level, while the ground floor entrance to the circus ring was flanked by midnight-blue velvet curtains.

A bare-breasted woman on a unicycle distributed glasses of champagne. Sinead nodded her thanks and swallowed hers in two gulps.

She might have been wearing more clothing than some of the other women, but her waist-length red hair, which Gabriel had insisted she tie up in a long ponytail, was attracting attention.

'Come, *chérie*,' he whispered. 'Let's see what's going on in the ring.'

A masked Pierrot drew back the curtain and they moved inside.

Sweet Sodom and Gomorrah. Sinead bit her tongue to stop herself whistling. She had been to plenty of burlesque clubs, but this was like no circus she had ever seen.

Above the crowd, two naked men and a woman performed a trapeze routine. In the centre of the performance area, a ringmaster displayed a skill with a single-tail whip that was mesmerizing. Instead of bursting the strategically placed balloons around a naked woman, he struck the woman while avoiding the balloons.

An announcement came over the PA and the crowd cheered. 'You'll enjoy this,' Gabriel murmured. 'Pony girls.'

'You're kidding me!' she hissed.

The team of six were tall, blonde and wore nothing but white feathered headdresses and long tails. 'Please don't tell me that the tails are . . .'

'Attached to their butt-plugs,' Gabriel confirmed as they watched the 'ponies' being put through their paces by their 'trainer' before leaving the arena. 'Let's go check out the rest.'

With her smile frozen in place, Sinead followed him. The risqué circus had no performing animals, but women and men sat in cages in the waiting area, eager to perform for their audience. Gabriel patted the head of a girl wearing nothing but a leopard-skin collar and she purred loudly.

A trio of acrobats played in a smaller ring, their skin glistening with sweat as they brought the female artiste to a shrieking orgasm that drew a round of applause from the observers. Sinead pressed her thighs together. Despite the talcum powder she had dusted inside her leather suit, a trickle of sweat ran down her back. How could the woman have an orgasm in public with people watching her?

She could barely have one in private.

Gabriel was her closest friend and one-time lover, but even with him she still found it difficult to let go. Despite having appeared almost nude on stage many times, she found it hard to relax and, unless a lover was particularly patient, she was sometimes left edgy and unsatisfied. She felt a small pang of jealousy at the obvious abandonment of the woman.

Even her short time with Niall had been a revelation. His touch, his kisses had made her fly apart. She wondered what it would have been like to spend the night with him. She pushed the thought away. Now she would never know.

The crowd dispersed, splitting into pairs and making their way to the stables. Soft moans and an occasional grunt of pleasure left her in no doubt as to what went on behind the half doors and bales of hay.

'Does this turn you on, *chérie*? Do you want to see more?' Gabriel's dark eyes were intent on her face. His mouth twitched. He was daring her to say no.

Sinead swallowed. She might never get to see anything like this again and if she was completely honest, her curiosity had been aroused. 'Lead the way.'

The wooden door opened with an authentic creak and they walked the length of the stable block. Some of the stalls were empty, but the tack that hung on the walls was definitely not designed with horses in mind. Role-play costumes hung from a chrome rail.

Sinead watched as a naughty milkmaid was spanked over her master's knee. Her wriggling and squeals had attracted quite an audience until the sound of a whip hissing through the air and striking flesh caught their attention.

Gabriel nodded and they moved away from the crowd and followed the sound. A half-naked man was tied to a whipping post and she tried not to wince as the whip's tail struck home with precision again and again. As the leather-clad Domme worked, red marks appeared, crisscrossing the man's back, but she was careful never to draw blood. The blonde crossed the floor to the man and pulled his head back by the hair before whispering in his ear. He nodded and she resumed his punishment.

'Do you think you could do that?' Gabriel whispered. 'Because if things go well tonight, you might have to.'

Sinead sucked in a mouthful of air, drawing in the sweet scent of hay mixed with sweat and arousal. Apart from the illusion on stage, she had never struck another person in her life. 'I don't know if I could hurt you.'

He smiled. 'Coming from you, it would only give me pleasure. Let's go to the bar and see if we can find you a playmate.'

The glass floor in the bar allowed the audience to see

what was going on in the ring below and Sinead realized why Gabriel had taken her for a tour. Even though she hadn't played, she had been on display. She hoped that someone would take the bait.

Projecting a confidence she didn't feel, Sinead sipped champagne at the bar while Gabriel pretended that he wasn't scanning the crowd. A young American approached them, the neat folds in his surgeon's tunic marking him as a newbie. Gabriel bristled, as if affronted by his stupidity, and the man scurried away.

The Doms were more difficult. Without knowing whether her sister was a sub or Domme, Sinead didn't know how to behave when a questioning glance was aimed in her direction. She kept her expression slightly bored, hoping it would be enough.

'*Roz? Mon Dieu. Roz.*' The blonde Domme from the stables enveloped her in a hug.

Without thinking, Sinead switched to French. '*Oui, c'est moi.*' Well, at least that solved one problem. Now that she knew her sister spoke French, she wouldn't have to worry about betraying herself with her Irish accent.

'Clothilde was expecting you two weeks ago,' the blonde said. 'She had to cancel a femdom party because Megan dislocated her shoulder during a Shibari suspension and you didn't show.'

Oh, feck. Her sister was a Domme.

The blonde darted an interested glance at Gabriel who immediately looked to Sinead for guidance.

'I haven't seen you train a new one for a while,' the blonde continued. 'How is he behaving?'

'Not bad,' Sinead admitted in a grudging tone as she

ruffled Gabriel's hair. 'Most of the time he's a sweetheart, but he needs a firm hand.'

'Don't they all?' She sighed in sympathy. 'It's hard to get a decent slave and the place is crawling with wannabes. I suppose I better get back to work.'

She slid off her barstool. 'Clothilde's not around tonight and we're a bit short staffed. You'll have to do a demo scene.'

'Sure,' Sinead nodded, trying not to let the shock show on her face. 'Let's get together later and catch up. I really need to find some work. I don't suppose there are any parties happening soon?'

The blonde threw back her head and laughed. 'You are such a joker. Hermione's party starts on Friday. Surely you haven't forgotten the biggest event of the year?'

'Sorry, I've been travelling. You know what it's like.' Sinead shrugged.

'Where are you staying? I'll get the office to send a courier with another invite.'

Sinead scribbled Gabriel's address on a napkin and handed it over.

'Great,' the blonde said, and she tucked the napkin into her cleavage. 'I'll let the ringmaster know that you're going on. I'll see you in the performance area in ten minutes.'

Sinead stared after her as she moved through the crowd. In ten minutes she would give her first performance as a Domme. What on earth was she going to do?

8

What the hell was Cirque Noir? Niall checked again, but that was definitely what Sinead had been looking up. He did a quick search and was appalled. Why would a respectable museum curator be checking out one of the kinkiest shows in Paris? Hell, in Europe. From the look of it, Cirque was hardcore and people travelled for thousands of miles to attend. Why would a woman who owned one small vibrator and a handful of racy novels want to go there? Sinead O'Sullivan didn't have a kinky bone in her body. There weren't even any nipple clamps in her apartment.

Those nipples should have nipple clamps on them. They jutted out proudly, begging for someone to tease and torture them. He would suck them, lick and kiss until they were stiff and erect, then catch one and . . .

Niall stopped that train of thought. Why did everything bring him back to the fantasies of things he wanted to do to Sinead O'Sullivan? Not sweet vanilla fantasies either. All his dark urges rose up when he imagined her naked. What was it about her that called to his most dangerous instincts?

There was a reason he didn't do serious relationships. He could fake vanilla for a while, but, sooner or later, his urge to dominate would rise and he would have to fight to repress it.

Sometimes he wished he were smaller, weaker. The trouble about being built like a Viking was that he was too strong. His Ranger training had only made it worse. He was all too aware of how dangerous he could be if he lost control. Deep inside, he was scared that if he relaxed, he could be worse than Darren Hall. He needed someone who was his equal, and what were the odds of ever meeting someone like that?

Fuck this, he had a bail jumper to catch, and before that bastard Hall did.

Niall looked at the posters for Cirque Noir and despite himself, his cock twitched. God, it looked like an orgy of wall-to-wall kink. Women in PVC. Women in corsets. Women wearing damn all. One old poster caught his eye – a masked red-haired girl in a tight leather suit, holding a bullwhip in a businesslike way. There was something about those eyes that looked familiar.

No, it couldn't possibly be Sinead. The O'Sullivans would have a collective heart attack at the idea of one of their family being involved in something like this. He checked the date of that event. It was two years ago, when Sinead had been working at Sotheby's. Of course it wasn't her.

For a moment, he considered her crazy story about a twin. An identical twin that she hadn't seen for twenty-three years and that no one ever talked about. It was such an extraordinary story that he hadn't considered if it might be true. Who would make up a story like that and have any hope of being believed? It was complete nonsense. And yet something made him wonder.

He typed a quick order to his Irish office, telling them to check it out.

Niall went back to the Cirque Noir website. There was a show on tonight. He'd missed most of it, but perhaps if he hurried he might catch the end.

'Relax, *chérie*.' Gabriel put his hand on her shoulder. 'You've done this a million times.'

'Not for real. And have you forgotten? We need a third for this routine.'

'*Pas de problème*. I know a little kitten who will be just perfect.'

The next ten minutes were the most nerve-wracking of her life. Leopard girl was amenable to joining them for the routine. She was eager to play with Gabriel later. The ringmaster, an amiable man from Picardie, organized some appropriate music.

Sinead stood at the edge of the ring, watching as the props were placed where she directed. It would be a demonstration, but probably not the kind that the audience were used to at Cirque. She closed her eyes, wiping her mind of stray thoughts, inviting the calmness to descend. The opening bars of the Argentine tango floated in the air and the audience fell silent.

Gabriel, deliciously inappropriate as ever, had borrowed a waiter's jacket, leaving it open to expose his tanned chest. Leopard girl – thankfully wearing something resembling a dress – sat at the small white-clothed table in the centre of the ring, looking suitably bored. He stalked to her table and tilted her chair backwards before lowering his face to hers for an open-mouthed kiss.

Balanced precariously on the chair, Leopard girl could

do nothing but submit to his ever bolder embraces. Sinead raised an eyebrow. Gabriel was enjoying this far too much. Slowly, he raised the chair to an upright position and pivoted around her, blocking her flight. Sinead doubted that Leopard girl really wanted to escape. When she stood up, Gabriel closed the distance between them. With languid grace, he leaned back across the table, pulling the girl on top of him.

It was time for Sinead to make her entrance.

As the music swelled, she stepped into the ring. A single crack of her whip caught Gabriel's attention and the audience cheered. Releasing the girl, he turned to face Sinead, the picture of an unfaithful lover caught in the act.

She flicked her whip again, catching him on the calf this time. The sound of leather against latex was impossibly loud in the silent ring. Leopard girl fled.

Gabriel eased out of his white jacket, letting it drop to the ground before approaching her slowly, his hands outstretched.

Bad mistake. This lady didn't do forgiveness. Sinead flicked her whip again. It curled through the air and wrapped around his forearm. She tugged sharply, dragging him to his knees. She was conscious of the cheers of the audience as she stalked towards him with the whip held casually in her hand.

Usually she held back, barely touching his skin, but tonight she would have to go for it if she was to convince anyone that she was Roz. Gabriel held out his arm and she unwound the whip slowly. She caught the hint of a grin. He was actually enjoying this. Maybe she should hit him harder.

She circled him before reaching out and fisting her

hand in his hair as she had seen the blonde woman do earlier. 'Are you okay with this?' she whispered in his ear. 'This is a heavier whip than the one I use on stage. I'm afraid that I'll hurt you.'

'Bring it on.'

'Cocky bastard.' She almost smiled and then schooled her face into a stern expression. Lover boy was going to be punished. She picked up a flail in her left hand and danced it over the bare skin of his back, alternating soothing strokes with light bee stings.

'You hit like a girl, *chérie*,' Gabriel murmured under his breath. 'Just do it.'

As if impatient, Sinead cast the flail aside and the audience cheered. It was time to take the gloves off. She prayed that she wouldn't lose her nerve. A practised flick of her wrist brought the tail of the whip to within inches of him and he flinched. Too short. The handle felt awkward in her grip. She adjusted, took a step forwards and raised her arm again. Success. A red stripe formed on his back and the crowd gasped.

After that she found her rhythm. She aimed for his upper back, taking care to avoid his kidneys. His grunts of pain spurred the audience on. She hoped that he was pretending, but the criss-cross pattern was testament to the pain she must be causing him. He cried out again, but this time his groan was tinged with pleasure.

Was he actually enjoying this?

As the music drew to a close she cast her whip aside. She tried not to wince as she closed in on him and saw the state of his back. She had really done a number on him. That would hurt like hell tomorrow. She grabbed his hair again and forced him to look at her. Her apology for the pain she had caused him froze on her lips.

His eyes gleamed with enjoyment rather than pain. A bad slave brought to heel by his mistress. She released his hair and he fell forwards, placing a kiss on her boot as the music ended. The spotlight dimmed. The crowd cheered. Sinead strode from the ring as if she owned it, leaving Gabriel to collect her whip and flail.

She was going to be sick.

Niall arrived at Cirque as it was closing up for the night. He managed to get in, but no one was keen to talk to him since he was delaying their departure. He kept going, showing the photo of Sinead to the bored and tired staff members who were cleaning up.

Just when he thought he was going to have to leave without any result, one of the cleaners blinked at the photo. 'That's a new look for her.'

'You know her?' Niall tightened his grip on the photo when the cleaner tried to take it off him.

'Sure. Well, I do not know her name, but I've seen her here a few times. She's good. She did a really hot scene here tonight. She – '

Niall cut him off before he could go into details. 'Where can I find her?'

The cleaner scratched his head. 'I don't know the name of the man she was with.'

What man? It hadn't taken her long to find herself a man. A red mist descended over Niall's vision and he had to take deep breaths to hold onto his temper. He wasn't going to pound this little bollix to a pulp.

The cleaner, unaware of his danger, went on. 'But Madeleine was also in their scene, she might know.'

'And what is Madeleine's name? Where can I find her?'

The cleaner shrugged. 'She's Madeleine. Someone will know.'

It was 7.30 a.m. when Niall managed to find Gabriel Bertrand's apartment in Montparnasse. He had been up all night, chasing one insubstantial lead after another, before he finally got a name and address.

He rang, leaning heavily on the doorbell. After the time he'd spent searching, he was not inclined to let Sinead sleep in. And if she was sleeping with this Gabriel character, he'd enjoy rousting her out of bed even more.

The bell rang and rang, and there was no sound of movement inside. He jabbed it, deliberately trying to be as noisy and annoying as possible. Nothing.

Well, they had asked for it. He bent to the lock to pick it and noticed faint scratches on the metal. It could be nothing, maybe wear and tear, but his gut iced.

Quickly he unlocked the door and thrust it open. A scene of devastation met his eyes. The room had been turned upside down, and the furniture was tossed in all directions. Cushions were ripped open, and the stuffing was a layer of white over the room.

There was no sign of Sinead. Carefully, trying not to disturb the apartment in any way, Niall picked his way through it, looking for clues. It was clear that a man lived here, one with a taste for designer clothes and hand-made shoes. These were scattered all over the main bedroom.

In a small side room, a camp bed had been made up, and Niall spotted a long strand of red hair on the ripped pillow. He breathed a little deeper. It was ridiculous. The apartment had been ransacked and the occupants had been taken away after a struggle, but all he was worrying about was where Sinead had slept.

He pulled out his phone. 'Andy? Get over here as soon as possible. Sinead has been abducted.'

While he waited for McTavish to get there, he examined the apartment more thoroughly and wondered whether to call the Gendarmerie.

His first impulse was to get all the help he could for her, even if it meant telling them that she had stolen the Fire of Autumn. But he had an ugly suspicion that he knew who was behind the abduction. If it was really Darren Hall with his shadowy connections, then alerting the authorities might be the quickest way to sign her death warrant.

Carefully, he examined the apartment, looking for clues to what had happened. The furniture was older than he was, but lovingly maintained. Too many clothes and far too much beauty product for a heterosexual man – at least in Niall's opinion. What kind of man needed four bottles of hair gel? And three different kinds of deodorant? Something on the bedroom floor glittered – a broken gold chain. Not a robbery then.

He noticed several pictures torn from their frames. One featured a grey-haired couple. Three others were of a handsome, dark-haired man – presumably Bertrand –

with his arms around Lottie LeBlanc. That didn't endear him to Niall at all. He still had vivid memories of Lottie's last performance. Of the way she had looked directly at him as she had peeled off that scrap of a stocking. Of the way she had kissed her fingers at him, holding his eyes as she had lifted her body towards him.

It looked as if Bertrand had been involved with Lottie. Fuck the bastard. Niall wanted to pound him to a pulp.

Apart from the single red hair in the spare room, there was no evidence that Sinead had ever been here. He looked around the bathroom and an elusive trace of fragrance teased him. It was the twitch of his cock that jogged his memory. It was the oil he had used when he was in Sinead's bathroom in Geneva.

Something tightened in his chest. By god, she might be a scheming, manipulative, lying little bitch, but he needed to know she was safe. And it was clear that she was not.

A ruby worth $50 million was missing. Sinead had stolen it. Oh, she denied it, but all the evidence said that she had stolen it. Niall picked his way over the shattered crystal glass in the kitchen, searching for clues and furious with himself for ignoring the obvious.

Every bad guy in Europe – hell, in the world – would want a crack at the Fire of Autumn. And that meant taking a crack at Sinead O'Sullivan.

His phone rang. 'Moore. What have you got?'

Andy's voice was cheerful. 'Good news. Her phone went on for a good ten seconds. I've got a fix. Fancy a trip to La Courneuve?'

The metal floor of the van was painful against her cheekbone, but not as uncomfortable as her wrists. The men had tied her hands behind her back with something thin and plastic and it hurt like hell. Beside her, Gabriel was still unconscious. She winced at each bump as his head bounced on the floor. A cut under his eye was livid against his skin. She wondered where the men were taking them.

She tried to focus, to figure out why she was in a van, but her mind refused to work. She felt drunk, and not the chatty drunk she hit after two glasses of wine. This was a horrible, earth-spinning-and-about-to-throw-up kind of drunk. One spot on her arm throbbed nastily. Had one of them injected her with something?

She knew why. Of course she did. She couldn't quite remember at the moment. A thump when the van climbed the footpath jolted her. Oh yes, that damned ruby. She had told them that she didn't have it, but the one with the dark hair didn't believe her. And Gabriel's beautiful apartment – they had smashed everything while they searched.

Gabriel had helped her, and she had brought him nothing but trouble. She wished that she had never come to Paris and that she had never heard of the stone.

'Take the next right and it's the last container on the left,' the tall one said. He sounded English. There was quite a little UN convention of nastiness in the van. Sinead clamped her eyes shut and pretended that she was still out. She had to fight to keep from slipping into unconsciousness for real.

The van screeched to a halt and the door slid open.

They took Gabriel first. Sinead gritted her teeth as an unoiled hinge grated.

'Be careful with the woman. We need her.'

Well, thanks a bunch for that. They hadn't seemed to care when they took them from their beds earlier. She opened her mouth experimentally and flexed her jaw. There was nothing broken. Yet.

She opened her eyes into slits and through her lashes she saw a man appear in the doorway, blocking the light. He put his arms beneath her and lifted her with a grunt.

'What's up, Max? Not back to fitness yet?' a voice asked.

'Fuck off.'

Max carried her from the van. She struggled to lie limp in his arms although her arm was caught at a painful angle. He wore too much cologne and she battled the need to cough. Keeping her lids lowered Sinead observed her surroundings as he carried her into a big storage container, one that looked like a lorry body. His footsteps rang out on the metal floor and then she was placed on a low camp bed. The blanket smelled new.

'How much of that stuff did you give them?' The dark-haired man asked the question.

'Enough,' Max said. 'They'll be out for a while longer.'

'Good. I need coffee.'

Sinead lay still until they moved away. She heard an electric kettle boiling and caught the scent of coffee. An occasional word of conversation filtered through but not enough to make sense.

Wriggling, she tried to free her hands but it was no use. Her phone was in the pocket of the workout pants she had borrowed from Gabriel. She had turned it off earlier to save the battery. But if she could switch it on, maybe she could make an emergency call. Niall would find her. Niall was good at finding things.

She couldn't reach the phone, but it sometimes made handbag calls to her friends. If she could apply enough pressure, it might dial random numbers from her contacts. She gritted her teeth and rolled over. It was her only hope.

9

Sinead wasn't sure how long she lay there before the door opened and she heard chairs scraping against the metal floor. 'It's time to go to work, gentlemen.' The voice was cool and authoritative.

She didn't like the sound of that. She kept her eyes closed but could smell Max's cologne as he loomed over her.

'No. Leave her. Wake the other one first.'

Her stomach heaved with a mixture of fear and relief mingled with guilt. They didn't want her yet, but it was her fault they had taken Gabriel. What were they going to do to them?

The sound of a hand striking flesh startled her. 'Wake up, buddy. We need to talk.'

Gabriel groaned. They slapped him again, harder this time. 'Wakey wakey, Frog.'

'Uhh.'

Sinead heard a chair being dragged across the floor.

'We can do this the easy way or the hard way. Understand? *Comprenez-vous?*'

Gabriel groaned again. Sinead winced as she heard another slap.

'*Oui. Oui.*'

'That's better. Now where is the stone? And don't bother lying to me. We know your lady friend took it.'

'I don't know what you are talking about.' A punch this time, then a second and a third until she lost count; each one was punctuated with a grunt of pain.

'Where's the fucking stone?'

Oh god. They were hurting Gabriel. She wanted to be sick. The punching stopped and there was silence except for the wheezing gasp of air being dragged into his lungs.

'I don't think he'll talk, boss.'

'Oh, he will.' The voice had the quiet confidence of a man who had done this many times.

Sinead bit down hard on her lower lip. Please don't let them kill him. Don't let them kill him. Somehow the silence was worse than what had gone before.

Gabriel's anguished shriek was torn from his soul. Sinead struggled against her restraints, torn between wanting to put her hands over her ears and wishing that she had a gun, a knife, anything that would stop them. What were they doing to Gabriel? She couldn't listen any longer.

She rolled over onto her back. Out of the corner of her eye she caught a glimpse of him, strapped to a chair, blood streaming down his face. His T-shirt was torn.

'Stop,' she screamed. 'Stop hurting him.'

The blond one approached her. 'Welcome back to the land of the living, Red.'

Sinead shivered under the cold gaze that raked her from head to foot. 'Pretty little thing, aren't you? But your boyfriend's not looking so pretty right now. Is he?'

'No.' She shook her head. Keep him talking. While he was talking he wasn't hurting Gabriel.

He fished in his pocket and produced a pack of

cigarettes. Clamping one between his lips, he lit it and inhaled, before blowing a puff of acrid smoke in her direction. 'Let's make a little deal. You tell us where the stone is and we'll stop.'

The tip of the cigarette glowed orange as he inhaled again, waiting for her response.

'I don't know. I didn't take it. I came to Paris to find the person who did. You have to believe me. Please don't hurt him any more. He doesn't know anything.'

Cocking his head to one side, he stared at her with narrowed eyes. 'Is that right?'

Sinead nodded frantically. 'Please believe me. He knows nothing.'

'Well, that's a damned shame.'

He sucked another lungful of smoke and exhaled quickly before examining the cigarette between his fingers as if he couldn't understand how it got there. 'My mom always told me never to doubt the word of a lady and if that's what you're saying, well, it must be true.'

His smile didn't reach his eyes. He didn't believe her.

'It's a little-known fact that the tip of a cigarette can reach between 400 and 700 degrees centigrade. Did you know that, Red?'

She shook her head. Terror welled up, freezing her insides. He wouldn't. He couldn't possibly do that to another human being?

'Maybe we should ask your boyfriend?'

Dread churned in Niall's guts. The journey from Montparnasse to La Courneuve had taken years off his life. He wouldn't have believed that traffic could move so slowly. He had wanted to get out and push the fucking slow trucks that clogged the roads on the way. Or ram them.

'It's all right, boss, we'll be in time,' Andy said. He checked the reading on his computer again.

Niall took his eyes off the road long enough to glare at him. 'Easy for you to say. You've never run into Hall. And it's not – ' He stopped abruptly, aware that anything he could say after that would be far too revealing.

Sinead O'Sullivan was a job. Nothing more. She was not personal.

Andy hooted derisively, but wisely said nothing. 'Brief me on Hall,' he said. 'I haven't seen him since those military games on Brona.'

Niall wanted to spit. 'Nothing much to add to what you already know. Bastard. Former SEAL, where, as far as I can tell, he got in on the basis of good genes, a bad attitude and family connections. I've met guys he worked with and they all hated him. He took brown-nosing to new levels, but gave the men under him shit.'

Andy grunted. They'd both met men like that before.

Niall overtook a lorry full of bleating sheep on the way to market by squeezing in between it and an oncoming bus of tourists. The gap was so small that the Jeep lost a layer of paint.

Andy gripped the door handle but knew better than to comment on his driving. 'So why do you think he has Sinead?' he said.

'I did a quick check. Blackstone was hired by an Indian businessman to find the Fire of Autumn. He wants it returned to its ancestral home. If they are looking for the stone, you can be sure Hall is looking for Sinead, and he's prepared to be creative about whatever it takes to find her.'

Andy relaxed his grip on the door, only to grab the dash and brace his feet against the floor when Niall swerved around a Citroën 2CV full of teenagers.

Niall pushed his foot down even harder, trying to coax more speed from the creaking Jeep. 'Anything?'

Andy shook his head. 'No, her phone is dead now. But I got a fix.'

'Are you sure?' Niall couldn't bear the thought of Sinead in Hall's hands.

'Sure as I can be with this crappy equipment. You need to upgrade. And why the fuck didn't you plant a tracker on her?'

'I didn't think she'd run.'

An eternity later, they turned into an industrial estate. 'Well?' Niall demanded.

Andy pointed him over to a quiet corner that backed onto a chain-link fence. Even at 8.30 a.m. on a weekday morning, it was almost deserted. 'That's it, I think.'

'You think?' More than ever, Niall missed having Flynn by his side for this sort of thing. Andy was good, but Flynn was the best second-in-command he'd ever had.

They prowled around, searching for the source of the interrupted phone signal. The park was full of old warehouses and containers. The sun struggled to break through the clouds, and a light rain fell, changing the sound of the engines in the area. Sweat trickled down his back, despite the coolness of the air.

Finally he heard something as he approached a large,

unmarked container. A thump, followed by a female cry. He and Andy exchanged glances, and they both went cold. Combat ready. They crept up, ready to attack.

At the door of the container, Niall paused to check his weapons. He would have given his right nut for his H&K submachine gun. Or his Glock. Hell, even the crappy SIG Sauers that he was permitted to carry in England. Instead he was stuck with a fucking baton and a torch. Some use that was when they were up against god knows how many armed men and a former US Navy SEAL who was a walking one-man army. Damned EU laws.

Another female cry. A grunt of pain. He nodded to Andy and together they burst through the doors.

The inside of the 40-foot container had been set up like an interrogation room. A dark-haired man, who had probably once been handsome, was tied to a chair. Sinead, her distinctive red hair loose, and wearing a torn T-shirt and pair of baggy sweat pants, was tied to another chair. Tears tracked down her cheeks and dampened her chest.

The sight threatened to derail Niall's calm. They had hurt her. They would pay.

He didn't bother hitting the dark man bending over the battered prisoner. He grabbed him by the hair and jerked back. At the last second, he managed to stop himself breaking his neck. It would be bad PR. But he hoped the guy had whiplash that lasted the rest of his life.

Andy had taken out a second man, whipping out his extendable baton so that he caught him in the solar plexus. A quick kick to the nuts finished the job.

'What the fuck?' Niall didn't hear the third man approach from behind until a blow like a slab of cement caught him on the side of the head. He grabbed Sinead's shoulder to keep from falling and managed to spin around in time to avoid another blow.

Hall. Fucking J. Darren Hall. And armed with a knife.

Niall gathered his reeling wits, ignored the throbbing from the blow on his head, and concentrated on Hall. He had to beat the bastard to keep Sinead safe.

Hall lunged.

Niall twisted, avoiding the knife and slicing down at Hall's wrist. His hand was useless afterwards, but the knife fell and Hall swore.

Niall stepped in closer, ramming his shoulder into Hall's chest.

Hall grabbed his hair, yanking back to expose Niall's neck.

Foot out, hook and pull.

Hall went down, taking Niall with him.

Niall twisted, landing on top of Hall, and used his weight to hold the bastard still for long enough to jab upwards with a single punch that freed him. His numb left hand still had enough power to smash his nose.

Then Andy was there, dragging Hall's arms behind him. 'Yours,' Niall panted, and turned to Sinead.

She was frozen, eyes and mouth wide with shock at the sudden violence.

He tried to talk and found he had to cough and spit out a mouthful of blood. He bent to untie her. 'Are you okay?'

She nodded.

Niall turned to Andy. 'Get that guy to hospital, and clean up this mess. I'll take care of Ms O'Sullivan.'

10

Sinead tried to collect her wits. She was in a Jeep beside Niall and she was safe. As they left, she heard the sirens of police cars speeding towards the container park.

He turned to give her a quick once-over. 'Did they hurt you?'

She shook her head. 'No, they didn't have time. I'm fine.'

'Are you sure? I can take you to hospital.' Why was he going on about this? She didn't want to go to hospital.

'They didn't touch me. I'm fine. Just get me away from here.' She shut her eyes.

Her mind, normally so active and dependable, had shut down. The surge of adrenaline had kept whatever they had injected her with at bay for a while, but now it was sweeping over her, making it impossible to focus on more than one thing at a time. Her head was foggy and she couldn't think clearly. The scrape in the wiper, which left a trail of water every time it swiped across the window, held her attention. She frowned at it. That could be dangerous. The smear on the windshield could obstruct the driver's view. They might have an accident.

Briefly her gaze skittered across to Niall, driving through the traffic with nonchalant skill. She thought about telling him about the smear and decided against it.

His face was set like stone. He might not want her to talk. He had to drive. He needed to pay attention.

She needed to concentrate. There were things she had to know. As soon as she remembered what they were, she would ask him. Then she would sleep.

She dropped her gaze to her hands, clenched in her lap, and gave a cry.

Niall flicked a quick glance in her direction. 'What is it?'

She held up her hand, index finger extended. 'I've broken a nail.'

He turned to glare at her. 'Are you fucking kidding me?'

He wasn't looking at the road. That was bad.

'I fished you out of a crap situation, with some of the nastiest scumbags in Europe, and all you can say is you've broken a nail?'

'The road.' That was important, wasn't it? She knew watching the road was important.

He obediently turned to glance at the road, but kept his attention on her. 'Lady, all I can say is that you have to be the coldest piece I've ever met.'

'Yes.' Yes, she was cold. How did Niall know that? Why had she not noticed before how cold it was? She gripped her hands together to stop them shaking. A dancer never shivered, no matter how bad the heating was or how cold the stage. She opened her mouth to tell him so, and stopped before she could form the words.

She wasn't supposed to tell him that. She couldn't talk about Lottie. She stifled an urge to giggle. Secret. Lottie was a secret. She felt drunk. Not giddy drunk but the next drink after one too many. Her head was fuzzy. What had they injected her with the second time?

Focus, Sinead. Try to remember. It's important.

'. . . and not even a single question about Bertrand?' Niall asked.

Reality crashed back. 'Gabriel.' That was the thing she was trying to remember. Gabriel had been hurt. And it was her fault. 'Where is he?'

'I don't know yet. Are you going to tell me what happened to him?'

She ignored his question. Gabriel. That was it. She had to help Gabriel. 'You have to go back. I have to find out how he is. They kept beating him and beating him and I couldn't stop them.'

Did Niall's face soften a little?

'I'll find out as soon as we're safe.'

They weren't safe? But she didn't have time to worry about that.

'We have to go to Gabriel. Take me to him.'

'Oh no, lady. I'm not letting you go anywhere again. He is in good hands. He's going to the hospital, but from now on, you are staying with me.' For the rest of the journey, Niall ignored her and concentrated on the road.

Sinead lost track of the roads circling Paris and had no idea where they were when he pulled off the five-lane carriageway and onto a small road leading to a side street. He drove down into an underground car park, its electronic gate permanently shadowed by the tall apartment block overhead.

The silence when he cut the Jeep's engine was shocking. She sat there, wondering what to do now.

Niall came around and opened her door. 'Out you get. This is where you'll be staying for the next few days.'

She followed him into the elevator. Niall entered a code and they moved upwards. She counted the floors – thirty-five of them – before the elevator stopped. She stepped into a carpeted corridor.

'This way.' He took her arm and guided her to a door at the end of the hallway. He entered another code and opened the door and stepped inside. Two walls consisted of floor-to-ceiling windows with a view over the city. A galley kitchen was panelled with dark wood. A large slate-coloured couch faced a plasma screen TV.

The normalcy of the apartment was a shocking contrast to the violence she had endured. 'Does the door lock?' she asked.

Niall had been pointing out features of the apartment, but he stopped, going from businesslike to tender in a heartbeat. 'Yes, it locks. It's a triple deadlock with a built-in alarm.'

'So I'm safe?' She hadn't meant to say that, but the words burst out before she could stop them. She winced. She hated feeling out of control.

There was understanding in his eyes. 'Yes, you're safe here. No one can get in, and I won't let anyone harm you.'

She wondered if she had imagined him saying, 'except me', under his breath. It was too bizarre, so she ignored it. Niall had come for her. He had rescued her. She was safe.

His voice changed abruptly. 'What's that?'

She looked down and saw a large, dark stain on her top. It had dried to brown, but she knew what it was. She shuddered. It was Gabriel's blood.

'Are you hurt? Let me see.' Without waiting for her permission, Niall was kneeling down beside her, lifting up the hem of her top to examine her. His fingers skimmed across a bruise, making her gasp.

'I'm sorry. I didn't mean to hurt you.'

'It's okay.' How could she tell him that the gentle brush of his fingers, so hot on her cold skin, had caused a spasm of pleasure to shoot through her? It was so intense it was almost painful. She wanted him to do it again.

But Niall was all business, checking out her bruises and scrapes, his knowing fingers moving over her head, looking for bumps and abrasions. He clicked his tongue over a shallow gash she hadn't even noticed. 'I don't think this will need stitches. I've some sticking plasters in the kitchen, they should do the job.'

He went into the kitchen and then reappeared with a packet of wipes and a small metal box. He dabbed her skin with something smelly, opened a pink sticking plaster covered with blue animals and put it on her shoulder. 'That should do it.'

He flipped the lid on the box of plasters and grinned. 'Sorry, they've got bunny rabbits on them.'

'Bunny rabbits?' She was finally losing it. Had he said bunny rabbits?

He ducked his head, making it harder to see the faint trace of colour on his cheekbones. 'My sister and her family were living here during the summer. My niece is going through a bunny rabbit phase. I'm actually hoping she moves on to boy bands soon, but if Jenny gets into One Direction, I'll have to avoid her until she's over it.'

His casual patter about boy bands and bunny rabbits

allowed something in Sinead to unwind. For the first time since she had been kidnapped, she began to believe she was safe. The events of the previous twenty-four hours crashed into her mind and she trembled. Grabbing the hem of the blood-stained top, she yanked it over her head.

'I need to wash.' She knew she sounded hysterical, but didn't care.

'Come on, the shower is in here.' Niall led her into the bathroom and turned on the large overhead shower. While it warmed up, he helped her take off the rest of her clothes. She was vaguely aware that she was naked in front of him, but it no longer mattered. All she wanted was a hot shower.

He guided her into it, but there was no rubber mat and she slipped getting in. He caught her before she could fall and held her upright. 'Niall . . .' She had no idea what she was asking.

She didn't need to. Niall kicked off his shoes and got into the shower with her. He held her securely while she allowed the water to cascade over her, washing away not only the blood and sweat of her ordeal but the fear that had clogged her ability to think. She made no attempt to wash herself. That could wait.

Niall was trying to stand out of the direct angle of the shower, but he was soaked too. 'You look funny,' she told him.

'Says the girl with the bunny rabbit sticking plasters.' He opened a bottle of shampoo and poured some into his hand. 'So what happened to you?'

The movement of his fingers in her hair, massaging her scalp, was so luxurious that she closed her eyes and gave herself over to it. 'I was asleep,' she told him. 'It was dark in the apartment. Gabriel has blackout curtains, can't sleep without them.'

For a moment, his skilled fingers stopped their mesmerizing motion. But now that she was talking, she couldn't stop.

'The first thing I knew was a hand over my mouth. I opened my eyes and there was a man standing over me. It was too dark to see anything. I fought. I bit him and he slapped me.'

Niall's thumb brushed gently over the bruise on her cheekbone. 'I shouted, but it wasn't enough. And I could hear Gabriel fighting too. The man put something over my head, and I was being carried.' She shuddered. 'He groped me.'

Niall stiffened, but his voice was calm. 'Go on. Were they speaking French or English?'

She leaned against him, her back to his chest, not caring that he was still fully clothed. 'Both. But later there was a man with an American accent giving orders. We were put into a van. The floor was metal and it scraped me.'

He dipped his head and brushed a kiss onto the plaster. Despite herself, she was warmed by the gesture.

'I couldn't see, there was something over my head. When I could see again, they were taking us into a container or something like that, and then they started beating Gabriel.' She shuddered again.

'Shh, shh. It's over. You're safe.' Niall rinsed the suds out of her hair, carefully directing the shower away from her face. He rubbed in conditioner and then scooped up a handful of lemon-scented shower gel and washed her.

126

He was keeping his touch gentle and non-intrusive, but as his big hands moved over her breasts and grazed her nipples, a shock of sensation streaked through her, breaking her out of memories of the attack.

She turned her head and her gaze rose to meet his. Those hands might be impersonal, but the heat in his eyes told a different story. Niall Moore wanted her. And right now, she wanted him too.

She pushed her breasts back into his hands. 'Again.'

His fingers flexed, tightening on her, but not giving her the pressure she needed. 'Sinead –'

She knew he was going to come out with some platitude about her being in shock and not knowing what she wanted. But she wasn't going to let him tell her what she wanted. She wanted him.

'I don't care. Do it again.'

His grip tightened. His fingers were long enough to contain her whole breast, and she revelled in it. She moved slightly so that her nipples grazed his palm, and hissed with pleasure. 'Oh, that's so good.'

'Better than this?'

Now he had her nipple in a slight pinch, the pressure just enough to cause twists of sensation to streak through her, travelling in a straight line to her core.

Her knees weakened, but it didn't matter. Niall was there, supporting her, holding her. He bent down and kissed her neck, his lips hotter than the water in the shower. She tilted her head to give him better access and he took full advantage, kissing his way up to her ear.

He caught her earlobe between his teeth and nipped delicately.

'Ah!' It was precisely what she needed, and yet nowhere near enough. She slipped forwards, and found herself against the tiles of the shower stall.

The contrast between the heat of the Viking at her back and the coolness of the white tiles was shocking. Her nipples hardened even more, becoming rock-hard points of sensation.

She had lost the ability to move, but Niall turned her. She looked up into his eyes and caught her breath. They were ablaze with emotion.

Sinead put up her wet arm and pulled him down to her, desperate to kiss him. His mouth was hot and wild, his tongue a delicious temptation that she couldn't resist. When he took her mouth, she welcomed him longingly, opening eagerly to him. He tasted of passion, and she sucked fervently at his tongue, unable to get enough of it. She chased it into his mouth, determined not to lose the connection.

In this position, her sensitive breasts were pressed up against his soaked shirt. There was something intensely erotic about being naked while he was fully dressed.

He gave a strangled half laugh as he lifted his head. 'Wait. We'll get out and –'

'No. I want you now.' The hoarse note of command in her own voice startled her. This wanton, demanding woman couldn't possibly be her. But the sensations coursing through her were strong and urgent and utterly new. This time there would be no waiting for arousal to build to the point where she could enjoy love-making. The searing lust filling her was burning so hot that she couldn't wait another minute.

His hands skimmed down her back, lifting her and pressing her against him. The shock of the contact made it impossible to think. She hooked one thigh over his hip, torn between pressing her demanding clit against him, and grabbing his erection with her hands.

'Now,' she insisted. 'Fuck me.'

'Oh god, I'm going to hell for this,' he muttered, but let her slide down his body long enough for him to reach into his back pocket. His wallet was as sodden as the rest of him, and he had to fight to get it open, but there – thank you, god – was a condom. She had a moment of shame that she hadn't even thought of it, before she gave herself up to Niall.

He opened his jeans, allowing his impressive erection to spring free. She couldn't resist caressing it with greedy hands. Hers, all hers. The tip was already slippery with arousal. She ran her thumb over it in wonder and he shuddered.

What would it taste like? She considered slipping to her knees to find out. But Niall had already put a condom on it, and was lifting her up. He pulled her right thigh back into position over his and lifted her. With a surge of his powerful hips, he pushed into her.

'Ahhh!' She had never imagined it would feel like this. She was stuffed, stretched, full of Niall. She almost forgot how to breathe. Every rational thought was driven from her head and all she could do was revel in the sensations of him inside her.

He paused for a moment, allowing her to catch her breath. His grey eyes were narrowed in concentration and passion. She could drown in those eyes, lose herself in him.

'More. Now.' She had a fleeting thought that for someone who was so literate, her vocabulary had been reduced to monosyllables. She stopped thinking. Niall was moving.

He surged into her, his hips pressing her against the cold tiles while his rock-hard cock filled her with enough heat to run a power station. Every movement sent electricity along her nerve endings. She could hear herself gasping and making silly noises, and she didn't care.

He moved again, thrusting in boldly, pulling back reluctantly. She lifted her other thigh, letting him take her full weight, so that she could tighten her legs around him and urge him on. Her heels dug into his buttocks, as demanding as if he were her stallion to command.

He grunted and picked up the pace, going faster, causing her to burn from the inside out. Hot water beating down added to the maelstrom of sensation. Could those breathless gasps of pleasure really be hers? She shuddered, torn between wanting this to go on forever and needing him to speed up now, now, now.

As if he read her mind, he gripped her hips tighter and thrust harder and faster.

She wrapped her arms around his neck and buried her face against him, licking and biting at the skin of his neck and throat, wanting to devour him. She had forgotten how to speak, or how to breathe, but it didn't matter. All that mattered was Niall and the things he was doing to her. He moved faster.

Her insides tightened like a spring coiled too tightly. Her core contracted, squeezed to the point of pain, but it was a pain she wanted to last forever. She dug her heels in more strongly and raked her nails on his upper back.

He grunted and plunged more deeply into her, touching something that she hadn't known was there, and she shattered into a million tiny pieces. Sinead screamed as she exploded in his arms, trusting him to make sure that she survived.

She was still shivering in the aftermath when he followed her with a roar. She had time for a tiny thought about whether they had neighbours, but then all rational thought disappeared. He was plunging wildly and shuddering.

And holding her as if he would never let her go.

Dazed, she continued to cling on to him, not caring that the water was cooling. Her skin was still on fire from his touch. Each nerve ending jangled for long seconds before easing away and leaving her in a boneless, languid aftermath.

She couldn't have moved if her life depended on it. So this was what it felt like. This was what all the fuss was about. This was sex.

Niall pulled away from her reluctantly. She was wrapped around him and he found, to his amazement, that he didn't want her to let go. But he was all too aware that the water was cooling and he had to deal with the condom. For one crazy moment, he wished he didn't need one.

He had to look after Sinead. She needed him to rescue her, and that was what he did. All his protective instincts roared to the fore.

'Better now?' he murmured to the top of her head.

Her arms tightened for a fraction of a second, before gradually releasing their grip on him.

'Yes, I think so.'

Niall held her while she got her feet under her, and reached out to turn off the water. Five more seconds and it would be running cold.

She was still unsteady on her feet, but Niall couldn't help a small smug smile. He was responsible for her quivering. He was prepared to bet a lot of money that she wasn't thinking about her abduction any longer.

He wrapped her in a big fluffy towel and mopped the water from her hair.

This was the first time he'd had a chance to examine the thick mane, and it fascinated him. 'Why do you keep this hidden?' he demanded. 'You should leave it loose.'

Under the bathroom lights, it was a dark red, thick and waist length. When it was dry, it would be pure titian.

'Are you mad?' She had been standing docile under his ministrations, but now she turned to glare at him. 'I have a mop of ginger curls. At best I'm like Little Orphan Annie's big sister. Most of the time I look like the punch line of the joke about gingers having sex in a spring factory.'

She pulled away from him and braided her damp hair into a neat plait that concealed its vibrant colour. She did this without looking in the mirror and the tighter the braid got, the more quickly she returned to her starched and prickly self.

He watched with regret. While he was glad to see her recovering from her shock, he missed the passionate woman who had demanded that he fuck her. At the memory of her words, his cock twitched again.

He backed away. 'I'll go and put on dry clothes and organize some food. There's a robe hanging on the back of the door that you can use.'

He rubbed his hair dry and dropped his wet clothes in the laundry basket on his way to the kitchen to see if there was anything edible. Alison usually left something in the freezer for him, in case he dropped in.

'God bless you, my darling sister,' he said under his breath. Two steaks, frozen frites and petit pois in the freezer, and milk and coffee in the fridge. UHT, but it would do.

He put the steaks and frites on to cook while he pulled on some dry clothes.

Sinead's clothes lay on the floor, filthy and blood stained.

He battled the rage that the sight of that blood aroused in him. He needed to stay in control of himself. Would it be worth sending them for forensic analysis? Hardly. Any DNA on them was likely to be too contaminated to be useful.

He threw them into the washing machine.

By the time Sinead came, bathrobe clutched tightly around her, the table was set and the food was ready. She was a little hesitant. He had no idea why. Surely after that amazing encounter in the shower, she should be at ease with him.

'Hope you're hungry,' he said.

'Starving.'

'Good. I love a woman with a good appetite.' He put a steak down in front of her. If he said it himself, he could cook steak well. It was char-grilled to perfection. A dark criss-cross pattern was seared into the surface and a tiny drop of red oozed from the meat where he had tested to see if it was cooked. The peas nestled in beside it, and the frites perfumed the kitchen.

Niall took his place opposite her. 'Eat up.'

She took a mouthful, and then another. 'I don't usually eat red meat. It's not good for you.'

He snorted. 'I think you can handle it tonight.'

She didn't speak again until the steak was almost gone. For someone who claimed not to like red meat, she ate with gusto. It wasn't the only thing she did with gusto. He forced himself to stop thinking about that.

Finally she stopped eating for long enough to say, 'I used some of the toiletries in the bathroom. I hope that's okay.'

'Please save me from them. Alison has more stuff than she can use.'

'Alison?' Her expression was politely interested, but her voice shook slightly.

'My sister, I told you. This is her apartment, but she's on temporary assignment in New York at the moment, with the UN. I suppose you could say that, technically, we're squatting.'

'You broke into your sister's place?'

He laughed. 'Relax. I have permission. And the security codes.' He cleared her plate away, waving her back to her seat when she tried to help, and made coffee. But by the time he returned to the dining room with it, Sinead's head was drooping and her eyes were drifting closed.

Poor girl, she'd had a rough day.

Niall scooped her up in his arms, enjoying the way she fitted against him. He carried her to the bedroom and held her while he pulled back the sheets. Reluctantly, he set her down but she clasped his neck and refused to let go.

He could break her grip in a second, and without hurting her. Niall knew that. But he didn't want to. It had been a long day for him too. He would rest beside her until she dozed off and he could get up and set the orders in motion to find out what the hell was going on.

He slid into the bed beside her. He would hold her for a little while, until she was asleep. She needed her sleep, poor girl.

Niall was in the middle of planning what he would cook her for breakfast when he fell asleep.

135

Sinead woke to the sounds of an unfamiliar place. Although she had kicked off the sheets during the night, Niall's large, warm frame was wrapped around her like a blanket. Her skin tingled deliciously where the stubble of his five o'clock shadow had burnt her. She was sure she would have a mark on her neck where he had nipped her with his teeth. She blushed. He would probably have his own share of marks too. What had come over her?

Their encounter was exactly the kind of sex she had always imagined with him – a rough, passionate taking. Except that she was the one who had demanded it. She couldn't believe that she had asked him to fuck her. What must he think of her?

Ignoring his sleepy protest, she eased out of his arms, grabbed her robe and went to the bathroom. She risked a look in the mirror. Apart from the bruise on her cheekbone, and the cuts that Niall had tended so gently, there was nothing to show that she had been kidnapped.

She smiled when she noticed the plaster. Lottie had hundreds of costumes designed to seduce a man, everything from thirties vamp to leather corsets, and what was she wearing for her finest hour? A bunny plaster!

Sinead nibbled her lower lip. She didn't know a thing about him. Niall might have a stable of girlfriends. She hadn't exactly given him a choice when she dragged him into the shower. But she couldn't forget the heat in his eyes as the rivulets of water ran down his face or the way that his hair had escaped its binding and hung over his shoulders. Through the sodden T-shirt, each muscle of his abdomen had been clearly defined. Niall had looked like one of her secret fantasies come to life.

The ache between her thighs told her that this was no fantasy. None of her previous encounters could match this. They were like clumsy boys in comparison. She closed her eyes and ran her fingertips over her skin, imagining that it was his hands. When had she developed this sudden and voracious hunger for Vikings?

A brisk tap on the door jerked her back to the present. 'Sinead, are you okay?'

'Fine.' She ran her fingers through her hair and opened the door.

'Just checking.' Niall brushed his index finger against the bruise on her cheekbone and his mouth hardened. 'I have some arnica. I should have used it last night. It will help the bruises heal more quickly.'

She submitted to his gentle ministrations, unsure what else to do. Had the previous night been no more than an adrenalin-fuelled reaction to the kidnapping? She had initiated what happened between them. Maybe he regretted it already . . .

His swift possessive kiss silenced her doubts. 'Come back to bed. I want you.'

Niall took her hand and led her back to the bedroom. He sat on the edge of the bed and pulled her between his outstretched thighs. Tugging on the belt of her robe, he eased it off her shoulders, letting it drop to the floor.

'You're beautiful,' he said as he palmed one breast, plucking the nipple between his fingers until it peaked.

Sinead gasped as a dart of heat flared in her abdomen.

He bent his head and took the other nipple in his mouth, suckling gently at first and then harder until she squirmed. Oh, that felt so good. She ran her fingers through his hair, letting the strands curl between her fingers as a flood of sensations washed over her. He nuzzled between her breasts before latching on to the other one.

His warm tongue lapped against the hardened bud until it became too much and she tried to pull away.

Niall's arm clamped around her waist like a vice and he continued to torture her until she was breathless. He raised his head, a wicked grin curving his mouth. 'Sensitive there, aren't you?'

'Very.' She wriggled again and was rewarded with a tap on her buttocks. Not a slap exactly, but a firm reminder that he was very much in charge.

'Where else are you sensitive? I wouldn't want any complaints.'

'From my other sensitive bits, you mean? I think that –'

Hooking an arm around her waist, he lay back on the bed, pulling her on top of him. He angled her head to his satisfaction and plundered her mouth with his lips and tongue until she was breathless.

The hard ridge along her abdomen created a delicious friction against her clit. Undulating like a cat, she rubbed against his shaft, seeking more pressure. His tongue thrust against hers as his kisses became more forceful. Sinead moaned into his mouth, 'Please.'

His rumble of laughter held a dark edge. 'The condoms are in the drawer in the bedside table.'

She wriggled away from his searching hands and tugged the drawer open, pouncing on the box. Straddling him, she opened one foil wrapper.

His cock was long and thickly engorged; a vein ran

down the underside and a small pearl of pre-cum shimmered at the tip. She licked her lips. 'Maybe I should –'

'Sinead.' Her name was an agonized rasp and she felt a warm rush of pleasure. So much strength and hard muscle, and yet Niall was helpless. What would it be like to see him lose control? Condom forgotten, she cupped his balls with her palm and licked his shaft from root to tip, flicking her tongue lightly against the head.

He fisted the sheet, holding on desperately. He said something, but all she heard was a low growl of agony. She ignored his strangled plea, focusing her attention on taking the crown into her mouth, swirling her tongue against the slit, tasting his musky flavour. She wanted to experience everything with him.

He sat up, startling her, and she pulled away. Heat radiated from his stare. She had pushed too far. With a show of strength that made her gasp, Niall lifted her and threw her onto the bed. Sheathing his cock swiftly with the dropped condom, he followed her down.

Insinuating himself between her thighs, he gave her a heavy-lidded glance before pumping one broad finger into her core, stroking her aching wetness. A second finger followed, preparing her. Withdrawing his fingers, he licked them, never taking his eyes from her face.

Raising her hips in wanton invitation, she writhed under his intent gaze until, with a groan, he plunged inside her. The size of him was startling and her muscles stretched to accommodate him. Without warning, he withdrew almost to the tip before driving into her again. Sinead gasped. Caged by his arms, she clung on, breathless at each invading thrust, revelling in his brutal possession. She wrapped her legs around his hips and dug her heels into his buttocks, urging him on. She nipped at his neck, tiny biting kisses, licking the marks she had made the night before. Each stroke found a home deep inside her. She clamped her muscles around him, pleasure spiralling low in her abdomen, fanning out in waves, touching every nerve ending. His name became a breathless entreaty, begging him not to stop.

Her orgasm caught her like a tidal wave, obliterating all rational thought, sending her senses reeling. Dazed, she clung onto him. His thrusts increased in momentum. Eyes clamped shut, his jaw clenched hard as he fought his own battle for control. A second wave of pleasure followed rapidly and he drove his shaft home for the final time. Afterwards he lay shuddering in her arms. His laboured breathing mingled with hers until he slowly came to his senses.

He raised himself and the sudden withdrawal from her body made her gasp. 'Jesus, Sinead. Did I hurt you?'

She reached for him, but he moved away, rolling onto his back and dragging her into his arms. Beneath her ear, she heard the racing thud of his heart return to normal. 'I'm sorry. I should have been more careful. I'm too rough and I –'

She grasped one of his nipples between her fingers and pinched hard.

'Ow.' He jerked and she laughed.

'I'm not made of china. Stop fussing.'

Niall captured her hand in his, preventing another attack. 'I can't lose control like that. I'm too big. I could have hurt you.'

'Maybe I like it rough.'

He raised his head and brushed his finger along the livid bruise on her cheek. 'No man should ever be rough with a woman. If I got my hands on the guy who did that to you, he wouldn't see daylight again.'

She snuggled into his arms. Niall was so much bigger than she was that he made her feel cherished and protected. Her cheek throbbed, but she could tell it was healing. 'I'm fine. It could have been much worse.'

'I was trying to help you. Why did you run?'

'I came to Paris to find my sister. I saw that tape, I know it was her. It has to be. If I don't find her, I'm going to prison. I know that she has some connection with that club.'

'Cirque? What makes you think that?'

She shifted her head to look up at him. 'You sound as if you don't believe me. Look. If I had the bloody stone, do you think I'd be lying here in bed with you?'

Ouch. She hadn't meant it to sound like that. 'I'm sorry, that came out all wrong. I meant that if I had broken into the Rheinbach museum, I would have done a better job of it.'

Niall snorted with laughter. 'Go on, I presume this gets better.'

'Any intelligent thief would have stolen the smaller stones. They're easier to dispose of. The Fire of Autumn is one of the most recognizable stones in the world. It will be impossible to sell – think of it as the Mona Lisa of jewels.'

A thoughtful look crossed his face. 'And you believe this sister of yours has it? Why?'

'Because the girl on the security tape wasn't me, so that only leaves her.'

'Okay.' But he didn't sound convinced. 'I'll check it out. See what turns up. What happened at the club?'

'We went there posing as my sister and her . . .' An image flashed into her head of Gabriel on his knees in the centre of the ring, her whip swishing through the air, leaving a red line on his back. Probably best not to mention that bit. '. . . Boyfriend,' she continued. 'We were hoping to find her and convince her to give the stone back.'

'That was a bloody dangerous thing to do. What did you think would happen when you met her?'

Sinead pressed on. 'I lost my family when I was four years old. My mum died, my dad left and he took Roro with him. You have no idea what it's like to know that there's someone out there who belongs to you and you can't find them. I know it was stupid, but I had to try. No one in Geneva believed me about the stone. Did you think that I was just going to wait around and end up spending the rest of my life in prison?'

'What happened at the club? I believe that there was a scene with you and Bertrand.'

She had hoped Niall hadn't heard about that. She shrugged. 'It was nothing really.'

'Really?' His arm clamped a little more tightly around her.

She wasn't ready to talk about this with him and she still didn't know how she felt about it. She performed in stage shows, where every move was choreographed and rehearsed. But the exhilaration she had experienced that night in the ring was like nothing before and Gabriel had felt it too. He had been on a high afterwards.

'It was a bit of playacting to convince them I was Roisin.'

There was no way that she could tell him that she and Gabriel had performed that routine before. 'Anyway, we met someone who knows my sister. She's going to be at a party on Friday night.'

Niall's chest shifted beneath her head as he went on the alert. 'Where?'

'I don't know yet. They're sending the invitation to Gabriel's place.'

'Friday? I'm not sure if . . .'

Sinead sighed. He didn't have to finish the sentence. If the Swiss police discovered that she had left the country they could demand that she be locked up again and her uncle Tim would lose his money. She sat up, full of renewed energy. 'Come on, we don't have any time to waste.'

I 2

After breakfast he opened his laptop and sat down to work. She had never before met a man who owned four phones – and he used them all. Niall moved from one call to another, requesting background checks and sending operatives off to interview potential contacts, the sound of the Tardis blaring out on one phone, signalling the arrival of an email.

'What age are you?'

'What?' he said. 'I happen to like the programme. All the guys on the team have *Doctor Who* ring tones.'

He opened the email and scanned through the list of high-class jewellers who might have information. Niall posed as a buyer for the stone, switching between French and English easily.

Sinead scanned the names. She wouldn't have bothered ringing any of them. A dozen calls later, they were running out of names. Sinead lost her patience. 'You're doing it all wrong.'

His eyes narrowed. 'I'm an investigator, Sinead. Let me do my job.'

'Nobody knows you. They're not going to talk to you, but they will talk to me.'

Niall shook his head. 'That's out of the question. It's too dangerous.'

'So is prison. But that's where I'm headed if we can't

find the stone.' It was maddening. Why couldn't he see what was so obvious? 'Let me make one phone call and you'll see that I'm right.'

Reluctantly, he handed over the phone. Sinead wished that she had her notebook, but it was buried somewhere in Gabriel's apartment. There was one person in Paris she could call but she didn't know his number. Her phone was dead until she bought a new charger for it.

Leaning across Niall, she did a quick search on his laptop for Parisian antique shops. She tapped the number into the phone and waited. She had almost given up when the phone was answered. '*Maurice Verdon, ici.*'

Sinead almost cried with relief. 'Maurice, it's Sinead O'Sullivan. I need to talk to you.'

Maurice was willing to talk, but not over the telephone. He invited her to his shop and settled a time. When she finished the call, she was on a high until she looked down at the bathrobe. 'I don't have anything to wear.'

'And the problem with that is?'

The prospect of more naked time with him was tempting, but they had work to do. Sinead rolled her eyes. 'Idiot. I can't go out dressed like this.'

'I've some T-shirts I could lend you and you could –' His voice trailed off when he saw her expression.

'Not a chance. This is Paris.'

Damn, she was right. He couldn't take her out in Paris dressed in his T-shirt and a pair of workout pants rolled up to stop her tripping over them. She would stick out a mile. He mentally flipped through the clothes he had here, but while he loved the idea of her dressed in one of his shirts and nothing else, he knew she needed clothes.

He braced himself. 'I'll buy you something. What size do you wear?'

She gave him the sort of look usually reserved for people who tortured kittens. 'I'm not telling you something like that.'

'Why not? How can I shop for you if you don't tell me?'

'Because it's personal, that's why. I don't go around telling people what size I take. Let me at your computer. I'll see if I can find a store that will deliver clothes today.'

'No. Not happening.'

She crossed her arms over her chest, daring him to argue, and also pushing her breasts up in a display that made him lose his train of thought. Her breasts were bare under his T-shirt. Lucky T-shirt. 'What size bra do you take?'

Sinead narrowed her eyes at him. 'Are you trying to be difficult? I'm not telling you that either.' He opened his mouth and she went on. 'And I'm not telling you my height or weight either. So don't bother asking.'

He held onto his patience with an effort. 'Unless you want to go out dressed like that, you'll tell me.'

She snorted. 'In your dreams. I'm not having a man pick clothes for me. Give me the password for your computer, let me order my own and we'll be sorted.'

'Yeah, right. Do you really want a credit card trail leading here?' And she would order more of those hideous suits she wore. 'Nothing doing. You stay here, babe, and I'll shop for you.'

He headed for the door, but was still able to hear her repeat, 'Babe? Babe? Is he crazy?'

Once he was outside in the street, Niall realized that he'd had so much fun aggravating Sinead that he might have outfoxed himself for once. He had no idea where to shop for clothes for a woman. He intended to dash in, pick up a few essentials, pay and get out, the way he shopped for himself, but he was pretty sure she wouldn't be impressed by jeans and a T-shirt from Tati.

When in doubt, consult an expert. And luckily he had one on the end of his phone. No one knew Paris shops like his sister.

'Hey Alison, I need a bit of help here. I've got to buy some clothes for a woman. What do you suggest?'

He held the phone away from his ear while Alison shrieked at him. 'You haven't called me for weeks, and now you want help with a woman?'

'Take it easy, Allie, it's not like that. I just need to buy her some clothes.'

'An evening dress? Something for the opera?' Alison asked. 'Is it for a date?'

'No, nothing like that, just clothes.'

'What sort of clothes?' He could hear Alison's two year old screaming 'Piggy! Piggy!' in the background. Alison had no trouble ignoring her.

'Clothes. She has nothing to wear. Literally.'

'And why are you buying them for her? Who is she?' Alison demanded. 'Hold on, is she a real woman?'

Niall switched his phone to his other ear as an open-topped bus full of tourists went past. 'Of course she's a real woman. What other sort of woman is there?'

'As long as she's not one of your charity cases. You've got to stop doing that.'

He took a breath. Now he remembered why he didn't ring Alison all the time. She could piss him off quicker than any of his sisters. 'I don't have "charity cases", as you call it,' he said tightly.

'Does this one need to be rescued? To be looked after?'

'I suppose so.'

'Charity case. Duh!' Her voice became muffled for a moment. 'Mommy's talking, we'll do piggy soon.' Then it became all too clear. 'You have to let Dr Burns go.'

'She was killed under my command. I can't let that go.' Fuck it, why did Alison always rake this up?

'She disobeyed your orders and took a stupid risk. Could you have stopped her?'

'No, but –' He shoved his hand through his hair. He had replayed that night in Afghanistan thousands of times in his mind, trying to work out how he could have saved the doctor.

'Then get over it. Not every woman is a charity case.'

'This one is a client, not a charity case, and she needs clothes. Just give me the name of a couple of good shops.' A thought struck him. 'And if you tell Mam, you're dead.'

'You and whose army?' It was funny that all 5'2" of Alison wasn't in the least afraid of him, while half the operators of Europe backed down when they saw him coming. 'Okay, try Agnès B or Le Bon Marché.'

He thanked her, and set off.

The shop was discreetly lit, with several assistants and an artistic window display. From the street, it was hard to see what sort of clothes it sold. This was a new kind of battle. He took a breath and went in.

'Can I help you, Monsieur?' The smiling assistant looked like a fashion model, skinny and polished and flat-chested. Not like the curves of Sinead, made for a man's hands. But she was offering to help.

'Yes, I need to buy clothes for my friend. A couple of dresses, skirts, tops, lingerie, you know what I mean.'

Her eyes gleamed. 'Certainly. For casual wear? Business? An evening of pleasure?'

Oh god, he would like to see Sinead dressed for an evening of pleasure. What could he dress her in? Pearls and a smile sounded good. Later. 'Business. But business in Paris. Clothes that make her look beautiful.'

She looked affronted. 'Of course, Monsieur. We do not sell ugly clothes.' She gave him time to apologize, before asking, 'What size is she?'

The question he dreaded. 'I don't know.' He didn't need to see the expression on the assistant Yvette's face to know this was the wrong answer. 'But she's a little taller than you.' Another assistant, this one behind the cash desk, snorted as she tried not to laugh.

Niall looked around. There were half a dozen assistants listening to him, all openly amused. He had an idea. 'If you could all line up, I'll know which one of you is closest to her shape. We can find out that way, yes?'

He tried not to listen to their laughter as they obeyed, having clearly decided that the tall Irishman was the day's entertainment. He walked up and down along the row of chic French women, comparing them to Sinead.

'She's the same height as you,' he told one. 'And I think her waist is the same size as yours,' he said to another. 'May I feel?' The feel of Sinead's slender waist was burnt into his hands. The assistant nodded, and he put his big hands around her waist. 'A centimetre smaller. Write that down,' he told Yvette.

Another woman had hips around the same size, but none of them had breasts like hers. The more he looked at other women, the more of a crime it was that she concealed hers. The assistants told him he had to pick one of them, but none were the right shape. A shopper came in, allowing her leather jacket to open. She had an hourglass figure and knew it. 'Madame, may I ask your bra size?'

By now, the atmosphere in the shop resembled a party. The assistants cheered and assured the woman that the mad Irishman was shopping for his wife.

His wife? Where had that come from? But he didn't argue.

'90D,' the woman told him.

Now he had the measurements, the serious shopping began. Every woman in the shop had an opinion about what he should buy, and Niall himself had ideas too. He vetoed a few suggestions as being too dowdy, and his eye was caught by a deceptively simple blue dress. It would bring out her eyes while highlighting her tiny waist.

That was wrapped up, along with everything else. 'Is that all, Monsieur?'

He snapped his fingers. 'Shoes.'

'Let me guess,' Yvette said. 'You don't know what size she takes?' One more line up, this time in stocking feet, for him to decide whose feet were the closest in size to his lady's. He picked out two pairs of elegant high-heeled shoes for her, and waited while the bill was rung up.

'That will be €5,345, please.'

He gripped his credit card. 'How much?' That had to be a mistake.

'You have an eye for quality, Monsieur. And quality costs.'

Reluctantly, he handed it over and tapped in his pin number. Sinead had better like his choices.

Sinead had been trying to watch the television, but was constantly distracted by worry about Gabriel and Hall and her sister. When the door opened, she gave up and switched it off. Niall had returned, laden with bags. She raised an eyebrow when she saw some of the store names.

'I don't know why women enjoy shopping. I'd rather run thirty miles in full kit.'

He dropped the bags on the couch. 'I'm going to hit the shower. Get dressed. We don't have much time if we're meeting Maurice at three.'

She picked them up and hurried to the bedroom. God knows what he had bought, but she would have to wear some of it, whether it fitted her or not.

Undies first. The pink striped box was tied with a black ribbon. She untied it and pulled back the layers of tissue paper. A rose-coloured silk bra and panties greeted her. Nice. They were proper French knickers too, not the teeny tiny thongs that she wore on stage. Two more lace-trimmed sets were individually wrapped beneath the first; one black and one the colour of old gold. A supply of stockings and matching suspender belts were wrapped together.

She checked the size – 34D, perfect. What else had he bought? The dress was deceptively plain but beautifully cut.

The top of it would fit her like a second skin and the skirt flared out, ending just above the knee. Another bag revealed two close-fitting skirts and a selection of long-sleeved tops in different colours. She searched the other bags and discovered a dark leather jacket, butter soft and expensive. She inhaled its scent. Where were the trousers, or the jeans and T-shirts? And there wasn't a baggy sweater in sight.

The shoe boxes were another revelation. She whistled when she saw the label on a pair of black heels. Even Lottie would have hesitated before spending that amount of money on a pair of shoes, but they were beautiful. She kicked off the borrowed woollen socks and slipped the shoes onto her feet.

It had been a while since she had worn heels. She wore sensible shoes at the museum. She hadn't had a date since she had moved to Geneva, so there didn't seem to be any point in dressing up. Heels really did something for a girl.

She pivoted on one foot and struck a Lottie pose. She had missed her so much. Standing before the mirror, a thought struck her. She had never gone on a date as her glamorous alter ego. Lottie existed only under the spotlight. When the performance was over, she always vanished. Maybe it was time to let her out to play again.

Sinead carefully removed the labels from the wispy pieces of silk and put on the underwear. She drew on the stockings and smoothed them over her legs, glancing in the mirror to make sure that the seams were straight. She fingered the dress. It seemed a shame not to wear it. This time next week she could be in a Swiss prison. She pulled the dress over her head and zipped it up. It flared delightfully around her legs. She almost looked like . . . Lottie.

Sinead pulled a face at the mirror. Well, not exactly like Lottie. Without the elaborate stage make-up, coloured contacts and raven wig, she looked like a glamorous version of herself – except for the bruise. The bathroom cabinet contained a half-finished tube of concealer. Not her shade but she needed something to cover the bruise on her face. She took a step back. It wasn't perfect, but it wasn't as noticeable as before.

Niall's silence said more than a dozen compliments. She was used to that kind of reaction from fans of Lottie but not for Sinead O'Sullivan. He had changed into a dark suit that looked as if it had been made for him. Given the size of his broad shoulders, it probably had. His shirt was pristine and the tie was an understated grey silk that matched his eyes and had probably cost a packet.

He caught her glance and adjusted the knot again. 'Damn things, I hate wearing them.'

'Here, let me.' She re-tied it, tucked it inside his jacket and rested her hands on the lapels. The heels gave her an added height advantage. She was tall enough to kiss him and she gave in to temptation, brushing her mouth lightly against his. 'You polish up well.'

'I was about to say the same to you.' He rested his hands on her waist and hunger flared in his eyes. If they didn't get out of here soon, they were never going to make their appointment.

Regretfully, she stepped out of his arms. 'Come on, we have to go. We can call the hospital about Gabriel on the way.'

Niall parked in a side street around the corner from the antique store. Sinead had been quiet since she heard that Gabriel was out of surgery. The surgeon was confident that he would make a full recovery, but there would be scarring.

'Are you sure you want to do this?' Niall asked.

'Don't be stupid. Of course I'm going to do it. I'm fine. I've known Maurice for years. Stop fussing.'

He kept his hand on the small of her back as they crossed the street and stopped outside the antique shop. Among the replicas and tourist tat were two nice water-colours; overpriced of course, but saleable. She paused at the display of jewellery.

Sinead couldn't be sure when she had first developed a fascination for jewellery. Her mother hadn't left any, and Granny O'Sullivan's collection was pure paste. But there was something about a ruby. The cold purity of the fire within always set her heart racing.

Lottie had a few nice pieces she wore mainly for photo shoots, but they were stored in a safe deposit box in London.

She caught a glimpse of their reflection in the window. They might have been a couple ready to make a very special purchase.

Niall fingered the collar of his shirt. 'Stop looking

at the engagement rings, Sinead. You're making me nervous.'

She threw back her head and laughed. 'You'd be lucky.'

He held the door open and the bell jangled as they stepped into the store. A middle-aged female stepped forwards, dressed entirely in black. A small cameo brooch at her throat was her only embellishment. Her attention focused on Niall, taking in the bespoke suit and polished shoes, measuring his worth.

'Monsieur.' She inclined her head in welcome.

The woman had probably already adjusted the prices upwards by 20 per cent. Sinead was tempted to throw him to the wolves but they didn't have the time. 'We're here to see Maurice,' she announced. 'I'm Sinead O'Sullivan. He's expecting us.'

Concealed behind an embroidered screen was a panelled door that led to a narrow staircase. On the second landing the woman rapped on an unmarked door. They heard a key being turned and a bolt being drawn back. Niall shot a dark look at Sinead. He didn't like this one little bit.

The Frenchman was barely 5'7". A brocade waistcoat covered a belly that was testament to his love of good food. Sinead kissed him on both cheeks and received an enthusiastic hug in return. 'Maurice, so good to see you.' She gestured to Niall. 'This is Niall Moore, my associate.'

'Come in, come in.' He motioned them into the room and locked the door after them. 'I've made coffee.'

'That would be lovely.'

She glanced around the room. The dark mahogany display cases came from another century, as did many of the pieces contained within. Necklaces, rings and tiaras glittered under the light and Sinead itched for a closer look. Maybe later.

'How are you?'

'Terrible.' Maurice shook his head as he poured three cups of coffee and offered one to her. He gestured to the cases. 'You see how it is. Since the crash, everybody wants to sell. No one wants to buy.'

She nodded sympathetically as she sipped her coffee. Things were always terrible with Maurice. He hadn't had a good day for a decade.

'And the rent.' He sighed. 'They must think I'm made of money. You saw the shop downstairs. Full of stock.'

Full of tat more likely. Sinead knew that most of his 'antiques' were made by his brother in Lyon. Even sold as replicas, they were vastly overpriced.

'You might have noticed the nice little pair in the window. I bought them from a dealer in Brittany. No provenance, but they're a steal at four thousand, don't you think?'

'You'd be robbing me if you looked for more than nine hundred.'

'For both? Impossible. I have a family to feed.'

Sinead laughed. She knew that his son had his own import business and that his daughter was married to a wealthy oil executive. 'I'm not in the market for a picture, Maurice. I need some information. I'm sure you've heard that the Fire of Autumn has been stolen. Could you –'

He set his cup down carefully. 'Not even for you. We are talking about dangerous men.'

'She's already met them.'

It was the first time that Niall had spoken since they entered the room and Maurice turned his head and gave him a shrewd stare. 'If you have, then you know what you are dealing with.'

He wasn't going to help them. 'Those men think I stole the Fire of Autumn. I have to get it back. Please, Maurice.'

He tapped one pudgy finger on the desk and sighed. 'You are not the only ones seeking the stone. There are at least two others searching Paris for it.'

'Who?' Niall asked.

'I've heard rumours that a certain Russian oligarch and a Chinese businessman are interested but it is also possible that the stone has been offered to the Rheinbach.'

'What? They want to sell them their own stone back?'

Sinead shook her head. 'It's not unusual. The museum will claim on their insurance, but for a lot less than the true value of the stone. What else do you know?'

'Nothing. There are other rumours of course.'

'Like?' Niall didn't bother to hide the impatience in his voice and Sinead flashed him a look telling him to shut up.

'Perhaps an auction; I really could not say.' Maurice shrugged.

Could not or would not? She couldn't be certain which. It was time to apply a little pressure. Sinead rose from her chair and pretended to examine the contents of one display case containing antique rings.

Maurice followed her. 'Have you seen anything that catches your eye? I will give you a good price.' He pointed to an emerald ring. 'That one came in recently.'

'I hope you didn't pay much for it.' The ring might have had an antique setting, but two of the smaller stones gave the lie. They were machine cut, not cut by hand like the other stones.

'You are cruel, but correct as usual.' He turned to Niall. 'Do you know that they call her the Ice Queen because of her love of stones?'

She hated that nickname. Some men in the business viewed it as a challenge, thinking it referred to her private life and not her passion for jewellery.

'Ah, I have the most wonderful thing for you. Not diamonds but sapphires – a perfect pair of Sri Lankan stones. Now where did I put them?'

Maurice moved a set of old wooden steps along the floor and climbed them to reach the top shelf. He took a bunch of keys from his belt and opened one drawer. 'Here.' He announced with a hint of triumph before descending the steps again.

'Sit. Sit and try them. They were made for you. They are the same colour as your beautiful eyes.'

Sinead brushed back her hair and allowed Maurice to fix the earrings in place. He handed her a mirror.

He was right. They were perfectly matched and exquisitely beautiful. She couldn't possibly afford them. Well, Lottie could, but museum curator Sinead O'Sullivan couldn't. She shook her head regretfully. 'They're too expensive.'

'But you haven't heard the price yet. Seventy.'

She unclipped one earring. 'Twenty.'

'You wouldn't want to see my children starve. Sixty.'

'Thirty-eight seven fifty. My final offer and I want to know who's running the auction for the Fire of Autumn and when it's taking place.'

Maurice smiled broadly. 'Done. And may I say it's always a pleasure doing business with you.'

There was one tiny little problem. She didn't have a credit card and the police had probably frozen her bank accounts by now. She glanced at Niall. 'Can you get these for me? I'll pay you back later.'

She had never noticed the tic on his lower jaw before, but it was jumping madly now.

'Thousands?' he croaked.

'Yes, sir. €38,750. A bargain.'

Niall was still smarting when they left Maurice's. He'd heard plenty of guys in the Wing complain about women who spent money like water. None of them could hold a candle to Sinead, that was for sure.

'I'm hungry, can we go for something to eat?' she asked.

'As long as you're prepared to eat table d'hôte. That little visit cost me almost €40,000, on top of your clothes. My credit card is pretty much maxed out.' He still couldn't believe how much money he had spent on her in one day.

'In that case, I'll have a house salad and glass of water.'

He didn't believe that demure tone for a moment. There was mischief in her eyes.

'I think I can run to a meal or two.'

'Lucky I know a cheap place that does excellent food. We can walk and enjoy the air.'

It was windy, and the clouds were drawing in, making the shadows darker than usual. A few drops of rain fell, threatening more. 'Enjoying the air?'

She shrugged, for the first time looking uncomfortable. 'I need to be outside for a while.'

Considering what she had been through, it wasn't unreasonable. But – 'Your hair is too noticeable. You'd better wear a hat.'

Hall was under arrest, but no saying how long they would be able to hold him. Niall knew that the bastard was an expert at weaselling through red tape. They stopped at a tourist store and he bought her a dark beret to match her leather jacket.

On her, it looked stylish. But with her hair hidden, there was something familiar about her. He eyed the high-heeled shoes. When he had bought them, he hadn't realized how high they were. He had been determined to put her in something different. He hadn't considered strolls along the Seine in shoes that made walking a party trick. Somehow she was coping.

The river was dark and sullen, but she smiled as she walked along. 'I love Paris. Not just the touristy things like the Eiffel Tower and the Louvre, but the river in the rain and the smell of garlic and cologne on the metro and the chatter of people in the markets.'

'Dublin is my city. Even when I'm living in England, there's something about Dublin that says home.' He hadn't planned to tell her that, it slipped out.

'Oh look!' Sinead stopped and leaned over the wall guarding the river. She waved at the bateau bus chugging up the river. A handful of people waved back. She stayed there, leaning a little further as it fought the current on the way to the next stop.

Niall was stunned. That position caused her dress, so

respectable when she was standing, to ride up, showing that she was wearing the stockings he had bought her. The flash of thigh at the top of the smoke-grey stocking was mesmerizing. And she had no idea.

He checked around. No one else within range. He allowed himself to enjoy the sight. She shifted again. 'Careful,' he called.

She turned to him, mischief in her eyes. 'Do you think I'm going to fall in?'

He had trouble operating his tongue. Now he could see the tops of both stockings. 'Be careful.'

'It's okay. I know what I'm doing.'

She hadn't a clue. Despite himself, his cock swelled. Why hadn't he noticed the purity of her profile before? Because she always wore glasses, he realized.

'We'd better walk on before it gets dark. Can you see or do you need to hold my arm?' It took everything he had to make the offer. Moving on would mean that she hid those enticing thighs.

'I'm just slightly short-sighted, I'm not blind.' She sounded a little offended, but straightened up and moved to his side. He didn't know whether he was relieved or disappointed.

They walked along the quay, pointing out sights to each other. Niall wasn't surprised when she knew about the architecture of the buildings, or that she usually had a story to go with them. A half hour walk through Paris with Sinead was an education. He didn't tell her that his version of the city usually involved catacombs and sewer systems.

'Who do you remind me of?' he asked. It was driving

him mad, an itch he couldn't scratch, that feeling that he knew her from somewhere.

She broke off her account of the dispute between Matisse and Picasso. 'I like to think I'm a unique individual, not a cheap copy of someone else.' She sounded annoyed and he couldn't blame her.

She shrugged. 'It's probably Summer. We are cousins, after all, and there is a family resemblance.'

The hairs on the back of Niall's neck stood up. There was a lie somewhere in that. But what?

14

The restaurant Sinead led him to was old and dimly lit. The menu was scribbled on a blackboard, in French. There was no translation and a limited choice. They arrived before the rush and the waiter found them a table. The patron came out and kissed her effusively while exclaiming at her paleness. He looked Niall up and down and sent out a bottle of Cahors that he swore he kept just for her.

Sinead didn't even bother to read the blackboard. 'Two of whatever you're having yourself, Manu.'

'Steak for me,' Niall said. 'They seem to know you?'

Sinead looked around her. 'It's one of my favourite places. I come here every time I'm in Paris. Sotheby's has an office here.'

She sat down, and her skirt rode up again, another flash of thigh, this one even more tantalizing than the last, because it was within touching distance. Niall shoved his hands into his pockets to prevent himself reaching out to see if that skin was as soft as it looked.

Get a grip, man. It's not as if you haven't stroked every inch of that skin already. But it was different when they were out in a restaurant and he was looking at the lure of the forbidden. She shifted and the skirt fell back into place. Niall took a breath. He could cope with this.

Their soup arrived, a rich onion soup, fragrant with

sherry. Sinead ate with enthusiasm. 'I had forgotten how good Manu's cooking is. He used to work in a two-star restaurant, but left to take over his father's zinc.'

'Zinc?'

She waved her arm around. 'This place. His family's restaurant.'

She stretched out when she had finished her bowl, clearly relaxing. That damned skirt rode up again.

'Are you enjoying your soup?' she asked.

'Hmm?' He couldn't drag his attention away from her legs. He should tell her. It was the gentlemanly thing to do. But then she would pull down her skirt. He could see one of her suspenders now. He had picked them out in the shop, thinking they would drive her mad. He had no idea how mad they would drive him.

'Niall? Are you feeling all right?'

He flushed and jerked his attention back to her face. 'Yes, fine. Perfect. Amazing.'

'You seemed a bit distracted.' She pushed a lock of hair behind her ear, the movement somehow as erotic as the stocking top. He didn't know where to look.

'I'm wondering how Manu can top that soup.'

She laughed. 'He'll manage it.'

The main course was *Andouilles et crozets*. 'Peasant fare,' said Manu. 'But tasty.' Garlic and spices wafted off Sinead's plate. Niall's steak was cooked to perfection, but he still hungered for a taste of her dinner.

'Lucky I won't be kissing anyone tonight,' Sinead said. 'This gives you wicked bad breath.' It couldn't have been clearer that she was not planning to invite him into her bed tonight.

'I've got garlic on this, so I'm immune.' It was worth a shot.

'You won't be scoring either then.'

Dessert was tarte Tatin served with crème fraiche, crisp and glossy with caramelized apple. He looked at it longingly. Most of the time he was quite happy with meat and vegetables, but this was torture. With the ingrained discipline of years of training, he ignored the temptation.

'Aren't you having any?' Sinead asked.

'I'm coeliac.'

'Really? You never said.' She scooped a bit of the golden apple off the top of her dessert. 'Have a taste of the apple. It's gorgeous.'

He shook his head. 'That would be enough to trigger a reaction.'

'In that case, I'll have to eat it all by myself.' She made a production of putting the spoon into her mouth, closing her eyes in simulated bliss and making purring sounds as she savoured it.

Watching her luscious lips curl around the spoon was setting off a different reaction. But he couldn't look away. Never had any woman in history spent so long eating a slice of tarte, or enjoyed it so much.

When the plates were cleared, Sinead suggested they move to the counter to have their coffee, and free up the table for the hungry people waiting. Niall was not in the least surprised that so many people were willing to stand in line. This was the sort of meal that food critics raved about.

Even the counter was crowded. Niall snagged the single remaining high stool and helped Sinead up onto it, while he stood beside her. She settled herself, crossed her legs – and her skirt rode up again, revealing the tops of both stockings. Niall began to sweat. He swallowed.

By the time he had control of his tongue again, Sinead was chatting away to the man sitting on the stool beside her. He was dark-haired, with smooth olive skin and a lot to say.

'I am French, not Canadian,' he was telling her. 'I choose to live here. This is a country where you can take your glass of wine outside while you smoke. In Canada, I told my friends about this, and the staff in the bar came running up. "Sir, are you planning to steal one of our glasses?" I said, no, of course not, but they still told me to leave. When I insisted on finishing my drink first, they banned me from that bar. So now I live in France.'

He introduced himself as Daemon and continued to chat, but Niall noticed that his eyes kept dipping. To where Sinead's stocking tops were clearly on view.

He wasn't the only one. The bar was crowded, and at least one other couple had noticed. They nudged each other and whispered, but did not speak to her.

Niall positioned himself to shield her from the eyes of the other patrons in the bar.

Sinead was oblivious. She asked questions, exclaimed at what Daemon said, and generally flirted like a professional. And her eyes never once dropped below her waist level.

Why, the little madam! She knew what she was doing. It was a deliberate tease. Niall had to admire the artistry of it, but he would never have expected it from Sinead. She was just full of surprises. He had no intention of letting her get away with it.

His inner Dom, usually buried beneath layers of iron-clad control, rose to the surface. He leaned over and whispered into her ear. 'Pull your skirt up another inch.'

She froze. For endless seconds, she didn't even breathe. Niall held his own breath, wondering what she would do. An eternity passed while their little corner of the café was locked in stillness. Without turning her head or acknow-ledging his order in any way, she moved, crossing her legs so that her skirt rose an inch higher.

Yes! She had obeyed. He had given her an order and she had submitted to it. His cock rose, rock hard. He moved behind her so that it wasn't visible. Sinead contin-ued to tease Daemon about his Canadian roots and resolutely ignored the inch of pale thigh. Niall managed to join in, asking the odd semi-intelligent question about the weather in Toronto.

Manu refilled their wine glasses, reminiscing about the last time Sinead had eaten there, along with a bunch of friends. He was not in a position to see her display. She cut across him at one point, changing the direction of the conversation.

'Pull it up another inch,' Niall told her.

This time, she obeyed at once. Now her skirt was so high that he caught a flash of her rose-pink panties. There was a muted buzz in the atmosphere as the table opposite them noticed Sinead's display. Niall moved so that he blocked their stares.

Daemon looked from Niall to Sinead and back again,

aware of something in the atmosphere. 'Say, what is it with you two? Are you boyfriend and girlfriend?'

'No!' They answered in unison.

'There's something between you.'

'Don't be silly,' Sinead told him. 'He's a business associate of mine.'

Nettled, Niall leaned down and murmured into her ear. 'Go to the Ladies room, take off your panties and give them to me.'

She turned shocked eyes to his. He held her gaze, silently commanding her to obey his order. He didn't repeat himself, just waited.

'Nature calls,' Sinead told Daemon. She placed her glass on the bar. 'Back in a couple of minutes.' She slid down from her stool and disappeared into the back of the café.

The seconds ticked by, turning into minutes. The minutes dragged on. Sweat dripped down his back, cold against his hot skin. He had almost forgotten how to breathe when she came back, smiling and cheerful, weaving her way in between the crowded tables as she returned to the bar. She apologized for taking so long, and as she climbed back onto her stool, she pressed something into Niall's hand. He opened it barely enough to catch a glimpse of rose-pink.

She had done it. His Dom roared in triumph. Sinead had submitted to him, obeying his orders, and was now naked beneath her dress. Only the two of them knew, and the knowledge made his cock swell.

The panties in his hand were damp.

He couldn't resist running his hand down her back,

caressing it gently. 'Good girl.' She shifted subtly, moving into his touch. He dropped his hand lower, below her waist. He could feel the curve of her buttocks, unobstructed by panties. He dipped his fingers inwards, pressing into her warmth.

'Mmm,' she said. Her skirt was rising up again.

'What's that?' asked Daemon.

'Oh, nothing. I'm getting a little tired. Perhaps it's time to go home.'

Niall couldn't agree more. He had a raging hard-on and needed to do something about it. He had to get Sinead to himself. He needed to get his hands on her.

She took her bag from him, let him help her into her jacket, kissed Manu goodbye, accepted a card from the Canadian and promised to ring him soon, and waved as she left the café. She had been centre stage all night, Niall realized, ruling the café as if it were her own personal stage. Again, that sense of familiarity nagged him.

He kept his hand on her back on the walk back to the Jeep. She was silent on the ride back to the apartment.

'That was a fun evening. We must do it again some time. I believe you have something belonging to me.'

Niall reached into his pocket and reluctantly handed over the panties.

'Good night.' She closed the bedroom door in his face.

Fuck! It was going to be a long night.

Sinead leaned against the door and closed her eyes. *Oh my god, I can't believe I did that.* She had meant to tease him a little in the bar. After all, it was his fault. He had bought the lingerie, and the stockings, and the impossibly high heels. What did he expect? To dress her up like Lottie and hope she behaved like a nun? He deserved payback.

The ardour in his eyes on the bridge had set her inner imp off like a rocket. After that, she couldn't resist. She fingered the scrap of rose silk and tossed the panties onto the bed. They were still damp, which was hardly surprising, given that he had switched on her libido and she couldn't seem to turn it off again. What had he done to her?

Watching Niall watching her was one of the most erotic things she had ever experienced. That ice-cool veneer of control that he always wore barely masked what lay beneath – pure dominant alpha male. After the previous night, she knew what passion Niall was capable of. In a way, they were both hiding what they were.

She had no idea how much like Lottie she really was, but Niall had tapped into her naughty side.

When he had ordered her to remove her panties, she had never been so turned on in her life. The heat in his eyes, that rough edge of command in his voice had sent the blood rushing south. She realized that her breasts were still tender, aching for his touch. Her nipples were standing to attention like two . . .

Stop that right now. Think cool thoughts. Ice. Snow. Frost.

A vision of Niall, a sliver of ice between his teeth as he . . .

She had a bad case of lust. A sudden attack of Niallitis. 'It's just sex. It can't possibly lead to anything,' she told the empty room. 'He is the head of a security firm and you are a . . . a criminal.'

Well, not quite. But after talking to Maurice, she realized how precarious her position was. Other people wanted the stone too and until she tracked down her sister, she didn't have time for romance.

And then there was the whole Lottie thing. There was no way that she could keep that hidden. But back at the lake, she had told him she wasn't hiding anything else. How could she tell him about Lottie now?

Stop thinking about him, she told her libido. It is not happening.

Sinead kicked her heels off. Her feet hadn't hurt this much since her last performance. Padding across the room she unzipped her dress and hung it carefully on a wooden hanger. She caught a glimpse of herself in the wardrobe mirror – stockings, suspender belt, half-cup silk bra.

If she opened the door and went to him now, she had no doubt that they would be in bed within five minutes. Bad idea. Very bad idea.

The ache between her thighs said something else. She wasn't going to get a minute's sleep unless she took the edge off. Where was her friendly vibrator when she needed it? She unclasped her bra and dropped it over the back of the chair before switching off the lamp and lying down on the quilt. The open drapes let the shimmering lights of Paris into the room. Here she was in the most romantic city in the world and she was sleeping alone.

She trailed her fingers across her breast, circling her still-erect nipple. Maybe she should cave in and invite Niall to share her bed. His lips would be so hot, so skilled and so very eager. The prospect of his talented mouth busy at her breasts sent another flare of heat to her core.

Spreading her thighs, she grazed between her soft folds. She was so wet. She moistened her fingers and rubbed lightly against her clit. The little nub was already swollen and tender.

Niall had really done a number on her. She couldn't seem to switch off this craving for him. She imagined his tongue lapping, his broad finger pumping inside her. Her pulse raced. Every nerve ending tingled as she pictured him between her thighs. His broad shoulders holding her legs apart and her own helpless murmurs mixed with his passionate groans.

He would look up at her with those stormy grey eyes of his. Maybe she would take that leather tie from his hair and run her fingers through his tresses, holding a fistful of his hair as his mouth did its magic between her legs. And while she was still catching her breath from one amazing orgasm he would press the head of his cock against her and –

'Sorry Sinead, I need to use the en-suite, the other shower is – Holy Fuck!'

She couldn't have put it better herself. A towel was slung low around his hips. Even in the dim light of the room, the muscles of his abdomen were clearly defined. His hair was loose about his shoulders in the way she had fantasized about. He looked edible. And now he had caught her and, from his smug expression, he knew exactly what she had been doing.

Reaching for a pillow, she flung it in his direction. 'What are you doing? Get out of my room.'

He caught it easily but his eyes remained focused on

her stocking-clad legs and bare mons. 'Need a little help with that?'

She dragged the quilt across her legs. She wished she had something hard and pointy to throw at him. Icy politeness was her only refuge. 'I'm fine. Thank you.'

'Really? It wouldn't take long. I don't like to see a lady in distress.'

'I am not in distress. I am . . .'

'Horny? Believe me, after your little display tonight, that makes two of us.'

'I did not –'

He dropped the pillow onto the floor. The lights from the street played over his bare skin as he approached the bed. Despite the heat in the room, Sinead shivered. His eyes raked over her bare breasts; her nipples peaked as if they had been exposed to a blast of icy air.

'Oh baby, you knew exactly what you were doing. Don't bother denying that you were as turned on as I was.' He picked up the discarded panties and brought them to his face and inhaled.

'You know what I smell? A little tease. If you want me, you know where I am.' He dropped the towel onto the bed and sauntered into the bathroom, closing the door behind him.

She hoped the water was freezing.

15

Sinead snuggled deeper into his embrace. She was back in her apartment again, the first morning they had woken up together. Niall's large hand cupped her breast, his fingers playing with her nipples. She wriggled her hips, savouring the feel of his warmth against her thighs and the sizeable bulge against her bare skin, wanting to prolong the moment before she woke up and had to face the world again. 'Mmm, that's good,' she murmured.

'Glad you think so,' his voice rumbled against the back of her neck.

Sinead opened her eyes. This definitely wasn't a dream. 'What are you doing in my bed?'

'I think you'll find that this is my bed.'

Niall nipped at the tender skin where her neck met her shoulder and she shuddered. His hand cruised along her hip and stroked her thigh with a feather-light touch that made her ache for more. Wretched Viking. How could he annoy her one minute and make her feel like this the next? Somewhere, she knew that Lottie was laughing at her. This was payback for teasing him the evening before.

'This is such a bad idea,' she said as she rolled over into his waiting arms.

'I know,' he murmured.

His lips brushed against hers and a rush of desire flared

between them. Sinead gave a happy little murmur and opened her mouth, allowing his tongue to sweep inside. God, the man could kiss. She parried her tongue against his, savouring the taste of him. Mint. Oh, hell, she probably had morning mouth. Breaking the kiss, she tried to wriggle away from him. 'Bathroom,' she pleaded.

'Two minutes,' he said, releasing her reluctantly.

She scampered to the bathroom. 'Two minutes, my eye,' she said, staring at the mirror. It would take a lot longer than that. At least the bruise was fading, but she probably reeked of garlic from Manu's special. She brushed her teeth vigorously and had the quickest shower ever before hurrying back to the bedroom.

'That was a long two minutes,' he said, running his eyes over her towel-clad body. 'You're lucky you're not under my command or I'd have you on punishment detail.'

Sinead laughed and pulled the towel higher around her breasts, watching as his eyes flicked over her bare thighs and back to her breasts. 'I'm not sure if I'd like to be serving under you.'

'Oh, I think you'd like it just fine. Now, lose the towel, soldier. It's time for your mission debriefing.'

She hesitated, wondering how long she could string out losing the towel. One of her favourite burlesque routines was the dance of the seven veils.

'Slowly,' he urged, as if he had read her mind.

Sinead closed her eyes. She had no stage, no props, no music, but her blood was on fire. She wanted to tease Niall; to rouse the sleeping giant. With sure-fingered grace, she un-tucked the towel and drew it away from her breasts, never taking her eyes from his. The towel dropped to the floor and she bent to pick it up, allowing him a perfect view of her derrière. Niall might think that he was in charge, but he didn't have a prayer against Lottie.

She swung her hips as she walked with deliberate slowness to the chair and draped the towel over it. 'Tell me, does Moore Enterprises do a lot of naked interrogations?'

A smile quirked his mouth and he patted the sheets, inviting her closer. 'If you come over here, you can find out for yourself. I handle all the important cases personally.'

'I bet you do,' she said.

As if she was performing on stage, Sinead walked slowly towards him, with a provocative swing to her hips. Standing naked before him was almost a bigger rush than appearing on stage. The dark promise in his eyes made her tremble.

'Is this the part where I tell you my name and rank and nothing else?'

He cocked one blond brow. 'Sure. If you want to end up over my knee. I'm fully trained in multiple interrogation techniques designed to extract the maximum amount of information from unwilling subjects.'

'Should I be scared?' She pouted. 'Tell me, what's the bad man going to do to me?'

With an almost feline grace, he rolled to the edge of the bed and sat up. He rested his hands on her waist. Their warmth was startling against her skin. He had big hands. Not quite large enough to circle her waist, but he made her feel tiny. Drawing her towards him, Niall pressed a kiss in the hollow between her breasts. 'Well, there's isolation, but then we'd both suffer. Or maybe sleep deprivation – but I had enough of that last night.'

She shivered as his searching mouth fastened on one erect nipple. A hot swirl of his tongue dragged a hiss of pleasure from her. 'What else did you have in mind?'

He drew his mouth away and she immediately felt the loss of his touch. 'Sensory deprivation,' he continued. 'The elimination of sensory stimulus – sights, sounds, tastes, smells and tactile sensation. But on second thoughts . . .'

He pursed his lips and blew gently on her erect nipple. 'You're very responsive there. Maybe I should try sensory bombardment instead.'

With a strength that surprised her, he lifted her up, and despite her giggling protests, dropped her onto the bed.

'Don't move,' he warned as he retrieved her stocking from where it had fallen the night before and looped it around her wrists. It wasn't tight enough to be uncomfortable but enough to make her feel restrained. Niall moved to the other side of the bed and opened a drawer.

'What are you going to do to me?'

In response, he tugged a sleeping mask over her eyes. Sinead lay perfectly still, her chest rising and falling rapidly, trying to figure out what he was doing. He whistled as he entered the bathroom and she heard the bathroom cabinet open and close. The edge of the bed dipped and she thought she caught the scent of mint.

She wriggled her arms. She could slip out of the restraint if she pulled hard but she wasn't sure if she wanted to. The thought of being helpless, of being at his mercy, sent a wicked thrill coursing through her. This was something she had fantasized about. She could trust him to let her explore.

'Let's see how responsive you really are.'

He crushed her against the quilt, ravishing her mouth with a possessive kiss. Niall's lips trailed along her jaw, his morning stubble leaving a tingling trail in its path. She wriggled beneath his searching hands as he stroked her from breast to hip. A growl of pleasure rumbled in his chest, sending a thrill straight to her core.

Slowly she spread her thighs, seeking his touch. 'Please, I . . .'

'Soon. Don't move.' Sinead held perfectly still, afraid that he would stop. Her eyelashes fluttered against the black silk mask but despite her best efforts she couldn't see what he was doing. All she could do was wait.

His hot breath teased one hard nipple before moving to the other. This was torture. Why couldn't he . . .

'Easy, baby,' he murmured. One broad finger traced a circle around her erect nipple, spreading something cool on her sensitive skin.

She arched into his embrace as he traced a similar circle around the other. He licked a path down the centre of her abdomen and for once she was grateful for all the hours she had spent rehearsing in front of a mirror. His hot mouth paused over her mons. A puff of breath against her tingling flesh made her writhe helplessly against the sheets. 'Niall —'

'Patience,' he said.

His tongue made slow circles on her heated flesh, circling the opening, ignoring her clit. She gasped aloud when it plunged into her core. The heady sensations continued until he used his finger, covering her tender nub with her own juices. A cool touch against her clit made her gasp. Then she felt the same touch against her nipples, which began to tingle.

'What are you . . .'

The tingling changed. It was still cool but it became maddeningly hot simultaneously. What had he used on her? 'Please, Niall. Oh god. What did you do to me?'

She wriggled, trying to close her legs against the pleasure, but his hands held her thighs apart. Her nipples burnt hot and icy cold at the same time. 'What have you . . . ? Stop it, now.'

'Say my name. Say, please Niall.'

She was mindless now, writhing like an eel. 'Please Niall.' She forced the words out through gritted teeth as the sensations flared maddeningly hot and cold.

The first sweep of his tongue against her nipple brought a hint of relief. She arched her back, seeking more of his tongue. He obliged, licking roughly, frustrating her even more. Niall turned his attentions to the other nipple and relief washed over her. It was so good. She never wanted him to stop.

The sensation between her thighs grew more heated. She raised her hips to him, rubbing herself against him like a wanton. 'Please, Niall.'

He ignored her plea, focusing on bringing relief to her breasts. She had heard of women who could come just from this and thought they were exaggerating. But his mouth, his merciless tongue, was making her change her mind. Except for the maddening sensation in her clit, she would have stayed like this forever, a prisoner of her own pleasure.

She rocked her pelvis against him, and was rewarded with a rumble of laughter. 'I'm heading there. Stay still.'

His slow, torturous path down her body had her pleading, until at last his mouth fastened over the tender pearl and she screamed. A rush of hot pleasure flooded her core. She could no longer hold back. Waves of ecstasy crashed over, sending tremors to every nerve ending. Her body trembled helplessly on the bed, wracked by a series of aftershocks that left her unable to move.

Finally, he removed the blindfold and she shut her eyes against the morning light and his smiling face. 'Bastard,' she managed to say with trembling lips. 'What did you . . . ?'

He waved a blue and white tube at her.

'Toothpaste?' He had used toothpaste on her. She could barely form the words to reprimand him further. How had he done this to her? Reduced her to a trembling pile of wanting? With *toothpaste*? When she recovered, she would make him pay.

Niall left her on the bed while he went to make coffee. The urge to make love to her there and then had been so strong it had frightened him. When had Sinead acquired so much power over him?

The sight of her sprawled on the bed, open and pliant and receptive to him had been an aphrodisiac so powerful that it almost broke him. He had to draw back from the temptation she presented or he would lose control.

Besides, a tiny part of him argued, if he left her wanting more, when she finally begged him to take her, it would be mind-blowing. He already knew that there was a furnace of passion locked away behind her staid exterior.

He poured coffee grounds into the pot and tamped it down. He needed something strong after the sleepless night and early-morning kinks. He screwed the two halves of the coffee pot together and cursed when he realized that even something like a coffee maker reminded him of Sinead's hourglass figure.

He licked his lips and tasted her again. Salt and honey musk. He wanted more. Could he go back and have another taste? The sound of the shower running made him frown. He liked the idea of her going around still wearing his kisses, still wet from his mouth. He wanted to mark her so that no other man would approach her.

The pot hissed as the water inside boiled up, forcing its way through the grounds. The smell of fresh coffee filled the air.

She had the most sensitive, responsive little body. It was a pleasure to see her writhing around on the bed, begging him to bring her relief. Maybe it wasn't time for breakfast yet.

He picked up the second cup, filled it and headed for the bedroom. 'Sinead, I've brought you coffee.'

16

Coffee? How could he think of coffee at a time like this? She had barely gotten her hands on him and he wanted to have breakfast? The bedroom door opened and a robe-clad Niall entered carrying two cups. He set them down on the bedside table.

She patted the quilt and pouted. 'Forget the coffee. Come back to bed, Sinead wants to play.'

'Does she now?' Niall sat down and lounged against the padded headboard, the picture of unconcern. Had someone pressed his 'off' switch? 'What games does Sinead like to play?'

There was an edge to his voice she didn't understand, but then he smiled and she was reassured. 'Maybe I could tie you up?' she offered.

He almost spat out a mouthful of coffee. 'Not a chance. Besides, there isn't a lot that could hold me.'

To prove his point he flexed his arm. She glanced at the width of his forearms and the wall of muscle visible where the robe parted. Niall really was beautiful and very strong. What would it be like to see that strength unleashed, to see him out of control with passion? The thought of it made her shiver.

'We're going to play Truth or Dare. Are you up for it?' Niall asked. The glint in his eye should have made her wary, but she wasn't going to back down.

'Of course. Sounds like fun.'

Sinead was discovering that a lifetime of being a good girl wasn't half as much fun as being bad. Niall was an experience she couldn't miss, and whose memory she would enjoy for the rest of her life. She wasn't going to wimp out because his eyes had darkened to a stormy glitter.

'Take off that bathrobe and get comfortable.'

'Comfortable? You really don't know much about women, do you?' Sinead said, even as she opened her robe with teasing fingers and allowed it to drop to the floor. As Lottie, she was confident, but since she had stopped dancing professionally, she had put on ten pounds, and was very conscious of them sitting on her belly. 'There are almost no women who are comfortable being naked in front of other people.'

'Don't be silly. You look stunning, and you know it.' Niall's eyes were on her breasts, not on her belly. She shimmied a little, making her breasts quiver, and watched him swallow. Lottie still had it.

'Truth or dare?' he asked.

'Truth.' That couldn't be too difficult. She had been telling him the truth.

'What's your name?'

She paused for a fraction of a second before she said, 'Sinead O'Sullivan.' Damn it, she had almost said Lottie LeBlanc. She watched his eyes narrow at her hesitation. Niall Moore was too sharp.

She tried to imagine Uncle Tim's reaction if he ever found out about Lottie, and shuddered. Some things were best left unexplored. 'Dare,' she said hastily. She wasn't giving him the chance to ask her any more questions like that.

'Have you ever had your breasts bound?' Niall picked up a length of rope.

It was thinner than the rope she had used around horses but thicker than baling twine, and it was orange. She shook her head. 'I don't see how you could.'

He stepped closer to her, so that she could feel his body heat and breathe in his unique scent. Shampoo, skin, a hint of musk, wholly male, all Niall. She would know him anywhere, just by inhaling his scent. He wrapped the rope around her right breast, tightened it to the point where there was a slight pinch but no pain. 'All right?' he asked.

She nodded. Her breast stood high, the nipple pointing out.

With dexterous fingers, Niall passed the rope around her back, criss-crossing it and tying a knot to hold it in place. He wound the rope around her breast, taking care to make sure the cord lay flat against her skin. Each twist of the rope increased the feeling of tightness. As the blood was trapped by the rope, her skin flushed and darkened. Her nipple stood out, rigid.

He stopped before he reached the now purple nipple, tied off the cord and stood back. 'How does that feel?'

'I have no idea,' she said truthfully. It was tight and constricting, but at the same time, she jangled with a combination of pain and pleasure.

He flicked her nipple. 'Now?'

Sinead gasped and her knees buckled. It was as if every nerve ending in her body had taken up residence in her breasts. 'I've never felt anything like that.'

Niall was there to support her. He set her on her feet and then gave her a wicked grin. 'And we're only half done.'

She watched, wide-eyed, as he bound her other breast. She was fascinated by the neat knots, the way her skin changed colour, the sensation of blood pounding under her skin.

When he was done, she looked at her reflection. 'You could put Wonder Bra out of business.' The rope bra gave her an uplift that even her Lottie stage bras could not. The woman facing her in the mirror was a stranger. A sultry, mysterious, decadent stranger.

Niall appeared in the mirror beside her. The combination of his robed strength and her bound nakedness made something twist inside her. Despite herself, moisture pooled between her thighs.

'Do you want to play another game?'

She nodded.

'It's a difficult one.'

Her competitive spirit rose to the challenge. 'Bring it on.' Her cousin Summer had learnt years ago that the easiest way to make Sinead do something she wasn't supposed to do was to tell her she couldn't do it.

'Pick a number.'

She had no idea what he was about, so played it safe. 'Five.'

'Good choice.' He handed her a sheet of notepaper. 'Tear it up into about six pieces and scatter them on the floor.'

Mystified, she did, taking care to spread them out evenly.

'How's your memory?'

She raised her eyebrows. 'Better than yours, I'm sure.'

'Then you'll have no problem remembering where the bits of paper are.'

She surveyed the floor again, memorizing the positions of the scraps. 'No, none at all.'

Niall moved behind her and put the sleeping mask over her eyes, then caught her wrists in his big hands. He tied them together loosely behind her back, before wrapping the end of the rope between them, so that she couldn't wriggle out. 'Now pick up the bits of paper.'

She wished he could see her glare through the mask. 'You bastard.'

Hampered by her hands being tied, she got down on her knees and moved to the place where she thought the first piece of paper was. She leaned over and picked it up with her lips.

'Good girl. One down, five to go.' Niall took the scrap from her.

Now it got more difficult. She was no longer exactly sure where the next piece was in relation to where she was now. But even if she couldn't see, her brain still functioned. She shuffled around the room, using her bare knees to feel for the paper. Got it. And feck this picking things up in her mouth. She was not a dog, she could do better.

Sinead lowered herself onto the floor, scrabbled around with her bound hands and picked up the next bit. She flipped it triumphantly.

Niall laughed and took it. 'Well done, four more to go.' He sat down on the chair. 'Oh, did I mention there was a time limit? And a penalty?'

She glared blindly at him. 'No, you neglected to mention that.'

'For every piece of paper you don't find in two minutes, you get ten spanks.'

'That's not fair! How much time has elapsed?'

'Thirty seconds.' How was that possible? It felt as if she had been searching for ages. But her competitive spirit was up and she got moving, searching for the rest of the paper.

Now it was hard. She had no idea where she was in the room, or where the paper was. Once more, Niall's hand stopped her. 'You're about to hit the dressing table.'

She changed direction and kept searching until, with a triumphant crow, she found one more, then Niall called, 'Time's up.'

'You're not really going to do this, are you?' She half laughed, not sure if she wanted to egg him on or tell him to stop.

She heard the creak of the chair as Niall seated himself. 'You bet I am. I've been dying to do this for the last week.' That was her only warning before a strong arm grabbed her and tipped her over his knee.

'Ow!' His thighs were thick with muscle, but she felt awkward. Without her hands to help her balance, she was dependent on Niall to keep her from falling. The position caused the blood to rush to her aching nipples, making her gasp. 'I'll fall.'

'No, you won't.' Niall held her securely, and despite herself, she relaxed. All that Viking muscle had to be good for something. He wouldn't drop her.

Swat! The first spank shocked her. This wasn't a pretend

slap. This was a real one that would leave a mark. 'That hurt.'

'Oh come on. That was barely a warm-up.' Another shocking spank landed, driving her into his thighs. It lit a fire in her breasts, making her moan.

The third spank cracked onto her ass. Despite her resolve to take whatever he could give her, she tried to put her hands back to stop him. He caught her wrists and kept going. Fourth, fifth, sixth. She yelled with each one and struggled, trying to twist off his lap, trying to wrench her wrists from his grip.

'Bastard.' She was panting and sweating now, her ass ablaze and her breasts on fire.

He laughed. 'You have no idea.' More spanks, hot and stinging. Her world had reduced to the muscular thighs supporting her, the merciless hand that was blistering her bottom, and the extraordinary heat that was running from her nipples to her clit.

'That's ten.' He paused. 'You know, I don't think you hate this as much as you pretend.' One broad finger eased down her thighs and between her lips. They were wet and slippery, and the added pressure of his finger opening her up was too much to bear. He touched the tip of her sensitive clit and she convulsed into an unexpected orgasm.

'Ahh!' When she regained control of herself again, she was surprised to find she was still over his knees, still blindfolded and trembling.

'You are a kinky girl, aren't you?' he teased, before returning to spanking her.

This time, she lay limply, allowing herself to absorb the swats without fighting them. Heat bloomed again and she found herself moving a little, trying to position the spanks where she needed them.

Too soon he stopped. 'All done. You were a brave girl.'

For a mad moment, she considered asking him to keep going before sanity returned. 'Can I get up? This is not a dignified position.'

He helped her to her feet. 'One more thing. Those nipples are far too tempting.' Something flicked one and the wet heat of his mouth closed over the other. The invisible string linking all her nerve endings tightened. The edge of his teeth tightening was all it needed to tip her over the edge into another orgasm.

She lost the power of speech as her world reduced to her flushed skin and convulsing insides. What did this man do to her? How did he do it?

Niall held her as she trembled until her watery legs were able to support her again. 'Let's take this off.' He fiddled at the knots before he said, 'Hold still.' She felt cold metal against her skin as he clipped open the cord.

The rush of blood to her breasts was enough to weaken her knees again. For endless moments, all she was aware of was the burn as her circulation returned to normal. He supported her, holding her against his now naked body. The brush of her ultra-sensitive nipples against the hot skin of his chest made her groan.

'Now, there is the little matter of five,' he told her, his voice a suggestive rumble in her ear.

She had forgotten. 'Five what?'

'Orgasms. Only three more to go.'

She groaned. The last two had nearly killed her. She had no idea how she would manage three more. She rubbed her wrists and cuddled her aching breasts. 'What is this, death by orgasm?' She still wore the blindfold and made no effort to take it off. Somehow, as long as she wore it, this wasn't real.

'Tell me where the Fire of Autumn is, and we can stop.'

Damn, that was far too real. 'I already told you, Roisin has it.'

'Yeah, I remember. You told me a lot of things.' He picked her up and laid her down on the bed.

She hadn't registered the short bars set into the headboard until he wrapped her hands around two of them. 'Hold on to those, or I'll have to tie you.'

Sinead gripped them tightly. She hated being out of control.

Niall let loose his sensual armoury on her. He kissed her until her head spun, alternating light teasing kisses with deep passionate ones that touched her soul. He nibbled his way down her neck, with a foray onto her earlobe, before finding her breasts. The nipples throbbed in time to her labouring breaths. Even the pressure of the air was almost too much to bear. Niall's hot breath and surgically precise teeth pushed her over the edge again.

She wailed, not caring if the people in the next apartment could hear. Hell, not caring if all of Paris could hear.

This time there was no tender embrace. Niall kept going, pushing her limp thighs apart to make a space for himself. 'Mmm, you smell so good. I could get drunk on you.' His tongue lapped at her, licking along her lips. It was too much, she was too sensitive. She tried to close her legs against him, but he was like a rock.

'Can't take any more,' she protested, though even to her own ears, it sounded weak.

He laughed. 'You can take anything I give you.' He teased her clit with the tip of his tongue. The little bundle of nerves jerked and she found herself lifting her hips to his mouth.

'So good,' he murmured and settled down to licking and sucking in earnest.

Sinead gripped the headboard desperately, trying to retain her sanity. Every time she thought she could cope with what he was doing, Niall changed it. Now he was swiping sideways over her mons, the prickle of his morning beard a delicious contrast to the softness of his lips.

She tensed, gathering again for another plunge into ecstasy, but her body was betraying her. 'I can't.'

'You can.' He sucked harder, his tongue flicking delicately, while one big hand pinched her nipple.

'I hate you,' she gasped before losing the ability to speak. Or breathe. Or think. Nothing existed except Niall and her traitorous body that constantly rose to his touch.

Then he was there, plunging into her, pounding into her, filling a void that she hadn't been aware existed. She gripped his hips, driving him on with her heels, desperate for more of everything he had to give.

This time it was short and fierce, both of them at the end of their control. The previous orgasm didn't have a chance to die down before this one rose, stronger than the others. With each ruthless lunge of his hips, he stole another bit of control from her. She was helpless to do anything except take what he gave her, and allow it to drive her higher.

She wailed as she came, the sound echoed by his roar as he followed her. He continued to thrust, still hard, still forceful and she continued to shudder around his length.

She vaguely felt him taking off the blindfold, but couldn't summon the energy to open her eyes to look at him. Sleep beckoned, irresistibly, and she gave herself up to it.

Sinead stirred. She could barely move, but the rumbling of her stomach was too insistent to ignore. 'I'm starving. What is there to eat?' She was pretty certain that they would not be eating out, but – 'Manu would make us something in a flash.'

A large hand landed on her back, pinning her to the bed. 'You're not going anywhere.'

Ah well, it had been worth a try. 'I'm hungry.' On cue, her stomach growled again. She stared pointedly at Niall. 'Are you planning to starve me into submission?' Under her breath, she added, 'As you can't do it any other way.'

Of course he heard. Niall Moore had ears like an elephant. She would bet that he could hear everything that went on in the entire block of apartments. 'Is that a dare?' he demanded.

She fluttered her eyelashes, allowing Lottie to come to the surface. In spite of the night that had passed, or perhaps because of it, she was filled with a sense of feminine power. 'Merely an observation. Now, are you planning to feed me? Or do you think I need to lose weight?'

Sinead stretched, undulating subtly as she did so. Judging by his hungry stare, Niall didn't care about the extra weight she'd gained.

'No, you don't. You're right, I need to feed you. Go to the bathroom and I'll get some food started.'

She allowed herself a brief moment of regret that he wasn't going to help her shower again. The memory of the last time he did still made her shiver. Eager to see what he had in mind, she bundled her hair under a cap and rushed through her shower.

She dashed into her bedroom when she was finished, determined to put together a combination of clothes that would have him on his knees. The wardrobe was empty. So were the drawers.

She marched into the kitchen, wrapped in a large bath sheet. 'Where are my clothes?'

Niall flipped the egg in the frying pan. 'I put them away safely.'

The yolk was a pure yellow, and the smell of the bacon made her mouth water. It almost distracted her. Almost. 'Well, get them. I need to get dressed.'

The heat in his eyes made her take a step backwards. 'No, you don't.' He looked her up and down. 'You can lose the towel. Naked is perfect.'

A tiny part of her thrilled to the thought of being naked in front of him, but she wasn't going to let him get away with this. 'I'll be cold. I'll get a chill and get sick and die on you.' In spite of the rain drumming against the apartment window, it was warm inside, and she was fairly comfortable, but she wasn't going to tell him that.

'Hmmm.' He considered her words, and then disappeared into his bedroom. A moment later, he handed her his bathrobe. 'You can wear this. It will keep you warm.'

It was large and fluffy and warm. She snuggled into it,

relishing the faint trace of his scent that clung to it. 'Where's the belt?'

His smile was positively evil. 'I have it for something else.'

She could imagine the uses he would find for the long, soft belt. It would be perfect for tying someone up. She shivered. 'But how will I close the robe?'

'Don't worry, you'll be fine.'

Standing there, watching him cook, it was easy to hold it closed from her chin to her shins. She admired the competent way he moved around the small kitchen, unhurried but everything so coordinated that all the food arrived on the table at once.

Sinead had never been interested in the preparation of food. It had always seemed so much hassle when it was quicker and easier to open a packet and eat on the run. But she had to admit that one of the benefits of sharing a flat with her cousin had been the food. Summer loved cooking, and Sinead had benefited from her skills.

When Summer was upset, she had used cooking as therapy. After one particular fiasco in her love life, she had run up a bill of over £2,000 at Fortnum & Mason, and Sinead had learnt not to eat the day before she visited. Or the day after.

Niall was no chef. She doubted he would recognize a caper, never mind know which fish it went with, but the coffee was hot and aromatic, the eggs were perfectly round and the bacon was crisp. And he put things away as he worked, leaving the kitchen neat and the worktops clear.

'Do you enjoy cooking?' She picked up her fork and

stabbed an egg. Yolk oozed out slowly. Exactly the way she liked it. Was he a mind reader?

Niall shrugged. 'It's a useful skill. I need to eat a lot, so unless I want to live on junk, I need to cook it.' His own plate had five eggs. Hers had two.

When she lifted her knife, Sinead discovered the problem with the bathrobe. She couldn't do any activity without it falling open. She pulled it across her, and tried to hold it closed with her knees.

Niall's gaze dropped to her chest.

'Hey, I'm up here,' she snapped. She hated guys who talked to her breasts.

But Niall gave her a slow, hot stare. 'Not all of you.'

She held the robe closed with her left hand while she took a gulp of coffee. Niall transferred his attention to his plate and ate enthusiastically. Where did he put it all? she wondered. He was a big man, but he really did eat three times more than she did.

'I don't eat egg yolks,' she told him.

'You should, they're full of good stuff that will keep you healthy.'

'And fat!'

He frowned at her. 'And you don't eat enough for someone of your activity level. Finish what's on your plate and I'll give you a treat.'

'What age am I? Eight?' But she picked up her fork again. She'd spent too many years of her life cutting back so she would fit into her Lottie outfits and look good on stage. There was something comforting about being told to eat.

'Oh no, I can see you're all grown up.' His words were

a promise that caused her pussy to clench. And filled her mind with ways to torment him.

Deliberately, she allowed the robe to gape while she ate a mouthful of bacon. It was crisp and she didn't have to feign pleasure as she chewed. 'Mmm. Perfect.' She half-closed her eyes in appreciation.

Niall's face was still, but his pupils dilated. Oh yeah, he liked that. He could be as dominating as he liked, but he wasn't immune to her. And he hadn't met Lottie yet. Not really. The performance in the café had just been a warm-up act.

She picked up her cup, the movement giving him a flash of her breast for a second before it was covered again. He swallowed. Poor baby. She was going to kill him.

She held the coffee in both hands, so that her robe parted, but the position of her arms prevented it opening all the way. He was transfixed. She sipped, and gave a subtle shift of her shoulders. 'You make good coffee.'

She considered herself something of a connoisseur of coffee, she drank so much of it.

'Thanks.' But his voice sounded preoccupied. Considering that he had already seen every inch of her body, what was it about her slightly parted bathrobe that had him so distracted? With a wicked grin that he didn't see because he was staring at the inside curve of breast, she set out to drive him wild.

She ate with gusto, as if she wasn't aware that her every movement translated into a new shift in her state of undress. She finished her breakfast long before he did. Something was keeping him off-balance. His Y chromosome. Men were slaves to it.

'I'm still hungry,' she told him, managing to put a pout and a promise into her voice.

Without a word, he gave her an egg and a slice of bacon from his plate.

'Perfect. I love a man who knows how to satisfy a woman.' Her smile was pure Lottie and a quick twist to pick up the pepper mill granted him a glimpse of an erect nipple.

'What? Oh yeah. Sure.' Niall had trouble getting the words out, and his upper lip was damp.

Poor baby. Lottie was going to make him sweat.

17

The insistent buzzing on the doorbell made Sinead jump. Niall was on his feet immediately, motioning her to be quiet. For a big man, he moved swiftly. He bundled her into the bedroom and through the door into the en-suite bathroom. 'Lock the door and don't come out until I call you.'

With shaking fingers she locked the door and slumped onto the tiled floor. Who could be looking for them? What if it was Hall's men again?

The tiny bathroom window wouldn't let a child through and, besides, what the hell would she do on the thirty-fifth floor of an apartment block? Nothing stood between her and Hall but the man outside. Niall might be a deceitful, manipulative bastard but he had sworn to protect her and that much she believed.

She didn't want to think about what might happen if it was Hall out there, but if there was a fight, she couldn't let Niall do it alone. She climbed to her feet and opened the door. Voices came from the outer room. Niall and another man, and she recognized that laugh.

Clutching the edges of her bathrobe around her, Sinead raced through the bedroom door and flung herself into his arms. 'Andy McTavish, you frightened the life out of me.'

He had been involved in the rescue of her cousin. During

those awful few days during the summer, she had met several of the other operatives from Niall's company, but Andy was the friendliest and the most flirtatious.

He kissed her on the cheek and embraced her enthusiastically. 'Sorry to scare you, babe, my phone was damaged during our encounter with Hall. It's been on the blink since, so I couldn't call to say I was coming over.'

Andy looked good, as tall and handsome as ever. He could have been a model, and he knew exactly how gorgeous he was.

Niall made a sound suspiciously like a growl and Sinead glared at him. He stared pointedly at Andy's arm, still wrapped around her waist. What was his problem?

'I suggest you fasten that bathrobe,' he said.

She looked down and realized it had gaped open, and Andy was enjoying the view. She resisted the urge to drag it closed, and instead made a production of it, one that captured Andy's attention as well as Niall's. Let him see he wasn't the only man in the world.

Andy coughed. 'I've brought you a few things from Bertrand's apartment,' he said.

Sinead pounced on the bag and tugged it open. Everything appeared to be intact. She had her ID and cash cards. 'I love you.'

'I know.' Andy winked at her. 'I have that effect on all the girls.'

Niall cleared his throat. 'If we can dispense with the mutual appreciation society meeting, I'd like an update.'

'Bertrand is recovering, but we should keep him covered until we find Hall.'

'What do you mean "find Hall"?' Niall roared.

'He disappeared before they got him to the police station.'

'Fuck.' Niall paced the floor. 'Find him. Bring in more operatives if we need them. I don't like the idea of that bastard being out on the streets.'

Andy nodded. 'I'm already on it and you might want to see this. A courier tried to deliver it to Bertrand's place and when they didn't get an answer, they left it with a neighbour.'

The seal on the back of the dark envelope had already been broken. It was simply addressed to Red. Sinead couldn't resist flashing Niall an I-told-you-so look. She snatched the envelope from his hand and pulled out the invitation. Madame Hermione de Montraforte cordially requested her presence for the weekend at her house in Ville d'Avray. The party theme was Mistress and slave.

'See!' She couldn't resist waving the invitation under Niall's nose. 'And you didn't believe me. I told you – my sister will be there.'

She was learning how to read him, and saw the doubt on his face.

He took the invitation from her and read it carefully. 'You're not going to this.'

'What do you mean I'm not going? This is the best lead we have. The woman who sent it knows my sister. I have to go.'

'It's too dangerous. God knows what you'd be walking into.'

Andy laughed. 'Some of those parties are wild. I know exactly what she'd be walking into.'

'You would.' Niall shot him a filthy look.

Sinead paused. She had been so focused on finding Roisin that she hadn't thought about what she would have to do to blend in. Andy had reminded her that she'd be diving in at the deep end in a scene she knew nothing about. This would be nothing like the routines she did on stage.

She took a breath. She had to go. She'd pump Andy for any information she needed and she'd fake it. She was a performer. She could do it.

Andy shrugged and smiled. 'Don't get your panties in a bunch. I'll go with Sinead. The invitation says Mistress and slave. It would be a bit odd if she turned up without one. What do you say, Sinead? Think you could keep me in line for a couple of days? I promise to be good.'

His wicked smile told her he would be anything but good. Andy was drop-dead gorgeous and the prospect of parading him on a leash for the weekend made her giggle. She would have to fight the other Mistresses off. 'I doubt if you know what the word means.'

'You could teach me. I'd be a very willing pupil.' He stretched out the last three words, leaving her in no doubt as to how he would behave.

Sinead rolled her eyes. 'Did anyone ever tell you that you're a —'

'I'll go.' Niall's statement put a sudden end to the conversation.

Andy snorted and his eyes crinkled with laughter. 'You on a leash? I'd pay money to see that. Besides, you haven't a submissive bone in your body. You wouldn't have a clue how to behave. It's better to leave this one to me, boss.'

He turned to her. 'We need to do some shopping,

Sinead. We need to be dressed to fit in. I'll have a look to see where we can get good play outfits.'

Sinead shuddered at the thought of letting Andy shop for her. 'I know the perfect place.'

They both looked at her.

Damn. She had spoken without thinking. Several of Lottie's stage outfits had been made in Paris and she knew specialist shops where she could buy something suitable. If she was going to impersonate her sister, she'd better look the part.

'A friend of Gabriel's is famous for this stuff,' she said. 'She'll sort us out.'

'I've said that I'll do it.' Niall's tone was clipped and his mouth formed a thin, hard line. He couldn't be serious. She shot Andy a pleading glance. He would be much easier to work with. Niall would want to control everything and that was hardly slave-like behaviour.

Andy eyed Niall dubiously. 'I don't want to point out the obvious, but you don't look or behave like a slave. You don't have any suitable clothes and you'd need a hell of a lot of man-scaping before you'd get through the front door.'

Niall scowled. 'We better get started.'

Sinead stopped him with an upraised hand. 'I want my clothes first.'

'Damn!' Andy said. 'I hoped she wouldn't ask.'

Clara de Lune was a six foot two cross-dresser from Galway who had settled in Paris some fifteen years before, but she had never lost her Galway lilt. Her French was atrocious, but that didn't dissuade her legion of customers.

Sinead knew her as one of the finest tailors of stage clothing in the business. She spotted her the moment Sinead entered the store and Sinead crossed the floor swiftly, trying to get to her before the others.

She swept her up in a bear hug. 'I didn't know you were in Paris.'

Sinead hugged her tightly, inhaling the smell of her face powder, which reminded her of her grandmother. 'Not a word to them about Lottie, promise me,' she whispered. 'And call me Sinead. I'll tell you everything later.'

'Mum's the word, pet. Now, what can I do you for?' She shot a glance at Andy and Niall who were hovering beside a costume that consisted entirely of feathers. 'They're not dancers, I presume?'

'As if! But we need some costumes for a party tomorrow night.'

'Fancy dress, is it?' Clara inspected Niall and Andy as if they were two mannequins.

'Sort of,' Andy chipped in. 'The theme is Mistress and slave.'

'Hermione's bash?'

'You know her?' Niall asked.

'Darling, I know everybody who is anybody.' Clara turned on her size ten heels. 'This way, don't mind the tat. I'll show you the good stuff.'

They climbed the stairs to the workshop and Sinead ran her fingers along the costumes lining the rails. Lace, rhinestones and feathers clamoured for her touch. Lottie would have been drooling. There was no way she could leave here without buying something.

'What about this?' Andy held up a scarlet leather cat-suit.

'Mimi Lorenzo is wearing one exactly the same.'

'This?' Sinead fingered a black corset. The fabric was soft and supple to the touch, a perfect casing for the rows of spiral steel bones beneath. It would fit her like a glove.

Clara considered it. 'It's too ordinary for you, my pet. Tell me, which one is the slave?'

Niall couldn't make up his mind which of them he was most pissed at – the big cross-dresser who looked him up and down like a side of beef, Andy McTavish who was enjoying this way too much, or Sinead O'Sullivan who was trying to hold in her laughter.

'I am her escort for the night,' he said through clenched teeth. 'And I'm not a slave.'

Clara gave a derisive laugh. 'They all say that.' She walked around Niall, inspecting him from all angles. 'Nice buns. And great legs.'

'He's got good shoulders too,' Sinead said helpfully. 'We need an outfit that shows him off.'

Clara dived into a box in a corner. 'I love a man in uniform, but he's too tall to fit anything that I have. Don't worry, I'll find something.'

Niall found a bundle of leather thrust into his hands.

'Try this on, see how it looks.'

He gritted his teeth. He was not in the least self-conscious. He was proud of his body, which was the result of thousands of hours of hard work. But seeing three pairs of eyes laughing at him put his temper on edge.

'Don't mind us,' Andy said. 'Pretend we're not here.'

Clara smacked Andy on the hand. 'Don't tease the poor man. It's his first time. I can always tell.' She pointed to a corner with a curtain. 'Nip in there, duckie, and get changed.'

Niall snapped the curtain closed and stripped down to his boxers. He held up the leather and discovered it was a pair of trousers, soft and supple. He could cope with that. He pulled them on and had to tug hard to get them up. The belt at the top fastened – almost – but the laces at the thigh were stretched dangerously tight.

'Come on out, sweetie.' Clara's head peered in around the edge of the curtain.

Holding himself stiffly, Niall left the shelter of the curtains.

Sinead and Andy didn't even attempt to stay silent. They laughed in his face.

'Sweetie, you're not supposed to wear the kaks under it,' Clara said.

'But –' He gave up the protest. The trousers were cut out front and back. Without his boxers, he would be committing indecent exposure. It was clear Clara didn't care. 'They don't fit,' he insisted.

'I can see that,' Clara said. 'Beef to the heel, like a Mullingar heifer.' She ran a finger under his waistband, and felt the tension across his thighs.

'We need something he can move in,' Andy said. 'He can't squat in those.'

'Or kneel,' Sinead said.

He glared at both of them, and turned to Clara. 'How about some sort of uniform? Cargo pants and a Kevlar jacket would be perfect.'

'Don't be silly, dearie. If you want to play toy soldiers at home, that's fine, but if you want to get into Hermione's do, you'll need a proper outfit.' Clara handed him another piece of leather. 'Try that.'

It was a lot smaller than those damned obscene pants and it barely covered Niall's hand. 'Where's the rest of it?'

A puzzled expression crossed Clara's face. 'Silly me. There's a collar and chain to go with it. Now where did I put them?'

Clara hurried to a back room in search of the accessories and the moment the door was closed, Andy burst into laughter. 'Please, can I go? I don't care if I have to wear a feather in my ass.'

'Fuck off.' Niall glared at him. 'If you want to stay pretty, I suggest you quit while you're ahead.'

The door opened and Clara returned carrying something that looked too small to be a costume. She held up a diaphanous piece of fabric and some jewelled pasties to Sinead.

'And this one is yours. Samson and Delilah. You'll be divine.' She handed the outfit to Sinead, then went back to the other room to search for Niall's accessories.

Niall allowed Sinead to take the changing corner and stripped off the trousers. The outfit was a loincloth. A fucking leather loincloth. 'I feel like a right dick,' he said.

Andy walked around him, admiring him from every angle. 'You know, in a weird sort of way, it suits you.'

'I have it.' Clara returned carrying a studded leather collar and a length of silver coloured chain. 'Would you like me to –'

'Not a chance.'

'Suit yourself. Now, let's have a look at you.' Clara walked around him, studying the effect of the costume. Sinead popped her head around the curtain to examine him.

Niall bristled under Clara's gaze and Sinead shot him a warning glare, urging him to be quiet.

'Hair down?' she asked Sinead.

When Sinead nodded, Clara chuckled. 'He'll make a perfect Samson. I'd love to see Hermione's face when you arrive with him in tow.'

Sinead retreated behind the curtain before Niall exploded. She hung her clothing up and examined the costume. The silk pants were almost sheer and the one-shouldered top barely covered her right breast. There would be quite a lot of flesh on display. The imp in her laughed as she pulled the pants on and fastened them at the waist.

She unpeeled one pastie from the backing sheet and fixed it over her bare nipple. There, it was almost decent. She studied her reflection in the mirror. Who was she kidding? She could stop five lanes of traffic around the Arc de Triomphe if she appeared in public wearing this. A familiar sense of power surged through her. Lottie LeBlanc was in the house.

'How are you doing there, pet? Do you need a hand?'

'I'm fine, Clara.' With a final glance in the mirror she drew the curtain and stepped outside.

'Holy fuck,' Niall exclaimed. 'You are not going out dressed like that.'

'Who are you? My grandmother?'

Sinead pivoted for Clara's approval and stood still as she made a tiny adjustment to the outfit and marked it with a pin.

'The waist needs to come in an inch. Drop back in an hour and I'll have it ready for you.'

Sinead caught Andy casting a discerning eye over her costume, lingering a little too long on her barely covered nipple. She raised her chin, daring him to keep looking, but he didn't bother to hide his interest and smiled shamelessly at her. 'Perhaps Mademoiselle O'Sullivan would like another slave? Clara, I don't suppose you have another loincloth?'

'Only if you don't want to see thirty-one.' Niall snapped.

Andy laughed. 'I'm joking. Besides, we can't all enjoy ourselves. Someone has to act as back-up.'

Sinead smiled, pure evil in her heart. 'Of course, you do realize that you're not ready to go out in public yet?' she said.

'Why not?'

Her grin was diabolical. 'In an outfit like that, you need to have what I believe is called a B, S and C?'

Niall shook his head. 'Never heard of it. What is it?'

'You're about to find out.'

18

The sign over the narrow doorway said 'Smile'. It was years since Sinead had been there but she knew a lot of dancers used the place. Niall grimaced when he saw the price list and she guessed that it wasn't the cost he was worried about.

'You can still back out, you know.'

Niall ignored her and held the door open. The walls on either side of the wooden staircase had a series of before and after shots, as well as advertisements for services that made Andy laugh.

'Shut up, Andy. Haven't you got anything better to do?'

'Better than this? Not a chance.'

Sinead stepped past him and down the stairs to the basement. She immediately caught the scent of warm wax. A sullen blonde dropped her magazine and stood up.

'Irina?' Sinead asked.

'Irina gone back to St Petersburg. I am Nadia. You want treatment?'

'Er, no thanks, but my friend does.'

Niall's face had turned the colour of putty. Sinead almost felt sorry for him as the no-nonsense Russian girl approached him with the keen eye of a woman who enjoyed her job. 'Gabriel says it's a piece of cake. You'll be fine.'

'He needs the works,' Andy interrupted her study. 'And a spray tan.'

'You can't do a tan after waxing,' Sinead corrected him. 'It will sting and he –'

'Is no problem. I have special gel to help with irritation. Tan will be fine. But first, open shirt.'

Sinead kept her eyes fixed firmly on the tiled floor and waited for the inevitable explosion. It didn't come. She heard the rustle of clothing and when she looked up again the woman was stroking Niall's chest. 'Nice,' she said to Sinead. 'You want to wait while I take care of him?'

She nodded, not trusting herself to speak or to look at Niall's face.

Nadia pointed to a brown-painted door. 'You – in the back, clothes off, lay down, turn over.'

'Want me to come and hold your hand, boss?'

Niall's reply was unrepeatable.

They took seats in the waiting area and Sinead tried to concentrate on reading a magazine, but it was impossible. The silence in the next room was broken by Nadia's voice, 'So sorry, so sorry, so sorry.'

From Niall, there was no sound.

Andy's eyes were filled with mirth. 'I can't believe it – Niall Moore getting a back, sac and crack. I wish Flynn was here to see this.'

'How is he?' Sinead hadn't spoken to him in months.

'He's grand. He still does the odd bit of work for Niall but no long-term stuff any more. Summer's dad is opening up an office in BA. He's offered him a job as head of security.'

Sinead missed her cousin. She had been more like a

sister to her, but she had found the love of her life and they were living happily in South America. 'Tell them I was –'

The brown door opened and Nadia stepped into the room. 'He will be ready soon. I think you will be pleased.'

As Andy settled the bill, Sinead kept her eyes focused on the door.

The tan did something for him. It made his eyes almost silver. The impassive expression on his face prevented her from offering a compliment. Niall walked with a stiff-legged gait that was different to his usual stride. She followed him outside.

'You could have warned me,' Niall said when Andy joined them. 'That woman poured glue stuff all over me and all of a sudden she lays something on me . . . and Jesus that hurt! I'd rather take another bullet than go through that again. I need a drink.'

'It's only lunchtime,' Andy pointed out unhelpfully.

'I don't care. Find me a bar.'

They sipped coffee in a café while Niall had a shot of brandy in his. After a while, he regained his composure. He set down his cup. 'Where to now? It couldn't be as bad as that.'

Andy was in his element now. 'It might be worth picking up a few accessories for the party.'

'Accessories?' Niall said, looking suspicious.

'Yes, boss – I know how you like to be fully prepared and tooled up . . .' Andy was smirking and Sinead guessed what he had in mind.

Twenty minutes later they were wandering around Avenue du Plaisir. The sex shop was as big as a supermarket, with rows of costumes down one wall, interspersed with sex toys of all kinds. Andy pointed out the various toys, and told her to ask him if she had any questions about any of them. Oh yeah, she just bet he'd be helpful and discreet, and not try to make a show of her.

Andy needed a keeper.

He stopped in front of a display of dildos and cast a sly glance at Niall. 'Will you be needing a strap-on, Sinead?'

'A what?'

Andy couldn't be serious. Some of them were monstrous. 'I couldn't possibly be expected to –'

'You should see your face.' Andy laughed and even Niall smiled at her naïveté.

'Don't worry,' Andy said. 'We just need a couple of floggers and maybe some movies.'

'Movies?'

The wicked grin was back. 'You might dress up like a Domme, but underneath you're like a nun in a brothel. You won't last five minutes before someone realizes that you're faking it.'

'Oh, but I . . .' She just closed her mouth before she could tell him about her scene in the club with Gabriel. Probably best not to mention that. 'And absolutely no movies.'

Andy studied the selection of leather flails with a practised eye. 'Nice,' he murmured. 'They can be used for pleasure or pain.'

Niall snorted. 'Don't give her any ideas. She needs a couple of toys for carrying around. Sinead won't get to use any of this stuff.'

'Wanna bet?' Sinead selected a whip from the stand and

flicked it experimentally. The tip cracked inches from his feet.

'Whoa.' Andy stepped back. 'You've done this before.'

She shrugged. 'My cousin was mad into horses so I had to learn too. Want me to show you again?'

'No,' both men chorused.

She left them studying a selection of movies while she wandered the aisles. The store had everything, from fun items for a hen party to the truly bizarre. She stopped at a glass-topped case and looked at the items inside. Pretty jewelled nipple clamps, some items that might have come from a gynaecology practice and a metal object that looked like one of the fabric tracing wheels from Clara's workshop. Except it was rimmed with small spikes.

'A Wartenberg pinwheel,' Niall said from behind her and she jumped. 'It was originally designed to test neurological reactions. I'm told some people find the sensation quite pleasant.'

Sinead shivered at the thought of the tiny metal spikes against her skin and she wasn't sure if it was from interest or nervousness. 'Would it hurt?'

'Only if you want it to.'

An image of being tied to Niall's bed while he ran the wheel along her skin popped into her head. She had always thought of herself as being pretty average in her sexual tastes, but the past few days had opened her eyes. Maybe a little too much.

Andy placed his selection of purchases on the counter and Sinead cringed when she saw them. Two days from now, she would have to pretend to be a Domme, just like her sister.

'Will that be all, Monsieur?' The assistant asked as he packed them.

'We'll take one of the wheels too,' Niall announced, ignoring Andy's knowing smirk.

Heat flooded her face and she couldn't look at either of them.

Outside, a gust of wind raced along the pavement, scattering brown leaves underfoot. She zipped up her jacket and shivered.

'Come on.' Andy threw his arm around her, ignoring Niall's disapproving glance. 'Let's pick up your costume and find a café. I'm starving.'

They headed to the nearest metro station, laden down with their purchases. Sinead couldn't stop thinking about the flogger that Andy had insisted she would need. It was heavy, with at least thirty strands of red and black leather hanging from the handle. What must that feel like hitting human flesh? She shivered. This was all getting too much for her.

She could handle a single-tail whip, mostly thanks to sharing riding lessons with Summer when they were younger. Her cousin had always been a bit lazy when it came to lunging the horses before they rode them, while Sinead relished the chance to concentrate on training the horse before she mounted it.

She had learnt how to handle the long whip, to crack it loudly and flick it so that it barely tipped the horse without hurting it. It was a skill that she had put into several of Lottie's burlesque acts.

Strange how men reacted to a woman holding a whip.

From nowhere, she had a vision of Niall with a flogger in his hand. He was dressed in smooth, supple black leather, and a collar and handcuffs hung from his belt. He handled the flogger with negligent ease and he was looking at her with heat in his eyes.

Whoa! Where had that come from? Before she met Niall, she would never have considered any of that stuff. Sinead O'Sullivan did not do kinky.

Studious, uptight, careful and hard-working, that was the real her. She wasn't the confident, shimmering seductress with a string of celebrity lovers. Lottie loved the tease. She adored the slow theatrical build-up, the drawing out of tension until she enslaved her audience. She might entice men with her eyes, incite them to desire with her body, but Lottie was a chimera. She knew that she would never have to make good on her sensual promises. When the lights went down and the curtains dropped, Lottie was gone.

Night after night, they both went home alone. Until now.

This experience of being in a state of near-constant arousal around Niall, of her imagination taking her to places she hadn't known existed, was disconcerting – and annoying. She wasn't Lottie, couldn't be her, not in a million years. But the vision of Niall with a flogger would not fade away no matter how hard she tried to suppress it.

She glanced up at the display board above their platform. The next train was an express on its way to Gare du Nord, and their RER would be along in five minutes.

'Is there a vending machine around here?' she asked Andy. 'I'm thirsty.'

She carefully did not look at Niall.

'Never mind, I see one.'

It was halfway down the platform and she fished out coins as she walked. She examined the selection of snacks and drinks.

Something brushed against her, but before she could make a sound, a hard hand was over her mouth and she was being dragged off the platform and through a dark doorway.

She was paralysed, the terror of the last time freezing her limbs until fury came to her aid. They would not do this to her again. She kicked out wildly and bit down on the hand.

'You little –'

There was a split second when his grip loosened but it was enough for her to open her mouth and scream. A lifetime of not making a fuss evaporated. She yelled at the top of her lungs, knowing that Niall was close by.

Next moment, she was free. She caught a glimpse of Niall's enraged face as he hauled the man away from her, then he was gone.

The other man was big, dressed in close-fitting black clothes that made it hard to see him in the dim light of the ancient metro station. His speed was shocking and he and Niall were engaged in a combat so fast and lethal that her brain couldn't follow it.

'Andy.' Niall's voice was calm, despite the speed of his movements. 'Get her to safety.'

'But –' Andy stopped his protest. 'Yes, boss.' He took Sinead's arm, grabbed the bags and pulled her away.

'We can't leave him,' she protested.

'My priority is getting you to safety. After that I can help him.'

Put like that, she had no choice except to obey. The sooner she was safe, the sooner Andy could go back. She hurried in search of a security man. She'd noticed the gun-carrying security staff on the way in. Where were they now?

Sinead looked back at the platform. Niall and the other man were on the ground, still locked in combat. The sign clicked over. The RER was now due in three minutes. How could all that have happened so quickly? The rush of the express train roaring into the station drowned out her shout for help.

Andy dragged her along, pulling her away from the platform, back up the corridor towards the exit. Her heels clicked noisily on the tiled floor, echoing under the barrel-shaped ceiling. 'We have to help him,' she told Andy.

He didn't stop. 'Niall can look after himself. Don't worry about him. I want you out of here.'

The noise from the platform increased. Screams mingled with metal screeching on metal. A bell rang insistently, deafening her. Moments later, six armed and armoured security men ran past them towards the platform.

A muffled voice on the PA system said something Sinead could not catch. 'What is that?'

Andy looked away.

'Tell me.'

For once, his mobile face was deadly serious. 'It said there was an accident and a man has fallen under the train.'

No. No. No.

Sinead's brain went blank. No. It could not be Niall. No.

She fumbled her phone out of her bag, and pressed his number. With a small, detached part of her brain, she noticed that her fingers were shaking. The number clicked through. Sinead waited for it to ring. A female voice told her, 'The number you have dialled cannot be contacted. It is out of service.'

Since she'd met him, she'd never known Niall to switch off his phone. He was always in contact.

What had happened to him?

Outside the station, Andy bundled her into a taxi, ignoring the protests of the Japanese tourist who had flagged it down. After giving instructions to the driver, Andy removed the phone from her shaking hands. 'Fuck, I'll have to risk it.'

He punched a number rapidly and Sinead heard a woman's voice on the other end of the line. 'Reilly, Niall is down. Check the metro station at Nation. I want the full team on this and I don't care where you have to pull them from.'

Niall is down. Niall is down. The words resonated inside her like a bell, each peal more mournful than the last. Niall is down. Niall is –

Andy shifted the phone to his other ear and pulled her against his chest. 'Breathe. Just breathe, baby. Don't fall apart on me now.'

He returned his attention to the call. 'Reilly? No. we don't know that yet. Get me confirmation asap. And send me a secure phone. This one is traceable.'

He disconnected the call and requested the driver to turn on the radio, urging him to find a news channel. Following an interminable report about the latest political scandal, a small item announced that services to Nation had been disrupted due to '*un incident*'.

She buried her face in Andy's shoulder, unable to listen to more.

Andy ordered the driver to stop around the corner from the apartment. He grabbed the bags before hurrying to open the car door for her.

Sinead stepped onto the pavement, swaying slightly when the ground appeared to move under her.

'I've got you.' Andy put his arm around her and held her steady.

She couldn't remember how they got into the building, but he pushed the door open and helped her inside. Niall was gone. She couldn't say the other word yet. He couldn't be dead. Not even if a dozen trains ran over him. God, she felt sick.

Sinead bolted for the bathroom, barely making it inside before she threw up. She slumped, shivering on the floor, arms wrapped around her knees, unable to move. She stared at the shower cubicle.

Was it only a couple of days since they had been there together, clinging to each other as the water pumped down on them? He couldn't be gone. *Please don't let him be gone.* She would put up with anything from the annoying Viking if he would return. Hell, he could question her non-stop for twenty-four hours and she wouldn't complain. *Please keep him safe. Keep him safe.*

A hot tear ran down her cheek and splashed onto her knee.

'Sinead.' Andy tapped on the door and entered the room. He rinsed a washcloth in the sink and used it to wash her face. His gentle, oddly intimate gesture brought her back to reality.

'Thanks,' she murmured, raising her face for his deft ministrations. A memory flashed into her head of attending Sunday mass in Castletownberehaven with Granny O'Sullivan. Her grandmother always carried a proper linen handkerchief – no paper tissues for her – and she wielded it like a weapon when confronted with a snotty-nosed grandchild.

Satisfied that she was clean, Andy tossed the washcloth into the linen basket. 'He's not dead.'

'You heard something?'

Andy shook his head. 'No, I've heard nothing and that makes me sure that he's still around. Besides, it would take more than a train to take down Niall Moore.'

He sat on the floor beside her and draped an arm around her shoulders and they sat in silence.

'For a womanizing flirt, you're actually a nice guy.'

Andy laughed. 'For a stuffy museum curator, you're not bad either. Everything will be okay, I promise.'

Her phone rang. Andy raced from the bathroom and she followed close on his heels. He snatched up the phone, knocking over a cup in his haste to answer it. Sinead stepped from one foot to the other, watching his face for clues, but apart from a narrowing around his eyes, his expression betrayed nothing.

'Fine. I'll let you know as soon as I hear anything.' Andy disconnected the call.

'Well?' Sinead poked him in the chest. 'Tell me, before I have to hurt you.'

'That was Reilly. There's good news and bad news – there's no body.'

'Oh thank god for that.' The urge to jump up and down was quashed when she realized that Andy wasn't smiling.

Sinead closed her eyes. She wasn't sure if she wanted to hear this. 'What's wrong?'

'The bad news is that no one knows where he is.'

19

Niall caught a flash of movement out of the corner of his eye, but it was enough. One moment, Sinead was there at the vending machine, the next she had vanished. Niall moved before his brain caught up with his reflexes. He had to find her.

An almost invisible maintenance door behind the vending machine was closing. Niall jammed his hand in before it could slam shut. Pain lanced up his arm, but he ignored it. He'd worry about broken fingers later.

He shoved his weight against the door, forcing it open and revealing a concrete corridor lit with intermittent red bulbs. And a large man whose form-fitting black outfit made him hard to see. He had his arm around Sinead, but she bit his hand, clenching her teeth hard enough to hurt him through his gloves. He cursed, a vaguely American accent that Niall couldn't place, and Sinead screamed.

Niall lunged forwards, hauling Sinead free of the kidnapper's grip. He pushed her out through the door onto the platform and turned back to the danger.

The other man didn't wait for Niall to get his bearings. He swung his fist, a fast lethal jab that rocked Niall backwards.

It didn't matter. Sinead was free. He spotted a familiar face. 'Andy, get her to safety.'

Niall ignored their protests and concentrated on surviving.

Because this would be about staying alive. One operator would always recognize another, and Niall had no doubt that he was dealing with one of the most highly-trained spec-ops warriors in the world. In fact, he was pretty sure he already knew who he was dealing with.

'Hall?'

The other man didn't answer, except by drawing a MK3 diving knife, but his flinch was confirmation enough. J. Darren Hall.

Niall curled his left hand, and the agony in his fingers confirmed his suspicion that he had injured them. Mollycoddling could wait until he had time. Now he had to get out of here alive.

Hall's blade flashed and Niall jumped back. In the closed corridor, he was at a disadvantage. He needed to get out onto the platform where he could use his height to advantage.

He lashed out with a front kick and feinted a punch. Hall dodged both with insulting ease, but came close enough for Niall to elbow him in the face. There wasn't enough force to do more than rock Hall back, but it allowed Niall to move closer to the door.

He reached out to open it and was caught when Hall's kick hit him in the nuts.

Fuck! He doubled over, fighting the need to puke. He saw Hall's knife glinting in the red light above him as it descended, and he dropped to the floor, grabbing Hall's knee and taking him down with him.

Hall fell through the doorway and Niall went after him.

They were evenly matched, both tall, broad shouldered and in remarkable physical condition. Except that Niall, dressed for a day out in Paris, was still smarting from the full body wax job, and had what felt like several broken bones in his left hand. And Hall was dressed in a Kevlar-reinforced bodysuit and armed with a diving knife.

It didn't matter. This was a fight that Niall had to win. He attacked Hall, using his weight and agility to make up for the lack of weapons. He gouged at his eyes, one of the few weak spots, and accepted a punch in the kidneys as the price he paid.

They rolled over, first Niall on top, now Hall, locked together as close as lovers, but in an embrace that would end with one of them dead.

From the corner of his eye, he saw commuters frozen, unable to take their eyes off the combat. Andy and Sinead vanishing through the exit. The roar of a train.

The instant cost him. A cold burn along his ribs. Hall's knife dripped blood.

Niall shoved his head up under Hall's chin, exposing his neck.

Hall hooked his leg around Niall's and heaved.

Fuck. Too late, Niall realized his danger. The edge of the platform caught him, and he tumbled onto the tracks, right in front of the oncoming train.

The train was the size of a mountain as it roared straight at him.

Desperately, Niall flattened himself onto the ground.

The electricity of the metro track half an inch from his arm made his hair stand straight up. The train engulfed him. The clearance was so tight he couldn't breathe. Any movement of his chest resulted in a scrape from the metal edge of the engine.

Who needed to breathe? It hadn't crushed him. Yet.

The train went on forever. Carriage after carriage raced by, moving incredibly fast, and yet far too slow. He didn't know how long he could take this. Would the train ever end? His chest burnt. He had to breathe.

Over the noise of the metro, he was vaguely aware of sirens and screaming. Someone must have seen him go under and raised the alarm.

Even while his lungs fought against the need for oxygen, he calculated the logistics.

He couldn't identify Hall with certainty as the man who had attacked Sinead and pushed him onto the tracks. Alerting the Gendarmerie wouldn't do much good. It would tie him up in hours and hours of red tape, hours in which Sinead would be alone. Or worse, she would be with Andy.

The last carriage was still passing over him when he decided he would have to make sure he was not detained by the authorities. He couldn't be around when the train was gone.

Fuck, this was going to hurt.

He grabbed a bar across the bottom of the train, and held on. The train dragged him along, and he held himself rigid against the bottom of the moving carriage, desperately trying to prevent his back touching the ground and being ripped open by the motion. He clung on grimly, ignoring the agony, until darkness signalled the end of the metro platform and the beginning of a tunnel.

Finally, he was able to let go and lay there in the dark,

dragging in deep breaths and wondering if there was any part of him that didn't hurt.

He might have lain there for hours if the lights of another train hadn't reminded him of where he was. Fuck, time to move unless he wanted to be run over again.

Painfully, he forced himself to his feet and flattened himself against the wall while the RER went past.

The rain beat incessantly against the windowpane and Sinead paced the apartment. She turned on the television again, desperate to see if there was any mention of what had happened in the metro station. Nothing. How was it possible that it wasn't a headline?

Andy was on the laptop, tapping away furiously, occasionally barking orders into his phone.

She turned off the television, paced some more. Stopped.

'Where could he be?' she asked again. 'Surely we should have heard something by now?'

Andy closed the lid of his laptop. 'Don't worry about the big guy. He's come out of tougher situations than this. He's a Ranger.'

'Tougher than being run over by an express train? Are you out of your mind? I don't care how amazing you Rangers are supposed to be, you can't take on an RER and expect to win. You're all flesh and blood, not titanium. You can be killed.' She was aware her voice was rising and that she was getting hysterical.

She didn't care. Niall had been run over by a train. She was entitled to a few hysterics.

'Here.' Andy sloshed some whiskey into a tumbler and gave it to her.

She took a sip and shuddered. It reminded her of the night she and Niall had sat in her apartment in Geneva drinking Bushmills. Was it really just a couple of days ago? She felt like she'd known him for a lifetime.

'Got any ice?'

'No, but I have something you'll like better.' Andy went to his room and when he returned he was carrying a bar of chocolate.

How had he known? Nothing would kill the uncertainty, but the sugar would calm her. Sinead pounced on it. 'I love you.'

'I know.' He flashed her a perfect smile. 'All the ladies tell me that.'

'Any lady in particular?' It was inconceivable that Andy didn't have someone special in his life.

He mouth tightened briefly. 'It's hard when you're in this game. I don't like the idea of someone getting the call to say that I won't be coming home. It's better to stay free and easy.'

She broke off a square of chocolate while she considered that. 'Do you all think that way?'

'Some do,' he acknowledged. 'Getting involved with a client can be disastrous, especially for the client. In this game you need to think clearly all the time. Emotions cloud your judgement. Speaking of which, what's going on with you and the big guy?'

Taken by surprise, Sinead coughed and had to set down her mug but she couldn't prevent the scarlet flush that raced along her skin. 'Nothing,' she said.

'That kind of nothing?' Andy smirked. 'Don't worry about him. He'll turn up.'

'I am not worried about him.' But her words sounded hollow, even to her own ears. She stared out the window. It was getting dark. Paris was lighting up and there was still no sign of Niall.

Please god, let him be safe.

Just then, the sound of a key in the lock startled them both. Andy was on his feet instantly, motioning her towards the bedroom. Sinead fled inside and closed the door. Her heart raced. It had to be him. *Please make it be Niall.* She opened the door a crack and peeked outside.

His clothing was stained and torn. A dark smear marked his cheek. He might have been a homeless person. She raced over and flung herself into his arms.

'Easy, easy there,' he murmured against her hair.

His clothing stank of oil and dirt but she didn't care. She had never been so relieved to see anyone in her life. Sinead raised her head, a question on her lips, but the exhaustion on his face silenced her.

'We can talk later. Right now, I'm shattered. I've spent hours in the underground wiring system, hiding from Hall's people.'

She nodded. There would be time enough to hear the details. In the bedroom he dropped his filthy jacket onto the floor. His shirt, which had been pristine the previous afternoon, was caked with scarlet.

'Andy,' she screamed.

Andy came running and winced when he saw the blood-soaked shirt. 'It's dried in. Let's get him into the shower.' He took Niall's arm and guided him into the bathroom.

It was then that she realized how unsteady Niall was on his feet. With the calmness of an ER doctor who had seen it all before, Andy untied the laces on his friend's shoes and unbuckled his belt.

Sinead couldn't have moved if her life depended on it. She hated blood, had always been terrified of the sight of it. Summer had teased her unmercifully about it when they were younger. A paper cut on her finger was almost enough to make her faint.

Niall swayed and braced his arm against the shower cubicle.

'Sinead,' Andy called. 'I need you now.'

She hovered in the bathroom doorway, unsure what to do. 'The b-b-blood,' she stammered.

'Jesus, get your act together, we don't have time.' He shook his head in disgust. 'Get his pants and shoes off while I hold him up.'

She blinked. She could do this. It wasn't the time to fall apart. Niall needed her. She focused on the buttons of his shirt. One, two, three. Each one accompanied by a shaky breath. The others were missing. What had happened to him? His pants were next. She unzipped them and then realized that she wouldn't be able to get his shoes off. Sinead dropped to her knees and lifted his feet one by one, tossing the badly scuffed shoes into the corner. He wouldn't be wearing them again.

'Good . . . girl.' Niall managed to get the words out.

While pulling down his pants a touch of black humour almost made her smile. She was kneeling before him, inches from his penis. On any other evening it would have been an erotic experience to be with him like that. *Oh, you have it so bad. Focus.*

She managed to get his pants off and reached for his boxers.

'Leave them,' Andy cautioned her.

'Oh.' The realization that they must be covered with blood, too, hit her like a mallet. She wanted to be sick.

'Hold him steady while I fix the shower.'

Sinead planted herself, doing her best to hold him upright, but he was heavy.

Andy adjusted the temperature of the water to his satisfaction. He half carried Niall into the shower and helped him to sit, unwilling to take a chance that Niall would keel over. Soaked through, Andy hurried to the bathroom cabinet and rummaged until he found what he was looking for. He filled a glass of water and popped three pills into Niall's mouth.

'Do you want to kill him?' Sinead said. 'Those things are strong. You should take only one of them.'

'He needs strong for what we have to do. We have to get that shirt off him. Fetch me a pair of scissors.'

Sinead swallowed. She wasn't a field nurse but the evening was turning into a battlefield.

'Sinead, now.'

She stood up automatically at the edge in Andy's voice and ran to the kitchen. A search of the cutlery drawer produced a lethal-looking pair and she hurried back to the bathroom. The shower tray was awash with red as the dried blood mixed with the running water. Her stomach heaved. She couldn't be sick. Not now.

Kneeling on the floor beside the shower, she handed the scissors to Andy.

Niall's eyes were glazed and she wasn't sure if it was from shock, or if whatever combination of pills Andy had given him was kicking in. Andy made deft work of the shirt. Cutting away the front and sleeves until only the back remained.

The red water turned pink and finally clear. 'This bit is going to hurt, bud.'

Niall clenched his teeth as Andy pulled the remains of the shirt away from his back.

Andy allowed the water to run for a little while before he turned it off. 'Towels,' he directed her. 'Lots of them.'

She hurried to do his bidding and, between them, they managed to staunch the bleeding. They dried Niall off and helped him to his feet before staggering to the bedroom and easing him face down onto the bed. Only then did Sinead see the extent of the damage.

The livid bruises ran the length of his back. An array of red scrapes criss-crossed the spaces in between. 'Jesus,' she yelped. 'You need a hospital!'

Niall groaned. 'It's nothing. Stop shouting.'

'I am not –' Then she realized that she was shouting and shut up. She wasn't much of a nurse, but as long as he wasn't bleeding, she could cope. While Andy went to get into dry clothing, she raided the medicine cabinet. Armed with an improvised medical kit, she returned to the bedroom.

Niall eyed her warily. 'What do you think you're doing with that? Can't you leave a man in peace?'

Of all the idiot men. Did she think that she could leave

him like that? Sinead rolled her eyes. 'Don't be such a baby. What happened to you?'

'An RER and I had a difference of opinion.'

'And you lost.' She found it difficult to keep the tremble out of her voice. This had happened to him because he tried to protect her. It was her fault.

'No. I won. If I'd lost, I wouldn't be here now.'

Sinead opened the kit and squeezed antiseptic cream onto her fingers. With soothing strokes and a few flinches from Niall, she covered the cuts on his back. Thankfully, none of them were too deep. Despite all the bleeding, he had somehow escaped any really serious injury. God, it turned out, had heard her prayers. She stroked his damp hair, raking her fingers between the tangled strands until they were smooth. Her touch seemed to soothe him. Gradually, the tight expression eased from his face and his eyes drifted closed.

Andy returned from cleaning up the bathroom. 'Want me to sit with him?'

Sinead shook her head. 'No. I'll do it.'

'Okay. Give me a shout if you need me.' He closed the door behind him and they were left alone.

She hadn't realized how much he meant to her until she thought she had lost him. And now he was here, safe, and though she ached to slip into bed beside him, she was terrified that she would hurt him. She pulled the sheet up over his buttocks and tiptoed out.

She settled herself on the sofa, cuddled up with Niall's bathrobe, and fell asleep.

20

The sound of Andy leaving his room woke her. He paused when he saw her on the sofa. 'You've been here all night?'

She nodded. 'I didn't want to disturb Niall.'

'You should have shared with me. I'd have made it worth your while.'

Despite herself, she laughed. 'Do you ever stop flirting?'

'Only when I'm alone. Not much point then.'

He headed to the kitchen and made himself a quick breakfast. He stuck his head into Niall's room.

'Still sleeping. Best thing for him,' he said when he came back. Then he headed out to get a new BlackBerry to replace the broken one.

In the silence, Sinead walked into the kitchen and poured a cup of coffee.

'Is any of that for me?' Niall's voice rumbled from the bedroom. 'I'm hungry.'

Sinead hurried to the door. 'You're awake?'

Niall hissed as he tried to roll over.

She winced in sympathy. 'I'm not sure if you should move yet. Stay still, I'll feed you.'

'You are not feeding me.' He carefully turned onto his back and tried to sit up. He grimaced and lay back down again.

'I'll give you some more pills, but only if you eat first.'

'Witch.' His scowl promised retribution when he was recovered, but Sinead didn't care. She had to find some way of making up for her squeamishness the previous night.

'I love you too.' She bustled around the kitchen, frying bacon and eggs quickly. It wasn't haute cuisine but it was food. 'Here we are.' She cut a small piece of bacon and offered it to him on a fork.

Niall opened his mouth reluctantly but as he chewed, his expression brightened. 'I suppose I could get used to having a maid.'

He wolfed down the eggs and bacon and looked expectantly at her. She had forgotten what a big appetite he had. 'More?'

He nodded. 'Thanks.'

In the kitchen she whisked up some more eggs and cooked the last of the bacon. They were down to their last egg. They would have to think about doing some shopping. She made a fresh pot of coffee and returned to the bedroom to find that the bed was empty.

Niall emerged from the bathroom. His face was ashen.

She quickly put the tray down and went to help him back to bed. 'What are you doing up?'

'I had to. I don't do bedpans.'

Sinead helped him into bed, trying not to wince at the sight of his back. The bruises were more livid than the night before and the scrapes on his flesh looked painful. 'I can see that you're going to be a very bad patient.'

'You can count on it.' Niall agreed. 'I hate being tied to the bed.'

'If you don't behave, I may have to do that,' she said.

He ate the remainder of his breakfast obediently and only when she was feeding him the last piece of bacon, did she realize that the neck of her robe was open. She was revealing quite a lot of naked flesh and Niall had a bird's eye view. Sinead pulled the edges together and glared at him.

'What?' he grumbled. 'Don't you want me to get better?'

'I'm sure you don't need to leer at my boobs in order to get better.'

'I was not leering. I was . . .'

'Yes?' she demanded, trying not to smile. He was worse than Andy – despite the fact that he had been run over by a train.

'You could make it up to me.' He flashed her a smile. 'How about a bed bath?'

'How about two painkillers? Because that's the best offer you're going to get.'

After making sure he took his meds, Sinead took a long, hot shower. Standing beneath the spray of water she had a vivid recollection of the night before – Niall struggling to stay conscious despite the pain and the way he had trusted her to look after him.

She had become accustomed to the strong Niall, the flirtatious Niall, the one who wouldn't take no for an answer. He might be a gigantic pain in the ass, but seeing him injured and vulnerable like that had made her heart flip.

Stop it. You are not falling for that man. He might be the most incredible lover she had ever had, but they were nothing more than ships passing in the night. Weren't they? Men like Niall and Andy were amazing but they didn't get involved. There was no way that she and Niall could have a future together. Well, not if she was in a Swiss prison.

She had to focus on finding her sister. She and Andy would go to the party tonight, find Roisin and get the stone back. Nothing else mattered.

When she returned to the bedroom, Niall was sleeping. Sinead dressed in some of the lingerie he had bought for her, smiling at the thought of him at the mercy of a Parisian shop assistant. He had good taste, she admitted, as she took out a close-fitting sweater and skirt. The clothes were very Lottie. She wondered if that was a coincidence or perhaps it was a style that he liked.

She really missed dancing. Sinead glanced over at the sleeping lump in the bed. He was sound asleep. Maybe she had time for a workout. She didn't have any workout clothes, but could always do one in her undies. There was no one around to see her. She undressed quickly and switched on some music.

Consciousness returned. With a groan, Niall shifted slightly in the bed and his body screamed in protest. Fuck, every inch hurt. A sense of urgency forced him to open his eyes. Was Sinead safe?

The shades were down and the shutters were closed, enfolding his bedroom in gloom, but he could see it was daytime. His internal clock, which never switched off, told him it was early afternoon, probably around two or so, and his finely attuned soldier's sense told him that there was only one other person around.

Music drifted from the sitting room, along with the occasional hummed note and the sound of uneven footsteps. Despite the pain, he smiled. Sinead was dancing.

He relaxed.

It was a sultry Latin-American tune, the sort made for lovers to dance to, but he would bet money that she was using it to keep fit. Women seemed to be always finding new ways to exercise and Sinead's knockout body was proof that she worked out regularly. He wondered if she danced for joy, or if it was nothing more than cardio for her?

Staid museum curators weren't the sort who danced because they couldn't resist the rhythm of the music, but Sinead constantly surprised him.

He wanted to see her in action, to know what she did when she was alone, but his first attempt at movement made him clench his teeth against a betraying groan. Fuck, he was in bits.

He took inventory of his injuries. His back was a blaze of agony, but there was none of the stabbing pain that indicated a broken rib. His hands were raw, and every attempt to flex his left fingers made him suck in a breath. He had bruises on his ribs, a tender spot on his jaw and a dull ache in his nuts, courtesy of Hall's kick.

Yeah, women could go on all they liked about how painful childbirth was. Eventually most of them thought about having another baby. No guy in the history of the world had ever said, 'I think I'd like another kick in the nuts.'

Tired of lying on his back, he tried to pull himself up. A betraying hiss slipped from between his clenched teeth. God, he hurt all over. A night at a party, trying to find this sister of Sinead's, was going to be even more torturous than he had anticipated.

The door opened and there was Sinead, her glorious hair scraped back into an untidy pony tail, and wearing nothing more than a pair of panties and a bra. Her skin was damp and a sheen of sweat glimmered on her breasts.

His unruly penis immediately took notice. 'That's my idea of workout gear,' he said.

She glared at him. 'You shopped for me. It's not like you bought me leggings and a sports bra.'

'Best move I ever made. Those things are ugly.'

She came over beside the bed. 'How are you feeling? Your colour is a bit better.' She leaned down to touch him, gifting him with a peep at her cleavage.

'Oh yeah, I'm definitely ready to get up.'

'No, stay where you are –' She stopped when she caught the innuendo in his words. 'Do men ever think about anything else?'

'Can't speak for all men, but if I ever fail to appreciate a beautiful woman, you'll know I'm dead.' He forced himself to move, anxious to be fit for action again.

'No, stay there.' Sinead put her hand out to keep him in place.

Her warm palm on his naked chest felt far too good.

She blushed. 'Do you really think I'm beautiful?'

'A total babe,' he assured her.

'I've got no make-up on.'

'That's good. It might smudge when you're giving me a

238

blow job.' He wanted to make her laugh, chase that vulnerable look from her eyes.

'I am not giving –' She broke off, seeing the laughter he was trying to keep hidden.

'If you're not going to play with me, I'll have to get up and make my own entertainment.' He threw off the single sheet that covered him. The apartment was warm, he noticed. She must have turned up the heat.

Her glance strayed down to his crotch, to where a noticeable bulge tented his boxers. 'Tell you what. I'll entertain you, but you'll stay in bed. Deal?'

He caught the hint of curiosity in her eyes. 'Not if you are going to talk about politics or something boring like that. I'm a simple man, I like simple pleasures.'

'Simple?' She snorted. 'How about I dance for you?'

Now that was an offer he hadn't expected. He nodded. 'Deal.'

She disappeared into the sitting room and turned up the music. It changed to something slow and sultry. When she came back, there was a subtle difference about her. She took up her position, struck an attitude, and allowed the music to take her.

Niall swallowed. This answered his question. She danced because she was in love with the music. Who would have thought it? He fought down a flicker of jealousy. He wanted to put that look on her face.

'Closer,' he said hoarsely.

Obediently, she moved closer to him. He could reach out and touch her, but sensed that if he did, she would stop dancing. And he didn't want anything to stop this. She was mesmerizing.

Her spine was made of elastic, so flexible it seemed able to move in any direction. Her hips moved independently, keeping the beat of the music while her hands caressed her breasts and floated down her body, outlining the sweep of her hips.

'You're good,' he said.

Her blue eyes were deep pools of mystery and mischief. 'No, I'm bad.'

She leaned over him, this time deliberately moving to allow his eyes to take their fill.

He swallowed. He could smell her, a tantalizing mixture of sweat, musk and female arousal. His cock hardened.

She noticed and her smile widened. She untied the knot holding her hair up and allowed it to fall down over his chest. It brushed him like a thousand butterfly wings.

'Do you like that?' Her voice was deeper, throaty, seductive.

'Oh yeah. Can't you tell?' There was no hiding the state of his erection.

'Then you will probably like this too.' She leaned forwards and planted a kiss at the base of his throat. It was light and delicate, not nearly enough, but he didn't move, determined to let her do what she wanted.

He nodded.

She kissed him again, this time on his chest.

His breathing deepened, but he forced himself to stay still and allow her to do whatever she wanted. Again, he figured that she would leave if he tried to touch her.

Sinead nibbled her way down his chest, stopping to lick his nipple on the way. Funny, he had never realized how sensitive it was. Now his hips moved involuntarily every time her teeth closed on his nipple. He groaned.

She checked his expression, then grinned wickedly and went back to what she had been doing. 'This is fun,' she told him.

She worked her way down his body, kissing and licking as she went. The wetness she left behind was warm and he cherished each kiss.

He tried to remind himself that she was not going all the way with this. She had said she wasn't giving him a BJ. He would enjoy whatever she did and not push for more.

His cock had other ideas. It reared up hard against his boxers, demanding attention.

She licked at his belly button, dipping her tongue in and making him shudder. Goosebumps rose wherever she touched, and he had to fight to keep from dragging her head down lower. She would stop soon.

Instead, she nuzzled her face into his belly, pushing aside his boxers. She took a deep breath. 'I love the way you smell.'

He forced his voice to work. 'How do I smell?' He couldn't be too sweet right now.

'Male, musky, like Niall.' She buried her face in his crotch, licking and kissing. She climbed up on the bed, moving so that she could look up at him while she played with him.

He spread his legs, allowing her all the room she wanted. She settled herself between them, kneeling up and staring down with a look of triumph. 'All mine!' She knelt back on her heels and took up where she had left off.

Sinead sucked one of his balls into her mouth. Thanks

to Irena, it was smooth and hairless. He groaned, unable to control himself.

Her hand kept a grip on his hips. 'Shh, don't make noise. You don't want to drown out the music.'

Belatedly, he realized she was kissing him in time to the music. He would never be able to listen to 'Straight . . . to Number One' again without getting a hard-on. He lay back, allowing her to do whatever she wanted, while he held on to the edge of the bed to keep himself from grabbing her.

She licked his balls, first one, then the other, and he forgot every ache that Hall had inflicted on him. His body was awash with pleasure, all centred on where her mouth was tormenting him.

She had been avoiding his cock, not even touching it. He lifted his hips. 'Please.' His voice was hoarse.

She smiled, a cat-got-the-cream smile, and blew. The puff of warm air was a torment. 'More, please.' He didn't care if he was pleading; he needed her to keep going.

She brushed her hair back over his penis, then finally – thank you, god – she took it in her mouth. It was hot and wet and he yelled, unable to control himself. She took a firm grip on the base of it and licked the head.

'Mmm, nice and wet already,' she purred.

He couldn't reply. Every single sense was focused on what she was doing. The only nerves in his body that still worked were in his cock.

Sinead licked and kissed her way around the head, lavishing it with attention and care. Every so often she took it deeper into her mouth and sucked, pulling ragged groans from him.

He lay back, desperately holding on to the bed, the pleasure she was giving him so sharp it was almost pain. He never wanted it to stop. Behind his eyelids, sparks flashed. His brain shut down and all he could feel was the lash of her tongue, the heat of her mouth and the edge of her teeth as she nibbled carefully along his length.

Her hands were moving too, he realized. They cupped his balls, and one thumb was pressing into that sensitive spot behind them. He lifted his hips to give her better access, and didn't care that he was pressing on all his bruises. Nothing mattered except that she keep going.

She sucked more deeply, gripped him harder. He needed to touch her, hold her, but the tiny bit of sanity he had left told him that she wanted to control this. He gripped the sheet, not caring if he tore it.

His entire body consisted of his cock. There was nothing else. He babbled nonsense, unable to control his voice. His spine tightened, the juices forcing their way down to his balls. He resisted, wanting this to go on as long as possible, but his body had other plans.

She sucked harder, holding his balls firmly, and he exploded.

'Ahhh!' Jet after jet of cum shot from him, pulling his body rigid. His mind blanked as sensation overpowered his brain.

She kept sucking, milking him, demanding everything he could give her. Vaguely, he was aware that she was swallowing him, and he allowed himself a single astonished thought. Who would have guessed?

He quivered as his penis softened, and still she held it in her mouth. Tremors ran over his skin and he felt everything around him, from the sheet underneath to the weight of the woman kneeling between his legs.

She looked up with an expression of triumph. 'I own you now,' she said.

He was too exhausted to argue. 'Later,' he told her and fell asleep again.

When he woke up again, he could tell it was late afternoon. He was stiff and sore and aching in places he didn't remember being injured, but overriding all that was a remarkable sense of well-being. Even his bursting bladder couldn't detract from the tiny aftershocks of pleasure that fizzed under his skin.

Sinead never ceased to surprise him. She hid a knock-out body under the most boring clothes money could buy, and concealed a talent for seduction behind a spinster librarian's manner.

Slowly, he sat up, creaking and wincing, but smiled when he made out the outline of a glass of water and two pain pills beside it. Andy must be back. It was time to get up and moving.

He just wished Sinead had been in his bed when he woke. After a blow job like that, the least she deserved was a lot of cuddling and pleasuring, which he would have been delighted to provide. When a man was lucky enough to find a woman who could blow his mind like that, he would be mad to let her out of his sight.

He made it to the bathroom under his own steam and cleaned himself up. Halfway through, he was struck by something that had been nagging him.

Why?

Why did Sinead hide herself like that? Okay, he could understand why she might dress older than her years in a profession that valued experience more than instinct. But she didn't dress down, she disguised herself. When they had first met, he had noticed nothing except her sharp tongue. And he was a trained investigator.

He might not be in the market for a new bed-mate every night – he had resigned himself to the knowledge that very few women could cope with him and his profession – but he was still a man, with a Y chromosome and the usual amount of testosterone. He should have noticed Sinead as a woman. And he hadn't.

And given her spectacularly talented mouth, she should have had men lining up around the block to go out with her. Yet his investigation had turned up nothing. There were no boyfriends and she hadn't had a date in months.

There were odd blanks in her profile too – evenings and weekends when she was off the grid. If she really was an old maid, he would have assumed she was at home, watching television. Or more likely, reading some obscure book about the history of jewels. God knew, she had enough of them in her apartment. But the woman who had seduced him so skilfully did not sit at home every night.

'So what time are we leaving?' Andy was asking. He was holding the invitation in his hand.

'We'll have to drive there, so about eight, I think.' Sinead cupped a bowl of coffee in her hand and took a sip. She caught a glimpse of him at the door and smiled. 'Niall, you're up.'

'Got any more coffee?' he asked. 'And some food? I'm starving.'

She jumped up to get him some. 'We're planning what we'll do at the fetish party tonight.'

'Yeah, I don't fancy the loincloth, I'm thinking that leather outfit would do me,' Andy said.

Niall held up his hand. 'We're not going there. It's too dangerous and there is no point.'

Before Sinead could protest, Andy handed him a sheet of paper. 'Before you decide that, you might want to take a look at the guest list.'

Niall read the thirty names on it and blinked. It read like a *Who's Who* of European politics, business, academia and science. And one name in particular made him whistle. Vadim Gorev, one of the biggest names in the Russian Mafia. If there was anyone who could dispose of a $50 million jewel, this was the man.

'Andy, I think you deserve a raise.'

'Yeah, boss, I keep telling you that.'

Sinead looked from one to the other. 'What's going on? Are we going?'

Doubt niggled at him. Finding a 'missing' sister was one thing, but throwing Vadim into the mix was something entirely different. Sinead looked so innocent, but he knew she was hiding something. If he wanted to get the stone back, he would have to let her go to the party. But he would be there, watching her for the entire weekend.

Niall looked from Andy to Sinead. 'We're going. I'm going with you.'

'Dude, have you looked at yourself?' Andy gestured at

the mirror over the mantelpiece. 'You look like a train wreck.'

Niall managed a smile at the choice of words, and grimaced. That hurt. 'Doesn't matter. We're not going to win a beauty contest. Have you forgotten what this is about? We're there to find Sinead's sister.'

'What are you going to do if you find her?' Andy asked.

Sinead looked at him in surprise. 'Get the ruby back, of course, and then bring her home to meet my family.' It was too obvious to need saying.

From the grim expression on their faces, the men did not agree. 'Sinead, it's not that simple,' Niall said. 'She stole a valuable jewel and framed you for the theft. We can't just let her go.'

'But —' She looked from one to the other. 'She must have had a good reason. She's my sister. She wouldn't try to hurt me.'

'She already has,' Niall said.

Sinead stood her ground. 'It's a mistake. You'll see. I want you to promise me you won't do anything to her without my permission. After all, you're working for me.'

Andy hooted with laughter, while Niall gave a reluctant nod. 'We'll consult with you. Fair enough?'

She nodded. 'And what happens if she is not there?'

'That's more tricky. We'll have to try to pass you off as her, and see if we can find out where she lives or what she does for a living.'

Andy handed Niall a mirror. 'Have you looked at yourself, boss? You'll never pass as a slave. I think I should do it.'

The mirror showed him that Andy was right. His face

was covered with bruises, his right eye was turning black and there was a cut under it. Hall had fists like anvils.

Sinead gasped. 'Your back!'

He twisted around and saw that it was a mass of livid cuts and purple bruises.

'No way are you going out in a loincloth, dude,' Andy said. 'You'll scare the ladies there. Now me, I'll be like the flower that attracts all the bees.'

'I hope they sting you to death,' Sinead snapped.

'But what a way to go.'

Niall scowled at both of them. 'I am going. Andy, you can drive us. And get me some more of those pills. I'll get through this and crash later.'

Andy opened his mouth to argue and then shut it without saying anything.

Sinead's eyes were narrowed. 'You are impossible, both of you. I feel like going on my own.'

'No!' both men said at once.

'Oh, very well. But Andy's right, you can't wear the loincloth. We'll have to find you something else.' She groped in her bag and found her phone. 'Hey Clara? L – Listen, Sinead here. We need a new costume for tonight.'

Damn. She had almost said Lottie. Sinead held Niall's eyes while she said, 'Turns out my date is not as pretty from the back as I had thought. We need something that covers his back completely, but we still need to make him look like a slave. He's going to be very servile tonight.'

She listened to whatever Clara was saying, occasionally commenting. 'Okay, that sounds great. I'll send someone to pick it up.'

She disconnected the call, an evil laugh in her eyes. 'Oh, you are going to love this.'

Niall closed his eyes. He had a feeling she was going to torture him. And in the meantime, he needed to track down Hall and find out what the bastard was up to.

While Niall was on the laptop chasing down a lead to Hall, Sinead permitted herself the luxury of a bath. It had been a while since her last public appearance and she needed the works if she was wearing that skimpy costume.

As she lounged in the warm water, memories of their earlier encounter flooded her head. What had come over her? She had almost let Lottie out of the box. Now, each time Niall looked at her, there was heat in his eyes that he didn't bother to disguise.

'You cannot do this,' she told the steam-clouded mirror.

Great. Now she was talking to herself. A relationship with Niall would be impossible. She couldn't possibly keep a secret like Lottie. And it looked like Lottie would have to come out of retirement until she found another job. It was lucky she hadn't sold her costumes and stage props.

She slopped a wet flannel over her arms, letting the soapy water dribble across her skin. She was falling for Niall and that was way out of her comfort zone. Her only long-term relationship had been with Gabriel, and that had been friendship and fun rather than passion. He knew the score. Keep it light. No promises and no tears when it was over. She could never surrender her heart to a man.

Falling in love was a big no-no. She needed to control her relationships, and she was never going to leave herself vulnerable to another person who might leave her. She'd already lost too many people. Sinead shut the lid on that memory. She was not going there. No falling in love. And definitely no falling in love with Niall.

'Sinead, have you fallen asleep in there? Andy is back.'

'Ten minutes,' she replied. She climbed out of the bath and oiled her damp skin. As she grabbed a robe from the back of the door, raised voices carried through from the sitting room: Andy's laughter and Niall's clipped tone. Oh dear. He had obviously seen his costume. She hurried outside.

'I am not going to a party dressed like Russell fucking Crowe. You can take it back and get me something else.'

'Clara says it's Spartacus and that all the women will –'

Sinead clapped her hands to get their attention. 'Boys, please. Stop fighting.'

'You.' She addressed her remarks to Niall in the sternest voice she could manage. 'The party starts in less than two hours. The store is closed. There will be no other costume.'

'And you.' She rounded on Andy. 'Stop laughing at him. God knows he's bad enough.'

Sinead picked up the new costume. Clara had done a fine job. The strips of leather were stitched together and studded to form a tunic that would cover the damage to his back. The gladiator-style skirt would barely come to mid-thigh on him. Andy was right. Even with the cuts and bruises, the women would melt when they saw him coming. Digging into the tissue-lined box, she found two

250

leather arm braces. They would barely go round his forearm, but they would cover some of the bruising there. As for the rest of the injuries, he would have to be content with looking dangerous.

A smaller box revealed a sheer stole to match her costume and a metal headdress that looked vaguely Roman. Clara had thought of everything. They were no longer going as Samson and Delilah but as a Roman lady and her gladiator, one of her favourite fantasies.

'I don't suppose Clara gave you a sword?' she asked, trying to lighten the tension.

'If she did, I know where I'd stick it.'

Andy snorted with laughter. 'Look on the bright side; it covers more than the loincloth.'

'Keep digging that hole and I'll be happy to bury you in it.'

Sinead rolled her eyes. They were worse than a pair of two year olds. 'You have half an hour to get ready. I suggest you hit the shower. Andy, you better change into your chauffeur's outfit. You get to be my servant for the weekend.'

21

Ninety minutes later, they were waved through the tall iron gates of the mansion near Ville D'Avray. Sinead reached for Niall's hand. It was too late to turn back.

He squeezed her hand. 'We'll be fine. Don't sweat it. We'll stay in the background, ask a few discreet questions and get out as soon as possible. It's only a few weirdoes dressed up like plonkers.'

Andy's snort of laughter could be heard from the driver's seat. 'Like you, you mean? I'd give my next pay cheque to see you wearing that outfit in public.'

'Keep that up and you might not be getting one.'

Sinead could feel the tension thrumming through him. The winding entrance road led through a screen of trees. The house was well concealed from prying eyes. Around the next bend, a gravelled forecourt was lit with lights strung through the branches of mature trees. Several limousines were parked outside, their drivers sharing banter and cigarettes.

'Here we are.' Andy pulled up at the entrance and hurried to open the rear door for them.

Niall released her hand. 'Ready?'

She managed a nervous smile. Her stomach was churning and she wasn't sure if it was the prospect of meeting her sister or getting the stone back. Or both.

When this was over, there would be no excuse for them

to be together. Niall would go his way and she would go back to her old life. The prospect made her spirits plummet. 'Yes, I'm fine.'

She accepted Niall's hand as she climbed out of the car and her heel wobbled momentarily on the stones beneath her feet.

'I've got you,' he whispered. 'You'll be fine. It's just a party.'

Andy opened the trunk and unpacked the bags containing their costumes and a few items he had purchased in the sex shop. Sinead closed her eyes and took a deep breath. It was show time and she had never felt so nervous before a performance.

The door to the mansion opened. A footman wearing a striped waistcoat descended the stone steps and took their bags from Andy. Niall moved to follow him and Sinead raised an eyebrow at his audacity. Chastened, he remembered his role as her slave and waited for her direction.

'This way, Madame.' The footman led the way into the house.

Sinead paused in the doorway, tempted to whistle. The black and white marble tiled floor was original, as were the array of mirrored doors leading in all directions. An unending series of reflections greeted them, her red hair cascading over the dark evening cloak that Andy had picked up in a local flea market, and Niall, tight lipped and serious, in a dark suit.

'Red! Darling. It's been far too long.'

The perfectly-coiffed blonde hairstyle matched the cultured Parisian accent. She was stick thin. The slanted cast around her eyes and slightly widened mouth was a clue to her surgeon's expertise. She might have been a well-preserved forty but was probably closer to sixty.

Would she recognize her as a fake? Could she pass for her sister? She worked to keep her French as perfect as possible.

'Darling.' Sinead air-kissed her cheeks. This could only be Hermione.

'I haven't seen you since Stockholm, or was it Helsinki?' She looked at Sinead expectantly.

Sinead stared blankly at her. Apparently her sister got around. She had a fifty-fifty chance of getting this one right. 'Wasn't it Stockholm at the . . .'

Hermione clapped her hands. 'Of course, George's party. Silly me. You did that fabulous routine with two subs.'

Apparently her sister had some pretty extreme tastes.

Hermione eyed Niall openly and ran an expert hand along his upper arm. 'He's new. Nice looking brute. But then you always did have good taste.'

She gave Sinead a perfectly even smile that did not crease the skin at her eyes. 'I look forward to seeing you put him through his paces.'

The door opened again and Hermione prepared to welcome her next guest. 'Your room is on the second floor. Philippe will show you. I'll see you in the salon when you've changed.'

Dismissed, they followed the footman up the wide staircase. One entire wall was painted with a mural of a heroic battle scene.

'Battle of Ulm,' Niall informed her. 'Karl Mack von

Leiberich, or General Mack as he was known, Commander of the Austrian forces. He surrendered to Napoleon, along with thirty thousand men.'

From the hallway below came the sound of another party of guests arriving.

'This way, Madame.' The footman was anxious to return to his duties and they followed him up another flight of stairs and along a carpeted hallway to a door at the very end. He opened the door with a flourish.

The room was large and filled with antique furniture. An enormous upholstered Corbeille bed was set beneath a gilded mirror. The picture windows were framed with heavy damask curtains. Outside, she caught a glimpse of an azure swimming pool surrounded by trees strung with lights. The faint tinkle of a piano carried on the air.

'Will that be all, Madame?' asked the footman.

'*Merci*.' She smiled her thanks at him and he departed.

Niall whistled. 'Nice bed. And the mirror is tilted at the perfect angle for –'

'Don't get any ideas. We're here to find my sister.'

Niall shrugged and loosened his tie. 'We better get changed. It looks like the party is already started.'

He unbuttoned his shirt and placed it on the back of a chair before going to his bag. The leather skirt looked impossibly small in his hands and Sinead was tempted to laugh. He unpacked the complicated array of leather armour that would conceal most of the damage to his back. The rest she would have to cover with make-up.

Niall frowned. 'You'll have to help me with this.' He pulled it on, cursing at the number of buckles and double rings. 'Give me a Kevlar vest any day.'

Sinead dropped her cape on the bed before she helped Niall to adjust the straps of his costume and stood back to admire her work. 'There. Once you lose the pants and put on the sandals, you'll be fine. Don't be shy.'

His scowl told her she was skating on thin ice. Niall toed off his shoes and turned his back to her while he unzipped his pants and stepped out of his boxers. He tied the studded skirt in place and tugged it down to cover his butt. 'Are you sure I can't wear –'

'No. Positively no boxers.' She laughed at his outraged expression.

He perched on the edge of the bed and gave her a narrow-eyed gaze. 'Fine, but I believe it's your turn.'

The memory of the impromptu tease with the bath towel flashed into her head and she flushed. That had ended in some of the best sex she had ever had but they didn't have time for that now.

'Come on. Don't be shy. Strip.'

With his hair down and his muscled arms visible beneath the armour, he really did look like a gladiator ready for battle. She had stripped on stage for strangers without a thought, but this was personal.

Niall's last word had an edge of command to it that sent a blaze of heat straight to her core. Keeping her eyes focused on his, she unbuttoned her shirt, taking pleasure in the way that his eyes followed each new inch of exposed flesh. She eased it off her shoulders and dropped it onto an antique chair. Slowly, she unzipped her skirt and shimmied out of it, noticing with satisfaction that the front of his gladiator skirt was tenting.

She kicked off her shoes, sat on the edge of the seat and unclipped her stockings from the suspender belt before rolling them down her legs slowly. A wave of feminine satisfaction surged through her as she watched him, watching her.

Standing up, she unclipped the silk bra and let it slide down her arms. Her breasts sprang free, her nipples two hard points.

Niall flexed his powerful thighs. 'Now the rest,' he said hoarsely.

Catching the lacy waistband of her panties, she pulled them off in one deft movement and stood naked before him, wearing nothing but a mischievous grin. 'We have a party to go to. Aren't you going to dress me?'

With a hungry smile, he stood up and fetched her bag. The tissue-wrapped parcel lay on top. Deftly, he opened the ribbons and shook the costume loose. If anything, it looked more outrageous than it had done in the changing room.

She stood as obediently as a mannequin as he slid the harem pants up her legs, his fingers lingering too long as he fastened the red button at her waist. He shook out the silken top before dropping it over her head.

She wriggled her arm through the single sleeve, trying to ignore the sensuous brush of his warm breath on the tender skin of her neck. Teasing him had been a very bad idea.

He eyed her exposed nipple. 'Maybe you should leave it like that.'

She ignored him and unpeeled the jewelled nipple cover

from its protective backing before fixing it in place in front of the mirror. She touched up her make-up, painting her mouth a dramatic scarlet, and bound her hair tightly into a pony tail before fixing the headdress in place. The severe style highlighted her cheekbones and eyes.

When she turned, Niall was looking at her, puzzled.

'What's wrong?' she asked.

'Nothing, but sometimes you remind me of . . .'

She hadn't thought of that when she chose the costume. Lottie's favourite colour was red and with her hair tied back from her face like this she looked more like her alter ego.

'One of your old girlfriends, I'll bet.' She tried to make light of it. Sinead picked up the 'tool kit' that Andy had packed for her. Inside was the collar and leash. That would definitely distract him.

She pivoted. 'Bend your head so I can fix this around your neck.'

His grey eyes flared with outrage at the prospect. Niall grasped her wrist, not enough to hurt her, but tightly enough to prevent her from attaching the collar to his neck. 'I'll do it. No one is collaring me. Let's check out the party and get out of here. We don't need to stay for the weekend.'

They made their way downstairs and into the salon. Sinead struggled to pretend nonchalance as they moved through the crowd. Groups of PVC-clad women perched on antique sofas, while their almost-naked male slaves sat at their feet. She tried not to stare as one Domme fed her slave from her hand and ruffled his hair like a pet when he swallowed obediently. He smiled adoringly at her.

'Good boy, Vadim,' the woman purred.

'And I'm not doing that either,' Niall muttered.

'Just act the part and stop sulking,' she hissed at him.

At the far end of the room, a crowd gathered to watch a mistress whip her slave using a matching pair of leather floggers. Sinead swallowed. There was no way that she could do that to Niall.

They passed through the patio doors to the pool area. A dark-haired woman lay half out of the pool, her breasts rising and falling with exertion, her moans of pleasure audible on the night air. Just then, a man's head popped up from beneath the water. The younger man was breathing heavily, but the expression on his face was beatific.

'Was he . . .?'

Niall grinned. 'Now that, I will try.'

'In your dreams.'

Up ahead, she spotted a familiar face in the crowd and waved. It was the blonde Domme from the club, who moved away from the group she was chatting to and came to greet her.

'*Chérie*.' She kissed her cheeks. 'I was beginning to give up on you.'

She turned her attention to Niall. 'Oooh, nice. I like this one. Lovely hair. Can I see it down?'

Sinead tried not to smirk at the barely concealed outrage on Niall's face as the diminutive blonde inspected him from head to toe as if he was a prize stallion.

She fixed him with her best imitation of a Domme-like stare. 'Let the Mistress see how well behaved you are.'

If looks could kill she would be dying in agony but their cover would be blown immediately unless Niall behaved. There was no way that she would permit him to destroy her one chance of finding her sister and the stone. She stared pointedly at him. He shouldn't have to think about it.

She waited, tapping her foot impatiently. If she was really his Mistress, her flail would have been in use by now. Slowly, Niall reached for the length of leather binding his hair.

Sinead held her breath, watching as his fingers opened the knot. His eyes never left hers for a second. Memories of the day they spent in bed together flashed in her head. Niall stroking her, his hair loose about his shoulders, bringing her to the edge over and over again without letting her come.

An angel couldn't resist payback for everything he had put her through – and she was no angel. She was willing to bet Lottie's entire wardrobe that Niall had never let a woman have the upper hand before. She was pushing it, she knew, but he deserved it.

'Take it off.'

His flinty gaze held hers and there was a mutinous edge to his expression. It promised a very special kind of revenge when this was over. With more nerve than she knew she possessed, Sinead took the leather tie from his hand and ran her fingers through his hair. 'Your Mistress prefers your hair loose. You'll wear it that way tonight to please me.'

A muttered curse was his only response.

'Pardon? I didn't quite catch that?'

'Yes, Mistress.' The words came out through gritted teeth.

Sinead ruffled his hair again. 'Good boy.'

The blonde smiled. 'Wonderful hair and nice biceps too. Good definition.'

'Yes,' Sinead agreed as she stroked Niall's muscled arm, mimicking the actions of another Domme who was trying to calm her sub. 'He's a real sweetie.'

'Hermione said that you'll be doing a scene with him later?'

Sinead's smile froze on her face. A scene? In front of all these people?

'Yes, she's dying to see you in action with the whip. I told her about the wonderful routine you did at Cirque recently. Not your usual style, but very hot. Everyone's looking forward to it.'

22

A waiter offered them a glass of pink champagne decorated with a sliver of strawberry and they continued their
journey around the pool. There was no one who looked
remotely like her. Roisin wasn't here. She nibbled her
lower lip, trying to contain her disappointment.

'Would you like to tell me about the hot routine with the
whip?' Niall's expression betrayed nothing. He might have
been admiring the charming seventeenth century architecture, but there was nothing charming about his tone.

'I told you already. Gabriel worked as a dancer and I
grew up around horses. We made something up.' Her
excuse sounded lame, even to her, and she knew from
Niall's expression that he didn't believe a word she had said.
Working with horses wasn't exactly the same as the hours
she had spent training and rehearsing for a dance routine.

'Is that what we'll be doing tonight? Making something
up? I'm afraid I don't dance.'

Sinead blinked. He was right. Why hadn't she thought
this through? She had been so wrapped up in what she'd
say to her sister that she hadn't thought about having to
pass as her.

'Niall? Niall Moore?' A tall man pushed his way through
the crowd. 'I thought it was you. What are you doing
here?'

Niall's face blanched beneath his fake tan as the man

gave him a frank stare. 'Same as you,' Niall replied levelly.

'But I had no idea you were on the scene. And I'd have figured you for a Dom.'

Sinead glanced around her. They were beginning to draw attention and not the kind that they wanted. She caressed Niall's arm with her nails, leaving a red mark along his skin. 'He's a switch, but he only subs to me. Don't you, sweetie?'

Niall flashed her a look that would freeze a volcano.

'Yes, Mistress.' He ground the word out through clenched teeth.

'Frederic?' A dark-haired woman arrived wearing the red leather catsuit Sinead had admired in Clara's work-room. She attached a leash to his collar. 'I hope he hasn't been a nuisance. He's very playful.'

'So I noticed.' Sinead replied. 'It's Mimi Lorenzo, isn't it? I haven't seen you since . . .'

'This time last year.' Mimi laughed. 'I presume you'll be performing for us again?'

'Er, I'm not sure about that. I –'

'Madame.' The footman who had shown them to their room appeared out of nowhere. 'The display area in the garden has been set up. When do you wish to start?'

Sinead looked to Niall for help, but he kept his expression inscrutably blank, like a good submissive. 'Fifteen minutes,' she said.

'*Très bien.*' He nodded his head. 'And will you require music?'

There was no point in having music if Niall couldn't dance. 'No. We don't need music.'

'*D'accord*, I will inform Madame Hermione.'

She wished Mimi good evening and watched the footman disappearing through the crowd. If they were putting on a display, Hermione would expect more than a simple flogging and Niall's back wouldn't take much punishment. They would have to do something more elaborate. 'What are we going to do now?'

Niall gave her a tight smile. 'We have two choices. We can go back to the car and get Andy to drive us the hell out of here, or we can put on a show.'

They had no choice. They had to go through with this. Sinead nodded. 'What do you suggest?'

Niall drained his glass and placed it on the tray of a passing waiter. 'That depends on you. Just how good are you with a whip?'

If they were going to get through the next hour, it was time for honesty. She couldn't let him face her and not know what it was going to be like. She gave him a level stare. 'I'm scary.'

One dark blond brow shot up in surprise. Niall hadn't expected that. 'You can tell me all about it later. Right now, I need to find a weapon. Or this display won't last five minutes.'

Ten minutes later, she stood at the edge of the circle of guests while Hermione performed the introductions. Two of the footmen had carried a velvet chaise longue from the main salon, the only prop she would need. Niall was armed with a flat-bladed sword, taken from an armoury display on the stairs. It wouldn't kill her, but it could certainly leave bruises if Niall was not accurate.

She took her place in the centre of the impromptu stage, lying down on the chaise longue. Behind the silken folds of her costume, her nipples peaked and she wasn't sure if it was from the chill that accompanied the deepening twilight or the prospect of coming face to face with Niall.

Excitement curled in her abdomen at the prospect of an erotic battle fought before an audience. They both knew the outcome. Niall must eventually surrender or their cover would be blown, but he wouldn't give in easily. His taming would be a battle that every mistress watching would relish.

She closed her eyes and turned her focus inwards, inhaling the scent of smoke from the burning torches. A flurry of autumn leaves whispered across the flagstone terrace. Glasses clinked and the low murmur of conversation drifted into silence. It was time.

A startled cry was the first indication that Niall had arrived. He vaulted silently over the low terrace wall. His hair was loose, his sword already unsheathed, a conquering warrior ready to do battle with an enemy, but finding none except her.

Sinead lay perfectly still, feigning sleep, trying to control a tremor of nervousness as he approached. When the blunt sword traced a path along her thigh, she sprang into action, rolling off the chaise in a graceful movement that clearly surprised him. She suppressed a laugh at his obvious dismay. Did he really think it would be that easy?

The audience cheered as, in a move worthy of Indiana Jones, she snagged her whip from beneath the chaise. The battle was on.

With a flick of her wrist, the tip of her single-tail whip cracked the ground beside his foot. Niall sidestepped fluidly, but his eyes narrowed and determination hardened

his features. He crouched, sword in hand, trying to antici-
pate her next move.

Sinead used the whip again, trying to dislodge the
sword from his hand, but he was ready, parrying with a
blow that sliced through the thin silk sleeve of her outfit,
leaving the shreds fluttering in the breeze.

She almost called him a bastard. She had been looking
forward to wearing the outfit again, but the amused quirk
of his mouth cautioned her. Niall wasn't going to make
this easy. Fine. If he wanted to play rough, they would
play rough.

Her next blow hit home. The red welt on his upper arm
drew a groan from several slaves and an approving murmur from the Dommes. The grim set of his mouth told
her that he didn't appreciate her skill and he lunged, determined to inflict more damage to her frail costume.

Sinead moved out of his reach and ripped away the
shredded silk. The entire sleeve was gone, leaving a jewelled collar and a scrap of fabric covering her breast. The
top wouldn't survive another blow. She was going to make
him pay for that one.

She feinted and he turned quickly out of the path of
the whip, the short leather skirt flaring out, giving a
glimpse of his taut thighs and butt. That was too much
temptation for her to resist. The follow-up blow caught
him soundly and he cursed. *She* would pay for that later.

He advanced, sword poised for attack.

With her next blow, she managed to curl the whip around
his blade and drag it from his hand. The audience gasped as
it sailed through the air, landing harmlessly among the
straggling late blooms of Hermione's rose display.

He evaded her next blow, but not the following one, which landed on his unprotected thigh.

'Witch.' His accusation was carried across the terrace, drawing a laugh from Frederic that was quickly silenced by his mistress.

She advanced, delivering a series of blows, most of which hit his leather tunic. At least she didn't have to hold back. The armour was strong enough to protect him. Out of the corner of her eye, she saw Hermione run her tongue along her lower lip.

The minute distraction was enough for Niall. Recovering himself, he parried the next blow and managed to grab the tail of the whip.

Sinead tugged but his grasp was too strong. He reeled her in like a fish, stopping when they were inches apart. They were both panting. A fine sheen of sweat glazed his brow, but his eyes showed a fierce determination to win. Grasping a handful of her hair, he bent his head and plundered her mouth with a kiss.

Sinead jerked away, using the opportunity to recover her weapon. With her left hand, she struck him, a move that raised a cheer from the crowd.

Niall showed no reaction to the blow. If anything, she would swear that her resistance turned him on. She wasn't as delicate as she appeared – something he was only beginning to realize. He turned away, searching for his weapon.

Emerging from the shrubbery with his sword, he stalked her with animal grace, staying out of range of the merciless tip of her weapon. They circled each other like prize-fighters in a ring, neither willing to give an inch.

His sudden lunge caught her by surprise and she didn't have to look down to realize that she had lost the remains of one leg of her costume. Sinead flashed him a look that promised revenge. Before he could recover she flicked the end of the whip and caught his weapon again. It sailed dangerously through the air, clattering to the ground inches from her feet. The crowd cheered their approval.

Let's see how you like it.

Keeping her eyes focused on his, she crouched and retrieved his weapon. She had never used a sword in a routine before, but she mimicked the fighting stance he had taken earlier, beckoning him with the sword, inviting him to approach.

Niall didn't refuse her challenge. He moved within reach of her and then stood still. The crowd held their collective breaths as Sinead let her whip fly, striking his torso over and over with precision, being careful to land the occasional blow on his arms and legs for show. A trickle of sweat ran between her breasts.

Niall didn't flinch. The heat in his eyes was unmistakeable. Their usual calm grey was replaced by molten steel. He trusted her not to hurt him too much. She nodded in a pre-arranged signal and he raised one arm as if to defend himself.

With a final flourish of the whip, she curled the leather tail around his arm brace and tugged hard, dragging him to his knees. This time he stayed down.

Sinead stalked forwards, her sword still in her hand. When she was within reach, she touched his throat with the tip. He didn't move a muscle. Only the racing pulse at his throat betrayed any emotion. Sinead flung the sword aside and grabbed a fistful of his hair in a move that mirrored his earlier attack on her.

Bending her head she took his mouth in an openmouthed kiss that branded him as her possession. Her slave.

As the crowd showed their appreciation, she continued to kiss him, her tongue tangling with his. The scent of sweat and leather mingled with the oil on his skin. Niall's soft growl of appreciation urged her on.

'I can see that you two have a lot more playing to do.' Hermione's words cut through the haze of desire and Sinead raised her head, still a little dazed by his kiss.

'Wonderful performance, my dear. A complete change of style. If I didn't know better, I would swear that you were another person entirely.'

The smile froze on Sinead's lips. 'You know me, I love trying something new.'

Hermione laughed. 'I'm sure you'll want to freshen up. I'll see you both later.'

Niall couldn't remember when he had ever been so turned on. The aches and pains he was suffering were gone, swallowed by pure, undiluted lust. The sight of Sinead with that whip in her hand, staring him down, eye to eye, strength to strength, had sent every drop of blood he owned straight to his cock.

He could barely remember his own name. Every thought he had was consumed with Sinead and how much he wanted to get her into their room and turn the tables on her.

Somewhere during that scene, a circuit in his brain had

closed. He couldn't believe how he had missed it before. The woman in front of him, still holding her whip, with her mouth swollen from his kiss, was *his*.

His mate.

His perfect counterpart.

His lover.

He didn't know all of her secrets, and there were a lot of things to be settled between them, but those were minor details.

He had finally found the woman he had been searching for, the one he needed, his equal.

He must have been crazy thinking he had to find one with his military expertise. It had nothing to do with the ability to shoot a target or carry a 50kg backpack. It was nerve and intelligence and strength of mind.

And Sinead had all those qualities in spades.

He inhaled, and realized he'd been holding his breath. He would settle things with Sinead when this mission was over, but that had to wait.

She beckoned to him.

He bowed to Sinead. 'Yes, Mistress.' His tone was subtly mocking, but his bow was that of one equal to another. 'I'll be happy to serve you your just deserts very shortly.'

Her expression of triumph morphed to one of wariness, as well it should. She really didn't think she would get away with that little scene without retribution, did she?

Niall turned away and grabbed a glass from the tray of a passing footman, gulping it down and realizing too late that it contained white wine, not water. He wondered how it would affect the pills Andy had given him, then dismissed it. Whatever happened, he had a job to do and he would finish it. But no one was particularly interested in talking about Sinead. They were all busy talking about him.

'But what a find!' One Domme looked to Sinead for permission, then ran her hand through Niall's hair. He gritted his teeth and stood still. The woman motioned him to his knees, and he resisted.

To his surprise, she flushed. 'I apologize.' She turned to Sinead. 'With your permission, Madame?'

Sinead nodded and the corset-clad Domme pulled his chain, forcing him down. He could have resisted of course, no one here had anything approaching his physical strength, but it would have blown their cover. He dropped down to the floor beside her, fighting the urge to knock her fingers away.

She patted his head and trailed her fingers down his chest. 'So beautifully trained. Truly a trophy sub.'

'A trophy sub?' Sinead said.

'Oh yes, one of those rare submissives who have everything. Beauty, brawn, intelligence, manners, even attitude. It's obvious that he's devoted to you.'

'That's his job, and he knows it,' Sinead said, but he could hear the tremble in her voice. Well she might tremble. His temper was growing hotter by the second.

He watched her drain her glass while avoiding his eyes. She stood up. 'I think it's time I put my pet to bed. Good evening, ladies.'

With that she beckoned him to follow her and walked towards the staircase. He would follow for now but when they got to the bedroom, it would be a completely different story.

23

As they headed up to their room – Sinead still in the lead, Niall following behind – his eyes never left her ass. There were so many things he wanted to do to her that he didn't know where to start.

And, he realized, he was free to do them. Sinead might look as delicate as a hot-house flower, but underneath, she was as tough as a dandelion. Knock her down and she would come back. He was looking forward to it.

As soon as he shut the door behind them, he unbuckled the collar and flung it off. Damned thing had chafed him for the last hour, and not just his skin. His pride hurt too.

He stared at Sinead, knowing his hunger showed in his eyes. He didn't care. He was through trying to hide who he was. Sinead could deal with the real Niall. The Viking. It was time to live up to his heritage and do some pillaging.

'Strip,' he told her. He made no effort to be polite. It was an order, non-negotiable. The atmosphere in the dimly lit room was electric. Sinead's breathing quickened. Holding his eyes, she unfastened the few bits of clothing she wore and dropped them to the floor.

Downstairs, in front of all the guests, they had been playing. Now playtime was over. It was clear that they both knew it.

He picked up the collar and stepped closer to her. 'Your turn now. Hold up your hair.'

Obediently, she lifted her hair up and held it out of the way while he buckled the collar around her neck. He checked that it was snug, but not too tight. It was a little wide on her, forcing her to hold her chin up higher than usual.

She started to lower her arms.

'I didn't say you could do that. When I give an order, you obey it until I say you can stop. Keep holding your hair up. I want to look at you.'

She glared but stood there, holding her hair up. She looked magnificent wearing a collar. She was born for it. Taking his time, he examined her from head to toe.

God, she was gorgeous. He feasted on the sight of her body, her voluptuous breasts – the perfect size for his big hands, topped by dark pink nipples. They crinkled and tightened under his eyes until they were rigid. His mouth watered to suck them.

He dropped his gaze, taking in her ribcage, now rising and falling with her quick breaths. The narrow waist, so small in comparison to the bounty above and below. He itched to encircle it with his hands. He bet he could fit them around it.

The rounded hips were a contrast to the delicate thrust of her hipbones. As he watched, she sucked in her stomach.

'Why are you doing that?'

'I'm getting fat.' Her voice was a little breathless.

'No.' He wasn't going to argue with her about silly stuff. Women obsessed about being fat, and he could never understand why. Did they not know that when a man looked at a naked woman, he was not looking for flaws?

Her mons was smooth, hairless. Not that he objected but again it struck him as out of character for the prim museum curator. Now, if she had been Red, the most sought-after Domme on the scene . . .

'Why are you smooth there?'

She flushed. 'I swim, and there was a special offer on laser at my local beauty salon, so . . .'

He nodded, not really believing her, but it wasn't the time to make an issue of it.

Her legs were smooth, lightly muscled and shapely, and tapering down to long feet with surprisingly crooked toes.

'Turn around.'

Still holding her hair out of the way, she did. In this position, her arms were elegant and graceful. Not that she wasn't graceful in almost any pose. She had a presence, a subtle something that drew the eye, even when she was cataloguing old books.

Her back view was as outstanding as her front, and showcased her magnificent ass. Pale and firm and rounded, it begged to be spanked. Oh, he would, but he had more in store for her first.

'Turn back to me again.'

She did.

'You can take your hands down now.'

Glaring, she dropped her arms, shaking them slightly. There was a limit to how long someone can hold her arms up before the muscles protested.

'Now, kneel down.'

'What?' Shocked, she jerked back.

'You heard me. Kneel.'

She didn't move. 'Or what?'

He could tell she was weighing the consequences of disobeying him.

'There is no "or what" option.'

She looked down at the chain hanging from the collar. They both knew he could use it to pull her down to her knees. He didn't. This wasn't about forcing her into anything.

He held her eyes and for endless moments, she stood there, not moving. He said nothing, waiting for her to obey him. Finally, still glaring at him, she slipped to her knees.

'Good girl.' She remained in position and he smiled at her. 'How do you feel?'

'Like an idiot.' But the flush on her face told a different story.

He picked up two sets of cuffs and handed them to her. 'You can get up now and put these on.' The cuffs were made of soft leather and had long chains attached to them.

She sorted them out and buckled one set of cuffs around her wrists, then knelt down again to put the other set on her ankles. He checked and was pleased to see she had fastened them tightly enough. 'I'm only doing this because I owe you one for the scene downstairs, you know.'

'Keep telling yourself that.'

He caught the wrist cuffs and attached them to the collar. Then he picked up the end of the chain dangling from her collar. She hadn't noticed the nipple clamps on it, but he had. Carefully, he attached one to each nipple. He tightened them, not enough to hurt, but enough that she'd feel it.

She gasped.

'Don't worry, I won't torture you,' he told her. 'Much.'
Her breathing was light, fast. Standing this close to her, he
could smell her arousal.

'You are so full of it,' she said. 'You're getting off on
this.'

'What red-blooded man wouldn't? But this is special.'
And it was. He was finally showing her who he really was,
letting the real man out to play. And she was loving it.

He pulled the big padded armchair out and told her to
get over the arm. She looked at it dubiously, not sure what
he meant. 'Lean over the arm, bum in the air, legs straight.'

She did, bending gracefully.

'No, legs apart.'

She turned to scowl at him, but obediently moved her
legs apart. The scent of her arousal deepened.

Niall ran his hand over her back, down over her magnificent bottom, then spanked it. Not hard. Not yet. She
gasped as the movements caused the clamps on her nipples to move, reminding her forcibly of their presence.
He increased the intensity of the spanks a little, noticing
how she moved back subtly into his hand. She might be
grousing and giving him dirty looks, but her body was
enjoying everything he was doing to it.

He put a steadying hand on her hips and felt between
her legs. Oh yes, so wet. He couldn't resist licking his fingers, just to enjoy the sweet, salty taste, then went back to
tormenting her. Her clit was hard and swollen, a lure to
his fingers. Every time he grazed it, she reacted. God, she
was so responsive.

His cock hardened. He was tempted to sink into her

right now, but he restrained himself. Tonight he was going to show her who was in charge. They had been dancing around each other for days, and he had been letting her get away with murder. It was time to establish who was the Dom in this relationship.

He deepened his caress, pulling moans from her. Her hips moved involuntarily, seeking a firmer pressure. Her rich liquid covered his hand.

'You have to ask my permission to come.'

'You're kidding?' She turned to stare at him.

'You can't come without permission. You have to ask.' Again, there was no 'or else.' She could fill in that bit herself if she wanted. He wasn't going to waste time doing it for her.

'You bastard.' She lapsed into clench-lipped silence for long minutes while he lavished more caresses on her. He pumped two fingers into her dripping pussy, and she gave in. 'Please may I come?'

'Of course. Good girl.' He was so pleased with her.

With the permission obtained, she relaxed into his touch, allowing him to push her higher and harder. She absorbed the pleasure he was pressing on her, enjoying it, wallowing in it. He pumped harder and flicked her clit with his thumb.

With a wail, she fell apart, collapsing into a shuddering heap on the over-stuffed chair.

He helped her to stand and hugged her, supporting her while she quivered. He felt like a god.

'Did you enjoy that?' he asked.

She nodded, her head tucked in under his chin. Sometimes he forgot how small she was. He tipped her face up to him with a finger under her chin. 'You forgot to ask permission.'

Indignation widened her eyes. 'I did ask.'

'Ages before you came. Did you think it was a rolling permission?'

Her face shifted slightly. She knew what she had done. 'Well, I thought if I waited until the last moment, you might not give it. And I'd be all worked up for nothing.'

He laughed. She was so smart. 'That's true,' he said. 'I have to admire your logic, but not your submissiveness. I probably will give you permission, but not if you ask too early. That's a punishable offence. So now I'm going to punish you.'

'That's not fair,' she said, but didn't move away.

He unclipped her hands from her collar, and then whipped off the nipple clamps. 'Ow!' She cupped her breasts in her hands before she glared at him. 'That hurt.'

She cuddled her abused nipples tenderly, the picture of indignation.

He grinned. 'That was the idea.'

He pulled her hands away and clipped the wrist cuffs behind her back. He spun her around so that she was facing the full-length mirror on the wall.

'What do you see?'

Niall stood behind Sinead, his body covered in the tough leather armour. Next to her, he was bulky and brawny, raw male strength in an extra-large sized package. Whereas Sinead was delicate and fragile, flushed cheeks and titian hair making her look younger than she was.

In a voice of discovery, she said, 'I look amazing.'

And she did. The heavy black collar provided a stunning contrast to her pale skin, and the red hair tumbling down behind it added to the picture. Clipping her wrists together pushed her breasts forwards, so that the pink nipples pointed at the mirror. The chain from the collar dangled between her breasts, the silver links clinking gently every time she moved.

'You were born to wear my collar,' he told her, his voice rough.

It was true. He knew this was special, a time out of real life, and they would go back to their own lives soon, but he didn't know how he would be able to let Sinead go. She had burrowed under his skin, become a part of him. Tearing her out would leave a gaping hole that would bleed and bleed.

He didn't want to think about that. They still had now, and he would make the most of it. He put his hands around her waist. Yes, with a little squeeze, his fingers did meet. His hands were dark against her pale skin.

'They would have loved you back in the time when women wore corsets. You have a tiny waist.'

She tensed.

'Don't be silly. Women then had no rights, couldn't vote, couldn't go to college, couldn't hold jobs. Typical man – wanting to go back to that sort of time.'

'You know, this is not the time for a political debate. I'll have to find a way to silence you.' He looked at the array of toys on the panel beside the door. One thing he'd say for Hermione, she provided great hospitality for her guests. He picked up a ball gag and a rubber snaffle.

Sinead stiffened. 'Don't even think about it. I am not a

horse, so I'm not having a bit in my mouth. And that ball is far too big. I'd choke.'

'There are holes in it, you won't have any trouble breathing,' he pointed out, but he put it back. It might be a bit much for her first time.

If it really was her first time, a nasty little voice in the back of his mind jeered.

'Let's keep things simple.' He picked up the chain dangling between her breasts and put it up to her mouth. 'Hold this between your teeth.'

'Bastard!' she said, but she opened her mouth and took it. Now she could speak, but was muffled, and certainly wasn't going to chat about politics.

He picked up a small riding crop and tapped it against her nipples. There was no weight behind it but she reacted beautifully, jerking back as if she had been shot. 'You're a softy, aren't you?'

She clenched her teeth over a retort, but the narrowed eyes warned him that she would remember his comment. He grinned.

He found a pair of magnetic nipple clamps, jewelled and pretty. He sucked each nipple, stroking it to a firm point with his tongue. When she was moaning and twisting restlessly, he slipped them on. She tensed, but they were gentle. At first. He knew that when she had been wearing them for a little time, she would feel them.

He slid his hand into the back of her hair and gripped it firmly, pulling her head back. She held her ground but the pupils of her eyes dilated. Oh yes, she liked this.

Niall kissed and nibbled his way up her neck, listening to her breathing roughen. He nipped her earlobe before he let her go. She swayed unsteadily, so he pulled some pillows from the bed and scattered them on the ground.

'Sit down,' he told her.

She didn't argue, but folded her knees, graceful as a faun, and settled on the silk-covered pillows. How did she do that, move so elegantly even with her hands clipped behind her? He unfastened them. 'Now play with yourself.'

'Humf?' Even around the chain in her mouth, her voice was full of indignation.

'I want to watch you come. I want to see your face. See the flush heating your skin. It's a huge turn-on for me.'

She clenched her teeth on the chain, but said nothing and nodded. He settled himself in the big armchair, ready to be aroused.

She tried. She slid her hand down along the side of her breasts, grazing the nipple clamp and hissing as the tiny movement sent a jolt through her. She moved down across her stomach and dropped a hand onto her mons. One finger dipped lower, and she moved it slowly and gently.

'Open your legs. I want to see what you're doing.'

She obeyed, but kept one knee drawn up, so that his view was obscured. He didn't care, what he really wanted was to see her face. She flicked a finger across her clit, and flinched. She continued, her face set, but he could see it wasn't working for her.

She spat out the chain. 'I'm sorry, I can't. I thought I could but . . .'

'That's okay. We'll just do something else.' He would have loved to have seen her pleasuring herself, but it wasn't going to happen. There were so many things he wanted to do to her, and he would. He made a silent vow that sooner or later, he would do everything his fertile imagination could conjure up.

He pulled her to her feet and picked up a small flogger. The handle was mahogany but the strands were rubber. He trailed the fine strands over her neck and she purred, pleased by their softness. Lowering it along her body, he used it to caress her before flicking it against her thigh. Now there was a hint of sting in it. She made a tiny sound but stood her ground, even when he repeated it a little harder.

'Since you won't play for me, you'll have to amuse me some other way.' He pulled the chair around so that the back of it was facing her. 'Lean over that.'

Now her back was to him, and he whisked the little flogger up and down. 'Legs apart,' he told her. When she had shuffled her feet apart, he flicked it up between her legs. She gasped, but didn't shift position. He did it again, and this time the sound she made was harsher.

He continued to flog up and down her back and legs, with occasional strokes between those luscious thighs. She moaned in protest, but her hips rocked back, seeking more.

His erection was like granite, harder than he could ever remember being, but he would not stop now.

He put his hand on her waist, holding her still. He didn't want to make any mistake. He struck a little harder, faster. And her voice rose, building up to a peak. The scent of her arousal was rich and deep, intoxicating. He dragged it into his lungs.

'Don't forget you have to ask.'

She gasped, then found words. 'Please, please, please.'

'Yes, you may come.'

She panted, twisted into the path of the flogger, trembling as he pushed her harder. He struck a little harder, again, again, and he flicked the nipple clamp.

With a wail, she climaxed, her whole body shaking and trembling.

Niall couldn't wait any longer. He grabbed a condom from the bowl beside the bed, rolled it on and got ready. He gripped her hips, took aim and thrust himself into her.

She was scalding hot and still throbbing. He plunged forwards, without finesse or grace, but he was too far gone to care. Thank god, so was she.

Sinead lunged back onto his cock, impaling herself and meeting him stroke for stroke, thrust for thrust. He held on to her even more tightly and rocked himself deeper into her. He could not wait and he didn't want it to end.

His vision went as he finally gave in to his climax and ejaculated in an endless stream. His roar of release was echoed by her high-pitched wail as she joined him.

Niall's legs were shaking almost as hard as Sinead herself when he picked her up and carried her to the bed. Tomorrow they would talk. Tomorrow.

24

Sinead struggled out from underneath the weight of Niall's arm and went to the bathroom. The mirror revealed the worst excesses of the night before. The side of her neck was coloured with the rasp of his beard. A bruise had already appeared on her right breast. Between her thighs she ached with the sensations of a woman who had been well used and well loved.

She climbed into the bath and turned on the overhead shower, allowing the water to find the other aches and pains that he had inflicted. Niall was a Dom. Why hadn't she seen that before? She must have been blind. His sheer size and power and the natural air of command should have been a clue. How on earth had she thought that she could get away with making him submit to her in front of a crowd?

Payback was a bitch.

His domination of her had been merciless. He had demanded her submission and she had given it willingly. Gloried in it. Even now she blushed at the memory of wearing his collar.

You cannot do this. It's completely impossible.

Her aching body told her otherwise. Part of her wanted to crawl back into bed and never leave it. She had known he was dangerous from the first moment she set eyes on him, but just not how much. And what about Lottie? Why hadn't she told him the truth when she had the chance? How could she explain her alter ego to him? Niall Moore wasn't the type of man who would let his woman perform naked on stage. He might enjoy watching, but she was willing to bet that he would never share his woman with anyone else.

You are in so much trouble.

She turned the water to cold, letting the icy pinpricks lash against her skin until she was shivering. Climbing out of the bath, she pulled an over-sized fluffy towel around her and used some of the scented moisturizer that matched the shower gel. Hermione obviously believed in spoiling her guests.

When she returned to the bedroom, Niall was still sleeping. She couldn't wait for him to wake up and, besides, he probably needed to rest. She dressed quickly and hurried downstairs. Following the sounds of cutlery against china, she located the sunny breakfast room. Apart from an older woman who was feeding her 'pet' from her plate, Hermione was alone.

'Come sit with me, Red. Isn't it a wonderful morning?'

Sinead took the seat beside her and a waiter hurried to bring her coffee. She inhaled the aroma and sipped the strong liquid gratefully.

'I see you had a good night.' Hermione eyed the bruise on her neck with amusement.

'Yes, he's quite something when aroused.' That was a serious understatement.

The waiter returned, carrying a basket of warm croissants and rolls. The scent made her mouth water. She tried to calculate how many calories she had used up the night before. If the ache in her muscles was anything to go by, more than in a full stage performance.

'Help yourself to breakfast.' Hermione gestured to the side table where a selection of covered dishes awaited.

Sinead piled her plate with scrambled eggs and smoked salmon and returned to the table where Hermione was picking at a small dish of exotic fruits. She gazed enviously at Sinead's plate and sighed. 'Oh, to be twenty-five again.'

They ate in companionable silence, Hermione greeting her guests as they gradually arrived for breakfast. Some sported bruises that were not covered by clothing; most looked tired from their exertions of the night before. Memories rushed through her head: Niall spanking her, Niall pinning her down, Niall taking her as if he owned her, branding her with his mouth.

'You got my email?' Hermione's question interrupted her reverie.

'Which one?' Sinead asked, startled.

'The party on Tuesday at the St Pierre? Surely you haven't forgotten? Mr Takahashi wants you to double-Domme him with Mimi. You agreed months ago.'

'Sorry, it slipped my mind.'

Hermione gave her a puzzled look. 'It's 10k for a couple of hours' work. Hardly to be sniffed at.'

'Ten?' Sinead almost spat out her coffee.

'Each.' Hermione snapped. 'That was the fee agreed. I don't know what's gotten into you lately. You used to be so organized.'

Christ! Roisin wasn't just into the BDSM scene. She was a high-class dominatrix.

'I'm sorry, things have been a little difficult . . .'

Hermione's suspicious expression softened. 'I didn't want to say last night, but you really should be careful. Falling in love with your submissive is never a good idea.'

In love? In love with Niall Moore? No, she couldn't be. She wouldn't.

'I've seen it before. A possessive sub is almost impossible to control. Best to un-collar him, my dear. Several of the other mistresses have already expressed their interest in taking him on.'

'I'll think about it,' Sinead agreed – anything to end this conversation. And she was still getting her head around the information that her sister was a professional Domme.

'Mimi, darling.' Hermione was distracted by Mimi and Frederic's arrival and Sinead sighed with relief. She saw the opportunity to make her escape and wished them a polite good morning as she got up from the table. She was surprised by the change in Frederic. All the energy of the night before had disappeared and he looked like a different man. Before she could ask, Mimi rustled in her bag until she found a dark red card that she pressed into Sinead's hand, saying that they really must see each other more often. And then she laughed, winked and said, 'But I'm forgetting. I'll see you Tuesday, *chérie*.'

Sinead did a double take. And then she remembered – they would be 'working' together.

With each step on the plush carpet her heart lightened. She knew how to find her sister. In a few days' time, somehow, she would get her life back. Whatever this was with

Niall would have to end, but until then she would savour every second of it.

Niall struggled up from the depths of sleep. The combination of an intense scene, pain pills and a glass of wine had wiped him out, and he had slept until mid-morning. When he opened his eyes, the sun was high in the sky and he was starving.

Sinead was sitting on the other side of the room, reading her Kindle. He must have made a noise that disturbed her concentration. She raised her head and smiled at him.

She looked damn good. His cock rose in response.

He moved to throw back the covers and grunted as pain hit him from all directions. He flopped back into the soft bed before he gathered himself to move carefully. It took a good five minutes before he could get out of bed.

Sinead put down her Kindle. 'You know,' she said thoughtfully. 'I think we should skip the entertainment today and the ball tonight.'

Niall itched to investigate everyone in the Château but had to admit she was right. He was definitely not back to full strength. And having Sinead here like this was not something he wanted to give up. 'Maybe we'll take it easy for a while. Get something to eat and enjoy the show.'

Grinning, she agreed, but couldn't resist giving him a push back into the bed. 'This is so tempting. I have you at my mercy.' She climbed on top of him.

He gave her his best evil grin. 'That's what you think, little girl.'

She giggled as he proved her wrong . . .

It was lunchtime the next day when he got a chance to chat to the other guests. He dodged a well-known political figure and a television presenter, and headed for a familiar face. Frederic Killy. He was perusing the selection on the buffet, still wearing a collar and an outfit that consisted of little more than straps. He looked way too much at home in it. Hard to believe he was one of the most respected scientists in Europe.

He looked up with a smile when Niall approached. 'Fantastic show you two put on the other night. You make an amazing pair.'

'Thank you.' Niall selected a devilled prawn and popped it into his mouth. 'I can say the same for you and your lady.' He deliberately kept his tone casual. Interrogation always went better when the subject didn't know he was being questioned.

Frederic chuckled. 'Go on, you can say it.'

'How the fuck did you end up as a sub?' Niall couldn't get his head around that. He had worked with him.

The other man shrugged. 'Just got lucky and met the amazing Ms Mimi.' He picked up a snail and used a tiny fork to extract the garlicky meat. 'I was always the top. I didn't bottom even for a play session. But I met her and we were messing about, and one day she said, "Enough of this, bring me that paddle." And that was that. Just like you and Red, eh?'

Niall paused with a prawn halfway to his mouth. 'You know her?'

'Well, sure. I met her here last year, when I was still a top. Even made a play for her, but she was in full Domme mode and wasn't interested.'

'You're certain it was her?'

Frederic's eyebrows lowered. 'I'm hardly likely to mistake someone I got that close to. Even if she wasn't famous on the scene as "*La Petite Anglaise Rousse*", she's very distinctive. How many women have hair and skin like that?'

'Maybe she's got an identical twin?' Niall fought to keep his face politely interested.

Frederic laughed. 'As if there could be two like her!'

Damn. Niall hadn't realized how much he had been counting on people here confirming Sinead's story. He didn't give up, but circulated, asking casual questions and getting the same answer from everyone. Little Red was a well-known feature on the French scene. She had a reputation as a formidable Domme.

What the hell was going on? Despite everything, he had really hoped that they would get here and find Sinead's twin. Or at least that he'd get to watch Sinead flounder as she was surrounded by some of the kinkiest people in Europe. After all, she was an innocent Irish girl who should be way out of her depth. Instead, she had slipped into place with ease, and everyone knew and accepted her as one of them.

He was a trained investigator. His instincts might scream that she was telling the truth, but the fact was that she was way too much at home here.

What was up with him? Sinead risked a sideways glance from beneath her lashes as Andy drove them to Gabriel's home in Montparnasse. En route, they stopped so she could pick up pastries at Bogato and some fresh flowers.

Andy dropped them off and she announced herself at the intercom at the gate. It was buzzed open, and Niall closed it carefully behind them. The shiny new lock on the door was more evidence of improved security at the house. The downstairs shutters also looked as if they had been repaired.

Gabriel waited on the step. The bruises had faded a little, but the white dressing above his eye was stark against his tanned skin. Although she had seen him only a few days before, tears welled up in her eyes. She ran the last few steps and flung herself into his arms, kissing him on the mouth and cheeks.

'Hey,' he cautioned her.

Sinead pulled back. How had she forgotten his damaged ribs? 'Did I hurt you?'

'*Mais non*, but I've spent an age ironing this shirt. I don't want you crying all over it.'

'Idiot. I've a good mind to eat all the pastries myself. I hope you have coffee?'

'For you, always.' He winked at her. 'Come inside.' He hobbled into the hallway and through to the sitting room. A rumpled blanket and an open copy of *L'Équipe* lay on the sofa.

'I'll make the coffee. You rest.'

Gabriel looked as if he was about to protest but demurred gracefully. 'You know where everything is.'

Niall followed her into the kitchen and watched as she found a glass vase for the flowers and set a tray with cups and plates while they waited for the water to boil.

'Can you fetch me the ceramic jar from the top shelf?'

Niall took down the unmarked jar and she opened it and put some of the beans it contained into an electric grinder. Gabriel wouldn't drink coffee unless it was freshly ground. He'd been disgusted by the horrible instant stuff they served in the theatre. She had almost converted him to tea.

'You do know where everything is,' Niall observed.

'Of course I do, I've been here a lot.' She regretted the words when she saw his mouth tighten. She had visited Gabriel's home when Lottie was working in Paris, and had even stayed overnight sometimes, but she couldn't tell him that.

'You and he shared this place together?' Niall asked.

What was his problem? He could hardly expect her to have reached twenty-seven without having a boyfriend. She shrugged. 'Gabriel and I are friends.'

'Do you share his bed when you come to Paris?'

Sinead huffed a breath. That question didn't deserve a response. What had put him in such a strange mood? He had been withdrawn and quiet since they left Hermione's. 'I slept on a camp bed. Not that it's any of your business.'

'What else haven't you told me?'

There was a dangerous edge to his voice but they had come here to see Gabriel, not to argue. She picked up the tray and brushed by him. 'Grab the coffee pot, will you?'

The visit was mercifully short. Gabriel was tired and she didn't want to impose on him for long. Once she was satisfied that he had enough food and medicines for the next few days, they left and returned to the apartment.

Niall checked the display on his phone. Four missed calls from the one person in the world he needed to talk to. He headed into his room and closed the door. This was not a conversation to have in company.

He hit redial. 'Reilly, what have you got?'

Reilly's voice was clear. 'Sorry boss, not a lot.'

'Well, spit it out.'

'I couldn't find anything.'

Niall gripped his phone. 'You mean you couldn't find her mother?'

Reilly sighed. 'No, boss, I found her all right. Maggie O'Sullivan. Born in 1968. Died in 1989. The birth of a Sinead O'Sullivan was registered the same year that Maggie died, but her date of birth was given as four years earlier. That was a bit odd, but I didn't find any other births registered for children of Maggie O'Sullivan for 1985 or any year after.'

'Are you sure?'

'Give me a break. I know how to read a record.' Reilly sounded offended. 'I even searched for an Irish twin.'

'Irish twin?'

'You know, when a woman has a second baby within a year of the first, they're called Irish twins.'

'Oh, right.'

'I searched several years forwards and back, just to be sure. Nothing.'

'Thanks for letting me know, Reilly.'

He ended the call and put down the phone. Sinead had lied to him. He hadn't realized how much he had trusted her until this moment. She had looked him straight in the eye and lied. And she had done it so convincingly that he had actually believed her stupid story about a missing sister. He had got Reilly to go to the Registry and search for the mythical twin.

How gullible could one man be? He had been bewitched by Sinead's blue eyes and innocent look.

She had deceived him. Hardened operators had backed down in front of him and told him what he needed to know. He could usually tell if a civilian was lying in about five seconds. And yet somehow, sweet Sinead O'Sullivan had lied to him, so convincingly that he had not only believed her, but believed everything about her.

He sat on the edge of the bed, barely able to support the weight of the disappointment crushing him. It was a painful lump in his insides, sending jagged darts of hurt out to stab him repeatedly. How could she have lied to him? He swore he would never put up with being lied to. He would not accept anything except the truth, and yet look at him.

He had swallowed everything that Sinead had told him. The redhead had managed to get under his defences, and make him ignore the facts and trust her.

The ache in his jaw made him realize how tightly he was clenching his teeth. With an effort, he loosened it. He would not allow her to affect him like this.

'Damn it!' He swore more violently than the situation demanded. The aching lump in his stomach got heavier, making it difficult to breathe. He wanted to throw up.

How could she? The deceitful little whore. She was way too good at this. How much practice had she had? How many men had she smiled at while she was lying?

Her performance in the bar came back to haunt him. At the time, he was convinced she was teasing him. Only him. Now he wondered if she had intended to drive the entire place demented.

Well, she wasn't going to get away with it. Two could play at that game. Now that he knew she was an accomplished little liar, he would be ready for her. He would get the truth out of her, and what's more, he would enjoy every minute of it.

She had the most sensitive, responsive little body. It was a pleasure to see her writhing around on the bed, begging him to bring her relief.

But suppose he used her own body against her? He could drive her mad, bringing her to the edge again and again, until she would tell him anything he wanted to know, if he would only give her what she needed.

Niall smiled, a hard smile filled with promises. He was going to enjoy this.

He hadn't finished contemplating what he was going to do to her, when the phone rang again.

'Niall Moore, what am I paying you for?' Tim O'Sullivan demanded. 'You had one job, keep Sinead from messing with the bail, and what did you do?' He paused. 'You made a bollocks of it, that's what you did.'

Niall winced. 'There were other factors.' It sounded as lame to him as it did to O'Sullivan.

'Your job was to keep Sinead in line.'

'And find the Fire of Autumn,' he reminded Tim.

'Yes, well, that's what I'm ringing about. What's this I hear about her being out of the country? That had better be a mistake. If she doesn't turn up for court, my million francs will be gone. So you'd better make damn sure she turns up. Understand?'

O'Sullivan was in fine form, determined to get his own way.

'Certainly sir. I'll have her there.' He paused. Some perverse part of him itched to ask a question he already knew the answer to. 'What can you tell me about Sinead's twin?'

There was silence on the other end of the line. 'Her what?'

'Her twin. She said she has a twin called Roisin.'

'Jesus man, it's too early to be drinking. Sinead doesn't have a twin. Roisin was her invisible friend. You know what kids are like.'

'Are you sure?' Niall knew he was grasping at straws. Sinead had played him for a fool.

Tim snorted. 'The poor child was traumatized. She was lucky she survived at all, considering the way – Anyway, enough nonsense. Just make sure you get her back to Geneva on Tuesday.' He hung up.

Andy was out. A scrawled message on the kitchen counter indicated that he was following up a lead. She was about to show it to Niall, when she realized that the colour had leached from his face. From the hard set of his jaw, Sinead could see he was fighting pain.

He poured a glass of water and popped three pills into his mouth. 'So, when did you meet Gabriel?'

Sinead scrambled for a suitable response. He wasn't

going to let it go. Was that what was eating him? How could she tell him about Gabriel without mentioning Lottie? She couldn't say that Gabriel was sweet and funny, with a wicked sense of fun. Or that he was intuitive when they were choreographing new routines, always knowing how best to display and entice. Of all her regular dancers over the years, he was the only one she had taken as a lover.

Yeah, she bet Niall would love hearing that.

That part of their relationship had ended a long time ago and she and Gabriel had settled into a close friendship, with occasional friendly flirting. Sinead sighed. 'We met in London a few years ago, at the theatre.'

That was technically correct, even if they had been auditioning, rather than watching.

'Were you lovers?'

There was an edge to Niall's voice that she didn't like. He had no right to ask her that question. They had shared amazing sex, but Niall had never pretended that it was anything more than that. He hadn't offered her any details about his former lovers. For all she knew, he could have a string of women back in London. Except for the niggling voice inside her that told her Niall didn't get involved.

'That's none of your business.' Damn it, she wasn't going to stay here. Niall had no right to pry into her past. She stormed out, slamming the door behind her.

Seconds later, it flew open. 'What is wrong with you? I asked you a simple question. What do you think it's going to be like when Interpol get their hands on you?'

'Interpol?'

'As soon as you left Geneva, it became an Interpol matter.'

Niall raked his fingers through his hair and she almost felt sympathy for him. He couldn't disguise the fact that he was bone-tired and that he had been operating on adrenalin and painkillers for far too long. But that still didn't give him the right to harass her.

'Tim rang earlier. He knows you've left Switzerland, and he wants you back there, keeping his money safe. I told him I would guarantee it.'

Her heart sank. How could she have forgotten Niall wasn't here to help her? She was a job, nothing more. He was working for her uncle.

'If there is any hope of getting you out of this mess, you have to co-operate.'

'I'm trying. Believe me. When I meet with my sister –'

Niall shook his head. 'Fine. We can play it your way if you want, but listen to me and listen carefully. Until we return to Geneva, you don't eat, sleep or move without my permission.'

She swallowed. His flinty gaze told her he meant exactly that. She sat down heavily on the bed. 'You can't do that. I'm not a prisoner. I have rights. I . . .'

'You've broken bail by leaving Switzerland. And Hall and his buddies are no doubt still looking for you. So feel free to walk out of here anytime.'

He was right. She had nowhere left to go. Sinead stared at him. The man who had kissed her and made love to her had turned into a cold stranger.

'The stone goes back to the museum within three days or you do seven years in a Swiss prison – that's the only deal that Rheinbach is offering.'

Seven years or more in prison if they couldn't get the

stone back from Roisin. She would be old before they released her. Old and in disgrace.

Logically, she knew that thirty-four was not that old, but she would never get another job. And all for a crime she hadn't committed. Sinead slid off the bed and walked to the window. Despite the late afternoon sun, she shivered. She had far too many secrets. She wished she had told Niall about Lottie at the beginning, but if she tried to tell him now, he would believe she'd been lying about everything. There had to be a way out of this.

Outside, it was a beautiful evening. Paris was laid out in front of her – the most romantic city in the world. It should be an evening for strolling hand in hand with a lover or having a romantic dinner. She pressed her palm against the glass and focused her attention on a bird that had landed on the window ledge outside. She shrugged. 'I didn't take the stone. I can prove it to you when we find my sister.'

A flicker crossed his face but it turned back into a granite mask. 'Look at me, Sinead. Let me make you a promise. By the time this is over there will be no secrets between us. I will know everything about you and I mean everything.'

'Why are you acting like this? What's wrong with you?'

His face had turned paler than before and he swayed on his feet. 'There is nothing wrong with me.'

'That's what you think. Now, lie down before you fall down. I'll be outside.'

In the sitting room, she threw herself onto the sofa. What had happened since last night? How could Niall have changed so much in twenty-four hours? It had to be more than the visit to Gabriel.

Their encounters in the Château had been mind-blowing. She had never known that anything could feel so good. But had it been nothing more than a ruse to get her to open up to him?

Was Niall so ruthless that he would make love to her to get the stone back? And what was all that Dom stuff about? What had he been trying to do? Turn her into an obedient little sub who would obey his every word? Get her so hooked on him that she couldn't think straight? Had it all been lies from the beginning? Get the girl into the sack and get her to talk.

A pity fuck for Plain Jane Sinead.

She remembered the way he had looked at her. The way his grey eyes had turned molten with passion. Could he really have faked that? Sinead punched a cushion and tossed it onto the floor. The only person who stood between her and prison was a man she couldn't trust and who didn't trust her. The only thing they had in common was a desire to find the stone and return it to the museum.

When she found her sister, she would show him. Niall Moore could go to hell in a basket. See if she cared.

She switched on the television. She was perfectly happy watching reruns of *True Blood* until it was time to make dinner. And Niall Moore could fend for himself. Damned if she was cooking for him.

25

The smell of coffee woke her. Sinead blinked and Andy came into focus. He waved a coffee cup beneath her nose. 'Glad to see that one of you is alive. What did you do to the big guy?'

Memories of the previous day came flooding back. 'If he's still alive, then obviously not enough.'

'That bad, eh?' His dark eyes held a hint of sympathy.

Sinead struggled to a sitting position and took the cup gratefully from him.

Andy collected his cup from the kitchen along with a bag from the bakery and joined her on the couch. 'Don't give him a hard time. This mission has been tough on him too.'

Sinead frowned. 'He's not the one who's likely to end up in a Swiss prison. I am.'

Andy set down his cup and raised his hands in mock surrender. 'Someone got out of the wrong side of the bed.'

'Someone didn't get to bed at all. In case you hadn't noticed.'

'Sorry, I didn't bother turning on the lights when I got in. I wasn't home 'til after four and I didn't notice you curled up on the couch.'

'Hot date?'

'As if.' He sighed. 'I got intel that Hall was checking out

some of the BDSM clubs. I did a trawl but there was no sign of him.'

'Oh.' She didn't like the sound of that. Hall was still out there and he was looking for her sister. The sooner she found Roisin, the better.

'Is there any coffee left in that pot?' Niall's voice came from behind them.

'I'll make some fresh.'

While Andy busied himself in the kitchen, Sinead risked a glance at Niall from beneath her eyelashes. His hair hung damply around his shoulders. He hadn't spoken to her or looked at her. She could do just the same to him.

She turned away and pulled a piece from her croissant. She hadn't bothered cooking in the end. She'd been too mad at Niall. Her stomach growled in protest. 'I don't suppose there's any jam?'

Andy opened the fridge. 'Afraid not. We need to shop.'

'We won't be here for much longer.'

Niall's statement made Andy raise an eyebrow. He looked from her to Niall and back again. 'Would someone like to tell me what's going on?'

The buzz of the telephone prevented Niall from responding. 'Yes,' he snapped. 'When?'

He darted an unreadable glance at her and she shivered. Something was very wrong.

'Stay where you are. I'll be there in thirty minutes.'

Niall disconnected the call and glanced at his watch. 'Holy fuck. You let me sleep for fifteen hours?'

Andy shrugged. 'Don't blame me. I wasn't here.'

He shot an accusing glare at Sinead and she couldn't

resist baiting him. 'Do I look like an alarm clock? I'm not the one who was popping pills for the past three days.'

'You're not the one who needed to.'

The edge to his voice silenced her. He was right. It was her fault that he had been injured. 'I'm sorry, I –'

Niall shook his head. 'I'm sorry too. I . . . Sinead, there's been an incident at Maurice Verdon's antique shop. He's dead.'

No, it had to be a mistake. Maurice couldn't be dead. But the expression on Niall's face told the truth. The funny little man she had known since her first year at Sotheby's was gone. 'What happened?'

'They think it was a break-in that went wrong early this morning. I'm heading over there now. Stay with Andy until I get back.'

Through the fog of shock, her brain continued to work. Maurice was trying to help her. He was looking for information to help her find Roisin. But why would Maurice be at his shop in the middle of the night? That didn't sound right. 'I'm going with you.'

'No.'

'You said you weren't going to let me out of your sight. Give me five minutes to get changed.'

Ignoring his protests, she hurried to the bedroom, showered quickly, changed her clothes and hurried back to the sitting room. Niall and Andy were deep in conversation and they stopped talking when she arrived. 'I'm ready.'

Niall was silent in the elevator and barely said a word to her on the journey. This just got worse and worse. She grappled with the idea that Maurice was dead. How was it possible?

They parked in the side street near the antique store, and as they turned the corner, crime scene tape fluttered against the scaffolding of the building next door.

The sign announced that the shop was '*fermé*' but the light was on. Inside, the shop assistant was sitting at the desk talking to another woman. Niall and Sinead pushed the door and the bell rang announcing their arrival. At the sight of them, Madame burst into tears and her visitor gave them a pleading glance. She patted Madame on the shoulder and left the shop. A grandfather clock ticked sonorously as Sinead approached the desk.

'*Je suis désolée*,' she began, but Madame wasn't inclined to be consoled.

'*Bâtards*. I warned Maurice not to have anything to do with them. He . . .'

'To do with whom, Madame?' Niall interrupted her.

She waved her arm. 'Them. Those men, he talked to them in secret. Told me it was better not to know. Maurice kept his own counsel about his business affairs. What am I to do now, eh? Nineteen years I have worked for him.'

She searched in the drawer of the desk and removed a packet of Gauloises and a lighter. She fumbled with the packet and Niall flicked the lighter when she finally got the cigarette between her shaking fingers.

'What time did you last see him?'

Madame shrugged. 'He said he was working late on his accounts. I went home as usual. This morning, the baker across the street phoned me that the door of the shop was open. It was around 4 a.m. He rang the police. When I got here . . .'

She drew heavily on her cigarette. 'The ambulance was here, but it was too late. The knife went too deep.'

'May we see the room, Madame?'

'I don't know. The police —'

'Have already been here,' Niall finished smoothly. 'It will only take a moment and then we will leave you to your grieving.'

She ground the end of the cigarette into a replica of a Chinese bon bon dish and removed the keys from the drawer. 'As you wish.'

As they followed her up the stairs, Sinead's heart thumped. She didn't want to do this. What if there was blood? What if there was —

'Sinead?'

Niall's voice brought her back to reality. 'I'm fine,' she insisted.

Madame unlocked the door of the office. Everything was as tidy as it had been the day that they had visited him. Apart from a new crack on one display case, the locks on the cabinets were intact. The tray on the desk was laid with a pot of coffee and two Limoges porcelain cups and saucers. Maurice had been expecting a visitor.

Sinead's stomach heaved when she saw the dark stain on the floor. The colour had already leached into the varnished oak. Niall picked up a bunch of keys from the desk. Sinead recognized the battered leather fob from the day they had been here. Robbery wasn't the reason for Maurice's murder.

From his expression, Niall was coming to the same conclusion. 'Do you know if anything is missing, Madame?'

She gestured to the cases. 'The police asked the same

question. Nothing appears to have been taken, but it will take time to do a full inventory.'

'The earrings you bought were the best thing he had in stock. He said you always had a good eye.'

Sinead nodded. 'I should have. Maurice was one of those who trained me.'

Madame nodded sadly. '*D'accord.* Me too.'

Sinead left Niall having a final check while she went outside for some fresh air. Outside the shop, Sinead inhaled deeply. It was starting to rain but she didn't bother to shelter. She wanted to wash all of this away.

'*Meurtrière.*' The shout came from the bakery across the street and an apron-clad man emerged. '*Meurtrière,*' he shouted again and she flinched. He was shouting at her and waving his arms. Murderess. Murderess.

'*Je t'ai vue hier soir.*' His shouts grew louder and he looked around him seeking assistance.

'*Appelez les gendarmes,*' he roared at a woman emerging from the flower shop to see what was happening on the street. '*La rousse s'est renvoyée.*'

The redhead had returned. She hadn't been here for days.

Her breath caught. Roisin was a redhead, just like her. Could he have seen Roisin? Her sister wouldn't hurt anyone, would she? Oh sweet god. They were staring at her, but her thoughts whirled, wondering if Roisin could be involved in Maurice's murder. No, it wasn't possible.

A small crowd gathered. A woman holding the hand of a toddler gave her a wary look and crossed to the other side of the street. Niall's hand on her elbow broke her paralysis.

'Sinead, are you all right? You're chalk white.'

She clutched his arm. 'We have to get out of here.'

Niall took Sinead's arm and guided her back to the Jeep. She had paled until even her lips had blanched, and her body was stiff. All the classic symptoms of shock.

Obediently, she climbed into the Jeep and fastened her seatbelt but her hands shook.

He glanced over at her. Poor girl, she was shaken by Maurice's death. Violent death was hard to take, especially when it was someone close. Maurice had been her friend, her mentor.

He wished she had been in his bed last night, even if he had been unconscious.

He drove carefully, allowing the pieces of the puzzle to fit themselves into place, but knowing he was missing something significant.

'Who do you think could have killed him?' he asked.

Sinead kept her eyes on the road in front of her. 'I have no idea. It must have been a robbery.'

And the hairs stood up on the back of his neck.

What the hell was going on?

26

Sinead gripped her hands together while Niall negotiated his way through the traffic, driving too slowly for her taste. When a siren blared, she froze, only relaxing when the sound faded into the distance.

He touched the call button on his in-car Parrot and the phone clicked on. 'Andy,' he said in a clipped tone. After a few moments, Andy responded. 'The situation has escalated,' Niall continued. 'I need to know everything about Maurice Verdon's death asap. Use your contacts, but discreetly. Our ETA is fifteen minutes.'

The authority in his voice reminded her of their night at Ville d'Avray. He demanded and expected that he would be obeyed without question. The flinty stare he gave her when their eyes met in the rear view mirror made her shiver. This was the Niall she remembered from London when her cousin Summer had been kidnapped. He had taken over her uncle's mansion and insisted on interrogating each one of the staff personally. This man was icily controlled. The man who had made love to her until she begged him to stop was gone.

He held her elbow as they entered the lift, smiling politely at an elderly lady carrying a Chihuahua in an over-sized handbag. His gesture was a parody of affection. Niall's grip was like a vice. When they left the elevator, he practically dragged her across the lobby to their apartment.

'Andy,' Niall said as soon as he walked through the door. 'The situation has become critical. We're returning to Geneva.'

Sinead swallowed. She was 'the situation' as he so crudely put it and she wasn't sure if she wanted to be under Niall's control right now.

Andy nodded and reached for his jacket. 'I'll sort out the travel arrangements.'

When Andy left, Niall locked and bolted the door. Ignoring her, he picked up a straight-backed chair and placed it in the centre of the room.

'Take a seat.' The silky voice held more than a touch of menace.

She tried for bravado. 'Thanks, but I'm not sure if I want to.'

'Sit.'

He barely raised his voice but it was enough to make her stomach flip. She hadn't felt so panicky since her first performance. She sat, stiff and upright in the chair, trying to quell her nerves.

Niall took off his tie and dropped it over the arm of the couch. 'Let's start with something simple, shall we? Tell me about your family.'

Simple? He had no idea. Sinead twisted her hands in her lap. 'There's nothing much to tell. My dad left when I was little.' Best hurry over that bit. 'My mum is dead. I was raised by my grandparents.'

'Ah.'

That loaded little word irritated the hell out of her.

She had been in therapy for a while and she knew the drill. Poor little orphan girl. 'Not everyone has a perfect childhood, you know. Lots of families break up.'

She hated the flash of pity in Niall's eyes; hated that she sounded so defensive. She was doing just fine. She didn't need anyone feeling sorry for her.

'Touched a sore spot, did I?'

She folded her arms across her chest. 'Feck off.'

'Okay, subject change. Tell me about school.'

She huffed out a breath. 'St Louis in Monaghan. Trinity College.' There was no need to tell him about her early years. Or how Granny O'Sullivan had intervened to make sure that she was educated with her cousin, Summer.

'After that, an MA at Sotheby's Institute of Art. They took me on before I graduated.'

'Impressive. Why was that?'

'Because I can spot a fake a mile away.'

'How?'

She shrugged. 'Some of it is science. I can analyse wavelet decomposition readings for paintings and check provenances of newly discovered "missing" old masters. But most of it is gut feeling and instinct.'

She didn't know how to explain the utter certainty when she looked at a piece of art or a jewel. She didn't need the equipment to tell her that it was the real thing.

'Tell me about the stone.'

At last. Something easy to answer. 'The Fire of Autumn. It is the world's largest ruby. At \$48.5 million, it set the record at Sotheby's for the most expensive single jewel ever sold at auction.'

When he didn't stop her, she continued on. 'Originally

from the Indian kingdom of Salkonda, it was a Sultan's wedding gift to his bride. King Philip of Spain purchased the jewel and included it in the dowry of his teenage daughter, Margaret Teresa, in 1664.

'The Fire disappeared and reappeared over the centuries, turning up as a centrepiece in the collections of the royal houses of Europe, including that of Archduke Ferdinand. After the First World War, the stone vanished, only to resurface as part of a secret Nazi horde at the end of the Second World War.

'Now owned by King Abdullah, it's currently on loan to the Rheinbach museum in Geneva.'

Sinead stopped. She was so involved in telling the story of the stone that she had almost forgotten about the theft.

'See, not a hesitation, not a flicker of doubt. You can tell the truth when you want to.'

'I haven't lied to you.'

The moment the words were out of her mouth she winced. She had lied to him. She had run out on him. She had left him carrying the can with her uncle Tim for a million Swiss francs. And while it had nothing to do with the theft of the ruby, not telling him about Lottie gnawed at her. The longer she left it, the harder it got.

'When I find my sister –'

Niall covered the distance between them in a flash. His strong fingers hooked under her chin and forced her to look up at him. 'You don't have a sister. You're an only child. Tim confirmed it when I spoke to him yesterday.'

Sinead closed her eyes. How could she tell him what it was like when Uncle Tim and her grandmother had found her at the camp? Of the nights that she cried for Roro.

But no one would believe her after their initial search for her twin found no trace of the girl. She was just a traumatized child with a vivid imagination. She stopped herself. It had been hard enough to tell Gabriel and he was her closest friend. Why should she tell Niall? He wasn't going to believe her anyway. She wondered what else had he asked Tim and what had her uncle told him? Sinead opened her eyes and stared back at him. Let him question her. She would tell him nothing.

Niall's gaze was cold and fathomless. If she hadn't been sitting down, she would have run. Instead, she sat frozen to the chair. Niall didn't believe her. He didn't trust her an inch.

'You stole the Fire of Autumn. You made me break my word to your uncle. And I hate breaking my word.'

Niall released her chin and stepped away. She watched him walk to the bedroom. When he returned, he was carrying the holdall he had taken to the party. He dropped it beside the chair and bent his head until his face was inches from hers. Following his angry accusations, his slow, tender kiss took her by surprise. In spite of everything, she couldn't resist him.

She whimpered softly as she leaned into it, opening her mouth, craving the taste of him. This was the Niall she needed right now.

Niall pulled away with a smile and busied himself with the bag. He pulled out a pair of steel handcuffs.

'Where did you . . .?'

'A gift from Hermione. Technically, you could say that it's a goodie bag. Although I think she meant you to use them on me.'

He fixed the cuff to her wrist and fastened her deftly to the chair.

'What are you doing?' He couldn't possibly want to do this now. Not when they were in the middle of an argument.

'You like playing games, don't you, Sinead?' He produced a second pair of cuffs. This time he attached them to her other wrist and clipped them onto the other arm of the chair.

Standing behind her, he pushed her hair aside and kissed the tender skin where her neck met her shoulder. 'This is a game called truth or dare.'

His deft fingers opened the top two buttons of her shirt and brushed lightly along her breasts, raising goose bumps where they touched. 'You tell me the truth, or I take it as a dare to do something to you.'

Her eyes flew open. 'What?'

She tugged against the chair, but they were serious cuffs, not the kind they used at hen parties.

Smiling, he returned to his task of dealing with her buttons, dropping a kiss on each inch of exposed flesh. His hair tickled as it came in contact with her skin. Niall couldn't be serious.

'You actually expect me confess all for a few kisses?'

He flashed her a smile that was tinged with wickedness. 'Of course not. I expect you to lie your head off.'

Niall tugged the sleeves of her shirt down over her arms, effectively imprisoning her. Sinead wriggled, but she couldn't move her arms. He was serious. He was actually going to torture her for information.

Her skirt came next but when he unzipped it she

refused to help him by raising her hips. Niall went to the kitchen and returned with scissors. 'Co-operate or I can cut it off. Your choice.'

It wasn't fair. She liked these clothes. 'Stop this.'

'Baby, I'm just getting started.'

She raised her hips reluctantly and he tugged the skirt off in one swift movement, leaving her sitting in matching bra, panties, garter belt and stockings.

He lifted the scissors to the lacy edge of her panties and then changed his mind. 'We'll leave them on for a while.'

Unhooking the front fastening of her bra, he exposed her breasts for his attention. When he circled her areola with his thumb, her nipples peaked.

'Nice and responsive. Just the way I like them.'

He rummaged inside the bag and pulled out something.

The small flogger looked as harmless as a child's toy. He flicked it experimentally against her exposed flesh. Tiny pinpricks of sensation bloomed along her breasts. It was nice. Not quite ticklish but good.

He knelt at the bag again and, without asking permission, he covered her eyes with a satin blindfold.

The sudden deprivation of one sense only heightened the others.

The next flick came in contact with her erect nipple and she jumped. 'That was —'

Another blow, this one harder than the last, caused her nipple to harden in response. 'You like a little pain with your pleasure, don't you?'

On and on it went, a tide of sensations, sometimes hard, sometimes ticklish, building warmth and tenderness in equal measure. The blows moved lower, along her abdomen and thighs. Sinead pulled her knees together and received a stinging flick and parted them again. The flogger gave her a pleasant buzz. Not quite pain or pleasure, but something in between.

He removed the blindfold and smiled down at her dazed expression. 'Like that?'

'I hate you.'

He raised one blond brow in amusement before opening the bag and pulling out a chain with nipple clamps on it. 'Good. Then I guess it's time for our first question.' His smile faded. 'Were you and Gabriel lovers?'

Sinead stared blankly at him. He could go to hell. 'None of your business.'

'That was the wrong answer.' He fixed a clamp to her right nipple.

That wasn't so bad. It only pinched a little. She could put up with it for a while, but when she got out of this Niall would pay. She would . . .

'We've got all night. I'll ask the question again. Tell me about you and Gabriel. Were you lovers?'

Sinead pressed her mouth shut and glared at him.

Shrugging, Niall attached a second clamp to her other nipple.

The first was beginning to burn a little, the tightness making her want to squirm, but she wouldn't give him the satisfaction.

Niall lifted the chain and gave it a gentle tug.

Heat bloomed in both of her nipples and she cried out as the pleasure/pain zinged through her. 'That hurts.'

'It's meant to. Let me know when you feel like talking.'

She was expecting another round with the flogger. Instead he sat in front of the laptop Andy had been using earlier and switched it on. That was it? He was going to ignore her? Minutes later, he was still sitting there. Sinead squirmed in her chair, but each swing of the chain only added to the aching sensation in her nipples. 'Take them off me.'

Niall ignored her. The apartment was silent apart from the tapping of his fingers on the keyboard. She shifted in the chair again, but each time she did, the tingling became worse. He had to take them off. 'Yes, we were lovers, but it's been over between us for more than a year. Now please . . .'

He finished typing and got up. She was going to kill him for this.

Slowly, he approached her. He ran his index finger along the valley of her breasts, brushing the chain as he did so.

'Ow,' she cried.

'Poor baby.' Bending his head, he nuzzled one breast and unclipped the tweezer clamp.

She gasped with relief but seconds later, the blood rushed back to her abused nipple and she cried out.

His hand fisted in her hair and Niall fastened his mouth over her burning flesh, sucking and licking, riding out the storm. Desire unfurled like a sail and she arched against him, seeking more of his mouth. God, that felt so good. She could almost come, just from this.

He released her nipple with a pop. The heat in his eyes was unmistakeable. He pulled on the chain, dragging her attention back to him. 'No, I don't think so. Shall we try another question?'

Dazed from the river of sensation washing over her, she nodded.

'Good girl,' he praised her, and she didn't know why the words sounded so good, so right to her ears. Planting tiny kisses against her heated skin, he traced a path upwards along her neck to nip at her jaw. 'Let's try another one.'

Sinead tensed, but under his teasing ministrations, she relaxed again. The sensation in her left nipple had settled to an insistent throb. When he removed the clamp she was going to scream.

'What was your father's name?'

'Peter,' she gasped.

'Peter what?'

'That's all I know. That's what mum called him – Peter.'

The picture of a smiling red-haired man popped into her head. He was laughing, lifting her skyward. Her sister clung to his leg, begging to be lifted too. It was just before he left, taking Roisin with him.

'He took her. He took Roro.'

He released the other clamp and the blood rushed back furiously. Heat shot out in bright arcs and even his suckling mouth couldn't hope to keep it at bay. Arms rigid, she rocked back in her chair and only his strength kept her from falling.

'Sinead, Sinead,' Niall's voice anchored her, bringing her back to him. 'Who is Roro?'

'My sister.'

27

Released from the handcuffs, Sinead was conscious of his hands briskly rubbing her wrists. Niall lifted her in his arms and carried her to the bedroom, setting her down on the cool quilt. Dazed, she watched as he picked up a pillow and placed it beneath her hips. What was he doing now?

Through her eyelashes, she watched as he unbuttoned his shirt and peeled off his jeans. Except for the bruises, he was perfect, as if one of the marble statues in the Louvre had come to life. Every inch of him was strongly muscled. Her mind might be confused, but her body knew exactly what it wanted. As if he had read her mind, he peeled off her panties.

The clank of metal told her he was at the damned bag again. She mentally added Hermione to her hit list along with her sister and Granny O'Sullivan. Surely Niall couldn't do anything more to a defenceless woman?

Apparently he could. He fixed a leather strap to one ankle and then a second one. She tried to close her legs, but couldn't. There was a long bar between the straps, holding her ankles apart.

'It's called a spreader bar. Like it?' His voice rumbled with amusement.

'No.'

Ignoring her response, he clipped her handcuffs to the bed.

'Sinead, focus on me.'

Bossy Niall was back. One by one, he removed more items from his kit bag – a length of soft rope, a ball gag, which he considered and replaced in the bag, a leather paddle and another flogger – this one heavier than the last.

Sinead swallowed. He couldn't use that on her.

'Nervous? We haven't gotten to the good stuff yet.' He smiled as he removed a tube of lube and finally a velvet bag. He emptied the contents onto the bed.

The purple G-spot toy she recognized. The large wand looked like the muscle massager that some of the dancers used when their legs were aching. The small, dark toy puzzled her until she remembered their visit to the sex shop. It was a butt plug.

'No,' she shouted and tried to sit up. The handcuffs kept her in place.

'Okay, we'll keep that one in reserve for now.' He dropped it into the bag and returned to stand at the end of the bed. Bending, he gripped the spreader bar and pushed it towards her. Sinead's knees bent automatically. He continued to push until the bar rested inches below her hips. In this position, she was open, exposed to him. Nervousness and excitement churned in her gut.

'Very pretty and very wet.' Niall dropped a kiss on her mons. 'Exactly the way I like my uptight museum curators.'

'Somehow, I wouldn't have thought that stuffy museum curators were high on your list.'

A long, slow lick the length of her pussy was his response. Niall raised his head 'You're not stuffy, just uptight, and I plan to fix that.'

'Oh.'

'But first, I have more questions.'

Sinead closed her eyes. Was he never satisfied? 'Ask them, but I've told you everything.' Except about Lottie, but that wasn't something she was going to tell him. Not ever. If he found out that she had concealed Lottie, he would presume she had lied about everything else.

Another slow lick followed by a puff of warm breath against her clit. This was a deliberate seduction. Niall wouldn't stop until he had extracted every piece of information he wanted.

'What happened to your mother?'

She tensed and received a sharp tap on her thigh.

'Eyes on me, Sinead. Focus on me and tell me the truth this time.'

'She died just after my dad left us.'

It had taken her years to discover the truth about her mother. Her grandmother had managed to build a wall around her past when they took her in. They meant well, but . . .

His touch changed to soft reassuring strokes, tender caresses that both soothed and inflamed her. Oh, he was good, better than good.

'So everybody went away?'

She nodded, not trusting herself to speak. Within twenty-four hours she had lost everyone she cared for.

'But you were a brave girl and you worked hard, maybe too hard, trying not to think about them?'

Sinead swallowed the lump in her throat. She couldn't explain why she was so driven to win, any more than she could explain Lottie. When she was on stage, the scared part of her switched off and she was free. She craved success and approval, but Lottie could destroy everything she had built.

'Sinead,' his voice dragged her back to him.

'Yes.'

'Poor baby,' he murmured against her heated core.

The vibrations of his voice added another layer of awareness. It was too much. More kisses, more licks, the exquisite pleasure of his mouth on her clit, sucking, licking, tormenting. Without warning, the sensory overload of the past hours tumbled her over the edge of a precipice, into a fast and furious orgasm. Breathless and helpless she lay on the quilt, shaking as she rode the last waves of pleasure until they ebbed away.

'See how good it can be when you tell the truth? That's all I want from you, Sinead. Nothing more.'

He pumped his finger slowly into her and her muscles tightened around him, straining to push her over the edge again.

'I can't,' she protested. 'It's too much.'

Niall silenced her with a kiss, taking her mouth with a slow passion that built to a relentless demand. She squeezed her inner muscles around his fingers and he laughed.

'I'll say when it's too much. Trust me.'

Removing his fingers, he returned his attention to Hermione's toys.

His wicked smile should have warned her. He plugged in the large white massager and switched it on, rolling it against her inner thighs. She tried to close her legs against the insistent vibration but she couldn't. Each pass brought it closer to her clit, but it never quite got there.

'Please.' She didn't care that she was begging. He had to let her come.

The rounded head of the wand brushed her clit and pinpricks of electricity shot along her nerves. She was close. So close.

He took the wand away, moving it down her legs and along her abdomen. Everywhere but where she needed it so badly. She arched her hips and clenched her inner muscles around the toy, but it wasn't enough. 'Let me come. Please, Niall.'

'You're sure you want to?'

'Yes. God damn you. Yes.'

His next kiss was soft against her mouth. She raised her head from the pillow demanding more. Thrusting her tongue against his, roughly taking his mouth, biting at his jaw, raking him with her teeth.

'Kitten's got her claws out.' He pulled away from her, but the flare of heat in his eyes was unmistakeable. She wanted him. Needed him. Why didn't he just –

He placed the wand against her and turned up the intensity. Sinead didn't bother to disguise her moans of pleasure. Helpless, she was swept up by a tsunami racing for shore. 'Oh, Niall. Oh god. Oh, Niall.'

Everything stopped. The machine was silenced and she could hear nothing but her own ragged breaths and her pulsing blood ringing in her ears.

'Where is the stone?' his voice was calm, matter of fact. He might have been asking her about the weather.

'Please,' she wailed, thrashing as wildly as her bindings would permit.

'Tell me where it is?' His seductive murmur came against her ear and she turned her face to him.

'I don't know. I tell you I don't know.'

Niall moved away. He switched on the wand again and drew lazy circles with it against her abdomen, venturing close to her throbbing flesh but never close enough to give her the satisfaction that her demanding body required. Mindless with need, she raised her hips, begging him to give her some relief. Urgency built, this time more quickly than before.

She clung to the pinnacle again, pleading for the tiny shift that would take her over. Her body was slick with sweat. She could smell the perfume of her own arousal. She would die if he didn't let her come.

'Where is the stone?' Niall asked again and this time she couldn't refuse.

'Roisin has it.'

The sharp vibrating intensity of electricity came directly into contact with her clit and she screamed as the wave of pleasure crashed to shore, obliterating everything in its path. Every nerve in her body was wracked by a flood of sensation that reduced her to a mindless, quivering heap. Pins and needles raced along each limb. Even her mouth numbed. Floating, she was aware of Niall unfastening the straps around her ankles and his hands massaging the muscles of her legs before rolling her onto her front.

He placed a cushion beneath her hips and positioned himself between her still-trembling thighs. He fisted a handful of her hair and with a single thrust he sheathed himself in her slick core.

'Mine.' His possessive grunt almost sent her over the edge again. It was too much, too soon. Her traitorous body told her differently. She arched back into his pistoning hips. She could die right here now from sheer pleasure.

Niall's body curved over hers, his mouth finding her neck, his teeth biting down on her tender flesh, marking her as his. She had never wanted anyone as much. Never known what it was to crave, to hunger for another's touch, until him.

'Yes,' she cried out as he withdrew almost completely and slammed home again. With disbelief, she felt another orgasm building. She couldn't come again, not after everything that had happened this afternoon.

His harsh thrusts increased in momentum. She revelled in the edge of pain that each one brought. He pounded into her, his breath coming in ragged gasps. He couldn't last much longer. Like tinder beneath a match, her senses caught alight in a blaze of pleasure that coursed through her blood, reaching every screaming nerve ending.

'Niall. Niall. Niall,' she breathed his name like a mantra each time he slammed home.

His hand in her hair only served to remind her that she was his. She was helpless and she didn't care. She wanted this, gloried in his rough possession. Fireworks exploded behind her eyelids and she fell into another vortex of pleasure.

Yelling her name, Niall followed her home.

When she came to, he was still covering her like a warm

male blanket. She inhaled the scent of his musky arousal and licked at the sweat on the arm that lay unmoving on the pillow beside her face. He rolled onto his side, taking her with him. She never wanted to be anywhere else, except in his arms.

'Love you,' she whispered as her eyes drifted closed.

What the fuck? Niall's eyes, which had been drifting closed, opened abruptly. What had she just said?

Sinead had just said that she loved him.

He allowed the knowledge to fill his head. She loved him. She loved him.

Until he heard the words, he hadn't realized how much he had longed for them. It seemed an age, even though it was only a couple of days, since he had realized that Sinead was his perfect mate.

He didn't believe in that 'Eyes meeting across a room' or soul mate nonsense. But every so often, two people just balanced each other so well that it seemed they belonged together.

Look at his friend Flynn and his fiancée Summer. On the surface, total opposites: the silent Ranger with the ability to blend into the shadows and the socialite who was the heart of every party. But when they were together, you could see the bond between them. They weren't at all alike, but they balanced each other. Of course, they still had some royal rows, but you could see them looking forward to the making up even when they were fighting.

Seeing them together filled Niall with envy. They had

what he had always wanted, and had resigned himself to never having. He had resigned himself to being alone.

He grinned into the darkness. Well, not entirely alone. His size and appearance always attracted women. Hell, it wasn't his fault that so many civilians were out of condition. All of the Rangers looked good in comparison, and they all carried themselves with a quiet confidence that attracted women. The trouble was, none of them were women who were in for the long haul.

They wanted someone to protect and care for them. That came naturally to Niall, but he had never been into the Daddy Dom thing. He wanted an equal, and had never found one.

Until now. Until Sinead.

She was as focused as he was. As good at getting her own way. She was used to being the smartest person in the room and took it for granted that she was always right. He must challenge her to a game of chess sometime. Maybe strip chess, just to make it interesting.

He'd like to see Sinead starting off all schoolmarm prissiness and stripping down to reveal that knockout body.

Niall loved the idea that he was the only one who knew what was under those god-awful clothes. He scowled. Apart from that little French bollix. He ignored the fact that he had admired Bertrand's fortitude until he discovered he had been Sinead's lover. She was twenty-seven. Of course she'd had lovers. He had no right to object. But something inside him snarled at the idea of any other man seeing her the way he had.

He just hoped Bertrand had a tiny dick and was a lousy lover.

Niall wanted to be Sinead's lover. He wanted to stand beside her and say, 'This is my woman.' He wanted to show her off, to watch her turn other men into putty.

The trouble was that he didn't trust her. Oh yeah, he burned for her. He wanted to make love to her, to drive her wild with passion. He wanted to lavish pleasure on her. He wanted to torture her until she begged him to fuck her until she saw stars.

He had seen the pain in her eyes when he asked about her family. She couldn't fake that no matter how talented a liar she was, but she was still holding something back. Sinead had been lying to him from the moment they met. He knew that. She was still lying. He couldn't trust anything she said. Not even when she said she loved him.

The pain made him clench his teeth against that knowledge. Sinead snuggled deeper into his embrace, and he lay in the darkness. He would make the most of now. He knew it couldn't last.

28

'You have to let me go to the St Pierre. It's the only way I can prove it. Once you see Roisin, you'll –'

'No,' both men chorused.

'It's too dangerous,' Andy explained. 'We still haven't tracked down Hall. You're safer here. And we have to bring you back to Geneva today. You are due in court this afternoon. Now, put on some more coffee, I'm starving.'

She glared at his retreating back and contemplated poisoning him. It didn't matter how pretty he was, he was still a bloody sexist. But she wanted to eat, too, so she headed for the kitchen. She put a pan onto the hob, melted some butter and cracked four eggs into it.

Niall was already at the laptop, his brow furrowed as he concentrated on the latest reports. Sinead sighed. She had to convince him to let her go to the St Pierre. This might be the last chance she would get.

The grill had turned her slice of bread to golden toast. She scraped a thin layer of butter over it, wishing she had some of her usual low-fat spread, and put on two slices of Niall's gluten-free bread to toast.

'Any chance of some breakfast?' Niall called.

'Yes, oh divine master,' she muttered under her breath.

'I heard that.' His eyes crinkled with laughter. 'You can practise saying it again later.'

Men! She wasn't sure which of them was the most annoying. She stirred the eggs, adding a large shake of black pepper and a dollop of cream. The coffee hissed and she turned the heat off under it, then snatched the toast from the grill just before it burnt.

She buttered it briskly, dumped the eggs on it and set the plate in front of him. He dug his fork into the eggs without taking his eyes from the screen. It was *him* she should have poisoned. Sinead poured herself a coffee and nibbled her toast. The eggs did look good.

'There's a report from Reilly about an unconfirmed sighting of Hall outside a hotel in the Marais. Can you check it out today?'

'Sure,' Andy said as he poured a second cup of coffee and added a lump of brown sugar.

Sinead sat back in her chair. So much for company. She might as well be invisible. 'I'm going to have a shower,' she announced. 'And it's your turn to clean up.'

She took her time, washing and conditioning her hair, oiling and buffing her skin. She hated the thought of having to appear in court, but at least she could make sure she looked good.

When she came back, the table was still littered with the debris from breakfast and Niall was hunched over in his chair. Sweat beaded on his face. 'What's wrong with you?'

Andy lifted his head from Google maps. 'Wow, boss, you look like shit.'

'Feels like a gluten reaction.' Even his voice was rough. 'Can't think what, though.'

Her mind raced, checking over what she had cooked. 'I

toasted your gluten-free bread. I know I didn't mix it up with my bread.'

Niall was pale. 'Did crumbs get onto it?'

She mentally rewound her breakfast preparation. 'I used the same knife to butter your toast and mine. There might have been a few crumbs.'

'Fuck,' Andy said.

'I didn't know. I didn't think that . . . it was just a few crumbs.'

'It doesn't matter. Any sort of cross-contamination would be enough.' Andy was about to add something when Niall made a dash for the bathroom.

When he came out, he was ashen. He grabbed the pain-killers and popped two. 'Okay, let's go.'

'Don't be silly,' Sinead told him. 'You can barely walk in a straight line. Go to bed and sleep it off.'

He glared at her, and she tried not to feel guilty. 'I can do whatever is necessary. I have to get you to Geneva.'

'I can get the train. I'm a big girl.' When he nodded curtly she realized he must be feeling really bad.

'Right now, what's necessary is that you go to bed and recover. No point killing yourself.'

She held her breath and was surprised when he nodded again and headed for his room. She was right, he wasn't walking completely straight. The rattle of the shutters being closed indicated that he was settling down to sleep.

She should have remembered from the night at the café. How could she have been so stupid? 'I'm sorry. I didn't mean to do it.'

Andy put his arm around her. 'I know you didn't. I have

to go out, but I'll get Reilly to look after you and get you to Geneva.'

Sinead shook her head. 'Don't be silly, I can take the train.'

Andy's stern expression was a contrast to his usual smile. 'Reilly will take you.'

It was a miserable, damp day and she pulled on her jacket as she got ready to return to Geneva. She hated this, leaving Paris when they were so close to finding Roisin and the Fire. She knew where she would be. It was madness not to make the most of it. Who knew when they would get a chance like this again? She tucked her hands into the pocket. Her hand brushed a card and she pulled it out.

Mimi Lorenzo.

She had forgotten about the card. And the client who was expecting a double Domme date this afternoon.

She fingered the card, twisting it between her fingers. Niall wouldn't know if she went there first. If she could convince Roisin to return the stone then this mess would be over and she would have her life back. Surely, the museum wouldn't hold it against her that her sister had stolen the stone? She hadn't seen Roisin for more than twenty years. Uncle Tim could confirm that. If she could get the Fire back, there might be a chance for her and Niall.

Sinead shook the thought away. They had made no promises to each other. Deep down, he didn't believe her about Roisin and he had been distant since she had foolishly told him that she loved him. There had been no 'I love you too'. No declaration that he had any feelings for her at all – apart from sex. *Me and my big mouth.* How could she have thought that Niall could possibly love her?

She stared at the card, trying to work things out. She should wait for Reilly to take her to Geneva. Of course she should. Uncle Tim had put up the bail for her, and if she didn't go, the money would be forfeit. Tim would never forgive her.

But if she didn't go to the St Pierre, she would never get another chance to meet her sister. For as long as she could remember, she'd had a Roisin-shaped hole in her life. All this stuff with the ruby, there had to be more to it. Her sister was a part of her. She couldn't have turned to the dark side, not really. And she knew that Roisin needed her, as much as she needed Roisin.

Sinead knew, with a bone-deep certainty, that Roisin would never have killed Maurice. She was in trouble, and probably didn't even know. Sinead had to help her.

And of course, she had to get the Fire of Autumn back. If she didn't grab this opportunity, she would never get another one. This was her chance to find the ruby and clear her name.

She punched the number into her phone. This was something she had to do alone. 'Mimi, darling. I'm afraid I have some bad news. Hermione asked me to call you. Mr Takahashi has been taken ill – he has to reschedule our play date.'

Mimi tsked. 'So annoying. And I just had my nails cut too. Still, I suppose I could fit in some shopping instead.'

Sinead made polite noises as Mimi rambled on about a darling little lingerie shop she had discovered.

Once she was off the phone, she grabbed Hermione's

party bag – it certainly gave a new meaning to that term, being filled with kinky gear – and the spare keys, then headed out of the apartment. She would get Reilly to bring her to Geneva as soon as she had got the ruby back.

She stopped at Clara de Lune's on the way and purchased the leather catsuit. Lottie could afford it and she had to look the part, otherwise she wouldn't have a chance of being admitted to Mr Takahashi's suite.

'Got a date?' Clara asked as Sinead changed into the leather suit.

'Sort of,' she admitted. 'I'm trying to find someone.'

'Ah.' A frown appeared on Clara's powdered forehead. 'I've heard a rumour that there's another little Red in town. Nothing to do with her, is it?'

Sinead hesitated, torn between keeping her own secrets and finding out what Clara knew.

'She's my sister.'

'Your sister! Why didn't you tell me?'

How could she tell Clara about the half-remembered flashes of Roisin, the family who tried to make her believe she had never existed, the constant fear that she was going crazy? 'It's a long story. Tell you another time. So what do you know about her?'

'I've never dressed her. She goes to George in London for her clothes. And to think that I could have been dressing the pair of you.'

'Forget the clothes. We don't see a lot of each other. What have you heard about her?'

Clara gave her a considered look as if she was deciding what to tell her. 'Well, she's quite a performer, but a lot darker than you, my pet.'

'I know. I have to see her today. She has something belonging to me. I need to get it back.' *Like my life.* 'What else?'

'She does private parties. Expensive ones.'

'I know,' Sinead said, glancing down at her costume. 'I'm going to one today.'

'Jesus, don't tell me that. I should put you over my knee.'

Sinead snorted. 'You're not my type.'

'Here, sit down in front of the mirror and I'll fix your make-up. You can't go to a party looking like that. The hairdresser down the street can style your hair. I'll give him a call.'

Clara's make-over took longer than she expected but when she finished, Sinead had to admit that she looked different – sexy but edgier, like a woman of the world who would take no nonsense from anyone.

She smiled at her reflection. 'Thanks, Clara. I owe you.'

'Don't worry. Next time you come back you can buy a whole new wardrobe and bring the two hotties with you.'

29

Niall gave up the battle to stay asleep, and made another dash for the bathroom. God, he hated this. He staggered back to his room, wiping his face. It had been a constant joke in the Rangers: the biggest guy in the Wing, the one who could defeat all comers, could be brought down by a few grains of flour.

He paused. Something was wrong. The apartment was too quiet. The television was still on, but there was no sound of human movement.

He forced himself away from the peace of his bed and checked. The apartment was empty. Where the fuck was Sinead?

He found his phone and called Andy.

'Hi boss, glad to hear you're back in the land of the living. But bad news, Hall is still in Paris but he's gone to ground. You should have seen the little cutie who saw Hall working out at the gym. She –'

'Shut up.' Niall didn't have the patience to deal with Andy and his womanizing. 'Did you put Sinead on the train?'

'No, I told Reilly to take her.'

Niall cursed, and hung up so that he could phone Reilly. 'Where is she?' he demanded.

Reilly's voice was muffled by what sounded like a pool

hall. 'No idea, boss. I came to collect her and rang, but there was no answer, so I got back to work.'

Cold froze Niall's ability to think.

She had been so determined to meet her sister. Niall didn't even have to check the location of her phone to know she wasn't on her way to Geneva. She had done a runner. Sinead had left him. Again. He fought the urge to throw up. It was the gluten. Only the gluten.

'Find her.'

'I'll get onto it, boss,' Reilly told him.

'Thanks.' He hung up and barely made it to the bathroom.

Where the hell could she be?

He forced his muzzy brain to function. She had been talking about going to meet her sister who was supposed to be taking part in some sort of Domme thing with a Japanese businessman. Where was it? Oh yes, the St Pierre.

He had to get there. No saying what Sinead would get up to. She had lied to him so often his head was spinning. And it wasn't just from the gluten she had fed him.

Shit, could it have been deliberate? Could she really have fed him gluten to get him out of the way? He hated to think she would have done that but the evidence against her was stacking up.

What were the odds that there really was a sister who had stolen the Fire of Autumn? Damned ruby. Every time she told him the story, he ended up believing her, in spite of all the evidence that the sister couldn't exist. She was the most accomplished liar Niall had ever met. And still he wanted to believe her.

He couldn't decide what he wanted. If he went to St Pierre and found the long-lost sister, the identical twin who had stolen Sinead's life, then his case would be over. But if he found just Sinead, he thought his heart would break.

He thought about going back to bed. Or back to the bathroom to heave his guts out. Either would be preferable to having Sinead rip his heart out again.

Niall took a breath. Fuck it. There was only one way to resolve this. He would go.

He wasn't up to driving through Paris in the rain. He'd take the metro.

Wearing his usual jeans and leather jacket, Niall knew from the doorman's supercilious glance that he wasn't dressed for this hotel. He wasn't in any mood to care. His insides were still churning and his head throbbed.

'Excuse me,' he said to the desk clerk. 'I'm looking for a friend. She's visiting a guest here.'

The uniformed man was perfectly polite, but without a flicker of warmth. 'Of course, Monsieur, and the guest's name?'

'I don't know.'

'That's unfortunate. What is the visitor's name?'

Niall paused. What would Sinead have done? Well, one way to find out. 'Sinead O'Sullivan.'

The clerk shook his head. 'I'm sorry, Monsieur, no one of that name has been here today.'

'She might have forgotten to give her name.' Even as he said it, he realized how stupid it sounded. 'You'd remember her, she has bright red hair.'

Ah! Even as the clerk shook his head, Niall saw a glimmer of recognition pass over his face. 'I suggest you try elsewhere, she is not here.' A twitch of his finger brought the doorman over to the desk.

'Monsieur is leaving,' he said.

Damn it. Niall cursed under his breath as he considered his options. Clearly he was not getting in the front door. That was all right, hotels had more than one way in.

He went around the back, climbed over a wall and slipped into the kitchen. It was insanely busy, with chefs shouting and waiters flying around, but even so, someone was bound to notice a big blond Irishman sneaking through the kitchen. He dropped his leather jacket beside the back door, and found a large apron hanging on the wall. He pulled it over his head, picked up a cardboard box that might contain food, and marched into the kitchen. A couple of the sous-chefs gave him a quick look as he passed, but he kept his eyes on the far door and no one challenged him.

Once in the uncarpeted corridor, he dropped the box and headed for the service lift. He needed to know where Sinead was likely to be and that meant tracking down the Japanese businessman she planned to see.

Security in a hotel like the St Pierre was decent enough. Not impossible for him to crack, but he didn't want to break into every room. He took the lift to the next floor. With a bit of luck, that's where the offices were.

Bingo. This corridor had hard-wearing beige carpets and a row of offices with windowed doors. He walked quickly, looking into each office as he passed. The one he wanted had four computers and was manned by three middle-aged women who managed to drip chic even in uniform. One or even two, he might have been able to cope with, but three was too many.

Time to be crude. He opened the matchbook he had picked up at the front desk, lit one and held it up to the smoke alarm in the ceiling.

Ten seconds later, the fire alarm was ringing and the sprinkler system had activated.

'*Merde!*' He heard the women cursing, but obedient to hotel directives, they left, locking the door behind them.

It took Niall a whole thirty seconds to unlock it and slip into the empty office. One of the computers was still on, which saved him having to bypass the password. He began a rapid search of the hotel's guest list.

Twelve Japanese guests. But ten appeared to be part of a business delegation and all had rooms beside each other. He ruled those out. That left two possibilities.

Both had deluxe suites with views of the Eiffel Tower. And the room key data showed that only one was occupied right now.

Mr Takahashi in the Bizet Suite. Niall was on his way. And just to make life really easy, he found a master key-card that would open all doors.

The alarm had cut off and the noise from the far end of the corridor indicated that the staff were returning. He collected his jacket. Time to make himself scarce.

Room 786 might have been on a different planet. The plush carpet and understated luxury of the corridors were a world away from the offices and kitchens. The artwork on the walls looked original.

He opened the door with his card. 'Room Service,' he called as he let himself in. He carried a bottle of champagne he had snaffled from another suite on his way here.

A flash of red caught his attention. Sinead stood there holding a blue rubber ball teasingly above her head. 'Who's a precious boy then? Fetch it for mommy.'

He'd never heard her use an English accent before, but it sounded natural. She tossed the ball and a diminutive man wearing a grey tracksuit bounded after it.

Puppy play. And Sinead was handling it like a master. Or a mistress.

She looked up when he came into the room. Her hair was pulled back in an elaborate twist, her eyes were outlined with dark smoke and her mouth was a dramatic red, but it was unmistakably Sinead O'Sullivan.

But when she met his eyes, Niall knew. This woman was almost identical, but she wasn't Sinead. He wasn't even sure exactly how he knew.

It wasn't just the lack of recognition in those blue eyes. Or the uncharacteristic firmness of the carmine painted mouth. It was the whole package. This was a different woman.

Relief roared through Niall. Sinead had been telling the truth. This must be the elusive Roisin.

The man in the tracksuit brought the ball back to the woman who looked so much like Sinead. She petted his head. 'Good doggy,' she said and threw it again. Then she turned to Niall. 'You can put that bottle down over on that table, and then I'll give you a personal tip.' Her tone and look of appreciation left him in no doubt about what she meant.

'No, thanks,' he said pleasantly. 'I don't take tips from whores.'

There was a split second with no reaction, then her eyes widened. 'What?' He had to give her credit for maintaining her sang-froid. Her breathing barely altered until she noticed the casual clothes he was wearing beneath the waiter's jacket. 'You're not –'

'You've just ruined your sister's life, and here you are, playing puppy with this moron.'

She threw the ball again but Niall knew she was paying attention to him. 'At least she had a life. Pampered little princess. She got the icing – I didn't even get cake. Do you know what sort of life I've had?'

The ball rolled beside his foot. Niall picked it up and tossed it over the balcony. 'I don't give a fuck.'

She gave a gasp of outrage. 'Now look what you did. That was his favourite ball.' The man whined and she petted him. 'Don't worry about it, sweetie. I'm going to run you a nice bath now while I talk to the dog trainer.'

Mr Takahashi looked at him through narrowed eyes and growled, but Roisin smacked him on the behind. 'Bad doggie. No growling. Now go and get into the bath.' Reluctantly, he headed for the bathroom.

'Give me the Fire of Autumn and I'll get out of here.' There was a tiny shift of her eyes that told him she knew what he was talking about.

Yes! He felt another surge of relief: Sinead had been telling the truth all along.

'You'll never have to see me again. Of course, you may find the police don't take the same attitude, but hey, those are the breaks.'

341

'Who are you?' she demanded. Funny, the longer he spent with her, the less like Sinead she looked.

'I'm your future brother-in-law,' he said. He had no idea where that had come from but it was so obvious he couldn't understand how he hadn't known it the first time he met Sinead.

She narrowed her eyes. 'Oh great, the princess gets a babe for a fiancé and all I get is a dog grooming service.'

A whine from the bathroom punctuated her words. She hurried in and he heard the shower being turned on.

His phone rang. He didn't recognize the number but answered it. This was his private phone, the one only family and friends had access to. 'Hello?'

A voice he knew answered. 'Mr Moore, I have something of yours.' There was a pause before Sinead's voice said, 'Niall?'

That was all. Hall spoke again. 'If you want her back, I suggest you bring me the Fire of Autumn. And no delays or tricks, or little Red will pay the price.'

'Niall.' Sinead reached for the phone again but her hand didn't seem to work properly. She flexed her fingers. Stupid hand. She shook her head. What the hell had they injected her with?

The journey in the taxi had been a blur. Why hadn't she checked before she got into the cab? Stupid Sinead.

'Take her back to her room.' American voice. The same one as before. The one who had asked her questions about the stone.

Why couldn't she focus? And why had she tried to tell

them everything? Her sister. The stone. Even that she loved Niall. The words had tripped off her tongue as if she was drunk.

'She's pretty out of it, boss. How much of that stuff did you give her?'

'Enough. Now, take her upstairs.'

He half carried her up the flight of wooden stairs and tumbled her onto the narrow bed. Sleep. She couldn't sleep. Not now. Niall would be worried about her.

She remembered being outside the hairdressers. Clara's friend had taken longer to style her hair than she had planned and she was running late. The torrential autumn downpour had been unexpected. Pools of water had formed in the street where the drains were clogged with autumn leaves and the Paris streets were teeming with shoppers trying to find shelter.

She had stepped into the street looking for a taxi and one had pulled out from a space further up the street. Her last memory was sliding into the back seat and directing the driver to Hotel de St Pierre.

Her face came in contact with the pillow and her eyes closed. Just a few minutes. A little rest. That was all she needed.

'No. No resting.' She pinched her hand hard. Ouch. That woke her up a little and she stood up and swayed, catching the iron bedstead for support. Put one foot in front of the other. You can do it.

Sinead staggered to the door and rested her forehead against it. She fumbled at the handle and the door swung open. She felt laughter bubbling up and put her hand over her mouth. Focus. Downstairs, the radio was playing Lady

Gaga, masking the sound of her footsteps. She hesitated at the open doorway of the kitchen. A low murmur came from the tall one and an Australian twang from the other.

The front door loomed ahead and she staggered towards it.

'What the fuck? Grab her.'

After that, there was no contest. The blond one bared her arm and the prick of a needle told her she had been drugged again. Everything was spinning.

Spinning . . .

Roisin led Mr Takahashi out of the bathroom by the collar around his neck and pointed him at the bowls on the floor near the balcony.

Niall didn't think he made a sound, but she spun around and frowned at him. 'What is it? You look like you just tasted dog poop.'

Niall's brain was still frozen. It wasn't possible. Hall couldn't have Sinead. But that had been her voice. And Sinead was one of the few people who could have given Hall his private number.

Sinead was in danger. The realization made his skin tighten and chill.

God damn it, he was reluctant to go up against Hall, even on a good day. The SEALS were among the most elite spec-ops forces in the world. Every single one of them was a one-man army. When a SEAL went bad, the way Hall had, he was a disaster waiting to happen. And he had Sinead.

His lungs seized at the idea of Sinead in Hall's hands.

Hall was a hardened sadist, with the training to inflict heart-stopping amounts of pain without leaving a mark. He would break Sinead if Niall didn't bring him the ruby.

Around him, the world slowed while he considered his options. His job was to find the stone. Roisin had it. If he didn't deliver it, he would lose the contract, and likely the agency. But none of that mattered compared with knowing that Hall had Sinead.

There was no decision to make. It was simple. He loved Sinead. He had to get her back. No matter what it cost.

Niall turned his most commanding glare on Roisin. 'Where is the stone? I need it.'

She rolled her eyes at him. 'Like I'm going to give it to you. You have no idea how much I've gone through to get it. I'm keeping it.'

Her blue eyes were dismissive. She had no intention of helping him.

All his inhibitions about hurting women left him. Niall put his hand around her throat, not tight enough to stop her breathing, but more than enough to let her feel his strength, and forced her to look at him.

'Let me put it this way,' he said. 'Right now your sister is in the hands of the meanest son of a bitch on the planet. If you don't give me that stone, I'm going to do to you whatever that guy is doing to your sister.'

She continued to meet his eyes, but her breathing shortened. Still, she kept her voice even when she answered him. 'Dad always told me that bullies were just lonely little boys in need of a hug.'

He stared down at her. 'I don't care what you call me.

345

Your sister has been kidnapped and the only way to get her back is with the Fire of Autumn.'

She said nothing while she processed that.

'Tell me where it is,' Niall insisted.

A stiffness in her spine alerted him. She had it with her. Made sense, she wouldn't leave something like that behind her.

'Never mind, I'll find it myself.' He dropped her and examined the room. It was a standard hotel room, if luxuriously appointed and decorated. There was an extravagant fruit basket, pink tea roses spilling their scent into the air. There were two dog bowls on the ground, one full of water, or possibly white wine, and the other full of sashimi. Niall raised his eyebrows. This was a puppy with expensive tastes.

But nowhere to hide a large ruby.

On the floor beside the couch lay a long bag, the sort used by hockey players to carry their stick. And by Dommes to carry their whips. He picked it up, ignoring Roisin's protest, and spilled the contents on the couch.

A riding crop. A cane. A dressage whip. A heavy horsehair flogger. A light leather flogger. And a supple single-tail whip whose handle was encrusted with coloured stones. A large red stone finished the handle and glittered in the sunlight.

He didn't need her instinctive grab at it to tell him he was looking at the Fire of Autumn. He lifted it up above her head, out of her reach. 'I'm taking this.'

'No, you're not. I need it. It's mine.'

Was she out of her mind? 'Your sister is in danger and this is what will buy her safety.'

'I need it more.' The grim set of her mouth told him she wasn't joking. 'I'm not letting it out of my sight.'

Whatever was driving her wasn't simple greed. Damn it, that was all he needed, a civilian getting in his way. He picked up his phone and briefed Andy on the situation. He promised to be over as soon as possible.

Then he called Hall back. 'I have the stone, and I'm prepared to give it to you. On condition that Sinead is not hurt in any way. If there is so much as a scratch on her, all bets are off.'

Hall laughed. 'Good boy. I do like a man who can obey orders.' Niall fought to hold onto his temper. He knew the other man was deliberately trying to make him lose control. 'Take it to the statue of the Virgin and Child in Notre Dame by 13.30. No police and no tricks, or you know what will happen.' He hung up before Niall could answer.

He glanced at his watch. Damn, this was cutting it tight. He shoved the whip into his pocket and headed for the door.

'Come back,' Roisin yelled. He ignored her.

'Wait for me.' She grabbed a pale macintosh from the back of the couch and pulled it on. Then she was beside him, holding his arm and refusing to let go. Damn it, he didn't have the time to deal with this.

'Woof,' said Mr Takahashi, in a questioning bark.

Niall ignored him. He headed for the lift, moving at a pace just short of a run with Roisin holding on tightly.

As the high-speed lift headed for the foyer, he considered his options. The timing was too tight to take chances.

347

'You might want to let go now,' he told Roisin. 'I'm going on foot and I'll be running.'

Her grip on his arm didn't loosen. 'Do I look like a cripple? I can run.' Beneath the mac, her thigh-high boots were covered with spikes and her figure-hugging catsuit was eye catching, but they were both serviceable.

'Not the way I do.' As soon as they were outside the hotel, he set off, heading for Notre Dame. He dodged through traffic to get across roads and wove his way through pedestrians on the footpath. His shadow kept pace with him. As they got closer, the crowds of tourists got thicker. He headed for a gap in a group and almost ran over two children feeding the pigeons grain from their hands.

'Sorry,' he said, and kept going.

Roisin grabbed a handful of grain as she went past and scattered it. The pigeons dived for the bounty and the grain seller shouted angrily at her.

'You're a damned trouble-maker,' Niall told her.

She grinned. 'More trouble than you can handle, that's for sure.'

He had to fight his way through a group of Americans clustered around a tour guide outside the cathedral. 'Remember this is a church, people will be praying. Be respectful and quiet and no photographs.'

Inside, his eyes took a couple of seconds to adjust to the dimness. He didn't have time to appreciate the soaring ceilings and incense-scented air. He had to find the statue where Hall was waiting. At the other end of the building, a choir was singing in plain chant. A priest was lighting candles on the main altar. It was a world away from stolen gems and threats of violence. Niall checked his watch. He had two minutes to spare.

He jogged around the perimeter of the church, checking the statues around the outside of the central space. Finally he saw the one he wanted.

The chapel it was in was deserted. There was no sign of Hall or Sinead. Wiping sweat off his forehead, he brought his breath under control and waited to see who would come. Two elderly American tourists stood, debating whether to tip the priest, and that was all.

He phoned Hall. There was no reply, but seconds later he got a text. 'Good boy, you're doing well, but you didn't think it was going to be that easy, did you? Be on the third floor of the Eiffel tower at 14.15.'

30

Niall knew exactly what Hall was doing. He would make him run all over the city, preventing him from setting up any sort of trap. And he had no choice but to go along with it.

'I hope you're in good shape, Red,' he said. 'We have more running to do.'

Outside, a row of bikes caught his eye. That would be faster. He keyed in the details and grabbed one. The saddle was too low, but he didn't stop to adjust it, just plunged into the maelstrom of Paris traffic, and headed straight for the Eiffel tower. He ignored the signs for one way streets and traffic lights and concentrated on getting there as quickly as possible.

On the way, he called Andy and told him to meet him there. Behind him, Roisin followed. She was on a bike, but it wasn't a Vélib'. He was pretty sure that she had stolen it.

From close up, the tower stood impossibly high, and the queue for the lifts snaked around the entire base. There must be close to a thousand people there. Damn it, he didn't have authority to get in ahead of the crowd, and couldn't afford to wait.

He dropped the bike and headed for the ticket booth on the South tower. Andy was there, holding two foot tickets. 'Way ahead of you, boss,' he said, grinning, then did a double take when he saw Roisin. She grabbed Andy's ticket and followed Niall right up the stairs. Behind him, Andy cursed a blue streak and headed back to the ticket booth to buy another one.

The stairs went on forever. Niall ran up them, his lungs heaving. They went in groups of twenty-five. Landing, twenty-five steps. Landing, twenty-five. Landing, twenty-five. Landing, twenty-five. Turn and up the next side of the tower. He pushed past tourists pretending to admire the view while trying to catch their breath. Roisin and Andy were at his back when he reached the first landing. He kept going, building a rhythm of stairs, landing, stairs, turn.

At the second landing, the stairs stopped. He had to go onto the platform and dodge workmen setting up an ice-skating rink. He followed a group of children clutching green Eiffel tower lollipops and found the closed-off stairs that led up to the third floor. He hopped over the gate and climbed.

He was wet with sweat and his breath laboured. 1,600 steps done and at least another hundred to go. He didn't have time to rest. He only had three minutes to get to the next floor. He forced his legs to move faster.

The third landing was cold and windy and he could feel the entire tower swaying. The lift stopped, disgorging twenty tourists, all chattering in different languages. Some compared the dramatic landscape visible from here to the maps in their hands. Two teenagers carried glass figurines of the tower that flashed different colours when they were switched on. A man and woman with Irish accents clutched the hand of four red-haired children, and the mother wore a sling across her chest. Another red head peered out with huge baby eyes.

None of them looked like Hall or his henchmen. Damn it.

Niall's phone beeped as a text arrived. 'Good boy. I admire punctuality. Now go to Place Denfert-Rochereau and be there by 16.00. And bring the stone. Red is not feeling too well.'

Fuck. Niall leaned against the railing, allowing the cold metal to echo the chill in his guts. Hall did have someone watching him.

Andy and Roisin appeared on the landing, wheezing with the effort of the climb. 'It's another dead end. He's going to run us all around the city. We have to go now.' He headed for the stairs, ready to go down. Andy grabbed his arm.

'We can get the lift down without a ticket.'

As the lift dropped down the shaft, Niall closed his eyes and breathed a silent prayer. Please don't let him be too late.

. . . Spinning.

The camp was a blur as Dada spun her around and around. His red hair flew out around his head when he laughed up at her.

'Me now, Dada. It's my turn now.' Roro tugged at his leg.

It wasn't fair. Dada was taking Roro with him on the boat while she had to stay at home with Mammy. The other children in the camp were smelly; she didn't like playing with them.

'Give your sister a chance, Roisin. It's nearly time for us to go.' He set her down on the grass and she swayed, tumbling in a dizzy heap amongst the daisies.

'Big kiss goodbye and we'll be off. I promise I'll bring you back a nice birthday present for looking after your mammy.'

Her sister's mouth was wet and sticky.

'Ugh,' Sinead pushed her away and they both giggled. 'Bye, Roro.'

She stood with her mammy watching the van go down the country lane. It went very fast. She pulled a dandelion from the grass beside the stony road and blew. The seeds caught on the wind and flew into the air. They mixed with the smoke from the back of Dada's van.

Her mammy rubbed her belly. Dada said that they would be getting a new baby. When Roro said she wanted a black one, Mammy had laughed.

'Go and play, Sinead. Mammy has a pain and needs to lie down for a while.'

Sinead nodded. She knew Mammy had a pain because she was very cross and her face was red all morning. She had slapped Roro on the leg when she said there was blue stuff on the bread again.

Sinead pushed through the gate into the back garden and walked through the high grass until she reached the swing. She pushed off from the ground and swung her legs. She threw her head back. She could see the blue in the sky. The blue went on forever. The wind made her hair fly around.

When she swung her legs up really high, she could see a hole in her sock. Mammy would be cross again. There was no money for socks. There was never any money. That was why Dada was gone in the van with Roro. To get some.

Her tummy growled. It sounded just like the puppies that slept in the broken greenhouse where they grew the special plants. She giggled. That was funny. Sinead climbed off the swing and made her way to the rhubarb patch at the end of the garden. The leaves were tall, almost as tall as she was. Sometimes she hid here with Roro. Sinead picked a stem and bit into it. The sour taste filled her mouth and she spat it into the grass. She needed sugar.

She carried the rhubarb into the caravan. Mammy wasn't there. She must have gone to see Myra the fortune lady in the next caravan. She climbed on a chair so that she could reach the shelf. The sugar bowl was orange and shiny. With careful hands, she lifted it from the shelf and put it on the table. Then she climbed from the chair. She dunked the rhubarb into the sugar and licked. It was nice.

She sat on the chair. Swinging her legs, she dunked and ate until the stem was gone.

She was still hungry.

Her hands were sticky as she carried the bowl of sugar outside and made her way to the end of the garden. She pulled up another pink stem and sat beneath the canopy of leaves.

She heard a loud noise outside and she froze. It was the police coming. Dada had warned them about the police. He said they were pigs. All Dada's friends hated the police too. If they came, she and Roro had to hide. She raced down the path, past the broken cars, towards the woods.

The sirens grew louder and then suddenly stopped. In the distance a man was shouting. 'Leave her alone, she's fine.'

'Ah, shut up, Murphy. She's needs to go to hospital.' It sounded like Myra.

Sinead kept running.

She ran until she found the hide and crawled inside, pulling the leaves and branches into place so no one would find her. Her tummy hurt. She shouldn't have eaten the green stuff, only the red. Mammy would be cross. She felt sleepy. She let her eyes close.

A large drop of rain hitting her nose woke her. She was shivering. She stood up and pushed the branches aside to watch the drops.

She hated the rain. It made scary noises on the roof of the caravan at night. Sometimes she thought it was monsters trying to get inside. Roro said that was silly.

When the rain stopped, she crawled out and went back up the path. As she passed the greenhouses she heard crying. The puppies.

One yellow bundle of fur sat outside the greenhouse. He was crying extra loud. Poor puppy. She called him, but he ran into the woods. She didn't follow him. She kept going. When Sinead climbed through the gap in the hedge, all of the vans were gone and all the people. All of the other caravans were gone, apart from the old one that had no wheels, and the one she lived in.

Three brown hens raced across the open space. Their wire run was broken and the cockerel was loose. She didn't like the big black bird, so she ran.

She saw that the door to their caravan was open. Sinead climbed the steps and went inside. 'Mammy,' she shouted. 'Where are you, Mammy?'

Mammy wasn't there. She pushed open the door to the room where she slept with Dada. It was empty. The drawers were all open and their stuff was on the floor. Yucky big flies buzzed in her face and she hit them away. The smell made her tummy ache. She closed the door behind her.

Where was everyone? Maybe the policemen took them away.

'Mammy,' she shouted, but she could only hear her own voice. Sinead went outside again, shouting louder this time. 'Mammy. Mammy. Mammy.'

But no one was there. Mammy was gone. Everyone was gone.

The next morning she waited for ages, but no one came back. There was a big black rat in Mammy's room. She couldn't go inside to get clean clothes so she wore the same ones again. Mammy said not to ever touch the cooker, so she didn't. She had cornflakes for

355

breakfast and for lunch, but they were almost gone. All day she wandered around, but it was no fun without Roro. She played with the puppies for a while. They were cuddly. At teatime she went to the allotment and ate some berries. The hens were in the vegetable garden. The black cockerel made noises at her every time she passed.

It got dark again and still no one came back. The rustling of the wind in the trees was scary. She sat on the couch eating the cornflakes. She shook out the box and ate the crumbs too. She fell asleep.

The next morning she woke when she heard a car outside. Then she heard voices. A man was saying, 'It's something my mam wanted to do. Thank you for bringing us.' And then another one said, 'I'm sorry we can't find out more about what happened. But everyone from the site has gone.'

Sinead wiped her hands on her legs and got off the couch to open the door. It was a big blue policeman. Like the ones her daddy called the 'pigs' and 'bastards'. He must have come to take her away. Like everyone else. At least she would see her mammy again.

A woman in a red cardigan came past the blue man. 'Jesus Mary and Joseph, there's a child here. What's your name, child?'

Sinead twisted the hem of her dress between her fingers, wishing they would stop staring at her. 'Sh-Sh-Sinead O'Sullivan,' she replied.

The woman lifted her up and burst into tears.

Sinead stayed as still as she could for a moment and then wriggled. She wanted to get away. But the woman held on tight.

The blue man and another man went into the caravan. She watched them from the woman's arms. Her blanket was on the floor beside the empty cornflakes box. The rat from Mammy's room was eating the crumbs on the couch.

'Sweet mother of Jesus,' the other man shouted. 'How in the name of Christ could they leave a child in a place like this?'

The man had eyes just like Mammy's.

The blue man took out a notebook. 'Mrs O'Sullivan, are you a relative of this child?'

The woman tightened her arms around her. She kissed her forehead and looked into her eyes. 'I'm your grandmother, child, and this is your Uncle Tim,' she said. 'You're coming home with us.'

Sinead's head jerked as the second slap to her cheek brought her abruptly out of her dream.

'I think she's coming round now, boss. I told you that you gave her too much of that stuff.'

'Get her up and ready. We leave in thirty minutes.'

Rough hands pulled her to her feet and she swayed unsteadily. Her mouth was as dry as the Sahara. She needed water. The dream had been so real, so vivid. Roro, her mother and the squalid little caravan in Mayo where she had spent the first four years of her life.

'Bathroom?' she croaked.

A muscular blond propelled her forwards to the landing and pointed to a brown door. The smell of his cologne triggered a memory. This must be the Max who had carried her out of the van when she had been taken from Gabriel's home.

The room had seen better days. The mirror was cracked and the tiny sink was stained brown with watermarks. She used the facilities and splashed cold water on her face. She was pale and hollow-eyed. Her hair was a tangled mess. If Niall saw her looking like this, he would probably give her back to the kidnappers.

A thud came on the door. 'Hurry up. We're leaving.'

She opened the door and he stood back to allow her to

precede him down the stairs to where another man was waiting in an old-fashioned sitting room. He flashed his teeth in a tight smile that didn't meet his eyes. How could a man who was so handsome have eyes so cold, Sinead wondered.

'So you are awake,' he remarked. 'Which one are you?' He looked her over carefully, taking in every detail. Those cold green eyes lingered on her hands and unpainted nails. 'Let me guess, you're the librarian.'

'Curator,' she snapped.

He shrugged. 'Same difference. Imagine my surprise to find out there were two of you. And both hot in a red-headed kind of way.'

Her breath caught. His expression was a combination of sadistic amusement and lust. All her female instincts went on alert. 'You have an advantage over me. I don't believe we've been introduced.' She was aware she sounded like Granny O'Sullivan at her worst, but she wasn't going to let this monster know how much he scared her.

He laughed and made a half bow in her direction. 'You don't need to know who I am.' He gestured to her to sit down.

Reluctantly, she took a straight-backed chair as far away from him as she could manage. He waited until she was sitting before he lounged on the couch.

This had to be the elusive J. Darren Hall that Niall and Andy had been talking about, the one that had fought with Niall in the RER station. The fact that he was allowing her to see his face sent a chill through her. She had seen enough crime dramas to know this wasn't a good sign.

'What do you want?' she asked. Get him talking, maybe he'd let something slip.

He laughed. 'As if you didn't know. I want that ruby, the Fire of Autumn.'

'I don't have it.' At least she could say that with complete truth.

'I know that. I already searched you. But if you don't, your sister does.'

She shivered at the thought of those hands on her body, but something he said caught her attention. 'How do you know I have a sister?' She had spent years trying to convince people that Roisin existed and now this – this psychopath just took it for granted.

'Your cross-dressing pervert friend told me all about it.'

For a moment, she scrabbled to work out who he could mean. 'Clara? Clara wouldn't tell you anything.'

He crossed one leg over the other. She couldn't help noticing the muscle in those long thighs. 'Is that his name? He was a little reluctant, but it's amazing how easily a knife to the nuts can loosen a tongue.'

'Did you hurt her?'

He laughed. 'Her? Oh, I have proof that fucking pervert is a man where it counts, and he's still fond of his tackle. He put up a good fight, I'll give him that, but he could have saved himself a lot of blood if he had told me what I wanted to know when I first asked. How do you think I knew where to find you?'

'How badly is Clara hurt?'

Hall shrugged. 'He'll probably live.'

Oh god, no. Gabriel, Niall and now Clara. Everyone

who came into contact with her seemed to get hurt. If she had stayed in Geneva, instead of running off to Paris to find her sister, none of it would have happened. She hadn't done it, but they were all hurt because they were involved with her.

Anger rose in her, keeping her fear at bay. 'Do you hurt everyone you meet?'

He smirked at her. 'Oh no. I'm very good to people who please me. And if you find me the ruby, you'll please me a lot.'

'In your dreams. I'm not giving you the Fire of Autumn.'

'No, your boyfriend will, if he wants to see you again. And if you misbehave, I'll kill him. It's not as if I need him for anything once I have the ruby.'

Sinead swallowed. She had no doubt that he meant every word.

'Do you understand?'

'Yes.' She nodded.

'Then get in the car.'

It was late afternoon as they drove through the Paris streets. Her favourite city in the world was turning into a nightmare. They parked behind a tour bus on Place Denfert-Rochereau and the driver switched off the engine. 'Last tour is at 4pm, boss.'

The blond glanced at his diver's watch and nodded. 'Remember what I told you, Red.'

She nodded. She had dragged Niall into this. There was no way that she wanted him to be hurt. They followed the tourists emerging from the bus and merged into the crowd filing into the catacombs.

'Ladies and gentlemen, *Mesdames et Messieurs*, we will

shortly begin our tour of the catacombs. Please note that there are no bathrooms or other facilities here and our visit will last approximately one hour.'

Sinead looked around her. There was no sign of Niall or Andy. Where were they going? As they descended a narrow spiral stone staircase into the darkness, the silence was broken by the sound of dripping water and the occasional cough from one of the tourists.

After what seemed like an age, the passageway opened out and they stopped before a stone portal over which were inscribed the words '*Arrête! C'est ici l'empire de la Mort.*'

'Stop! Here lies the Empire of Death,' Sinead translated. She only hoped that it wouldn't prove true.

The tour guide continued, '*L'Ossuaire Municipal* holds the remains of more than six million people. Opened in the late eighteenth century it has been a tourist attraction since 1874. On your right you can see . . .'

They followed the shuffling crowd of elderly tourists along the dark passageways of the catacombs. When a bespectacled man ventured down a poorly lit path he was cautioned by the guide. 'Monsieur, I would ask you to stay with the group. Philibert Aspairt was lost in the catacombs in 1793 and not found for eleven years. We will see his tomb later.'

That drew an uneasy laugh and there were no further attempts to wander. They paused at a semi-circular wall made from skulls and femurs arranged in rows with a stone cross set into the middle. Sinead shivered.

The tour guide rambled on, 'Since their opening, these passageways have been used by the communards in the nineteenth century and members of the French Resistance during World War Two.'

Further on, they filed past a rusting gate guarding a dark passageway. More endless passageways led off in different directions; someone could be lost here for years. Is this what Hall had planned for them when he got his hands on the stone? She risked another glance at her fellow tourists – a mix of wealthy Swiss, Germans and Americans. Not one of them was under sixty. She couldn't count on them for help.

Hall appeared to be perfectly relaxed, he might have been a tourist enjoying a holiday, but the slight bulge in the pocket of his jacket told her differently. Hall was armed.

Sinead glanced at her watch. They had been here almost forty-five minutes. The place would be closing soon. She checked the crowd again. There was no sign of Hall's buddy. When she risked a sideways glance, Hall draped an arm around her shoulders as if in a lovers' embrace.

'Don't try anything,' he murmured against her hair.

31

Niall looked around. Why had Hall sent him here? It was a nondescript Parisian square, with an elaborate metro station and a couple of official looking buildings on the other side of the green. There was nothing remarkable except a tour bus parked under a tree. Fuck Hall. He was laughing himself sick watching Niall run ragged around Paris while he had Sinead all to himself.

The thought of Sinead at Hall's mercy made him feel nauseous. Now he understood why doctors were not allowed to operate on family members. He was ice-cold during an operation, able to balance risk and reward analytically. Of course he knew what would happen if the op went wrong, but it didn't affect his planning. Now all he could think of was the ruined face of Gabriel Bertrand. Hall would do that, and more, to Sinead if Niall didn't get there in time.

'This is a dead end. Give me back my whip,' Roisin demanded. Damn, she was like a burr, sticking to him no matter where he went or what he did. With a detached part of his mind, he wondered how she kept in shape. He and Andy had been trained by the Irish Ranger Wing to be able to run for hours in all conditions, and they were sweating and panting. Roisin's skin was flushed and sweaty strands of hair straggled down her neck, but she was coping.

'When Sinead is safe, you can have it.'

Giving away that stone could well end his career, but he didn't care. The only thing that mattered was getting Sinead back safely.

His phone beeped. 'Good boy. Now get down.'

Niall snarled silently. 'He's fucking with us,' he said, showing Andy the text message.

'Or maybe not. Look over there.' A small sign said '*Catacombes de Paris.*'

That made sense. The catacombs went on for miles, and whoever got there first had the advantage of picking the spot for the handover.

The little kiosk selling tickets looked old, but the credit card machine was modern. The bored attendant pointed at a spiral staircase and went back to watching Jack Winter playing Superman on the television.

This was it. All his instincts told him that now they would meet Hall. 'Are you carrying?' he asked Andy.

His second-in-command snorted. 'Are you kidding? I've got a torch and a night-watch stick. That's all I'm permitted to carry in France.'

Grimly, Niall nodded. He didn't even have that. He would have to depend on his training and strength. And ignore the throb from his recent injuries and the nausea from his breakfast. 'Let's go.'

He led the way down the stone staircase that wound its way into the bowels of Paris. Halfway down, he got another text. 'Meet you at the tomb of Philibert Aspairt.'

As he descended, the bars on his phone disappeared. No calling for help now. They were on their own against Hall and his men. The only priority here was getting

Sinead back safely. And, he realized, keeping Roisin safe as well. She might be an immoral thief, but she was a civilian, and had no business going up against a psychopath like Hall.

'Andy, your job is to keep Roisin out of trouble.' He didn't bother looking back over his shoulder as he spoke. He could hear the pair of them bickering behind him. He ignored the curse under Andy's breath, but Roisin didn't.

'And the same to you, asshole.'

The stairs ended and the tunnel stretched out in front of them, silent except for the gurgle of water. He followed the signs and headed down the unpaved tunnel. It was warmer than he had expected, and electric lights picked up the dull sheen of bones.

A large circular cavern was lined with bones, piled neatly from floor to ceiling. A row of grinning skulls watched from amid the piles of femurs.

Roisin muttered, 'Bloody hell,' in a subdued voice. Finally, something that silenced her. But Niall himself was unsettled by the thousands of bones in this chamber alone.

He pressed on, hearing voices ahead of him. A tour group was plodding along, discussing last night's television, the price of eating in Paris and occasionally remarking on the bones that lined every wall.

Niall pushed past them, heading for the tomb of Philibert Aspairt.

'Monsieur, be sure you do not get lost,' the tour guide shouted after him, but he kept going.

The tunnel opened out into another bone-lined cavern, this one with a thick column of bones in the centre. Just how many people were buried down here? Millions, he suspected.

He found the exit and kept going, with Andy and Roisin following.

Something, a change in the air, a half-heard sound, alerted him. He flattened himself against the wall, and listened. Nothing. But he knew Sinead was near. The tomb of Aspairt, who took getting lost to a whole new level, was near. He merged with the shadows and approached soundlessly.

The stone marking Aspairt's death was deserted, but within sight of it was a padlocked gate. That was where Sinead was. Niall knew it. And if Sinead was there, so was Hall. He longed to kill the bastard, but Sinead was more important. It didn't matter what he wanted, this was about getting Sinead out safely.

He hand signalled Andy to stay where he was, and broke cover. He walked forwards boldly.

At the tomb, he stopped and waited. His back itched. He knew, just knew, there was at least one gun pointing at him. Sweat trickled down his back, but he kept his face bored. 'Are we done playing hide and seek, or are you finally going to show yourself?' he asked the air.

'Hands in the air,' Hall told him.

Niall obeyed.

He turned slowly, carefully, and saw Hall and two goons in the short tunnel behind the gate. Sinead was there too, looking eerily like Roisin in a red catsuit and with her hair slicked back into a sleek hairstyle that showed the dramatic bones of her face. And the large bruise on her right cheek.

Rage boiled up and, despite himself, his fists clenched. They had hurt her.

Hall's SIG Sauer pistol was aimed at him, and one of the goons, a thickly muscled blond, held a similar one pointed at Sinead.

'You couldn't have sent a SWAT team, could you?' Sinead asked him, as if they were the only ones there. 'You had to come yourself, without any backup.'

'Living on the edge,' he agreed.

'Next time, I'm looking for a man with a brain, not just a pretty face, muscles and long hair.' Her words were pure bravado but he heard the tremble in her voice.

'Don't forget the ten inch cock,' he said.

She gasped. 'It is not ten inches.'

'You never measured it.'

Hall cut across him. 'Enough with the billing and cooing. Have you got the Fire of Autumn?'

Niall nodded.

'Toss it on the ground.'

'Can I take my hands down? My ten inch cock is not prehensile,' he said.

'Fucking comedian,' Hall said. 'Take your hands down and toss the stone on the ground. And remember I have a gun on you, and my friend has one on your little slut.' It was a deliberate taunt, designed to anger him.

He would pay for that.

Niall lowered his arms and slowly took the whip out of his pocket. He held it up so the light glittered on the stone in the handle, and heard Sinead suck in her breath. She recognized it. He threw it on the ground, close by his feet. Let's see what Hall did now.

'Hands back in the air.'

Niall obeyed.

'Okay Red, go and fetch the whip. And remember that I have a gun on your boyfriend.'

'Does he look like anyone's boyfriend?' she snapped. God, he loved that she still had her wits and spirit, even in the hands of a certified loony like Hall. She walked towards him, her eyes on his face.

'Did you find her?' she whispered.

'Yes, she had it.'

Sinead crouched down to pick up the whip, glancing briefly at the stone that had caused so much trouble for her. 'I want to meet her.'

'I'll introduce you.' They might have been talking about the weather. Both of them knew they might die at any moment.

Hall interrupted. 'Back here, Red. Now!'

Slowly, Sinead turned away from him, back to the tunnel where Hall and his men were sheltered. Niall saw Hall's eyes flicker from him to the fiery ruby for a split second.

That was all he needed. He launched himself at the American, not caring that he might well get shot. Hall wasn't going to leave witnesses, Niall knew it.

A bullet whirred past him, leaving a streak of pain along his shoulder. Not enough to slow him down. He hit Hall with a rugby tackle, taking him to the ground and his gun with him.

The two of them grappled, struggling to get the upper hand, fighting for grip and pressure points. Niall wedged his forearm under Hall's chin, forcing his head back, but Hall grabbed his nuts and squeezed.

He twisted to break his grip, and hooked his leg around Hall's. This time, he wouldn't let go. Hall had gone too far. He had pointed a gun at Sinead, and that was unforgivable.

Hall slammed his head into the ground, causing his vision to black over for vital seconds. He groped and found Hall's head, then aimed his fingers at his eyes.

When his vision cleared, Hall had a knife in his right hand. Fuck. Where had that come from? He grabbed his forearm, holding on tightly to prevent that lethal knife from getting too close to him. His shoulder burnt and blood made his grip slippery. He and Hall twisted, as close as lovers as they fought for the upper hand.

Somewhere in the background, old ladies screamed. The minute distraction was enough and Niall lashed out, knocking the knife from Hall's grasp.

Sinead bit her lip as a woman in a floral dress screamed again. The tall Englishman held onto her but Max had pulled a gun and pointed it at the corner where Niall and Hall were fighting. He moved around, trying to aim, but the two men struggling on the ground were moving so fast that he couldn't risk firing.

With the knife gone, Hall had acquired another weapon, a blackened bone from the ossuary. He swung, and the bone walloped into Niall's head.

Niall hissed, and a gash opened on his scalp. Blood

flowed, obscuring his face and getting into his eyes. How could he fight when he couldn't see what he was doing? He used one forearm to wipe the blood from his face. The pause allowed Max to take aim at him.

She had to help him.

Squirming in her captor's grasp, Sinead bit down on his hairy wrist and he roared and released her. She couldn't let Max kill Niall. Not now. Not when they had found each other again.

The man who had been holding her reached for her but she caught a glimpse of something glittering on the floor – her sister's whip. She ducked down from his grasp and snatched at it. Missed. How could she miss?

Sinead realized that her brain was still foggy from the drug they had pumped into her. She focused. She couldn't miss this time. Lunge, grab, got it. *Please god let me be able to use it.*

When she was upright again, the fight had progressed. Niall and Hall were grappling again. Hall had regained his knife and Niall was struggling to hold it away from his neck.

Max had moved again, lining up his shot. He cocked the gun.

The dark man who had been holding Sinead reached for her and grabbed her right wrist. His grip was so strong she could not hold the whip. She caught it with her left hand.

Niall was on top now, slamming Hall's hand into the ground, and Max had a clear shot.

Fuzzy brain or not, she had no choice.

Sinead flicked the whip as precisely as she could. In agonizing slow motion, the lash moved out. It seemed that Max had endless time to avoid it as it took so long to arrive. Finally, finally, it went where she had aimed it and hit Max on the wrist.

He howled, dropping the gun and clutching his wrist. The gun discharged as it hit the ground.

Time resumed its normal speed.

The screams of the tourists echoed around the chamber.

Sinead kicked back, her spike heels raking down the shin of her captor. He cursed and his grip loosened. Too bad for him. In her hands, a single-tail whip was a weapon and she was ready to use it again. She struck out.

Niall was vaguely aware of movement above him. A gun being cocked. He braced himself, as if a tense muscle was any defence against a 9mm bullet. Hall had his hand around Niall's windpipe, tightening it.

There was a flash, a loud crack. '*Merde!*' someone yelped. A gun slid along the ground, landing beside him. He didn't waste time wondering where it came from. He grabbed it and pointed it at the side of Hall's head.

'Game over,' he panted.

Hall went rigid. He knew when he stared death in the face. It would take no more than a twitch of Niall's finger.

Then Andy was holding a gun on the group. 'Hands in the air.'

Still pointing his own gun at Hall's head, Niall backed away.

Sinead was there, holding the whip in a businesslike grip, and the blond gorilla was nursing his hand. A red welt marked the back of it. The tall, dark-haired man had a matching welt on his face.

'Did you do that?' he asked Sinead.

'Yes.' Her voice quivered a little. 'He was going to shoot you.'

'God, I love you.' It wasn't how he had meant to say it, but, hell, it was true, and he didn't care who knew it. Carefully, never letting up the pressure on Hall's skull, he levered himself to his feet.

'Roisin,' he called. 'Come and tie Hall up. Something tells me you're very good at knots.'

She came forwards, pulling the long leather thong from her hair. As she knelt beside Hall, she got her first good look at him and recoiled. 'You!'

'What is it?' Sinead asked. She still held her whip like a weapon.

'I saw him kill someone.'

He saw Hall's eyes meet hers and Roisin flinch. She rallied and tied his hands behind his back, ruthlessly tightening the thong until the circulation was almost cut off.

'Who?'

Before she could answer, a voice shouted from the passageway. '*C'est la police. Déposez vos armes.*'

'Fuck,' Hall spat.

Sinead quickly wrapped the tail of the whip tightly around the handle. She couldn't lose the Fire now. It was the only way of getting her life back. She crammed it inside her catsuit and zipped it up.

'Sinead, get on the ground and stay there.' Niall's voice cut through the anxious cries.

She obeyed without thinking, dropping to a crouch. After that, there was chaos – men shouting, the tramping of heavy boots on flagstones and flashes of green light.

Moments later, the emergency lights came on, bathing the catacombs in an eerie light. A row of skulls grinned at her from only feet away.

'*Déplacez-vous à l'extérieur s'il vous plaît*. Move outside please.'

The traumatized group hurried to obey the armed policeman's order. Sinead looked around her. On the far side of the cavern, Niall stood talking to a pair of men wearing riot gear. He gave his report calmly while the men nodded. They might have been discussing the weather.

Ignoring a shouted warning, Sinead crossed the room and threw her arms around him. He was bloody and bruised, but alive. 'Thank god you're okay.'

Niall took her mouth in a fierce kiss. 'I'll tan your hide when I get you home.'

'Yes, please.' She grinned up at him.

'*Madame, s'il vous plaît*. You must come with me now.'

The policeman took her arm and led her through the passageways, up the steep stairway and into the night. She drew in a lungful of air. A small crowd had gathered, drawn by the flashing lights and the sirens. It wasn't every day there was a shooting in the catacombs. Trying to look nonchalant, she took a seat in the waiting police van and craned her neck, trying to see Niall and Andy emerging from the catacombs.

She was in a heap of trouble but they were alive. Nothing else mattered. The van pulled away, jerking her back against the headrest.

Sitting in the seat opposite was her sister.

32

'You,' Roisin snapped.

'I might say the same to you, sister.' Sinead sat up straight in her seat, ready to do battle. How dare she talk to her like this? Roisin had wrecked her life and now she was giving her dirty looks, as if she was the injured sister?

Roisin ignored the interested looks of the other passengers. 'Where's that arrogant ass boyfriend of yours? This wasn't part of the deal. Tell him I want out of here.'

Even with the different accents, their voices were similar. While hers had a hint of Irish, Roisin's was English. London, if she wasn't mistaken.

She stared at her twin's face. The similarities were uncanny, but Roisin's cheekbones were stronger and her mouth was different. When she lifted her hand to her mouth and bit the nail of her index finger, Sinead could see that her teeth were slightly crooked, with a small overbite. Well, that was one way of telling them apart. She half smiled but Roisin didn't smile back. If anything, she looked pissed off.

Sinead struggled to contain her temper. This was nothing like the reunion she had imagined. Hugs, tears, lots of 'I missed you so much', but not the scowling woman sitting across the aisle from her.

This wasn't the Roro of her dreams. This was a thief and a liar. She had stolen the Fire of Autumn and her life and she didn't even have the decency to apologize. 'Nice to meet you again. How long has it been? Twenty years? More?'

Rosin sat up in her seat. 'Is that all? It seems like a century. I'm sick of Dad boring me about how wonderful your life is.'

'Really?' Sinead didn't bother to keep the sarcasm from her voice. 'So you felt it necessary to ruin it?'

'You bet. It's amazing what you can find out on the internet – if you're interested. Perfect little princess Sinead. Rich uncle who owns an airline. Posh job at the museum. Yada yada yada.'

Sinead kept her voice low with an effort. 'If you knew who I was, why didn't you contact me? You knew more about me than I knew about you. At least you knew I was alive. Do you have any idea what it was like when no one would believe you existed? I thought I was going crazy.'

'You did?'

'I kept telling them about you, and everyone told me I was imagining you. I almost started to believe them.'

Roisin's face didn't soften. 'Oh yeah? Well, boo fucking hoo. I was on the run with Dad most of the time. I went to fifteen different schools under four different names.'

The venom in Roisin's voice stunned her.

'You should have contacted me. I could have helped you.' She had no doubt the O'Sullivans would have taken Roisin in.

'Yeah? Sure you would. You were always the favourite. The one Mammy wanted to keep with her. She begged Dad to take me away.'

Sinead had been so obsessed with finding Roisin, she

hadn't thought any further. Now she did. 'Dada? Where is he?'

Roisin's eyes slid away from hers. 'None of your business. I'm taking care of it.'

'Tell me, please.' She had a father. Sinead had to know more.

Roisin looked bored. 'He's in prison. Can you believe his hard drive crashed on one of his computer scams and he got caught?'

'Computer scams?' Sinead winced.

'Sure, if you know what you're doing, you can make computers do anything for you.'

Something clicked into place. 'Like find the access code for the Rheinbach's security system?'

Roisin grinned. 'That job was fun. It was a real challenge, dressing up like you and then cracking their system.'

'Fun?' Sinead couldn't believe it. 'You stole the Fire of Autumn for fun?' Roisin nodded. 'How did you not leave fingerprints? Even identical twins have different fingerprints.'

'Easy. Superglue on my fingertips. Nothing to see and no fingerprints left. All it takes is a bit of practice to get the amount right.'

A tube of superglue?

Roisin shrugged. 'I needed the money. Dad pissed off some nasty people. Not that you'd understand anything like that. I wasn't going to keep the stone. The museum would have bought it back from me.'

Sinead closed her eyes. She couldn't believe she was hearing this. 'You thought it would be okay to destroy my career, and see me end up in jail, because you were strapped for cash?'

'Don't you dare judge me! You have no idea what my life has been like, Little Ms Perfect.'

'I didn't mean . . .' Damn. She hadn't meant to insult her. She had searched so long for her sister. This was not how it was supposed to turn out. No matter what Roisin had done, she didn't want to lose her again. 'I'm sorry I –'

The van stopped and the door opened. A baby-faced policeman motioned them to get out. The street outside the Parisian police headquarters was in an uproar. The press had got hold of the story and the Île de la Cité was thronged with reporters. Sinead kept her head down, ignoring their shouted questions and flashing cameras. On the pavement, an elderly German tourist remonstrated loudly about police incompetence and how she had almost been killed. While she delivered her lecture to the young officer, nobody could get out of the van.

Roisin sniggered. Sinead wondered what was so amusing about the mess they were in. In the few minutes they had spent together, she had realized how different they were. They might look the same, but Roisin was a petty criminal with a cynical outlook on the world. She wondered how much of it was down to her father. If he had taken both of them to England, would she have turned out the same?

She watched Roisin pull a dark wool hat from the pocket of her mac and tug it over her head.

'Time for me to bail,' she said, pulling the collar up around her, so that her hair was concealed.

'You can't be serious? What are you going to –?'

Sinead was distracted as the angry German tourist was joined by another and then a third. A dark flush swept up from the policeman's neckline and over his face. Roisin had moved ahead of her and was among those jostling for position at the open doors of the van, trying to get out.

Afterwards, Sinead wasn't sure what happened. One moment, a grey-haired woman hovered on the step, the next she had toppled to the ground. She lay there – clutching her arm, crying loudly – while her husband tried to comfort her. The policeman looked around for assistance, before getting on his radio and requesting help. As he was swallowed by a horde of anxious tourists, she almost felt sorry for him. Two policemen arrived, one carrying a first aid kit. Suddenly Sinead realized that Roisin was gone. She scanned the crowd, but her sister was nowhere to be seen.

'This way, please. *Venez ici, s'il vous plaît.*' A blonde policewoman clapped her hands to capture their attention.

Those left in the van climbed out and followed her obediently into the building. Standing on the pavement, Sinead looked around, but there was no sign of Niall or Andy. The police must be holding them separately. She trudged into the foyer of the station. Exhaustion was catching up with her. She was hungry and badly needed a shower.

Inside, they huddled in small groups; some were shocked, but others were angry. The woman in the floral dress pointed her finger at Sinead. 'She was one of them. She was with the men who had the guns.'

Damn. Sinead pretended she hadn't heard. She didn't need this right now. What she did need was to get Niall and get out of here. A glance around her revealed that more than one person had heard the woman's accusation.

The blonde policewoman motioned her forwards. 'Madame, if you would please come this way.'

Sinead sighed. There was nothing she could do except obey. Forcing a smile, she followed the woman along the corridor and into a small interview room.

'Wait here, please.'

Sinead slumped into a plastic chair. The tiny room was overheated, but she was afraid to open her suit a little in case they saw what she was carrying. Would this night-mare never end?

The mirrored wall on the other side of the room was undoubtedly a viewing point. She stared nonchalantly at it, as if she didn't know what it was. Ten long minutes passed before the door opened again. By that time, she could smell the sweat in her own hair.

'Miss O'Sullivan? Miss Sinead O'Sullivan?' The portly man pronounced her name 'Shin-ad' and she gave him a tight smile. The fact that he already knew her name didn't bode well. She was busted.

'Nice to meet you.' She stood up and offered her hand. There was no point in giving up yet. Not without trying. 'Do you need a statement now? I'm exhausted, so is there any chance we could do this tomorrow?'

The tight-lipped blonde detective who accompanied him raised a disapproving eyebrow.

Okay, so there would be no deferral.

The detective took the seat opposite her and smiled. 'I've spoken to some of the other tourists and there appears to be some confusion about your role in the events that occurred earlier.'

He laced his fingers together, the very picture of

patience and interest. Blondie shifted to her other foot. He hadn't invited her to sit.

What could she tell him? Anything about Hall would only lead the conversation back to the stone and she had no idea if they were holding Niall and Andy or what they had told the police. Sinead swallowed. 'Can I have some water please?'

'Of course.' He nodded to the blonde, who disappeared in search of water.

They sat silently staring at each other. Was it her imagination, or had the room become hotter in the last few minutes? She fingered the collar of her leather suit.

'Please,' he gestured with his hand. 'Make yourself comfortable. You look a little flushed.'

'I'm fine thanks.'

She sat unmoving in the chair and almost cried with relief when the blonde returned carrying a bottle of Evian and a plastic cup. She murmured her thanks and gulped the water down eagerly.

The detective smiled. 'As you seem disinclined to discuss events in the catacombs, perhaps I should inform you that we have received a request from our colleagues in Geneva for assistance.' His smile disappeared as quickly as it had come. 'Where is the Fire of Autumn?'

His words were almost a relief. All the running, all the danger was over. She had the stone in her possession. All she needed to do was convince them that she hadn't stolen it. Sinead unzipped her catsuit and drew out the whip, laying it across the white Formica table.

Small and dangerous, the coiled leather whip exuded a promise of very naughty things. The studs set into the handle were dull and discoloured with use. A faint smell of leather pervaded the interview room. Blondie stepped forwards to take a closer look.

Set into the base of the handle was a large red stone. Sinead's heart leapt every time she saw it. A fabulous jewel with a dark history and now she was a part of it.

The first sultan who had owned it had named the ruby The Heat of Desire. He had presented it to each of his seven wives in turn on their wedding night, to mark their joy in their surrender to him. It was rumoured that he had used it to pleasure them when they –

'Do you have anything to say at this time?'

Sinead jerked her attention back to reality at his question. 'Yes, I want a phone call and a lawyer.'

33

Niall waited while the security guards at La Brenaz checked his documents. He used the time to examine the newest prison in Geneva, built to catch the overflow from the notoriously overcrowded Champ-Dollon.

La Brenaz looked like an industrial office block, all red and white and security fencing. There were no bars at the windows that he could see, but he knew this place would not be easy to escape from.

Finally the guard was happy, and he was allowed through the security area into the prison proper. He followed his escort along a white corridor that reminded him of prefabs at school, to a small room with a table and two plastic chairs. Sinead was sitting in one chair, facing the door.

He took a moment to look at her, to drink in the sight of her beloved face. She was paler than he was used to seeing her and the plain skirt and top she was wearing were unflattering.

'Come in,' she said, with what sounded like forced cheerfulness. 'I'm only allowed visitors for an hour a week. Let's not waste any of it.'

With long steps, he reached the table and swooped down to kiss her. It felt like months since he had kissed her in the catacombs, not days.

Her mouth was warm and welcoming and she clung to

him tightly. He held her head in his hands, tilting it so he could kiss her more deeply. He had only meant it to be a quick, reassuring kiss, but when she was in his arms, passion took over. Kissing her was like coming home, warmth and passion all wrapped up in one splendid package.

His tongue tangled with hers and he slid his hand into her hair. His world narrowed down to Sinead. Her unique scent filled his head, inflaming him.

'Ahem!' A fake cough recalled him to his surroundings. He hadn't even noticed the prison guard standing there watching them. 'If you will please sit down? Thank you.' She indicated the plastic chairs.

Reluctantly, he released his grip on Sinead and was surprised at how much it hurt. She belonged in his arms. And his bed. And his heart.

Funny how thinking they were both going to die had made things so clear. Stupid stuff disappeared. All that mattered was that Sinead was his lady. His girl. His woman. The mother of his children.

'How are you?' he asked, conscious of the prison guard nearby.

She folded her hands on the table, clearly trying to keep control of her emotions. 'Not bad. This is a new prison, so I gather it's fairly nice as prisons go.'

'Are you lonely?' Niall hadn't realized how much he hated the idea of her being a helpless prisoner until now.

She smiled. 'No, I'm sharing the cell with a very chatty woman from London. She's awaiting trial too, and is very funny about the Swiss.'

He hated to think of Sinead being forced to mingle with criminals. 'What did she do?'

'Put her bins out on the wrong day.'

He stared at her. 'You're kidding!'

She shook her head, enjoying the story. 'No. She put them out on the wrong day and got a charge for littering that she refused to pay. Then she was arrested for that, and she resisted and it escalated.'

Niall took a moment to digest that. 'Crap. Even if I manage to prove that Roisin stole the Fire, you could still be in trouble for all the other laws you broke.'

'Yep.' She attempted a smile that did not meet her eyes. 'The Swiss police are nothing if not thorough at dotting i's and crossing t's.'

He shuffled his chair a little closer and held her clasped hands. 'I swear, I will find Roisin, and make her admit to her part in all this.'

'Any luck with that?'

He shoved his hand through his hair. Sinead's fingers twitched as if she wanted to do it for him. 'Nothing. If I hadn't seen her with my own eyes, I'd wonder if she existed. She has disappeared into the ether.'

'I only wish she'd told me more in the police van. All I know about my father is that he's some kind of con artist who's serving time for a computer scam. Roisin said that they moved around a lot. I don't even know his surname. Let's face it, we haven't a prayer. Funny, isn't it? I'm one of the best forgery detectors in the world and my sister is good at disappearing.'

He loved the simple confidence in her voice when she told him she was good at her job. 'So, I heard you're going to see Arnheim soon about your plea? And you can't remember any clue about where Roisin might have run to?'

She shook her head. 'Nothing. Who did she see Hall kill?'

'I'm guessing it was Maurice. Remember the way that man reacted to you when we left his shop? It looks like Roisin was there that night. She must have needed someone to broker the ransom of the ruby.'

Her eyes slid sideways, away from his. The prison warden leaned forwards, as if she was as anxious as Niall to hear what Sinead had to say. 'What about the trial? If you can't find Roisin, it's not looking good.'

'Fuck the trial. That has nothing to do with us.' Niall gathered his courage. 'Sinead, no matter what happens, I love you. I want to be the only man in your life.' He took a deep breath. 'Will you marry me?'

Her eyes were impossibly blue as they stared into his. Tears formed, making them larger and more luminous. 'Do you mean it?'

'I don't know why it took so long to realize how much you mean to me, how empty my life was before you came along. I need you, Sinead.'

Sinead sat up straighter, putting on her museum curator air. 'Niall, if the trial doesn't go in my favour, I could be facing seven years in jail. That's not exactly happily ever after.'

He knew it, and refused to let it put him off. 'You'll get time off for good behaviour.'

She snorted. 'Oh yeah, that's great. Five years instead of seven.'

'Doesn't matter. I'll wait for you.'

'For seven years?'

'Five with good behaviour,' he reminded her. 'But yes,

of course I'll wait. I love you. Say you feel the same way.'

She examined his face without saying anything. He wondered what she was thinking. Then she dropped her eyes to her hands, still silent.

Finally, Sinead lifted her head and met his eyes. 'I'm sorry, Niall. I don't think it would work.'

An invisible fist punched him in the gut. 'What?'

Sinead shrugged. 'I can't make plans while I'm facing seven years in jail.'

She looked out the window, where grey clouds veiled the mountains in the distance. 'I'm not the marrying type anyway. But thank you for the offer. It was sweet.'

Niall wanted to howl. He had no idea how much this would hurt. He had laid his heart at her feet, and she thought it was sweet?

'You mean a lot to me.'

The voice of doom. The brush off. She went on. 'I love you, Niall, but I don't think it would work.'

'We could make it work.' He didn't care if he was begging. Damn it, it had taken him years to find her, and now he wasn't going to let her go without a fight. 'We can build on what we have. And I love you.'

She held his eyes. 'You don't know me. You don't know anything about my life. I'm not what you think.'

Niall sat back in his chair. Every instinct told him that something bad was coming. What was it? Was she worried about her dad being a jailbird or her sister working as a paid dominatrix? Hell, he could deal with that. It meant nothing to him. 'If this is about your family –'

She gave a little sniff, the kind that usually signalled tears and he dug into his pockets for a tissue. Sinead blew her nose and tucked the tissue up her sleeve for later. That wasn't a good sign. She cleared her throat and fixed him with a blue-eyed stare.

'It's not about my family. It's because I'm Lottie Le-Blanc.'

Like fragments of glass from a shattered mirror, a thousand images exploded inside his brain. His incendiary attraction to her from the very first night at her apartment. How she moved and danced. The way she had teased him with her exhibitionist display in the restaurant that night in Paris. Even the way he had dressed her. The clothes he had chosen for his very own pin-up girl.

His libido had known all along. The truth had been staring him in the face from the very start. He wanted to bang his head against the wall.

A whole team of investigators on her and not one of them had made the connection to Lottie. Bertrand was her best friend. Sinead had known him for years, been his lover. He had pictures on his wall of Lottie. Of course he had – he was Lottie's lead dancer. The truth had been staring him in the face the whole time and he had been too dense to see it.

Sinead O'Sullivan was his dream girl and his fantasy girl.

Sinead O'Sullivan was also a liar and a chameleon.

And Sinead O'Sullivan had played him. Right to the end. A wave of jealousy washed over him when he thought of Lottie's legion of lovers and admirers – the actors, princes and other showbiz types. He wanted to kill each and every one of them.

'Jesus fucking wept.' He thumped his fist on the table.

The prison officer stepped forwards. 'Sir, if you do that again I will –'

Sinead reached for his hand. 'Don't. Please don't.'

Niall jerked his hand away as if her touch burnt him. 'What the fuck did you expect? Do you have an honest bone in your body? I told you that you could trust me. I asked you to tell me the truth. But you were lying to me all along.' He pushed the chair back, not caring that they were attracting the attention of the guard or that Sinead's eyes were welling up with tears.

Niall did what he always did when life fucked him over. He compartmentalized. With immediate effect. He shoved the pain into a deep hole where he would deal with it later, and he became the impersonal investigator again. He waved to the prison officer signalling that he wanted to go.

Before leaving, Niall leaned over the table, caught Sinead's face between his hands and kissed her hard. 'Remember this. Remember what we could have had.'

He left without looking back.

34

The dark blue suit had been delivered by the female prison officer after breakfast. It was accompanied by a pale fitted blouse and a pair of black heels. The tissue-lined box that arrived with the clothes had already been opened and searched. She fingered the silk contents and her heart leapt. There was only one person who could have sent them. Niall.

Stop it. Don't think about him now. She had barely held herself together since she last saw him. She'd had to battle tears every night. She'd lost weight, too; abject misery was better than any diet.

Niall. Niall. Niall. She couldn't get him out of her thoughts for a moment. His smile, his look, his touch. There were nights when she woke up sweating, imagining that he had been there with her. She craved his caress like a drug. She didn't care if he tied her up in a thousand different ways. The endless, wanting hours until dawn were unbearable.

Her Niall. Her lover. She still called him that even though their time together had been so brief. She had explored with him, shared with him, but he had shared much more. While she was with him everything had been about her, in a way that she had never imagined. She didn't want to put a label on it, hadn't understood until now that, in its own way, Niall's code of sexual dominance had always been focused on her happiness and her pleasure.

Her grandmother often said that it was folly to be wise,

but hindsight was also a curse. She had fallen for her fantasy man, forgetting that underneath he was just a man and in the end, she had hurt him badly.

She had spent her life hiding. Behind Lottie, behind her job, behind the frumpy clothes she wore. She had never expected to find someone who would accept all of her. But Niall had broken the law for her. He had risked his life and his livelihood. He was that type of guy. And yet, what had she risked for him?

She had always held something back from every relationship. She was worse than a liar – she was a coward. And she couldn't blame that on a fucked-up childhood. She had managed to destroy her future all by herself.

Niall hadn't been to visit her since he found out about Lottie. She told herself it was better this way, that he would find someone else, someone who loved him. Someone who would have his children, do all the things she had fantasized about while she was lying awake in her prison bunk.

She had lied to herself that she would be okay with that. But she was still lying.

The thought of him touching another woman, kissing her and making love to her made Sinead's heart ache. Blinking away the threatening tears, she shook out the blouse and draped it over the edge of her bunk. There was no question of borrowing an iron, but she would wear the suit for him.

A sharp rap came on the cell door and the guard shouted, 'You have thirty minutes before your transport arrives.'

Sinead nodded. She dressed quickly, pulling on the stockings and smoothing the fabric of the skirt over her hips. There was no mirror in the cell, and the deceptively plain suit was a little big, but she felt more like her glamorous alter ego than the plain Jane museum curator she had hidden behind for years.

The prosecution would probably drag Lottie into the trial. There was nothing she could do about that now. As long as she wasn't sent to prison, she could learn to live with it.

A small parcel at the bottom of the clothes bag caught her attention. The leather of the clutch bag was butter soft and inside was a pair of sunglasses and a tube of red lipstick, still in its cellophane wrapper. Niall had thought of everything. Sinead painted her lips, using the cover of the lipstick as a mirror. She needed all the help she could get to face the hostile court hearing ahead of her. She would have to do.

This would go down in Swiss history as one of the fastest trials ever. Why not, since there was so much evidence against her?

The entrance to the courtroom was thronged with reporters. It looked like Oscar night rather than a trial, as teams of international news crews gathered to cover the story. The prison van halted at the gates and she put on her glasses to shield her eyes from the flashing cameras.

It was showtime.

After the opening statements, Sinead was summoned to the witness box. She scanned the courtroom, eager for a sight of a familiar face, but there was no sign of Niall or Andy. A pale hand waved frantically from the back of the courtroom and she craned her neck to see who it was.

It was her cousin Summer, and if she wasn't mistaken,

Summer's fiancé, Flynn Grant, was sitting beside her. He looked suave and tanned in a dark suit. Despite the police presence, his eyes moved constantly around the courtroom, ever watchful. A bodyguard was always on duty. Sinead felt a pang of jealousy. The gruff Scot was crazy about her cousin.

The clerk called the court to order and she stood up. 'Mlle O'Sullivan. You are charged with the following . . .'

The clerk's voice droned on; theft, leaving the country while on bail, the list seemed endless. It was a wonder that they hadn't charged her with jaywalking too. Sinead was sure they must be making some of it up.

'And how do you wish to plead?'

She shot a questioning glance to her lawyer. Surely there must be some news about Roisin? He shook his head. She wasn't giving up without a fight. All she could do was play for time and hope that Niall and Andy could find her sister.

'Not guilty,' she said firmly.

An excited buzz filled the courtroom. Following some preliminary questioning by the judge, the defence presented their case.

By late morning, her new shoes were pinching. The defence strategy was not going well. She had watched the expressions on the faces of the observers varying between disbelief and scorn. At the prosecution table, they passed notes back and forth to each other, but they didn't bother to interrupt Arnheim's presentation. They didn't need to. He was doing their job for them. Her heart dropped, she didn't have a prayer.

Sensing that things were not going well, Arnheim

signalled to the judge. 'If I might have a brief consultation with my client?'

'You may.'

Sinead was ushered into a side chamber. Her guards remained on duty outside.

'Will you have something to eat?' Arnheim asked.

She couldn't have managed food if her life depended on it. 'Nothing, thank you. But perhaps some water?'

He nodded to his associate, who returned with a frosty glass of water. Sinead downed it in two gulps. 'Has there been any word?'

'I'm sorry, but there has been no news from them.'

'Oh.' Despite the water, her throat was suddenly dry. Maybe Niall wasn't coming after all.

Arnheim pressed on. 'I have tried to seek some concession from the prosecutor. You left the country to recover the stone and it has been returned to its rightful owner. But –' he gave her a tight-lipped smile '– we have little to bargain with and he has nothing to lose.'

'I understand.'

'Do you wish to change your plea? The judge may look kindly on you, even at this late stage.'

Sinead shook her head. 'I didn't steal the jewel.'

'Very well. In the meantime, my associates will begin preparing your appeal.'

Appeal? That didn't sound very hopeful. Her spirits plummeted even further. She wished she had never seen the damned ruby. The Fire of Autumn had brought her nothing but trouble since she set foot in Geneva. She wondered if the stories were right. Maybe the stone was cursed.

Following a miserable lunch break, Sinead was escorted

back to the courtroom. With typical Swiss efficiency the prosecutor got straight down to the business of demolishing her character. 'How long have you been a stripper, Mlle O'Sullivan?'

'Objection!' Arnheim stood up.

Sinead glanced at her lawyer for guidance. He pressed his lips together in a tight line. She knew that he had been hoping that Lottie wouldn't emerge at the trial but it was too late now.

Arnheim shrugged. The ball was in her court. There was nothing for it. She would have to tell the truth. 'Seven years,' she replied, trying to keep the quiver out of her voice.

'Seven years,' the prosecutor's voice boomed out, in case everyone in Geneva hadn't heard it.

'So you've been stripping since you were a twenty-year-old college student.'

Two elderly observers near the front of the courtroom exchanged glances. One of them, a dragon with iron-grey curls, reminded her of Granny O'Sullivan. Uncle Tim had sent a message to say that he was closing another deal and would be here soon. She was just grateful he wasn't bringing her grandmother.

Sinead sat up straight. Let them stare. 'That's correct,' she replied.

Lottie wasn't on trial, but she might as well have been – the stripper who passed herself off as a curator to steal from her employer. 'And when you're not dancing naked on stage, you work at the Rheinbach museum.'

What a horrible, piggy little man. Her palm itched to slap him. Stripping wasn't illegal – even in stuffy Switzerland.

'No. I have never . . .'

She hated that her voice shook. She remembered the hundreds of hours of rehearsal, the aching legs and bleeding feet and the smile she had forced onto her face for her audience when she was bone-tired from studying for her college exams. She had worked her butt off to become one of the best burlesque performers in the business. She didn't owe anyone an apology and certainly not this horrible little man. Sinead cleared her throat. 'That's not true. I've never performed in Switzerland.'

She tilted her head to one side and flashed him her best Lottie smile. 'Would you like me to?'

The first titter of laughter turned into a roar that echoed around the courtroom. Even the usually sedate Arnheim smiled. The judge banged his gavel on the polished wooden desk and called for order.

Two red patches flared on the prosecutor's cheeks.

Sinead sat back, waiting for more questions along the same line.

Instead, he strode to the prosecutor's desk and held a whispered conversation with his associate. From the side of the courtroom, a man wheeled a trolley bearing electronic equipment. 'At this time we intend to proceed with CCTV footage from the museum.'

The next thirty minutes were damning. She almost felt like convicting herself. By the time the clerk announced a recess, a pool of sweat had collected in the small of her back.

Sinead risked a sideways glance at the judge. He was barely listening, his decision was already made.

'Stop.' The shout from the courtroom guard dragged her attention back to the entrance.

The woman's eyes were covered by large sunglasses. The dark-blue suit was identical to the one she wore. Titian hair fell loosely about her shoulders. Her mouth bore the same slash of lipstick in exactly the same shade as her own. Sinead's eyes filled with tears as she watched her sashay to the front of the court. Her sister's voice carried clearly around the room.

'I'm Roisin O'Sullivan and I didn't steal the jewel either.'

For the second time that day, the reporters fled the courtroom in a pack. Some didn't even wait until they reached the exit to switch on their phones, much to the consternation of the clerk. The spectators at the rear of the court stood up, craning their necks to see the latest arrival. The judge banged his gavel uselessly, as he called for order.

Sinead permitted herself a laugh when she saw the prosecutor slump into his chair and mop his brow with a handkerchief.

Roisin took off her sunglasses and gave her sister a wink. Sinead had no idea what she was up to, but she had certainly blown a hole in the prosecution case.

Arnheim seized his chance. 'If I might be permitted to speak. I would like to recall one of the witnesses for the prosecution.'

Museum security guard, Jean-Baptiste Moutier, was clearly nervous. He fiddled with the collar of his white shirt as if someone had sprinkled it with itching powder. Sinead gave him an encouraging smile.

He frowned at her, glanced at Roisin and frowned again.

As Arnheim stood up and strolled to the front of the

court, the rotund prosecutor sat forwards in his chair. The courtroom fell silent.

'Monsieur Moutier, perhaps you would be so good as to relate the events of the evening of the theft for us again.'

Moutier nodded, pleased to be on familiar ground. 'I had done my usual rounds and I was back at my desk when Mlle O'Sullivan arrived. She often worked late.'

'Are you sure it was her?' Arnheim asked, darting a pointed glance at the front row of the court where the sisters sat side by side.

He cleared his throat nervously. 'I saw Mlle O'Sullivan every day. She often stopped to ask about my daughter. She's studying ballet.'

'I see. So there was nothing unusual about that evening,' Arnheim asked. 'How long did you chat for?'

'We didn't talk at all that night. She just signed in.'

'I see,' Arnheim said. 'But you did see her and there is no doubt in your mind whatsoever that it was Mlle O'Sullivan.'

'None,' Moutier agreed.

Arnheim smiled. 'Thank you Monsieur. That will be all.'

The relief on the security guard's face was palpable. He stood up and exited the witness box. As he prepared to return to his seat, Arnheim turned. 'One last thing. Perhaps you would be so good as to place your hand on the shoulder of Mlle O'Sullivan please.'

'I object,' the prosecutor rose to his feet.

Arnheim threw out his hands in a gesture of bewilderment. 'I fail to see the problem. The witness has stated

397

that he knows Mlle O'Sullivan. He has spoken to her frequently and has no doubt that she was at the museum that night. It's a simple question of identity.'

'This is preposterous. I must object.'

Sinead held her breath. Beside her, Roisin reached for her hand and she clutched it gratefully.

Sensing the closing of a trap, the judge shook his head. 'Mr Arnheim?'

'Your honour, this whole case rests on the question of identity. You have seen the footage. You have heard from Monsieur Moutier. I am simply asking that he formally identifies the accused. Nothing more.'

'Very well, if you will oblige us, Monsieur Moutier.'

Her heart pounded as the security guard approached, but she schooled her face into a mask of indifference. Jean-Baptiste was a good man and a proud father. He didn't deserve to be dragged into the middle of this, but then neither did she.

When this was over, she and Roisin were going to have a reckoning.

The guard stopped less than two feet from where they sat. Beads of sweat had popped up across his brow. He looked intently at her face and back to her sister, then back to her again, before glancing back at the judge.

The prosecutor tried again. 'I object to this . . . this –'

'Sit down,' the judge said in a tone that brooked no argument. 'Monsieur Moutier, please continue.'

As the guard stepped forwards, Sinead closed her eyes. Her heartbeat thundered like a runaway horse, she dug her nails into her sister's sweating palm. Roisin clutched her hand tightly.

Nothing happened. Sinead's eyes flew open. Roisin released her hand and stood up, facing her accuser for the first time.

'Thank you, Monsieur Moutier,' the judge said. 'You may resume your seat.'

He inclined his head. 'Mademoiselle, please approach the bench.'

Cool as an iceberg, her sister stepped forwards. The clicking of her heels on the wooden floor was the only sound in the otherwise silent courtroom.

'My name is Roisin O'Sullivan,' she announced.

'I see. And were you in Geneva on the night that the Fire of Autumn was stolen?'

'I was,' she replied.

'And did you steal the Fire of Autumn?'

'Of course not,' she said. 'Do I look like an idiot?'

A ripple of laughter ebbed around the courtroom and even the staid Arnheim was forced to smile at her audacity.

'The court will rise for a short recess.'

When the judge left the bench, the courtroom erupted. Sinead scanned the crowd seeking the one person she wanted to see more than anyone else in the world. She thought he had abandoned her, but he hadn't. How could she have doubted him for a second?

He stood inside the door of the court, big and solid and so gorgeous that he took her breath away. How had she survived without him?

'I'm sorry,' she mouthed the words to him. 'I do love you.'

Ignoring the guards, Niall forced his way to the front of the room and took her in his arms. His mouth found hers in a rough kiss. He was unshaven. His hair had escaped its bindings and he smelled of rain and leather. She held on tightly, ignoring the voices around them, focusing only on his kiss and the strength of his arms around her. She didn't need words to tell him that she had missed him and that she never wanted to be parted from him again.

A cough interrupted their reunion. Andy. Sinead extricated herself from Niall's arms and hugged him.

'Thank you so much for everything you've done and for finding my sister.'

Andy scowled over at Roisin who was sitting, still wearing her sunglasses, looking every inch the diva.

'She's quite a handful. If I had my way she'd –'

'Just keep an eye on her,' Niall said. 'Don't let her out of your sight for a second. Cuff her if necessary.'

Andy smiled. 'Now that would be my pleasure.'

'All rise,' the clerk barked out the order and silence was restored as the judge took his place on the bench.

Niall moved into the row of seats behind her while Andy pushed Roisin ahead of him into a row of seats in the opposite aisle.

'On the basis of the evidence presented today, it appears that I must dismiss the charges against Mlle Sinead O'Sullivan.'

Niall rested his hand on her shoulder and she squeezed his broad fingers gratefully. Sinead closed her eyes. The nightmare was over.

35

Like a scene from a movie, the courtroom erupted. Sinead raised her arm as she tried to defend herself against the flashing cameras, but eventually gave up. As Niall and Andy fought a fruitless battle to keep the reporters back, her cousin Summer fought her way to the front of the crowd.

'Oh, Sinead.' She threw her arms around her. 'I knew you didn't do it.'

'Of course she didn't feckin do it.' Tim O'Sullivan appeared behind his daughter. 'But your grandmother is having forty-seven fits about that dancing lark. Those damn photographers and hacks have shown up on her doorstep.'

Great. Now the whole of Castletownberehaven knew she was a stripper.

'Yes, you dark horse.' Summer poked her in the arm. 'And I thought I was the wild one. You were supposed to be going to ballet lessons.'

'I um –'

Tim looked around him. 'Where's the other one? We need to have a chat about her.'

'Roisin? She's here somewhere.' Sinead looked around the crowd and caught a glimpse of a mane of titian hair disappearing through a doorway at the back of the court-room. Surely her sister wouldn't try to escape through the judge's chambers?

'Mlle O'Sullivan.' Sinead felt a hand on her shoulder and she turned to find her lawyer was waiting.

Arnheim was wearing a broad smile. He blushed when Sinead planted a kiss on his cheek.

'How did you know that Moutier would pick Roisin and not me?'

'I didn't. We had a fifty-fifty chance. Sometimes a lawyer needs a little luck. There is some paperwork to be tidied up in the registrar's office when you are ready. I will send you my bill tomorrow.' He inclined his head and disappeared into the crowd.

Ouch. She hadn't thought about the bill. Her team of Swiss lawyers had probably cost a pretty penny and there was no way that she could expect Tim to pay for them. She had already cost him a million francs and would never forgive herself for that.

Niall handed her an iPhone. 'Go ahead, do what you have to do. I'll wait for you outside. Text me when you're done.'

She hadn't known that the paperwork would take so long. Even though she was no longer on trial, the Swiss made it more difficult to get out of custody than into it. She pulled the phone Niall had given her from her pocket.

She texted him, 'I'm done.'

A second later, the screen lit up. 'I'm outside.'

She closed her eyes with relief and smiled. When she emerged from the court building it was already dusk. Ignoring the flashing cameras, she climbed into the back of the dark Jeep and was dragged into his arms.

'Drive, Andy,' Niall said before he plundered her mouth with his. She wound her arms around his neck, stretching against the confines of the seat belt. He tasted so good. Like mint and warmth and Niall. Opening her mouth wider, she tangled her tongue against his, revelling in the flood of sensations that washed over her.

A guttural noise came from his throat and his fingers moved through her hair until he found the offending clasp that held it in place and tossed it to the floor. 'God, I've missed you.'

'Remind me to get locked up more often.' She gave him a teasing smile.

'Don't even think about it,' Niall said.

Andy cleared his throat. 'So, what will it be for your first night of freedom? A bar, a club, I've heard there's a good burlesque place that –'

'No,' they both chorused and Sinead laughed. She'd had enough trouble with Lottie and she wasn't sure if Granny O'Sullivan or Uncle Tim would ever forgive her for that one.

Sinead stroked Niall's thigh, savouring the feel of the rock-hard muscles beneath her palm. She couldn't seem to stop touching him. His grey eyes narrowed into that molten stare she knew so well. She wouldn't get a wink of sleep tonight. The thought of being in his bed again made her giddy. She gave him her best Lottie pout. 'You know what I'd really like?'

His warm hand covered hers, 'I can just imagine.'

'A bath,' she announced.

Weeks of pent up frustration showed in his face. He was so easy to tease, it was almost a sin.

'A bath,' he repeated.

'Yes. I haven't had one since Paris. It was the one thing

I dreamed about while I was in prison – a nice warm, deep bath, with a glass of something chilled. Oh, and a book.'

'A book?'

'Sounds like a fun night.' Andy snorted with laughter and Niall darted a warning look at him.

'Well, if you're sure . . .'

'I'm certain.'

Andy pulled up outside the hotel and they climbed out of the car. Niall held onto her hand tightly as they entered the lobby, as if he was afraid she would disappear again.

'Wait here, I have to check my messages,' he said. He let her go reluctantly.

Sinead watched the receptionist tilt her head to one side and then begin to write, raising her head from time to time, before finally nodding.

Niall returned and pressed the button, summoning the elevator.

'Is everything okay?' she asked.

There was enough anticipation in his answering smile that she became a little wary. What was the Viking up to now?

The penthouse suite was sumptuous. Sinead crossed the room and opened the glass doors that led onto a terrace. She didn't care that it was freezing. It was wonderful to be outside again, to breathe the clean frosty air into her lungs. She stared at the lights of the city twinkling like stars below them. A giant Christmas tree stood in the middle of a square. She was free and she still couldn't quite believe it.

Niall followed her, wrapping his arms around her and drawing her against his chest. 'Don't get cold.'

She rested her head against his shoulder and tilted her head, inviting his kiss. 'How could I, when I have you?'

The sound of a buzzer shattered the moment and Niall released her. 'That will be room service.'

She smiled as three uniformed women entered the room. One carried a pile of fluffy towels, another held a tray with a bottle of sake and some tiny ceramic cups, and a third, wearing a beautician's uniform, deposited a box on the table and left. Next came room service with a tray of chilled melon and lychees, and two pairs of chopsticks.

They were gone as swiftly as they had arrived and Niall gave her a smug smile. 'I believe it's time for your bath.'

She watched from the doorway as he filled the tub, testing the water to make sure it was the perfect temperature before adding some of the oils from the beautician's box. Rose, geranium and the tang of eucalyptus filled the steamy air.

'Won't you come in?'

Obediently, she entered the room and began to unbutton her blouse.

'Let me do that.' His words were a command, rather than a statement, and she stood perfectly still as he removed her clothing. Niall took his time, stroking her skin as he removed each piece, kneeling before her to remove her shoes, until she was naked before him.

He planted a light kiss on her belly and reluctantly came to his feet. 'Climb in. I'm going to bathe you.'

She stood in the warm water, staring up at him. Without the added advantage of height from her heels, she felt tiny and vulnerable before him. It wasn't fair. He was still fully clothed and she had missed the touch of his skin against hers. His mouth quirked. She had meant to tease him, but the Viking was going to drive her crazy.

'What if I said I wanted to go to bed and make out like rabbits?'

'Too late. You only get one wish.'

He scooped up water in his large hand and poured it slowly over her skin before taking a washcloth and immersing it in the warm water. No inch of her body was spared as he gently washed her, arms first, then around her neck, sliding the warm cloth down her back and between her breasts, never quite giving her the touch that she needed.

Her nipples formed aching points but Niall ignored them. Maddeningly, he turned his attention to her legs, focusing on her feet before sliding the warm cloth upwards again. His attentions were slow and deliberate. He was touching her, but not the way she wanted. If he didn't kiss her soon, she would scream.

He gestured for her to sit in the bath and left the room. She really was going to kill him. When he returned, he was carrying the tray of sake and fruit.

She raised her hand to take one of the cups and he frowned. 'No touching the food.'

Using the chopsticks, he picked up small bites of fruit and fed them to her one by one. He raised a cup of sake to her mouth, allowing her only tiny sips. She relaxed. She was actually beginning to enjoy this.

As if he had read her mind, he placed his hands into the ice bucket. She winced. He wouldn't. She would kill him if he put ice on her. Instead, he used the ice to cool his fingers and placed them on her nipples. The jolt of cold against her skin made her yelp.

'Had enough yet?'

The smug smile was back. It was time to turn the tables on him. 'Not quite. I seem to be missing a bath toy. Do you know where I might find one?'

'I thought you'd never ask.'

Niall peeled off his clothes with deliberate slowness, toeing off his shoes, unbuttoning his shirt and shedding it to reveal his muscular chest. If anything, he was more ripped than before.

'Been working out, soldier?' she teased him.

'I had to find some way to work off the frustration.' He unzipped his jeans and pulled them off along with his socks. The tenting in his boxers was unmistakable.

'Looks like you missed me.'

'What makes you think that?' With a grin, he dropped his boxers on the floor and eased into the bath. The water level rose dangerously; if they weren't careful, they would cause a flood. She smiled. To hell with being careful.

Rising onto her knees, she stalked her prey, sliding along his body until they were chest to chest. His wet hands stroked her back, coming to rest on her buttocks, and she squirmed against him.

'If you don't stop doing that we might –'

'Shut up,' she said before cupping his face in her hands and capturing his mouth. The kiss in the car hadn't been nearly enough. She devoured him, her tongue duelling with his in a long, open-mouthed kiss that went on for-ever.

His hands tangled in her damp hair, holding her hard

against him, crushing her breasts into his chest. His erection nudged hard against her abdomen. He was more than ready and so was she. She pulled away, breathless. They were never going to make it to the bedroom. Flattening her palms against his chest, she pushed to a crouch.

The hunger in his eyes was unmistakable. He grabbed a condom from beside the bath.

'I want you.' Her voice was husky. Reaching between her thighs she seized his cock and slowly lowered herself onto it, gasping at the feeling of fullness as he entered her.

Niall gritted his teeth and closed his eyes. 'Sinead,' he gasped out her name.

Slowly, she began to move, rocking tentatively back and forth until she became accustomed to him again. Niall gripped the edge of the bath as her movements increased in speed.

Water splashed over the edge of the bath. She didn't care. All she was conscious of was the sensation of him inside her. The sensation of warm water against her as she rocked against him, squeezing her inner muscles each time she rose before plunging onto him again.

Niall groaned. Neither of them was going to last. As her movements became more frantic, the water sloshed over the edge of the bath onto the marble floor. They were going to drown the place. Maybe they should move into the bedroom.

As if he read her mind, he said, 'Don't you dare stop.'

Sinead bent her head for another kiss and as she drew away, she spotted the sake bottle on the ledge behind him. A half-remembered tale from a dancer who had returned from a Japanese tour came to mind, and she wondered if it was true. There was one way to find out.

Reaching for the bottle, she tipped the contents into the warm bath.

'Holy fuck,' Niall roared.

The sake bath made her skin tingle and her blood feel like champagne. Mindless, she rode him hard, her eyes tightly shut, gasping his name with each downward stroke. Fireworks exploded behind her eyelids and her climax slammed into her, obliterating every rational thought. She was dimly conscious of Niall's arms locked around her and his hips driving hard into her, prolonging her pleasure, until he followed her climax with his own.

She collapsed onto his damp chest, wondering if she would ever move again.

He managed a smile. 'Did anyone ever tell you that you're a witch?'

Sinead pouted at him. 'Only when they're being nice to me. What's the matter? Can't the big strong Ranger cope with a helpless little exotic dancer?'

He threw back his head and laughed. 'You'd give a platoon of Rangers a run for their money.'

'A whole platoon? What if I said I only wanted one?'

'Any Ranger in particular?'

Sinead hesitated. If she didn't do this now, she might lose courage. She pressed on. 'I've had a lot of time to think about our relationship while I was in prison.'

'And?' The single word held an uncertain edge.

'I think that you should marry me.'

During their time apart, she had imagined Niall's response. He would kiss her passionately and say yes.

They would find a hotel room and not leave it for twenty-four hours. Instead, he was silent. She had already refused him once. Had she left it too late?

Niall's arms tightened around her. 'I accept, but there are conditions.'

Conditions? What was he talking about? This was a marriage proposal, not a contract negotiation.

'You know that I'm demanding, possessive and kinky as hell?'

'I do.'

'And that Lottie will have to come out of retirement on my birthday until you're at least sixty?'

Sinead giggled. He had worried her for a moment, but these were the kind of conditions she could cope with. 'Only 'til I'm sixty? I was hoping for some hot geriatric sex with an older guy.'

Niall raised a warning brow. 'I'm only five years older than you. Keep it up and you'll pay for that remark. Now, where was I? Oh yes. I want to be in charge in the bedroom.'

'Always? Every night?' Her voice rose. She couldn't believe Niall was trying to make her agree to this.

'Yes. Every night. Starting tonight.'

He was serious. She was looking at a lifetime of being . . . his . . . his sexual submissive. 'You are such a . . .'

She couldn't think of a word horrible enough to call him.

'Dom?' Niall flashed a dark smile that promised wicked things, and stroked the length of her back. Her eyes drifted closed in pure pleasure. He had such big hands, and they were so very talented.

She remembered the night Niall had tied her to the bed and made her come until she was too limp to move a muscle. He would always want to be in charge, whether she agreed to this or not. But there was no way she was giving in easily. She was an O'Sullivan after all. 'I was going to say pain in the ass.'

'I can be that too.' Niall agreed. 'But only if you ask nicely.'

'I'll fight you.'

'I'm counting on it.' He grinned. 'It wouldn't be any fun if you didn't.

36

The discreet buzzing of the hotel telephone woke her the next morning. Sinead stretched, luxuriating in the width of the bed and the warmth of the man she was cuddled against. She would never get enough of Niall.

Life was good. Proposing to Niall had been a terrifying gamble, but he had accepted and now she could look forward to a lifetime of waking up beside him.

Her stomach rumbled, reminding her that all she'd had to eat the night before was fruit. Niall had promised to feed her to replace the weight she had lost in prison. She looked forward to it.

The phone buzzed again and he reached out a long arm to pick it up. The muscles flexed and she couldn't help smiling as he lifted the receiver to his ear. How had she managed to find someone so beautiful? And she was going to marry him.

'Yes?' He was plainly annoyed by the interruption.

'Monsieur Moore?' Sinead could hear the receptionist clearly. 'There are some members of the police here who wish to speak to Mlle O'Sullivan. Shall I send them up?'

Police? Damn.

His eyes met hers. He shook his head to indicate he didn't know why they were here. 'Send them up in ten minutes, we're still in bed,' he said, then hung up.

'Why?' Sinead asked. 'I was cleared of the theft, I was found not guilty.'

'I've no idea, but unless you want to talk to the police in your birthday suit, I suggest you get dressed.'

She bolted for the bathroom, splashing through a quick shower and dressing as fast as possible. That was one benefit of her past as a burlesque dancer: she knew how to dress quickly. Thankfully, her cousin Summer had visited her apartment and packed a small overnight bag for her. She was pulling on her old conservative pants and unflattering jumper when they heard a knock on the door.

Sinead recognized the tall Swiss officer from the trial the day before, but the small brunette was French. She introduced herself as Antoinette St Michel and spoke in perfect English. 'I'm sorry to question you when I know you must be tired,' she told Sinead. 'But you are a person of interest now.'

Sinead gestured the two detectives to the armchairs and she sat at the small writing table to give herself an advantage in height. Niall stood behind her, a subtle message to everyone that she belonged to him. His presence grounded her more than anything else.

'Interest in what? I was cleared.' She was proud that her voice was steady, and hoped that no one noticed the slight tremor that ran through her.

'Yes, we heard about that. Congratulations on the outcome of the trial,' the Swiss detective, Captain Cenis, said. He did not sound that pleased about it.

'We are investigating the death of Maurice Verdon and

we have uncovered a possibility that you are involved with his murder,' Officer St Michel said.

Sinead sucked in a breath. 'No, that's impossible.'

Niall put a hand on her shoulder, steadying her.

The French officer continued, 'We have found CCTV footage of you running away from the shop on the night Monsieur Verdon was murdered, and an eyewitness says that he saw you coming from the shop at 4 a.m.'

'That's ridiculous, Maurice was my friend. I interned with him.' Sinead fought the quiver in her voice. She wasn't going to dissolve into hysterics.

'Do you have a key to his premises?'

Sinead sat up straighter. 'Of course not, I gave it back when I left his employment.'

'So you have had his keys in the past?' Officer St Michel continued.

'Well yes, but –' Sinead stopped. When she had been his intern, she had keys to the outer doors and to Maurice's office. She was certain she had given them back. Of course she had. But could she prove it?

Niall straightened up. 'Where is this going? You can't possibly suspect Miss O'Sullivan.'

'We have to investigate,' Captain Cenis said, taking out his notebook.

Officer St Michel put a small recorder on the table. 'Do you mind if I tape this interview?'

Sinead looked at it as if it were a snake. 'Do I need a lawyer?' she asked the French detective.

Officer St Michel switched the recorder on. 'Of course not. We are just investigating. There is evidence that links you to the murder. Your fingerprints were found at the scene, and we have unconfirmed reports that Monsieur Verdon was brokering an auction for the ruby you were accused of stealing.'

There was a stunned silence as they digested that. The police actually thought that they had a case against her. She had drunk coffee with Maurice, and touched various pieces in his office. Her fingerprints would be all over the office.

Officer St Michel asked, 'Do you have an alibi for that night?'

'I – I –,' Sinead stuttered.

She remembered that night. Niall had accused her of lying and it was true, but he hadn't known what she was lying about. That evening, he had taken painkillers and gone to bed, leaving her watching television in the lounge alone. She had fallen asleep in front of the box. The lounge was closer to the apartment door than to his room. She could have sneaked out and he would never have known.

And Niall knew it.

More and more, she regretted not telling him about Lottie from the beginning. If she had, they might have spent the night together, and Niall would be her alibi.

As it was, there was no one who saw her that night, and no one who could vouch for her presence when poor Maurice was murdered.

Could they arrest her for that? She hadn't killed him, but she hadn't stolen the Fire of Autumn either and look what had happened since then.

No, she couldn't tolerate being arrested again.

Niall's hand tightened on her shoulder.

'She has an alibi,' he said. She turned to stare at him. His eyes were calm, as if he were telling the truth. 'She was with me all night.'

'All night? Are you sure, Monsieur?'

'Absolutely positive. There are some things a man does not forget. Sharing a bed with Lottie LeBlanc is one of them.' There was a trace of irony in his voice, but she hoped she was the only one who would pick up on it.

'All night?'

Niall nodded.

Captain Cenis closed his notebook. 'If you are certain, Monsieur, then it appears we need to interview the other Mlle O'Sullivan.'

'An excellent idea.' Niall gestured them to the door. The two detectives stood up and shook hands with him and Sinead. 'Do you know where she is?'

Captain Cenis shook his head. 'No, but we shall find her.'

In the silence that echoed when they left, Sinead turned around. She leaned against the door and pinned him with her magnificent eyes.

'You lied,' she said simply.

'I –' Niall stopped. There was no point denying it. It was true. 'I know you didn't do it,' he said instead.

She didn't move, but her eyes shone more brightly, as if through tears. 'No, of course I didn't, but I can't believe you lied for me.'

He stepped closer, so that he was looking down into her upturned face. Her beloved face. 'You are mine now. I would never let anything happen to you.' He tipped her face up to his. 'Do you believe that?'

She smiled, her lips quivering slightly. 'Of course. You always tell the truth. But what about Lottie?'

How could she do it, pin him on the one thing he hadn't wanted to talk about? He shifted, trying to gather his thoughts. He had thought about little else for weeks but was still searching for the right words. Lottie still had the power to turn his mind upside down.

'For years I'd had a thing about Lottie. Flynn and I used to joke about how one day we'd get lucky and get a BJ from Lottie LeBlanc. In my mind, I had turned her into this superwoman, an impossible vision of perfection. I never actually expected to meet her.'

He stopped and grinned at her. 'Mind you, I did try. I used to go to all her shows, and would wait outside after-wards, hoping to catch a glimpse of her. And when she stopped dancing, I tried to track her down. No wonder I couldn't find her, she was in the Rheinbach museum in Geneva, the one place I never looked for her.'

'But you know Lottie isn't real, don't you?'

He tilted her chin higher, forcing her to meet his eyes. 'She is real. She's a part of you. She's just not what I was expecting. But this is better. She's not a figment of my imagination, she's a living, breathing woman who kisses like a dream and has an ass I want to redden.'

Sinead gave an outraged gasp. 'Saying something nice might help you more here.' But there was a sparkle in her eyes that told him she was interested.

'Look, I was an asshole when I found out. I couldn't

get over the fact that you had been lying to me. That you didn't trust me.'

She put up her hand and held onto his wrist. 'I wasn't lying so much as not telling you. I've spent years keeping Lottie and Sinead separate. It was a habit that I didn't see any reason to break. And the thing is that as hot and sexy as you were, I'd only known you a short time. I didn't have reason to trust you.'

Niall nodded. It seemed that they had spent a lifetime together, but it had only been a few weeks. She was right. He hadn't given her a good reason to trust him. 'And now?'

'Now I know you'd go to the wire for me.'

He couldn't resist kissing her. 'I'd walk on coals for you. Go to hell and back for you. Even eat bread for you.' She laughed, as he had hoped she would. 'But please, don't feed me bread too often.'

'I promise.' Then she was serious again. 'Have you forgiven me for not telling you about Lottie?'

'There's nothing to forgive. Sinead and Lottie are both fantasies of mine. I'm getting two for the price of one. It's every man's dream. And now that I've found you, I'm never letting you go.'

37

Her mobile phone rang and Sinead glanced at the display. It was Gabriel. He had visited her every week at the prison, trying to keep her spirits up. The last time she had seen him was at the courtroom, where he'd been swallowed up by reporters and Lottie supporters.

'Have you seen the papers, *chérie*? Your fans are delighted that you'll soon be wielding your whip again.'

Sinead laughed. 'Do you think it will protect me from Niall?'

'You have never been a woman in need of protection, only love.'

How well Gabriel knew her. She glanced across the room at Niall, who was tapping the keyboard of his laptop. Sinead lowered her voice. 'Thanks, Gabriel. For everything.'

It was an acknowledgement that their relationship had changed again. Over the years they had been friends, lovers, friends with bens – or as Gabriel called it *'une aventure'* – and friends again.

'For you, anything, always.' His voice sounded husky.

'Silver-tongued Frenchman,' she said, trying to lighten the moment. 'So, what's new?'

'A certain American has made us an offer.'

'Oh?'

'Three months in Las Vegas as part of his Legends of Burlesque revue.'

'You know I don't . . .' She had been about to say 'share a stage with another woman', but beggars couldn't be choosers. She had lost her job at the museum and she hadn't seen Arnheim's legal bill yet.

'Relax, *chérie* – you will have your own stage. Two shows per day, three days a week, and you haven't heard the best part yet. As I am no longer pretty enough to be on stage, I am to be your new choreographer.'

'That's not true. You are still pretty.'

She heard Gabriel's sigh over the phone. 'Your eyes are blinded by friendship. You know I can't dance on stage any more. Not without a mask.'

She wanted to reject his words, but they were true. She listened as Gabriel recounted the conversation with the American producer. This was an offer she couldn't refuse. Even factoring in the time it would take to develop a new show, the whole thing could be done in less than six months. She would clear her debts, get some money behind her and move on with her life.

There was no way she could refuse it, but how was she going to tell Niall?

'When do they want me?' *Please say a week. Let us have a few more days together. She prayed.*

'As soon as possible, *chérie*. There's a flight leaving Geneva tonight at 8 p.m. How many seats shall I book?'

Sinead glanced over at Niall. How could she leave him so soon? Regretfully, she sighed. She had no choice. 'Two. I'll see you there.'

She disconnected the call.

'Everything okay?' Niall asked.

'Not really. There's good news and there's bad news.'

He patted his knee. 'Come here.'

'I think I better –'

'I said come here.' The edge in his tone warned her not to argue and she crossed the room and perched on his knee.

'Who was that?'

'Gabriel.'

'And it wasn't good news he was giving you. What's the story?'

She cuddled into his embrace. God, she would miss him so much. She didn't know how to tell him.

Niall gathered her into his arms. 'This is about money, isn't it? Are you broke?'

As he gazed at her, her heart flipped. Of course, he knew. She hadn't had a salary cheque for months, but the bills still needed to be paid. She owed him €38,750 for sapphire earrings that she could no longer afford and her legal bill would hit five figures, maybe even six if she was unlucky. The kind of lawyers Tim knew didn't come cheap, and she wasn't willing to let her uncle pay her legal bills. Not after everything he had done for her. She needed to deal with this herself.

'Apart from some jewellery in London and £50,000 worth of costumes in Paris, I am pretty broke. Arnheim –'

'I can take care of Arnheim.'

She shook her head. 'No. I've already cost you enough. But thank you.'

'So what did Gabriel say?'

'Lottie is in demand. I can make enough money to pay

all my bills and have a nest egg to start my own business. But I'm going to have to travel.'

His grey eyes clouded and he sighed.

'Where to this time, and for how long?'

'Vegas,' she whispered. 'For three months, four allowing for rehearsals.'

'Ouch,' he said. 'I've got a job starting in London next week. The client asked for me personally. And your uncle wants me and Flynn to sort out some security issues in Buenos Aires after that. I had kind of hoped that you'd come with me.'

Misery bubbled up inside her. This wasn't going to be easy. Another separation on top of the one they'd already had would be devastating.

Niall's arms tightened around her. 'When are you leaving?'

'Tonight.'

He seemed to stop breathing.

'Tonight?'

She couldn't restrain the tears that threatened.

'I'm sorry.'

Time stood still for what felt like an eternity, though it was just a few seconds. Then Niall gathered himself.

'You can go, on two conditions.'

More conditions. She mustered a half smile. Even when he was down, Niall never gave up control. 'Anything.'

Niall picked up her hand and kissed it, never taking his eyes off her face. 'We get married six months from today and we spend the rest of the day in bed. What do you say?'

Her fingers were shaking slightly. 'Are you sure?'

'Surer than I've ever been. I'll travel to Vegas every chance I get. All you have to do is say yes.'

She wound her arms around his neck. 'In that case, take me to bed and prove it.'

Even though she had challenged him to do it, she was startled by the speed with which he scooped her up in his arms and headed for the bed. He lowered her onto it, and followed her down for another deep, drugging kiss.

There were so many things she had wanted to tell him about her life, about Lottie, but they were running out of time. Would Niall ever grow bored with her? Lottie was a part of her, but only a small part. At heart she still felt like Plain Jane Super Brain, the timid girl who hid in corners at parties and envied the confidence of her cousin, who could charm a room with a smile and a wink.

Niall had been fascinated by Lottie for so long. Now he had the real thing.

'I haven't had a string of lovers, you know,' she blurted out before she lost her nerve. 'And the Omani prince did offer me diamonds, but I didn't accept them.'

He had been ripping off his shirt, but her words stopped him. 'So we'll have to do without the diamonds? Bummer. That would have solved your money problems.' His voice was light, as if it was all a joke.

'And I did bathe in champagne at that party, but I was wearing a thong.'

He leaned over, holding her face between his hands. 'What's all this about? I don't care what you wore.'

His face was stern, the dim light making his cheekbones

harsher and his mouth a firm slash. She had never seen anyone so beautiful. How could she compete? Or even keep up?

'I'm afraid you're going to be disappointed. Everyone thinks I'm some sort of temptress, but I'm not. I'm just plain Sinead O'Sullivan. I'm ordinary.'

He threw back his head and laughed. The movement caused the muscles in his stomach to flex, highlighting the chiselled abs and the tight line of hair that disappeared into his pants. 'Ordinary? Have you seen yourself in a mirror? You're the least ordinary person I know. You're beautiful and you're smart and you turn me on.'

'Really?' She knew she sounded pathetic.

'Oh yeah. No doubt.' His eyes pinned her, allowing no escape.

She tried to lighten the atmosphere, not sure if she could cope with what she saw in his face. 'You're just saying that to get your way with me. But don't worry, I'm a sure thing.'

He held her still. 'You are. I've never been more sure of anyone in my life. But never doubt that you are a temptress. I'm just grateful that you hide so much of your beauty so that I'm not fighting off every man we meet. It's bad enough worrying about Bertrand and warning Andy to keep away from you –'

'Andy?' As if she would be interested in him when she had Niall.

Niall kissed her, a swift, punishing kiss. 'Forget about him. This is between us. You turn me inside out, and I'm determined that I'll be the only man you do that to from now on.'

Sinead hooked her arms around his neck. 'Then how about I do some of that now?' She tugged him down on top of her. She only had control for a moment, then he took over the kiss, ravaging her mouth, pressing her back into the bed and leaving her nowhere to go.

'Mmmm,' she purred, revelling in the strength and passion of the man who seemed bent on dominating her.

His kiss became more gentle, nibbled at her lips, teasing her with licks and nips so that she raised her head, determined to deepen the pressure. But Niall was in charge, and he was intent on showing her that.

He trailed kisses across her face, up to her eyes, where he muttered a complaint about her ridiculously long eyelashes, and down to her ears. He swirled his tongue around the contours, making her giggle and twist. 'Hold still,' he growled, then nipped the lobe of her ear.

She squealed and jerked, but he held her still and did it again.

'Oh god.' The things he was doing should be illegal. She couldn't bear to look away from him, but she couldn't keep her eyes open. The sensations that washed over her were coming too fast; she had no control over them.

His long fingers traced down her collarbone, along her sides, up around her breasts. She held her breath, waiting for them to touch her nipples, but instead they dipped down to her belly button. She gasped. When had that turned into an erogenous zone?

Those tormenting fingers continued on their path, touching lightly on areas where she wanted more pressure, skating around places where she would have welcomed any pressure at all.

When he just grazed her mons for a fleeting second, leaving her bereft and aching, she opened her eyes and glared at him. 'You know, if you are not going to get on with this, I can find someone else to take over. Andy, maybe.'

Niall's eyes darkened, the playfulness replaced with something much more dangerous. 'Oh no, darling, you're mine now. Now and forever.' He traced a line from her hip to her nipple. 'This is mine. Soft and delicate. And mine.'

He grazed her nipple, making lightning flash through her, but took his thumb away too soon. 'Mine. Get used to it.'

Sinead had to look away from the naked possession in his gaze. The sheer strength of his will was overwhelming. But she wasn't going to let him have everything his own way. 'You think so?' She was proud her voice didn't shake the way her insides did.

'Oh yeah.' He nudged her thighs and, helpless, she allowed them to fall apart, granting him access to anything he wanted. He stroked up the seam of her lips, forcing a moan from her. 'This is mine.'

He moved back just far enough to unfasten his belt and shove his trousers down. His erection sprang free, hard and fierce.

Sinead followed it with her eyes. She had done that to him. Niall's control was legendary. If she could make him that hard, she had power over him, too. She reached for it.

He caught her hand. 'Not this time. I'm going to show you how much you mean to me. And you are going to lie there and let me.'

'I am?' She tried to sound challenging.

'Yep. Now lie back and let me work.'

She couldn't help it; she giggled. He sounded so much like a surly workman. But she lay back obediently.

He gave her a mock glare, then caught her hands and wrapped them around the bed frame. 'Keep them there,' he told her, then proceeded to drive her out of her mind.

He kissed and licked and sucked, moving from one sensitive spot to another, never letting her catch her breath. His hands were equally busy, caressing and teasing and stroking.

She twisted, trying to contain the pleasure he was lavishing on her. Her eyelids would not stay open, as if her brain were unable to process all the stimulation and operate her eyes as well. It seemed impossible that he was only one man. She registered a nip on her neck, a pinch on her nipple and a lazy circle on her inner thigh. The Rangers were known to be resourceful, she thought dimly, before abandoning the effort.

The heat that emanated from him was a caress in itself, and she ached to be closer to it. She let go of the bed frame to reach for him, but he caught her hand.

'Please, I need to touch you,' she pleaded.

He held her hand in a strong grasp. 'Not this time. I need to concentrate on you.' His voice was strained.

Even while he caught both her hands in his and held them above her head, she exulted. She was driving him to the edge of his control, and she would drive him to lose it.

He drove his tongue into her mouth in a possessive, dominating kiss. She allowed him to exert his command, then she sucked delicately on it, tangling her own with it and shifting so that she rubbed his chest with her nipples. The feeling of his hot skin against the hard points was almost too much for her, but the groan that ripped from his chest was worth it.

She undulated against him, caressing his rock-hard cock with her belly, and she treasured the muttered curse he couldn't conceal.

'You're a bad girl, Sinead,' he said.

'I know. What are you going to do about it?'

'This!' That was all the warning she had before he moved between her thighs and surged into her in one smooth, powerful movement.

All the breath left her lungs. Her nerve endings went into overload. How had she forgotten the size and strength of him? The heat and power? He filled her, completed her. She wanted to spend the rest of her life like this.

'More,' she managed.

'Yes, ma'am.' Then he was moving, slowly at first, the friction so deliciously dizzying that she forgot how to breathe. He sped up, going faster and faster. She twisted, desperate to hold onto him, but he still held her hands, so she gripped his hips with her legs and drove him on with her heels.

Niall had obviously intended this to be a slow seduction, but he was no more able to resist her than she was him.

'Niall, Niall,' she gasped, not able to form any other words.

She had no idea where he stopped and she began, who

was moving, which of them was groaning. It didn't matter.

Now his hips were moving powerfully, driving her higher and higher. She fought to get breath, and expelled each one in a scream. The tension inside her tightened harder and harder, until she began to fear she would not survive what he was doing. But she would have killed him if he had stopped.

'Sinead, I love you,' he gasped, then surged into her in a last series of thrusts. Knowing that she had broken his control was all it took to push her over the edge. With a wail, she fell apart, her body convulsing around his in spasms of pleasure so intense she could not contain them.

When she recovered, he was holding her tightly. 'Never forget how much I love you,' he said, and kissed her, a tender kiss that told her everything she needed to know.

She snuggled into him and yawned. 'I have a terrible memory. I expect you'll have to remind me several times a day for the next fifty years.'

He laughed. 'Deal.' Then he tucked her against his body and settled down to sleep.

Epilogue

'I've never spanked anyone at a wedding,' Niall said thoughtfully.

'And you won't be starting now.'

Sinead cursed as she tried to fasten the tiny clasp on her necklace.

'Here, let me do that.' Niall took the platinum chain from her and deftly fastened the ends together.

Sinead gave him a sly grin in the mirror. 'You're still not spanking me. Come on, the others will be waiting.' She headed for the door.

'Ahem, haven't you forgotten something?'

Hearing the laughter in his voice, Sinead pivoted on her high heels and returned to where he was waiting. Cupping his face in her hands, she brushed her mouth lovingly against his.

Despite the hectic months of Lottie's last revue, she had never been so happy. After the wedding, they would finally set up home together instead of snatching weekends in hotels or overnights when Niall came to Las Vegas on business.

Niall's broad hands grasped her waist and he pulled her closer, deepening the kiss. His tongue plundered her mouth, and she gave herself up to his passionate embrace. It was easier than fighting him. She would save that for later.

In forty-eight hours' time, they would be sailing in the azure seas off the coast of St Martin. There would be nothing to do but laze around, eat and swim in the crystal Caribbean waters. She couldn't wait.

The telephone beside the bed rang and Niall reached for it. Sinead saw the number on the display and snatched it from his hand before he could answer. She put her finger to her lips, warning him to be quiet. Granny O'Sullivan was horribly old-fashioned. If she even suspected that they had spent the night together before their wedding, she would have a fit. As it was, they had booked adjoining rooms, one of which hadn't been used.

'Yes, Gran? Okay. I'll be there in two minutes.' She put the phone down and glared at Niall. 'She wants to see me.'

Niall laughed. 'She probably wants to give you a few tips about your wedding night.'

'Oh you . . .' She raised her hand threateningly and he ducked out of the way. 'I'll be back in five minutes. Make sure you're ready.'

Sinead hurried down the corridor to her grandmother's suite. Her uncle had spared no expense to ensure his mother's comforts on her first transatlantic trip. It was just a pity he hadn't arrived yet. Tim O'Sullivan was in the middle of acquiring another airline. If he didn't make it on time for the wedding, she would have no one to give her away.

She knocked on the door and her grandmother answered, resplendent in pale mauve silk. She was a small woman who radiated energy and authority. No one argued with Granny O'Sullivan.

'Come in, pet. I won't keep you long. I just wanted to give you a little something.'

From a folded envelope, she produced a silver St Christopher medal on a piece of faded blue ribbon. 'I wanted you to have this for your something blue.'

Sinead didn't have the heart to tell her that she was wearing a blue garter beneath her Forties-style ivory dress, or that Niall had insisted on putting it on her thigh earlier.

'It belonged to my own grandmother. I had hoped to pass it on to your mother, but . . .' Her voice shook. She pressed the medal into Sinead's hand and closed her fingers around it. 'My grandmother was working as a nurse in Cobh when the *Lusitania* sank. One of the passengers she looked after gave it to her as a remembrance.'

'Thanks, Gran. I'd be honoured to wear it.'

'You do that. They say that St Christopher looks after travellers. You've done a lot of travelling already and you'll probably be doing more with that dancing lark.'

Sinead's eyes filled with tears. Her grandmother was right. She had come a long way, from an encampment in Mayo to the bright lights of London, Paris and Las Vegas. 'Lottie is retiring,' she said.

'Is she now?' Her grandmother's eyes twinkled. 'We'll see. Now, dry your eyes and go fetch that chap of yours before we're late.'

Sinead was about to open the door and then stopped. How did Granny O'Sullivan know that Niall hadn't left for the church already? A soft laugh came from behind her and she turned.

'Your grandfather was a passionate man too,' her grandmother said with a smile.

Fighting the blush rising in her cheeks, Sinead fled from the room. Her cousin Summer was right. Granny O'Sullivan was a witch.

Sinead hurried back to the room and found that Niall was tapping away on his laptop. 'Five minutes,' he said. 'I have to get this done before we go.'

Sinead tapped her foot impatiently. They would be the last to arrive at the church. 'Mr Moore, I do believe we have a date at noon. You remember? Church, priest, wedding rings?'

Niall patted the pocket of his jacket. 'Everything is under control. Trust me.'

'That's what you said when you found my sister. And she's gone AWOL again.'

'Don't worry. I'll put Andy on it. He'll track her down.'

It was the one shadow on a beautiful day. She had so wanted her sister to be at the wedding, but Roisin had gone to ground – last seen somewhere in Ireland. She didn't like to think of her being without protection with Hall still on the loose.

'Stop frowning. You'll ruin the photographs,' Niall said.
'Feck off. Come on, hurry up.'

They arrived with minutes to spare at the white-painted Pilar Basilica, one of the oldest and loveliest churches in Buenos Aires. Outside the portico, a kilted Scotsman paced, drawing curious glances from passers-by. He tapped the face of his watch as they raced through the gates.

'What time do you call this? Everyone else is inside, except Summer and Tim. She had to dash to the airport to pick him up,' Flynn said, exasperated. 'They'll be here any minute.'

Niall dropped a quick kiss on Sinead's mouth. 'I'll see you inside. Don't keep me waiting.'

As the first strains of music drifted through the open doorway of the church, Sinead lifted the bridal bouquet to her face, inhaling the sweet scent of the exotic blooms. She couldn't believe that this day had come, that she was actually here. She tied the medal her grandmother had given her around the stem of the bouquet, then glanced at her watch. It was almost time for the ceremony to begin.

A red sports car circled the garden in front of the church and screeched to a stop at the doorway. Sinead smiled. Thank god. She thought she'd be on her own walking up the aisle. A beaming Tim O'Sullivan climbed from the rear of the car and gave her an enthusiastic hug, but took care not to crush her dress.

Her cousin Summer got out of the driving seat. Her mop of chocolate-brown waves had been tamed into an elegant up-style and the simple bridesmaid's dress had probably cost a fortune. 'Sorry Sinead, we had to race from the airport. Dad's flight was late.'

Tim O'Sullivan snorted. 'It wouldn't have happened if it was one of my planes.' He glared at his daughter. 'They have speed limits here, you know.'

'It doesn't matter. I'm so glad you're both here.' Sinead handed over the bridesmaid's bouquet. 'Flynn's like a scalded cat. You'd think it was his wedding, the way he's carrying on. We better go in and put him out of his misery.'

'Niall's misery is only starting,' Tim chuckled.

Two pairs of blue eyes glared at him.

434

'Can a man not crack a joke? What's wrong with women these days?'

Summer laughed and shook her head. She straightened his bow tie and checked him over. 'Come on, Dad. You've got a niece to give away.'

Just before they went in, Sinead fingered the ring on the third finger of her left hand – a platinum band set with a dark blue sapphire. She slipped it off and handed it to Summer. 'Don't you dare lose it.'

The Viking had surprised her last night with an engagement gift to match the earrings he had bought for her in Paris. He had also been thinking of something blue. Sinead smiled. How well he knew her.

The simple ceremony was probably costing him a fortune, but his sister Alison had been posted to Buenos Aires and her only cousin lived here too, so it had been the logical place to hold the wedding.

Sinead tucked her hand through her uncle's arm and they began the slow walk up the aisle. Sinead concentrated on putting one foot in front of the other, smiling when she reached the guests occupying the pews at the front of the church. Her uncle patted her hand and passed it to Niall. 'Mind you take good care of her.'

Niall nodded and Sinead tried not to laugh at the hint of a threat in Tim O'Sullivan's words. He was more of a father to her than her own had ever been. He had raised her, educated her and, in his own way, loved her almost as much as he loved his own daughter.

Niall squeezed her hand and mouthed, 'I love you.'

No matter how many times he told her, his words always made her catch her breath. Niall loved and accepted all of her. Both Lottie and Sinead. She didn't need to hear him vow to love, honour and protect her for the rest of his life. She knew the big Viking always would.

Sinead blinked away a tear. It didn't matter that her father was in prison or that her sister was on the run. None of that was important now. For years she had searched for her missing family, but her real family had been here all along – Tim, Summer, Granny O'Sullivan, and now Niall.

Her family. The only ones she would ever need.

Acknowledgments

Thanks to:

Our beloved families, who put up with our absence, without complaining too much.

Cover artist for the Touch novellas, Claire Chilton.

Our agent, Madeleine Milburn.

Our editors Patricia Deevy and Davina Russell, the wonderful staff at Penguin, and online publicist Catherine Ryan Howard.

Website designer and IT support, Seoirse MacGabhann.

John Colgan, for information on weapons and all things military.

Our FL friends, for kinky inspiration – particularly Apulia, Elftitch, JackC, Jeneie, JMagee, MCat, QueenHoneyBee, Suarach, Tenjiku and Zytex.

Our beta readers, Mary, Silje and Claire.

The Corner Table Writers' Group.

Patricia O'Reilly of UCD.

Caroline's baby sister Elizabeth McCall and her husband, Michel Guinand, for all things Parisian.

For assistance with the Swiss legal system, journalist Clare O'Dea.